ACCLAIM FOR
TED DEKKER'S NOVELS

"...highly charged suspense drama that shows Dekker at his best."

—*Library Journal* review of *Adam*

"As always with a Ted Dekker thriller, the detail is stunning, pointing to meticulous research in a raft of areas: police and FBI methods, forensic medicine, psychological profiling—in short, all that accompanies a Federal hunt for a serial killer. But Dekker fully reveals his magic in the latter part of the book, when he subtly introduces his darker and more frightening theme. It's all too creepily convincing. We have to keep telling ourselves that this is fiction. At the same time, we can't help thinking that not only *could* it happen, but that it *will* happen if we're not careful."

—David M. Kiely and Christina McKenna,
authors of *The Dark Sacrament*

"If you read one thriller this year—make it *Adam*. It's a high-octane thriller that lays bare the battle between good and evil in a way that will stun readers."

—Lis Wiehl, Fox News Legal Analyst and cohost
of *The Radio Factor with Bill O'Reilly*

"Ted's words leap off the page with a whole new level of crackling intensity and frightening realism. You can feel him relishing every word, and each time you think this is as intense as he can take it, he tightens the screws even more. I don't say it lightly: *Adam* truly is the best work of Ted's career. I was obsessed from the first page."

—Robin Parrish, author of *Relentless*

"Young and old alike will enjoy this latest offering. Dekker fans will love this new story from the Circle universe and new readers will undoubtedly be sucked in to the greatness that is Ted Dekker. [*Chosen*] is a superb beginning to what is sure to be a fantastic series."

—*Bookshelf Reviews*

"As a producer of movies filled with incredible worlds and heroic characters, I have high standards for the fiction I read. Ted Dekker's novels deliver big with mind-blowing, plot-twisting page turners. Fair warning—this trilogy will draw you in at a breakneck pace and never let up. Cancel all plans before you start because you won't be able to stop once you enter *Black*."

—Ralph Winter, Producer of *X-Men*, *X2: X-Men United*, and *Planet of the Apes*

ALSO BY TED DEKKER

Boneman's Daughter

ADAM

TED
DEKkER

CENTER STREET

NEW YORK BOSTON NASHVILLE

Copyright © 2008 by Ted Dekker
Excerpt from *Thr3e* copyright © 2008 by Ted Dekker
All rights reserved. Except as permitted under the U.S. Copyright Act of 1976, no part of this publication may be reproduced, distributed, or transmitted in any form or by any means, or stored in a database or retrieval system, without the prior written permission of the publisher.

Published in association with Thomas Nelson and Creative Trust, Inc. Thomas Nelson is a trademark of Thomas Nelson, Inc.

Unless otherwise noted, scripture references are taken from the King James Version of the Holy Bible.

Drawing of children by Mary Hooper

Center Street
Hachette Book Group
237 Park Avenue
New York, NY 10017
Visit our website at www.centerstreet.com.

Center Street® is a division of Hachette Book Group, Inc.
The Center Street name and logo are trademarks of Hachette Book Group, Inc.

Printed in the United States of America

First mass market edition, July 2010
10 9 8 7 6 5 4 3 2 1

ADAM

Reprinted from Crime Today *magazine, 2008*

MAN OF SORROW:
JOURNEY INTO DARKNESS

by Anne Rudolph

Crime Today *magazine is pleased to present Anne Rudolph's nar-rative account of the killer now known as Alex Price, presented in nine monthly installments titled "Man of Sorrow: Journey into Darkness." Rudolph's award-winning investigative reporting pro-vides us with a rarely seen glimpse of good and evil at work within our society today.*

1964

NO ONE—not the migrant workers who remember seeing the baby kicking stubby legs while he lay on a brown blanket next to the fields, not the Arkansas farmers who chuckled while poking the child's belly, certainly not his adoring fa-ther and mother, Lorden and Betty Price—could possibly imagine that the brown-eyed baby boy named Alex Price, born August 18, 1964, would one day stalk innocence like a wolf stalking a wounded lamb.

Then again, 1964 was more than four decades before Alex Price be-gan the calculated cycle of terror that would end the lives of so many young women.

As the children of migrant work-ers themselves, Lorden and Betty Price had grown up with the same strong work ethic many migrant field workers shared throughout the south in the 1940s and 1950s. Devout Catholics, they planned on instilling love and sound moral sen-sibilities into whatever children God blessed them with.

They regularly attended Mass at a small cathedral in nearby Conway off Route 78, where the faithful con-gregated each Sunday. With just a little more fortune, a little more edu-cation, a few more helpful people, Lorden could have opened up his own mechanic shop, according to those who knew him. He had a way with machines that impressed the local farmers.

The small family of three lived rent-free in a trailer on the back side of the Hope farm, a deal brokered with Bill Hope in exchange for Lorden's extra help maintaining all of the farm vehicles. Bill even loaned Lorden his 1953 Dodge truck for transportation. All things considered, the Prices were doing pretty well for themselves when little Alex came into the world.

"Cutest little bundle of boy you ever did saw," Constance Jersey recalls with a soft smile and tired eyes. "They used to tote him around in one of those wire buggies Lorden had found in the dump and fixed up. Didn't matter what they put him in, you couldn't make that boy stop smiling and cooing as if he was the luckiest soul in the whole wide world."

Other workers remember Lorden racing up and down the cotton-field roads late one day, sticking his head out of the truck, hollering for Betty and demanding to know where Alex was. Seems he'd misplaced both of them and panicked. He found them in the barn, taking a break from the hot sun.

When Alex was one year old, Betty gave birth to a beautiful, blonde-haired, seven-pound, two-ounce baby girl whom they named Jessica. Lorden was the kind of man who made sure every person he met knew just how adorable his children were, and he didn't have to work hard to accomplish this task.

"They're going to college," he announced to his coworkers one hot day in the cotton field. The cotton industry was taking a downturn in the midsixties, replaced by the more profitable corn market. The work was hard and the pay was hardly enough to keep a family alive. "I swear, they're going to college if it's the last thing I do."

The coworkers gave him no mind. The idealist in Lorden frequently made such bold announcements, but life as a blue-collar worker in Faulkner County in 1965 didn't hold out much hope for anything so extravagant as attending the University of Central Arkansas in nearby Conway. Still, Lorden repeated his intentions often, claiming that they would one day make some real money in the factories up north, and send their children to college.

Just over a year after Jessica's birth, as winter set into central Arkansas, Lorden announced to his wife that Bill Hope had agreed to let him take the truck up to Chicago for an extended visit with relatives who'd left Arkansas several years earlier, hoping to work in the factories. The Prices packed their belongings in two large suitcases, bid their neighbors farewell, and headed down the dusty road.

The Dodge pickup returned nearly five weeks later laden with gifts from the north. José Menendez, who lived with his wife, Estella, in a second trailer near the Prices, remembers the day clearly. "You gotta understand that them Prices was a frugal bunch. They didn't spend money on much unless it was for the kids. The smiles on their faces when they came back with that haul had us all thinking about going up north to work in the factories."

A perfectly good washing machine. Two new suitcases full of clothes, mostly for little Alex and Jessica. But the chainsaw was Lorden's prize. He cut enough firewood that first week to last both them and the neighbors two winters, José recalled.

The first four years of Alex Price's life can only be reconstructed from the memories of people like the Menendezes and the Hopes. Hearing it all, one has to wonder what would have become of Alex had his parents been allowed to continue their slow but deliberate gain on a happy life.

Would they have moved to Chicago and sent the children to a public school while they saved up the money for a secondary education? Would Alex have grown up on the farm, then finally opened the shop his father only dreamed of?

The night of January 15, 1968, was warm by Arkansas standards, a balmy 51 degrees according to the weather service records. Heavy, dark clouds hung over most of Faulkner County.

Betty tucked Alex, then four, and Jessica, who was three, in their twin beds in the back bedroom, sang them a soft song as she did every night, said their prayers, and turned off the lights. José Menendez recalled that the Price's mobile home, which stood only fifty yards from their own, was already dark when he went out for wood at eight thirty.

The crickets sang in the nearby forest; otherwise, the night was quiet. At approximately 1:45 a.m. Lorden was awakened by a creaking noise, a fairly common sound in the Price house, which was set on an unstable foundation and easily shaken by wind. Only when it occurred to him that there was no howling wind did Lorden open his eyes and listen more carefully. It was the absence of wind that awakened him, he later told the police.

The screen door squealed in the dark, and Lorden sat upright. A faint, muffled cry reached his ears.

Now panicked, Lorden threw off the blanket and ran into the tiny living room. He saw that the front door was open, but his mind was on the children's bedroom. Barging through the doorway, he saw a sight that would haunt him for years to come.

Two empty beds.

"I couldn't think. I just couldn't think," he later recalled. He stood frozen in the doorway, staring at the empty white sheets for a few long seconds before crying out and sprinting out of the house.

A Ford pickup truck was parked on the gravel driveway. The driver's door slammed and for a moment Lorden saw the shapes inside: an adult wearing a cowboy hat sat in the driver's seat, and another with long hair was shoving Alex and Jessica into the truck from the passenger's side. Freed from the hands that had muzzled them, both children began to cry.

Lorden ran toward the truck but was only halfway across the lawn when it rumbled to life and jerked forward, spewing gravel.

Now in a mindless panic, Lorden ran for the Chevy, started the engine, and took off after the disappearing pickup. Betty ran from the house,

screaming his name. He had the presence of mind to shove open the passenger door and call out for her to report the kidnapping to the county sheriff. She would have to call from the main ranch house.

Lorden had a difficult time remembering what happened next. "I couldn't think!" he repeated later. "I just couldn't . . . couldn't figure it, I couldn't think!"

In an understandable state of anxiety, the father raced down the driveway, took a hard left at the first fork, following the Ford pickup's dust, and pushed the old Chevy to its limits. His eyes were on the set of taillights two turns ahead.

The next corner turned ninety degrees to the left, and Lorden overshot it in a full slide. The truck came to a crashing stop in the ditch beyond.

Unable to restart the truck, Lorden exited the vehicle and ran after the distant taillights, calling out to the Menendez trailer on his right. José ran out, and a breathless Lorden yelled that someone had just taken Alex and Jessica.

But without a truck, José was powerless to give chase. And by the time he got to the Hope ranch house to call the police, the Ford pickup was long out of sight.

Bill Hope reported the kidnapping

to the Faulkner County sheriff at 1:56 a.m., then jumped in his car with José and headed for the county road nearly a mile away. They found Lorden Price at the intersection pacing, staring down the long strip of empty asphalt that stretched empty in both directions.

"It was the most horrible sight I'd yet seen," José recounts. "The man had run about a mile and was near a breakdown. He had that look of death on him."

Without a clue as to which direction the kidnappers had fled, Lorden couldn't decide where to take the chase, so Bill Hope headed east. The road ran through a forested region without streetlamps, and the dark clouds blocked the last hint of light from the sky. They raced east, following the spread of their headlights, nothing else.

They couldn't have calmed Lorden Price in those first ten minutes if they'd wanted to. But as the road yielded nothing of promise, he soon grew silent in the backseat. Bill slowed the car after fifteen minutes and asked Lorden if he wanted to try the other direction.

Lorden didn't respond. He just lay down on the backseat and sobbed. "It was horrible," José said. "Just horrible."

Sheriff Rob Green received the call to investigate a kidnapping at the Hope Ranch at 1:59 a.m. He tossed

The Prices' home in Arkansas

his cold coffee and immediately headed out. Officer Peter Morgan from the Conway police department also responded to the call. Both had arrived on the scene by the time Bill Hope, José Menendez, and Lorden Price returned.

While Lorden did his best to calm his hysterical wife, the officers started processing the crime scene. An all points bulletin was immediately issued for a truck matching Lorden's description. Although kidnapping was not a common occurrence, all of the law-enforcement officers knew how critical the first few hours of search were. A trail is only a trail as long as it remains discernible.

With the help of the highway patrol, hasty blockades were established on four of the six country roads in and around Conway. The FBI's Little Rock field office was informed of the incident at daybreak, and Special Agent Ronald Silverton agreed to assist the local sheriff in prosecuting the search. Kidnappings qualified for federal involvement, but for the most part, the FBI only pursued those cases they determined to be successfully prosecutable. The Price kidnapping wasn't promising, but Silverton thought that if they moved quickly, they might have a chance.

With Agent Silverton coordinat-

Police sketch of Adam and Jessica Price

ing FBI resources and Sheriff Rob Green leading the investigation on the ground, an exhaustive search for the missing children was launched. Field and ditch, canal and culvert: no evidence found. The word of Alex and Jessica's kidnapping was heavily circulated through dozens of Arkansas newspapers and radio stations. The Prices had no photographs of their children, the simple reason being that they didn't own a camera. They had saved for a family portrait to be taken in Conway for Christmas that year, but it was still late harvest.

An artist was brought in from the Little Rock police department, and his sketch of the two children was printed in newspapers and on flyers, which were tacked to hundreds of posts covering a two-hundred-mile radius. Meanwhile, the authorities constructed a likely kidnapping scenario based on the evidence gathered at the crime scene.

The Unknown Subjects, or UNSUBs, as unknown perpetrators of crimes are commonly called, evidently approached both the Hope ranch house and the Menendez trailer before proceeding to the Price house. Multiple boot impressions matching those outside the Price children's window were also found on the ground outside windows at both the Hope and Menendez homes.

"We knew then that we were dealing with the worst sort of kidnapping," Special Agent Silverton recalls. "The evidence suggested that the perpetrators passed up valuables in clear sight of the Hope windows and moved on to the Menendez house. Finding nothing of interest, they approached the Price house, where they found what they'd come for: children."

There are two primary classifications of kidnappers: those who kidnap victims as leverage for ransom, and those who kidnap victims for their own personal use.

It became immediately clear to Silverton that they were dealing with the latter classification. The Prices obviously had little or nothing to give a kidnapper in exchange for their children. They didn't hold positions of influence or have access to information that any kidnapper might be seeking.

In all likelihood, Alex and Jessica were taken by someone who either wanted but could not produce children, or by someone who intended to use the children for some unidentified enterprise.

In addition, the evidence suggested that the perpetrators were not new to the crime they'd committed. Once they found the children, they painstakingly removed the window frame from the wall, one screw at a time, a task that may have taken up to an hour.

No fingerprints were lifted from the room. There had been no cry of alarm from the children until they were outside the house, suggesting they'd been carefully lifted from their beds while deep asleep. Like many parents, the Prices sometimes allowed the children to fall asleep on the couch and then moved them to their beds, which could account for the reason neither Alex nor Jessica made a fuss sooner than they did. The cold outside had likely woken the children, but by then their mouths were covered and their abductors were running for the truck.

Guessing that the kidnappers were not of the variety who holed up nearby while they issued their demands for a ransom, Silverton broadened his search to the states surrounding Arkansas. An extensive search of the FBI records for abductions with a matching profile was immediately initiated. Casts of the tire marks and the boot impressions were sent to the FBI's crime lab at Quantico for detailed examination.

A week passed without any solid leads. Lorden and Betty grew even more frantic. Hope of a quick recovery gave way to a resolve for a long search.

The fact that only the vilest kind of human could possibly take a child wasn't lost on Lorden. His fear of what the children might be facing was replaced by a sleepless rage against the animals who preyed on such young, innocent children.

A month passed, and Silverton visited the Prices with some advice that they refused to accept. The number of cases in which abducted children were recovered after being missing for more than a month was negligible. He gently encouraged Lorden and Betty to prepare for a life without their children.

Two months went by, and not a single solid lead to the UNSUBs' identities or location surfaced. The authorities knew what shoes they wore—size 11 and size 6 Bigton work boots, likely worn by a man and a woman. Perhaps a husband-and-wife team. Based on the tire casts, they concluded that the vehicle used for the kidnapping was a Ford F150 pickup manufactured between 1954 and 1957. A file full of circumstantial evidence suggested the kidnappers lived in a rural setting, were handy with tools, likely lacked formal education, and would go to extraordinary lengths to acquire a child. But none of this evidence led the FBI or the local authorities to the abductors themselves.

Two months stretched into six, and Lorden slowly gave up hope and began to take Agent Silverton's advice. Betty wanted to have another child immediately, but he insisted they wait. "Lorden was afraid they'd come back and take that child too," José Menendez said. "I'm telling you, he never recovered. He was a shell after that. Like you couldn't pull no life from the man if you tried."

Alex and Jessica were gone. For all Lorden and Betty knew, their children were dead.

But Alex and Jessica were not dead.

They were in Oklahoma.

And they would not rejoin the world for thirteen years.

ONE

2008

A HOT, STICKY EVENING in Los Angeles. Out-side, the city was clogged with traffic and a million souls fighting their way through another rush hour, pre-occupied with bloated mortgage payments and impos-sible social pressures. Inside the FBI's Los Angeles field office, the air conditioner's hum had more significance to Daniel at the moment.

Special Agent Daniel Clark stared across the broad maple desk at Frank Montova's dark eyes, set deep behind puffy cheeks, like raisins. The man's neck bulged over a collar two sizes too small. Of the fifty-six domes-tic FBI field offices, only four were large enough to be helmed by an assistant director in charge, or an ADIC, as opposed to a special agent in charge. LA was one of those four. The running joke was that Montova fit his profes-sional acronym at times.

"I'm not saying I wouldn't use other resources at our disposal," Daniel said.

"You don't catch a methodical pattern killer who's left a trail of fifteen victims across nine states without a *lot* of help. I don't care how good you are. You go rogue, you break the chain-of-evidence custody, and you'll blow our chances of getting a prosecution altogether, let alone a conviction."

"This isn't just about getting a conviction," Daniel said. "It's about stopping the killer in the Eve case before he kills another woman. It's about getting into the mind of a killer without him knowing it. I think I can do that better alone than with a team. We follow protocol, we may never find him. We have to anticipate him, not just chase him."

"You sure this isn't about Mark White's death?"

Mark was the forensic pathologist who'd worked with Daniel, uncovering what clues they could from the victims' bodies. Two weeks earlier he was killed in a car crash that hadn't yet been ruled accidental. Daniel had considered Mark a friend more than a partner.

"I can understand how you might come to that conclusion, but no. Mark and I had discussed going dark. This is about trying to get an investigation ahead of Eve, not just waiting to catch up with his crime scenes."

"I'd be more concerned with legality and judicial precedence." Montova's lips turned down. "The director doesn't like it. There are reasons why the bureau investigates the way it does."

Daniel took a slow breath, calmed himself. "You're denying my request?"

The chief eyed him carefully. "It's my call. And, yes, I'm leaning that way."

Daniel stood from the green upholstered guest chair and stepped over to the window. Like many of the bureau offices, the furniture was dated, held over from the last round of budget cuts. Two bookcases stuffed with black case logs and leather-bound legal briefs. A fake rubber tree plant in one corner. Round oak conference table with four metal chairs. Gray industrial carpet.

The city towered outside, gray piles of concrete jutting to the sky beyond Wilshire Boulevard like a dusty three-dimensional bar graph.

"Fifteen women are dead because of our bureaucratic inability to do what is necessary. He kills every lunar cycle, which means he already has his next victim. And if pathology's correct, he's already exposed her to the disease. Twenty-eight days is tomorrow. And we have no breaks, am I right?"

"Go on."

"If we get nothing this time, let me go dark. Give me access to whatever information I need—I work strictly through a channel of your choosing. Officially take me off the case. Put a legal layer of protection in play so that we don't endanger the evidence or the case, and then prosecute as you see fit. But let me do what I do best. *Alone.*"

Montova regarded him with a long stare. Shifted his eyes to the bookcase on his left. Daniel followed his gaze. Two spines stood out from the long row of books, a red one and a black one, side by side.

Inside the Criminal Mind
Fixing the Broken Among Us

Both were authored by the same man. Daniel Clark, PhD.

He'd written them after receiving his doctorate at age thirty-five. The subsequent five years of lectures and tours led to his divorce from Heather, after which he requested and received a reassignment to the field. That was nearly two years ago.

At first the Eve case gave him an avenue of escape from the pain of the divorce. But the case soon developed into an obsession because, as Heather insisted, Daniel knew nothing *but* obsession.

It was why he understood the obsessive criminal mind as well as he did. It was why he'd gone back to school for his doctorate. Why he'd ignored his wife in favor of dishing out a hundred lectures on the same subject. It took an obsessive mind to know one.

Behavioral patterns, like forensic evidence, could lead them not only to a conviction but also to a new understanding of the psychology of serial killing. ViCAP, the federal Violent Criminal Apprehension Program, had a continually evolving database about the intrinsic natures of violent criminals. A pebble of prevention against a landslide of future psychopaths.

The Eve killer was a poster child for the conclusions presented in both of Daniel's books if there ever was one.

Montova's eyes were back on him. "Do what you do best, huh?"

"Yes."

"And what *is* it that you do best, Daniel?"

"I work alone best. Without all the distractions that keep me out."

"Out?"

Daniel hesitated. "Of his mind."

"Eve's mind."

"Yes." Few understood the discipline and focus required to enter the criminal mind.

"Isn't that a dangerous thing to do? Alone?"

Daniel shifted in his chair, uncomfortable for the first time. Heather's words came to him. *They're your addiction, Daniel. You live your life in their minds!*

"If not me, then who?" he said. "You want this piece of trash off the streets, you take some risks."

The assistant director clasped his hands on the desk calendar in front of him. His straight hair, normally slicked to one side, curled down over one ear. Montova was a respected man—a throwback to the previous generation, preferring a pen and a calendar to a Palm Pilot. As he liked to put it, the mind was sharper than any brain power a computer could muster.

"You're more concerned about beating Eve at his own game than you are about the victims," Montova said.

Daniel crossed his legs. "You're forgetting that I was on the Diablo case in Utah. I've seen what a compulsive killer can do in the space of seven hours. Don't tell me I don't care about the victims. I care about stopping the killer, not just wandering behind him with a dustpan and filling out Uniform Crime Reports."

"I'm not saying you don't care about the victims. I'm saying they're not what drives you."

Daniel started to object, but the words caught in his throat. "Does it matter?"

"Actually, it does," Montova said.

His desk phone beeped twice.

"It tells me *why* your motivation runs so deep. This isn't just a job to you, and that makes you a risk to this investigation, even a liability. Your allegiance to protocols—I don't care if you wrote them—is critical."

The phone rang twice more before he reached for the receiver and lifted it to his ear. "Yes?" He listened, interrupting once for clarification.

Daniel glanced at the books he'd written. Heather had repeatedly made the same accusation Montova had. The truth of it had cost them their marriage.

Montova hung up and pressed another extension. "Send her in." He set the receiver back in its cradle.

"Send who in?"

The door opened and a woman stepped in. Closed the door behind her.

"Daniel, meet Lori Ames. Lori, meet Daniel Clark, our major crime SAIC."

Daniel stood and shook her hand. "Nice to meet you."

"I know your work," Lori said. "It's great to finally meet you."

Daniel turned to the bureau chief. "I take it this conversation is over. I hope we can—"

"Sit down, Clark," Montova said. To the woman: "Have a seat."

Lori brushed past him, wearing a gentle smile. Soft brown eyes and a slender body wrapped in a dark business suit. Black heels. Blonde hair that hung just past her shoulders.

But it was the way she looked at him that caught Daniel's attention. Like she knew more than he might assume she did.

He followed her back to the guest chairs and sat.

Montova eyed them both and spoke when neither

offered comment. "Agent Ames is a pathologist from the Phoenix field office's evidence response team. She knew the fourteenth victim, Amber Riley, and has since become quite familiar with the case. We'd like to reassign her to you."

They were replacing Mark White two weeks after his death. But why not with a local? There were at least five qualified pathologists at the LA field office. He glanced over at her. Skirt tight against one toned leg crossed over the other. Not exactly the dress of a field agent.

"I suppose that's your call, sir."

"It is, and I've made it. She starts now. And I've changed my mind. I'm granting your request. Assuming, that is, you don't object to working through Lori. She'll remain on the case but shadow you in all respects."

Daniel didn't know what to say. "Just like that?"

"Just like that. Working within these new parameters you suggested, of course. Who do you suggest I turn the case over to?"

"Brit Holman," he said without thinking. The man was competent and nearly as familiar with the case as Daniel was. "You're saying you'll let me go dark alone, as long as my sole contact is an agent who's new to the case?"

Montova looked at Lori, who evidently took his stare as an invitation to share.

"The first believed victim was discovered sixteen months ago in the basement of All Saints Catholic Church in Cincinnati, Ohio. Maria Stencho, a twenty-three-year-old tasked with cleaning the church. Her body was bruised and blistered, and traces of a previously unknown bacteria similar to *Streptococcus pneumoniae* were found in her blood. SP is normally associated with meningitis, which infects the fluid surrounding the brain and spinal cord and can kill a host within hours in a manner consistent with Maria Stencho's death. No signs of struggle, no evidence of blunt-force trauma. No evidence of harm caused by any weapon. According to the local medical examiner, cause of death was acute encephalitis, most closely associated with symptoms consistent with ICD-10, code A-85, *meningoencephalitis*. The lab work detailed leukocytes in the cerebrospinal fluid after a lumbar tap, and confirmed that the disease was present and in full effect at the time of death. It was first assumed that Stencho died from a form of meningitis. Shall I go on?"

"I get the point," Daniel said.

But Montova held up his hand. "Please, go on."

"The next victim was found twenty-eight days later in San Diego. A Mormon, age twenty, female. This time in the basement of an LDS church. Nearly identical set of circumstances except this time the name *EVE* was painted in red on the cement wall next to the body. Lab came up with the same results in the spinal fluid, and the local coroner found evidence of the same intracranial pressure, as well as advanced infection of the meninges. She died of brain pressure leading to cerebral hemorrhage. A new victim has been found every new moon—the killer evidently likes the dark. All fifteen have been female, between the ages of nineteen and twenty-four. All found underground: seven in church basements, four in abandoned cellars at abandoned farms, four in natural caverns preselected by the killer."

Lori switched her gaze to Daniel. She was unique, he'd give her that much. Fresh. Her eyes sparkled with an infectious mystery. If he wasn't mistaken, in her late thirties.

"Evidence recovered from each scene includes size 13 shoe impressions—Bigton boots available at any one of several large chains across America. Stride indicates a height of six-six, and indentation puts him between 220 and 250. Different white vans were recovered near two of the sites. Hair and skin cell samples from each identify the killer as Caucasian, blood type B-positive, male. The lab cross-checked him through Combined DNA Index System (CODIS), and his DNA profile has appeared in no other investigations outside of this series. Hair indicates he is in his forties. There were no latent prints. No saliva, blood, semen, or any other fluid that could be traced to any other source than the victim. The killer's not a secretor. He's effectively either a newcomer or a ghost."

A pause. Then she went on delivering the data with practiced precision.

"The fact that he's gone to such great lengths to avoid leaving any prints suggests he believes his prints are in the Automated Fingerprint Identification System (AFIS) database. Which in turn suggests he's a professional. His killing is organized, patterned, premeditated, and clearly religiously motivated. He's killing with motives that are consistent with a classic psychopathic profile—he knows right from wrong, and he chooses wrong. He will continue until he is captured or killed. His profile indicates that he will likely never be taken alive. Nothing else is known about Eve."

Beat.

"Would you like me to tell you about *you* now? An even more fascinating case."

"I know myself, thank you," Daniel replied, offering her a polite grin.

"Do you?"

Lori said it with complete sincerity, as if she were his therapist and was only interested in the truth. Then she smiled. "I hope not. My mother always told me that men who think they know themselves are only stuck-up versions of those who don't."

"Smart lady."

The soft hiss of the air conditioner settled the room.

"Like I said, Lori has familiarized herself with the case," Montova said. His phone rang and he took the call. He nodded curtly and dropped the receiver back in its cradle.

"You'll have time to fill in the blanks on the way."

"Sir?"

"Local police in Manitou Springs, Colorado, just received a report of an abandoned white van found by two spelunkers near the Cave of the Winds. They found an entrance to an unmarked cave nearby. The report drew a flag from Eve's ViCAP profile. Local enforcement is setting up a perimeter, but they've been told to stay out of the scene until you arrive."

Daniel sat still, breath gone. *Eve*.

Ice crept through his veins.

Daniel stood and crossed the room in three long steps. He grabbed the doorknob and was halfway through before Montova's voice stopped him.

"Lori goes with you."

He spun back and saw that she was already right behind him.

"Fine."

TWO

HEATHER CLARK GLANCED at her watch for the fifth time in as many minutes. *Eleven o'clock,* the note had said. *Information you will kill for. The bar at the Emerald Dive. Limousine.* Which was why she was here for the first time since the divorce.

Her friend Raquel Graham, one of the better defense attorneys in Santa Monica, sat at the bar next to her, rocking subtly to the rhythmic tune blaring over the Emerald Dive's sound system. The new music, she called it. As opposed to the old music, which had filled the radio waves when she and Raquel were tearing up Santa Monica in their twenties.

They all liked the new music, they just didn't know the names of the bands. Or the songs, for that matter. Nothing as sensible as Red Hot Chili Peppers, which made a clear, definitive statement. What did names like Sky Block Streak say? Probably more than she cared to know.

The Emerald Dive catered to the professional downtown crowd—smart-dressed lawyers and such, half of whom Heather recognized from the major firms around town. She'd made partner at Biggs & Kofford a year earlier, ten years after signing on as a defense attorney. Another two years and her name would join Jerry Biggs and Kurt Kofford on the stationery. Assuming she stuck around.

Honestly, she doubted she would. The last year had ruined her for run-of-the-mill litigation.

Raquel tossed her dark hair, took another sip from the Tom Collins in front of her, and eyed Simon—a prosecutor from Los Angeles—as he crossed the room headed for the bathroom. They'd been dating a full month, something of a record for Raquel, who was thirty-nine and had yet to settle into any semblance of a permanent relationship. She tended to approach men the way she approached cases: moving from one to the next, always hoping for the next big payday.

"So this is the one, huh?" Heather asked, glancing at the clock on the wall.

Raquel offered up a whimsical smile. "Could be, you never know."

"One month and counting."

"I wouldn't talk, sweetie." Raquel raised a brow and took another sip. She nodded at a blond man across the bar, engrossed in a conversation with a friend. Jake Mackenzie, whom they both knew by reputation as an up-and-comer.

"There you go. You always did like blonds."

"Please, he's not a day over thirty."

"And that's a problem? You're only thirty-seven, babe, and any guy in this place can see you put the rest of the competition to shame."

Heather's eyes shifted to the clock.

Raquel set her drink down. "Will you stop that?"

"Stop what?"

"You got a hot date I don't know about? The clock!"

"It's a sin to look at a clock?"

"I'm trying to help you out here, sweetie. You've been divorced—"

"Please, not the divorce talk again," Heather said.

"Exactly. Forget the divorce already. You left that egotistical maniac almost two years ago for good reason. But no, you won't let go, will you? No, we shall be called Heather *Clark* because we were once married to a god named Daniel *Clark*. Why did you leave him?"

"Because he was an egotistical maniac"—she took a sip—"that I fell in love with."

"Listen to me." Raquel turned Heather's face toward her with a gentle hand. "Look at us. What do you see?"

"Two women, in a bar, at eleven on a Wednesday, when most reasonable lawyers our age are in bed."

"Since when were you reasonable? You know what I see? The smartest defense attorney in Southern California, who's so wrapped in the sad past that she's forgotten how to live for the future. The fact that she happens to have a body that looks as tempting in a tank top and holey jeans as it does in a business suit only makes her misplaced desperation more tragic. Learn to live, sweetie. Trust me, you were born to sweep 'em off their feet."

"Spoken like a seasoned litigator."

Raquel turned back to the bar. She was right, of course. Time was marching on, and Heather had allowed the past to suck her in. If anyone knew just how deeply, they would probably arrange for therapy.

The Budweiser clock's long hand tripped the large twelve at the top. Heather scanned the patrons once again, but saw no one focused on her. Whoever had left the note would approach her.

Unless they didn't want to be seen by Raquel. Heather had been working the Mendoza case for the last three months, a high-profile drug case involving a sixty-year-old Mexican woman who was being charged with laundering drug money through a dry cleaning business she owned. All the evidence pointed to an open-and-shut case, but after spending an afternoon with Marie Mendoza, Heather couldn't bring herself to believe the woman was capable of, much less guilty of, the crime.

Someone else was pulling the strings. Someone who had a lot to hide.

If the note referred to information on the Mendoza case, as she assumed, it would likely come from a source interested in the strictest confidence.

Then again, she just might be meeting with someone who wanted her off the case and was simply luring her into an alley where they intended to whack her.

"We've got to get you a date, Heather. Give me that much."

"I've had plenty of dates." Her contact was late. She eyed the room for a sign from any man or woman who would acknowledge her.

"What, two since Daniel split?"

"Daniel didn't split. I left him." A dark-haired man with a strong jaw and thick brows entered the bar, scanned the crowd, and settled on her. His face looked like it had been pistol-whipped a time or two. Heather considered bailing.

"So you left him. What's the difference?" Raquel said.

"The difference is, he still loves me." She picked up her purse. "And you're right, I do need more dates. Like the one I have tonight."

Raquel faced her. "You have a date? Who?" She followed Heather's stare across the room.

"Limo driver by the door. Don't stare."

"Him?"

"Him," Heather said, standing. "If I'm not back in half an hour, call me. If I don't answer, call the police."

She left Raquel staring after her.

THE LIMO DRIVER with the grisly face led Heather from the bar without speaking. Where he intended to take her, she had no idea, but she found the idea that she should follow him inadvisable. What was she thinking?

She stopped on the sidewalk ten yards from the bar's front door. "Where are we going?"

He kept walking, offering no explanation, as if it made no difference to him whether she followed. He was simply doing what he was ordered to do.

She took a few more steps. "Excuse me, maybe I have this wrong, but I won't just follow you without knowing where you're taking me."

He walked on. A younger man and his girlfriend or wife angling down the sidewalk stared at her, then back at the man she was talking to. She nodded politely, and, not eager for a scene, walked on.

The man veered to his left, walked up to an old black sedan, opened the door, and stared back at her. Still not a word.

Curious, she glanced back, saw several passersby

watching, and decided to approach the car. She'd never get inside, of course. But to turn back now would only leave her clueless as to this information she would kill for.

She stopped five feet from the opened door, removed her eyes from the man who was now staring at her, and peered inside.

The car was empty.

The driver motioned to the backseat. "Get inside."

"What is this?" she demanded.

"Please. I'm only doing what I've been paid to do."

"You left the note?"

"Please—"

"If you have information, I'll take it. Otherwise I'm afraid I have to get to my friends. They're waiting."

"I was told to tell you it's about Daniel Clark," the man said. "This could save his life."

Dread replaced her annoyance.

"What is this? Who sent you?"

"That's all I know. Please, lady, I don't get paid unless you get inside."

Several others on the sidewalk were now watching, whether curious or concerned she didn't know or care. Ignoring the onlookers, Heather stepped into the black car and shifted to avoid being smacked by the door as it thudded closed.

The driver slipped behind the wheel and pulled away from the curb. He punched a number into his cell phone, listened for a moment, then disconnected without speaking.

"Where are we going?" Heather asked.

"Home."

"You know where I *live*?"

A cell phone flashed on the seat next to her.

"Answer it," the driver said.

She hesitated, then picked it up slowly. Flipped it open and lifted it to her ear.

The voice on the speaker was soft and low. "Do you love your husband, Mrs. Clark?"

"Who is this?"

"Do you love your husband?"

"We're divorced."

A static-filled pause.

"Is that why you've kept his name?"

"I really don't see how it matters to you."

"It doesn't," the voice said. "It matters to you. Please, tell me."

The whole business was unnerving. But there were much easier ways to hurt someone. She doubted whoever was behind this had her harm in mind. They'd gone to some trouble to get her in a controlled environment and on an untraceable cell call.

She saw no harm in giving him an answer. "Of course."

"Yes, of course. Would you kill for him?"

The question caught her broadside.

He clarified. "To bring him back, healthy, without this ridiculous obsession he has with...Eve. To have your husband's love and affection. Would you kill?"

Maybe, she thought, then rejected the idea.

"The truth is, you love your husband very much."

This time she said what came to mind. "Yes."

"You may need to before it's over. There's more to this than what they all see on the surface." The caller breathed into the phone. "Eve cannot be stopped."

She didn't have the words to reply.

"If Daniel tries to stop Eve, he will die. He'll be dead tonight, or tomorrow, or in a week, or in a month, but in the end he will be dead."

This was Eve speaking to her? She became aware of the tremble in her fingers. "You can't know that."

The caller waited before dismissing her in a soft voice. "You're as obsessed with Eve as he is."

The caller knew about the basement?

"Eve's a sadistic killer who's preying on young, innocent women," she said.

"Not innocent, no. But this isn't about sixteen young women. It's about Daniel. It's about you. It's about me. And it's about what the world thinks of all of us when this is over."

"Sixteen?"

No response.

The car stopped in front of her house.

"Even if this were all true, I don't see how I can do anything. What you're suggesting is...It has nothing to do with me!"

"Good night, Heather." The line went dead.

She closed the phone, stunned.

The driver put his hand out. "Give me the phone."

She did.

"Don't waste your time trying to find me. Just the messenger who left you a note for a lot of money. Never met the guy and never will. Get out."

Heather opened the door and climbed out. Without further explanation, the driver took the car into the night.

The suburban neighborhood was dark except for a few scattered porch lights. She felt light-headed. Confused. Sick.

THREE

MIDNIGHT

THE TOWN OF Manitou Springs nestled in the shadows of Pikes Peak an hour's drive south of Denver.

The FBI Citation had flown Daniel, Lori, and three other field agents to the municipal airport in Colorado Springs, where they'd met up with the tactical unit from the Colorado Springs PD. Three black Suburbans snaked their way up Highway 24 toward the Manitou Avenue exit.

Daniel followed the lead car. Lori sat to his right, Brit Holman behind. The car's tires hummed beneath them. No one spoke. They'd said what needed to be said on the flight over the Rockies. Success today would all come down to luck, and the hope that in his boldness the UNSUB had made a mistake.

The stakes were clear. Assuming the hikers had identified the next murder scene, Eve was either present or not.

Either he had a victim with him or he didn't. If he had a victim, she was likely dead, like the other fifteen they'd found.

If she was alive, they would have their first real break in the case. An eyewitness.

If she was dead, they would be back where they started: armed with another dead girl but no further evidence of who Eve was beyond the fact that he wore boots, was white, drove vans with false registrations on occasion, was in his forties, knew a thing or two about disease, and had a rather substantial issue with young women.

They needed a break—if not an eyewitness, at least a better shot at evidence collection, which was why the local authorities were holding the perimeter without closing in. The last thing they needed was a SWAT team contaminating a virgin crime scene.

The walls in the FBI's LA Major Crimes offices were plastered with a profile of Eve, most of it speculation based on what they did have, and most of it Daniel's doing. Psych profiles, religious profiles, education profiles, physical profiles. Enough to flesh out a living being who could stand up and walk out of the room to kill his next victim.

But speculation did not flesh make.

"This is it," Lori said, staring at the Manitou Avenue sign ahead.

Daniel followed the lead vehicle through a tight right-hand exit loop and merged onto a deserted street that angled through the small, sleeping town. The scattered streetlights glowed with a yellow hue above them, diffused by a thin night fog.

They passed through the center of Manitou Springs,

turned up Canon Avenue, snaked back under a highway bridge a hundred feet overhead, and entered a narrow canyon, leaving the last glimmer of light behind.

Darkness. Eve had a penchant for darkness.

Daniel glanced at Lori, now dressed in black slacks and tennis shoes. She wore her gun in a shoulder holster, a Heckler & Koch .40. He'd learned on the flight about her career with the bureau. Nine years on the force following medical school. A string of other details that he'd been too preoccupied to register.

With any luck, none of it would matter. If they failed tonight, he would take the time to understand his new partner, but for now Lori was just along for the ride.

Williams Canyon narrowed. They drove deeper, following the red taillights of the tactical vehicle that held Manitou Springs police officer Nate Sinclair, who had first confirmed the abandoned van's location with the help of the two hikers. Evidently the hills surrounding the canyon were occupied by squatters who holed up in a system of caverns and caves that was still being mapped. Cave of the Winds was a tourist trap, but undiscovered cave systems were the draw for serious spelunkers.

Pine trees and aspens emerged from the fog on either side, just visible by the vehicles' glaring lights.

Daniel lifted his radio. "How far?"

A voice he assumed belonged to Sinclair crackled back. "Half a mile."

The canyon twisted around bends every fifty yards, hopefully cloaking their approach.

"Kill the lights," Lori said.

Daniel caught her stare. She'd read his mind.

"I believe he waits nearby until he's sure that his

victim is dead," she said. "Not *with* the victim, but close enough to maintain the surveillance."

"I know, I wrote the profile." He lifted the walkie-talkie again. "Kill the lights."

The radio remained silent for a few seconds. "It's gonna be hard to see with this fog." No one outside the cars could possibly hear the radios, but Nate's voice barely broke a whisper anyway. Big day for Officer Sinclair.

"Kill the lights," Daniel repeated. "Stop a hundred yards from the site. We go on foot. The tactical team can use their night vision, but they *do not close* until I say so. You have that?"

"Copy."

"Roger." The tactical unit behind them.

The lights ahead blinked out. Daniel twisted a knob he thought controlled the lights, was rewarded with a swish of the wipers instead. He reversed the switch and tried another.

Night smothered them.

"You see them?" Lori asked.

He slowed to a crawl until his eyes adjusted to the darkness. The profile of the vehicle ahead broke the lines of the forest as it slipped around the next bend.

"Slower," Daniel ordered.

"Copy."

Red brake lights glared ahead.

"Okay, friends. It's game time," Brit said, speaking for the first time since they left Colorado Springs behind.

"Remember, no one crosses my lead. That includes the tactical team. Keep them back, Brit. Way back. I want zero site contamination. Zero."

Daniel had made no secret of the fact that he didn't think they should use a tactical team on this one, much less a team he didn't know. Brit had agreed, but protocol won the day: armed suspect plus hostile scene equaled tactical purview.

Brit chambered a round in his Glock. "Alpha team is taking half a squad up the flank. The rest will stay twenty yards to my rear unless otherwise directed."

"Just keep them out of my scene until I'm in," Daniel said, glancing up at the rearview mirror. The hardened special agent who would officially be handed the case if Daniel went dark was nothing more than a ghostly figure by the amber light of the dashboard. Dark hair, strong chiseled jaw—a college receiver who'd graduated with honors before being recruited by the FBI.

Daniel had trusted the man with his life on several occasions. Given a choice of partners, he'd choose Brit Holman over any other without a moment's hesitation.

"Outside it is," Brit said. "To my rear. I'm going in behind you."

Daniel nodded. "Just keep them out of our way."

"And me?" Lori said. A simple question asked without any expectation. One Daniel hadn't considered. In a case so dependent on information gathered from the victims, some would argue that she was more important to the investigation than he.

"How many raids have you been on?"

"Eight," she said almost before he'd gotten the question out. There wasn't a breath of hesitation in her.

"You're with me," he said.

She nodded. "They're slowing."

Daniel stopped the vehicle just behind the lead,

shrugged into a Kevlar vest, took an H&K MP5 from behind the seat, chambered a round, and flipped off the safety. Engaging weapons on approach was an easy way to an early grave. Clanking chambers carried to all ears.

Lori had engaged her pistol already.

She waited for him to slip out before easing out of her door. Daniel rounded the car, ignoring all except Nate Sinclair, who was crawling out of the cab.

"Stay on the asphalt," he whispered. "Don't speak unless directed. How far?"

Nate's eyes were white in the night. "Around the next bend. To the left, fifty yards off the road. You do realize that I haven't actually seen the van. We were told to stay back. Way back."

"The cave, not the van. I was told you can get us to the cave."

Nate pulled out a GPS unit and switched it on. "Assuming the coordinates the hikers gave me were right. Quick thinking on—"

"Let's go." Daniel glanced at the team that had gathered behind him, waiting in tactical fatigues and helmets, armed for entry, ready for engagement. Ready to start a war.

He nodded.

The soles of their boots padded over the black asphalt. Crickets chirped, a song of life or death, Daniel didn't know. But his mind was in the tomb already.

Who are you, Eve? What drives you to take the lives of young women? Are you there in your hole, standing over another dead body?

The trees parted on the left and Nate stopped. He looked at Daniel for approval and veered for the gap when Daniel fixed on it.

The van sat in the clearing, dark and cold with a rusted white paint job. Windshield cracked. Balding tires. It was an old Dodge Caravan from the nineties. Serial numbers on the glass, the chassis, and the engine undoubtedly filed like the other vans he'd found. It would keep the evidence response team happy for a few hours.

Daniel motioned Brit and each took one side of the van, peering inside the windows without luck. He waited for Brit's cover, put his hand on the sliding door, and jerked it open, rolling right to give his partner a clean shot inside.

The van was empty. No rear seats, no tools, no rope or restraints. No Eve.

No girl.

Lori stepped close, scanned the dark trees ahead, and spoke in a voice that no more disturbed the night than a moth's wings. "He's here."

With those words Lori stepped into his space. She felt the scene in the same way he did. "You're right. Go easy."

A cliff rose to the sky at the end of a deer path, fifty yards farther. The cave opening was precisely where the GPS coordinates had placed it. A large pine and a boulder twice Daniel's height protected a two-foot fissure in the cliff face.

Daniel motioned Brit to send the tactical team along the length of the cliff in both directions, then cast one long look at Lori, who had her eyes locked on his.

I hope you're ready for this.

Then he slipped inside.

He pressed his left hand against the smooth stone surface along the southern wall and inched forward in the dark. Gun ready at his shoulder, muzzle low. Lori right behind, breathing steadily.

Her leading hand touched his elbow. Released it. Touched it again.

The sound of water dripping in a cavern was the first evidence that they'd entered more than a long, thin fissure. A musty odor of earthen mildew filled his nostrils. A scent that had permeated the root cellars Eve had used on two other occasions.

The ground suddenly sloped down. And it was down there that he first saw the faint hint of light. Hardly more than a shift in the darkness, from the thickest black to a shade of dark brown.

He instinctively reached back to stop Lori. His hand found her belly. He held her shirt and eased her close, heart in his throat.

"He's here," he mouthed. "Watch your feet."

Then he let her go and picked his way down. To a wall, where the tunnel made a sharp right.

The light glowed at the end of a long passageway, flickering orange on granite.

Daniel fought the impulse to run around the corner to the source of that light. He waited until Lori and Brit were by his side. Rattling stones announced the presence of two men from the tactical unit close behind. Daniel tried to wave them back, but even if they could see his hand, they were already down the slope.

He opened a palm at Brit and mouthed for him to keep them back.

Montova's voice haunted his mind. *What do you do best, Daniel?*

I work alone. I go into Eve's mind alone.

Why do you go into Eve's mind alone, Daniel?

Because I know him. I know how he was made, and I know how to unmake him.

Daniel hurried down the long passageway. The ground was mostly clay, blown in by the wind over the centuries. He avoided loose stones, advancing in a crouch, weapon ready.

Then he was at the next bend, facing a wall that flickered with light that could only come from flames. Daniel raised his weapon and took the corner low, cutting the pie in increments with the front sight of his MP5, breathing and scanning, high and low, left to right.

The wide cavern ran fifty yards and ended at a flat wall. Two flaming torches hung from wire fixed to the ceiling at the far end.

Stables, the kind you might see in a barn, ran along both sides. Marked off by two-by-fours that ran from ceiling to floor. No scent, sound, or indication of any animals.

An image of a hermit flashed through Daniel's mind. A whole tribe of them were reported to inhabit these canyons. This wasn't Eve. The den was occupied by squatters. They kept their animals here.

A hot vise of panic seized his shoulder blades. They'd been wrong?

"A prison," Lori whispered.

His mind snapped at the words.

Water dripped steadily on rock somewhere. He stepped forward, swung his muzzle to his right, into the first cell. The light on this side was dim at best. He pivoted, swept the cell.

Stone floor. Empty.

He spun and searched the cell along the opposite wall. Same.

Daniel hurried down the cavern, peering into the cells on either side. Empty. All empty.

But the fourth wasn't. A dead goat lay in the center. He knew it was dead, not sleeping, because it was on its back, four legs jutting to the ceiling. The carcass was intact, but the thorax had been sawn and spread, and the internal organs appeared to have been removed in a macabre display of pathology—a classic Y incision. No blood on the floor. The beast had either been killed elsewhere and brought here, or killed here with exacting precision.

He moved on, fixed on the cells to his left, walking laterally, nerves strung like bowstrings, palms now wet on his gun. More light here. The flames licked at the smoke they spewed.

The cell next to the last on this side was empty.

And the last cell, too, except for a gray blanket that hung from a wire stretched between the wood posts and the back wall.

He jerked his head back and saw that Brit had already checked the cells on the other side. Brit mouthed the word at him: *clear.*

Meaning what? Eve had taken this victim with him? Or that this wasn't Eve?

"Daniel?"

He turned back and saw that Lori had advanced past him and was staring into the corner of the last cell. Where the gray blanket hung like a curtain. Not against the wall as he'd assumed, but several feet from the wall. He moved closer to see what had arrested her attention.

Propelled by something close to panic, she ran in front of him, slapped up the crude wooden latch, and rushed inside the pen.

He peered between the two-by-fours and saw the victim then. Seated on a metal chair between the blanket and the stone wall with *Eve* scrawled in red behind her. Dressed in the same dirty white hospital gown that all of Eve's victims had been found in.

Only this victim had a gunnysack over her head.

And she was shivering.

Alive.

"Wait!" Daniel advanced, rotated into the cage, and moved past Lori.

Heart hammering like a steam pump, he stepped up to the blanket, pulled it all the way back, and stared at the girl.

"She's in shock," Lori whispered.

Daniel spun to Brit, who'd entered behind them. "This is him. Set up a perimeter south to Pueblo, north to Monument. Lock down 24 in both directions, fifty miles out. Get that tactical team scouring these cliffs. I want them to find routes up or down, specifically toward the highway. Have them spot and flag any large footprints, anything similar to our profile."

Brit snapped orders at the two men who'd followed them down the tunnel.

"He was here in the last thirty minutes," Lori said, pointing toward a wet spot of blood on the floor. "We need to glove up. For that matter, she could be contagious. One sneeze, and she could turn this sickness into an aerosol."

"We don't have time," Daniel heard himself say. Eve

had never left a victim like this; they couldn't risk losing her. Lori made no objection, despite the break in protocol.

Silence filled the cavern except for the dripping of water. And the faint rattle of the metal chair under Eve's victim.

She was thin—not an ounce over a hundred pounds. Pale. Blue veins traced the flesh beneath her arms' translucent, blotchy skin, symptomatic of the meningitis variant that had killed the others. Dirty, trembling fingers hung loosely by her sides. Bare feet.

No sign that she was aware of their presence.

Lori broke the stillness. "She's dying. We have to get her to a hospital, Daniel. We may already be too late!" She reached for the girl's arm and gently touched the blotchy skin with a gloved hand. "It's okay, honey. We're here to help. Can you hear us?"

Daniel eased forward, took the corner of the brown bag between his fingers, and pulled it up. They had to keep the girl alive—she was their only living link to Eve.

The sack slid up, revealing her slender neck, then her chin. Quivering lips, glistening with spittle. Jaw clenched.

Daniel pulled the bag free.

The girl's eyes were wide open but had rolled back into her head so that her irises were hidden. Her white eyeballs stared ahead, sightless.

Mucus ran from both nostrils and mixed with foaming spittle that seeped from her mouth. Stringy blonde hair hung below her ears, trembling.

The girl's head moved. Turned slowly toward them. Her mouth parted and she began to suck air in short, tight gasps. Her nostrils flared with each inhalation.

The sight of this victim tortured by such an abnormal

condition rooted Daniel to the ground. A thousand discussions about cause of death in the Eve investigation hadn't prepared Daniel for actually seeing a live victim being ravaged by the disease.

Lori backed away.

"Her eyes..." Daniel wasn't sure how to express his concern over the severe rolling of her eyes.

"Photophobia is a classic symptom of meningitis," Lori said. "She's reacting to the light."

The girl's mouth opened wider and she growled at them. Foamy bubbles popped in the corner of her mouth.

And then her jaws clamped shut and she began to whimper. A desperate cry for help from a wrinkled face. Her eyes righted themselves for a moment, irises grayed by whatever disease was killing her, then rolled back into her skull again.

Daniel felt his heart rise into his throat. His own fingers were quivering, perhaps more than hers.

Lori walked behind the girl, eyes wide. "We have to help her." She tentatively placed a hand on each of the girl's shoulders.

No response. Just the grimacing hyperventilation.

"Daniel!"

"How?" His voice sounded like a gravel mixer.

"We have to get her to the hospital."

He'd never seen a condition that presented in such a disturbing way, and he didn't know what the girl was capable of, but they didn't have time for caution—they'd wasted enough time assessing her condition already.

He stepped in, slid one of his arms under her legs and the other behind her back. She didn't resist. Neither did she calm.

He lifted her trembling form and stood awkwardly. Her jaw stretched in a silent scream; her body shook with such force that for a moment Daniel thought he might drop her.

Lori had both her hands on the girl's cheeks. "Sh, sh... it's okay, honey. It's going to be okay." But tears brimmed in Lori's eyes. Dealing with the dead was one thing. Seeing a living human so tormented was another, even for a pathologist.

"Her axial muscles are completely relaxed," she said. "She's not seizing, she's not convulsing." He didn't know the significance of her assessment. Her eyes met his, clouded with concern.

Then they were moving, running through the gate. Back down the chamber. Up the dark passage by the light of Lori's torch. The girl shook in his arms like a blender.

Eve was killing his victims with an exotic disease related to meningitis—they'd established that much over a year ago. Murder one, which included intentionally exposing another person to any life-threatening substance.

They burst from the cliff wall to find Brit Holman in an urgent discussion about Highway 24 with Nate Sinclair. Nate was trying to get the Colorado State Patrol to close the pass.

"Call FBI–Denver," Daniel snapped. "Tell them to lock down this location and perimeter."

To Nate: "How far to the closest hospital?"

Nate's eyes were on the shaking body in Daniel's arms. "Twenty minutes."

"You're with us. Lock it down, Brit, I don't care what it takes. He's close."

"What about you?"

"She's an eyewitness. I have to keep her alive."

FOUR

I NEED THE FASTEST route," Daniel snapped.

"It depends on—"

"The fastest, now! Back the same way?"

"Yes, back."

Nate sat in the passenger's seat next to Daniel, still in shock over the girl's condition. Behind Nate, Lori cradled the girl's head in her lap as she prepared an intravenous syringe with the cephalosporin-ampicillin antibiotic cocktail they brought for precisely this reason. They would soon know if the meningitis was viral, bacterial, or even existent at all. If Lori was disturbed by the girl's grunting, her white eyes, the foaming mouth, she showed none of it. Her medical training had kicked in.

Daniel squealed through a tight turn and floored the accelerator. They had to reach the hospital before the girl's internal organs hemorrhaged. High doses of antibiotics could stave off bacterial assault, but only if administered before irreversible damage had taken its toll, and only if it was, in fact, a bacterial infection. This was only a fraction of what Daniel had learned about meningitis over the past year.

Lori slapped the girl's arm to distend a vein. "Light, I need light!"

Daniel reached back and switched on the dome light.

"Hold on, honey. Stay with us. It's going to be okay." She pressed the needle into a peripheral vein and administered the full dose. Hopefully enough to slow the infection.

At this point he didn't care what they tried, as long as it increased the girl's chance of survival. He might even try a priest, if one could administer psychiatric therapy. Despite his disdain for religion, Daniel was all too aware of the soothing effects it afforded the mind. And the mind needed soothing at times.

He glanced at Nate Sinclair. "Get a priest on the line. I need a priest at the hospital when we get there."

"A priest?" Lori asked. "This is a disease."

"She may not know that," he shot back.

Nate snatched up his radio and barked the demand across the open channel.

The car careened down the narrow asphalt road, leaning with each turn. Daniel wiped his wet palms on his slacks and gripped the wheel.

"Is she responding?"

"I don't know. It's too early. No, not yet."

"Can you give her more?"

"She needs a transfusion. We're in a vehicle, not an ICU."

"Give her more. Will more—"

"Stop, stop, stop, stop!"

Daniel jerked his eyes up and saw what had set Lori shouting. The car's beams illuminated a man in the middle of the road, walking toward them.

Nate was on an emergency hotline; his words caught in his throat.

Daniel was on the gas, muscles frozen solid.

Lori was screaming bloody murder. "Stop! Stop!"

He switched his foot to the brake pedal and jammed it to the floor. The wheels locked, sending the car into a long squealing skid. Lori slammed into the back of his seat.

Still the man walked, deaf and blind, or uncaring that he was facing an onrushing hulk of metal that would grind him into the asphalt.

Nate spoke into his radio, rushed. "We have a civilian in the road. He's right in the middle of the road! He's walking toward us."

Everything slowed in Daniel's mind, minute details popping to life.

The man was tall and gangly. Dressed in dark cargo pants and a dirty long-sleeved shirt that hung open to his pale, naked chest. He wore brown work boots. His hair was disheveled and thinning. Dirty blond.

His right arm hung by his side. A metallic reflection. He had a weapon.

The car fishtailed to the left, then corrected to the right and squealed to a stop fewer than thirty yards from the man. Nate hit the dash, lost his radio. Rummaged about, dazed.

Still the man came, striding, gaunt face calm and deliberate, weapon held loosely by his side. His eyes were deep-set, hooded by a protruding brow, accentuated by a square jaw and high cheekbones.

This was Eve, wasn't it? It had to be.

For a brief moment he considered shoving that accelerator back to the floor and heading straight for the man, but he knew if he tried, Eve would simply step aside and be gone.

Daniel had shoved his sidearm between the seat and the armrest in his hurry to get the vehicle on the road, and he grabbed for it now. There was still time for a clean shot.

But the Kydex holster filled his hand, not the pistol. He had to get the gun out!

"Shoot him!" he screamed.

Ripping his own gun from the holster, he saw that Nate Sinclair was still disoriented. Lori was facing the back of the car, working with the victim, who'd spilled to the floor with her. Brit's voice crackled on the radio, demanding more information.

He had to get his gun clear of the car for the shot. Shooting through a tempered windshield would deflect the bullet from the target.

Daniel fumbled with the door latch, shoved the door wide, threw his left leg to the ground, and whipped his gun up and across the steering wheel as he leaned out between the vehicle and the doorframe for a supported shot.

He was aware of Lori clambering onto the backseat. Aware of Nate, staring silently with his radio pressed up to his lips. Aware of his own heart hammering.

The killer moved his arm then, while Daniel's gun was just clearing the windshield for a shot. Without slowing his stride, Eve calmly lifted his gun and fired directly into Daniel's face from a distance of ten yards. The bullet hurled from the muzzle blast couldn't possibly miss him.

Daniel felt no fear, only a split second of regret.

And then a searing flash of pain as the bullet struck his head.

In the moment before his life ended, Daniel wondered if Heather would take him back. And then he was dropping into a pool of darkness.

LORI HEARD THE door open, and twisted on one knee. She couldn't get a clear view of the killer's face. Only his body and the gun in his hand.

Eve.

The girl in her arms prevented her from any effective motion, but truth be told, she wasn't sure she could stop him even if she had a gun in her hand already.

An icy calm settled over her. The girl was too young to have life snatched away just when it had begun.

An image of Amber Riley, the redhead she'd grown close to in medical school, flashed through her mind. Eve's fourteenth victim. Before receiving the call that Amber had been murdered in California by a serial killer known as Eve, the Eve case hadn't even crossed her horizon. Staring at Amber's fair complexion badly discolored by the disease, Lori's world had changed.

And now her world was about to end.

These are the thoughts of people staring death in the face, she thought. Fruitless thoughts that replaced the ones necessary for survival. This was why so many died when death could have been avoided.

"Daniel?"

Her eyes were glued to Eve's gun as he lifted it. The muzzle stabbed fire, and Daniel's head snapped back as if it were on a spring. Blood sprayed the side window, which shattered from the impact of the deflected bullet.

Like a puppet on a string, Daniel went limp and collapsed. His chin hit the armrest on the door as he fell. She'd seen more than a few dead bodies and knew that she was looking at another.

The killer never broke stride. He veered out of the lights' glare to the passenger door and shot Nate Sinclair through the side window as the police officer fumbled for his own weapon.

The side door swung open, and Lori instinctively pulled the girl in front of her. Light splashed on the seat molding. A car was coming up from behind—someone had responded to the call.

He's going to kill me, Lori realized. *He's going to kill me and take his victim.*

She moved with only a moment's thought, shoving the girl up, toward the open door. Her only hope for survival now was to force his hesitation.

Eve scooped the girl into one arm, tore her from the car as Lori dropped to the floor, cowering.

Tires screamed behind them. The crash of the killer's shot boomed through the car, and Lori felt a tug of pain in her left arm.

If Brit Holman hadn't arrived when he did, a second shot might have killed her. But the victim was evidently more important to Eve.

Lori lifted her head and saw him pass from the ring of light cast by the other car's headlights into the trees, with his victim slung over his shoulder. As if the tactical team, the state patrol, and the FBI were little more than an irritant, an interference.

And then he was gone.

Lori clambered out and tore around the car. She grabbed the driver's door and yanked it wide. Daniel's body slumped into a pool of blood on the asphalt.

"Daniel!" Brit Holman sprinted forward, gun gripped in both hands. "Daniel?"

"Help me!" Lori dropped to her knees and tugged Daniel's limp body. "He's been shot, help me!"

The body rolled. She quickly felt for a pulse on his neck. Found none.

Brit stared. "What happened?"

"He's dead!" Lori screamed. "He's dead, that's what happened. Don't just stand there, help me!"

She felt the wound on the side of his head. The bullet had left a superficial radial gash, causing instantaneous unconsciousness, but it hadn't penetrated the anterior medial portion of the skull. The hydrostatic shock of the impact had likely concussed the brain tissue and put Daniel's nervous system into shock, followed by ventricular fibrillation.

He'd been shot in the head and was dying of a heart attack.

Had died of a heart attack.

Brit dropped to one knee, felt for a radial pulse, then stood. "He's dead." He was already moving, yelling orders at men behind them. "Suspect is in the perimeter. Get the team mobilized. In pairs. Night vision and spread. Now! Report every hundred yards. Get me some light. Move!"

Brit played his light over the windshield. "We have another officer down!" He hurried around the car to check on Officer Sinclair.

For a brief moment Lori stared at the body by her knees. Red blood matted the short waves of hair on the right side of his head where the bullet had struck him. Otherwise he looked like a man at peace.

His skin was smooth, boyish but firm. He was dressed in the same black knit T-shirt and blazer he always wore. Dark-brown slacks. A man who lived with careful attention to detail as much in his grooming as in his work.

She'd come to know him through his books, watching him from a distance over the last three months, studying every case he'd ever worked on, every lecture he'd ever given. And in the process she'd come to respect his obsession with the Eve killer.

Lori took a deep breath and let resolve fill her veins. Working quickly, with practiced deliberation, she tilted his head back, pinched his nostrils between her thumb and forefinger, lowered her mouth to his, and flooded his lungs with her breath. Again.

Then she leaned over him, pressed both palms over his sternum, and pumped at a rate that approximated one hundred beats per minute.

One, two, three, four... thirty times before she would give him more of her breath.

Come on, Daniel! She set her jaw. *Live!*

No response.

Her own heart beat in her eardrums. His remained stone. She needed a defibrillator, and she needed it now.

Brit Holman ran around the car, speaking into his radio. "You're saying he just disappeared? Find him!"

He pulled up when he saw her working feverishly over Daniel's dead body. "Anything?"

She blew into his mouth again. Then pumped his chest.

"We have to get him to the hospital." She grabbed Daniel's jacket and tugged him up. "Get me to a hospital."

"An ambulance just left…"

"We don't have time to wait for an ambulance. It's twenty minutes to the nearest hospital. We'll meet the ambulance." She dragged his limp body around the hood. "Help me. Get him into the car. Hurry!"

Brit hesitated only a moment, then grabbed Daniel's legs. They waddled around the Suburban, shoved him into the backseat.

"I need someone to take me."

"Lori…"

"Now. Now!"

Brit ordered one of the local officers to the car.

She climbed in, saw that they'd already removed Nate Sinclair's body from the front seat, and continued administering CPR on Daniel. It had been five minutes. She knew the statistics: fewer than two percent of adults who suffered cardiac arrest came back after five minutes—and that was in hospitals, under emergency care. Among those, fewer than one in twenty eventually left the hospital alive.

"Hurry!" She caught herself hyperventilating. He could not die, not now.

One of the plainclothes police officers who'd accompanied the tactical team slid behind the wheel.

"There's an ambulance on the way," she snapped. "Find out where."

"They'll meet you on 24," Brit said, filling the door. "Channel 9." He slammed the door and slapped the side of the car as it surged forward.

FIVE

HEATHER CLARK SAT AT the kitchen table at 1:00 a.m. with a cup of mint tea, trying to ignore the haunting voice of the phone call two hours earlier. The Mendoza file lay open, but it refused to offer a distraction.

How many times had she sat here, staring at a file, telling herself to let it all go, focus on the future, defend the case, get a life, quit being one of those weak women hollowed by divorce? Why walk through the pig slop of life when you could find a new path, walk around?

Her therapist, Dr. Nancy Drummins, had drilled the best advice into her rather thick skull a dozen times; Heather knew the self-sufficiency mantras as if she herself had written the book.

She'd been tempted to tell Raquel about the phone call but held off, not entirely sure why. All was fine. Yes, she did get some good information. Thank you, Raquel.

"You sure you're okay?" Raquel had to shout into her cell over the bar noise.

"Of course. Just good to have a friend. I'm fine, really."

And here she sat, almost two hours later, knowing that nothing was fine.

Heather stood from the table, hiked up her gray sweats, two sizes too large after her loss of twenty pounds, and poured herself another cup of tea. The porcelain spout clinked against her cup. The set had been a gift from Raquel, a delicate black pot with a single rose on each side—an image that would have drawn endless analysis from Daniel over breakfast.

She returned to the table. The voice whispered through her memory for the hundredth time.

Eve cannot be stopped.

She should tell Brit. He'd stuck close to their friendship after the divorce—closer than anyone could possibly know. But Eve had come to her, not to Brit. Nor to Daniel.

The cell phone on the table chirped. She sloshed the tea. Eve?

She set her cup down and snatched up the phone. Brit Holman. She opened the phone.

"Hello?"

"It's Brit."

Not the usual tone.

"What's wrong?"

"It's…Eve…"

"He took another girl," she said, half guessing, half knowing.

"We found him. Yes. He—"

"You found *Eve*?"

"We found the victim. And Eve. But he's gone. We're still not sure…" The agent's voice faltered.

Heather stood up. "Where's Daniel?"

"Eve shot him."

"What do you mean? That's…what do you mean, *shot*?"

"He was shot in the head, Heather. He's dead. They're working on him, but it doesn't look good. I'm sorry. I know—"

"When?" The emotions started to roll up her chest, first benign, then ferocious.

"About ten minutes ago. I'm sorry, Heather. I know how much—"

Heather snapped the phone shut. Her world tipped. She slowly turned to face the living room. All Daniel. The furniture she and Daniel had purchased with the home five years earlier. The fireplace he insisted they needed despite the mild winters. The portrait above that fireplace; the green plush rhinoceros that sat on the sofa, Daniel's since the third grade; even the shelved set of law books Daniel had purchased for her during her second year of law school.

All Daniel. And now he was dead?

Heather forced her legs to take her across the living room, down the hall to the door that led into the basement.

Confusion and pain washed her mind. The door thudded shut behind her and she stood in the dark stairwell, wavering on numb legs. She flipped the light switch and started down the stairs.

Eve had taken his sixteenth and seventeenth victims tonight. And now his eighteenth, because she, too, was dead.

Eve.

Tears broke through the pain as she stumbled down the stairs. Across the dark recreation area. Into the unfinished room at the southwest corner of the house. She stood in the doorway, pulling at the stale air. Then fanned her hand over the switch on the near wall.

Lights blazed overhead.

Long tables with folding metal legs ran the length of each wall. Two high-speed computers to her right, screens now black.

The concrete walls were covered with corkboard, and the corkboard was covered with photographs of Daniel and news clippings. Case files for each of the fifteen victims, provided by Brit Holman.

Eve. The latest in a long line of killers who had robbed her of her husband. This room was all about Eve. Every move he'd made, retraced here by Heather.

How many nights had she spent here, methodically combing through the minutiae, searching for a clue to the killer's motives, his next move, his identity? She hadn't been able to win Daniel back from his obsession, so she'd done the only thing that gave her any comfort.

Unbeknownst to Daniel, she'd joined him in his obsession after the divorce. Eve was as much her enemy as he was the enemy of every victim he'd set out to murder.

Heather sank to her knees and sobbed openly.

SIX

THE OFFICER CAREENED around corners, as if the car was a go-cart on a protected course, but vehicular safety was the farthest thing from Lori's mind. She continued the CPR, begging with each breath, each pump of her palms against his sternum, that Daniel Clark would climb out of the dark hole he'd been thrown into.

She would soon have access to the oxygen, epinephrine, and defibrillator that were in every ambulance. She would prefer a cardiac monitor, but time was now more important than the additional equipment a hospital could offer. Resuscitation was a game of long shots in short time.

And what if you're wrong? What if he is meant to die today?

The thought stopped her midstroke. She thrust her hands down. The bench seat shook each time she shoved her palms. She slammed her fist on his chest.

"Wake up!"

He did not wake up. She glanced at her watch.

Ten minutes.

The siren's wail reached her as the car tore down Highway 24, halfway between Manitou Springs and Colorado Springs. The officer was on the radio with the driver of the ambulance.

A calm male voice spoke over the speaker. "Okay, we have you. Pull to the shoulder and wait for us. How long has the victim been in arrest?"

"Just over ten minutes," Lori snapped.

"Just over ten minutes," the officer repeated.

"Age?"

"Forty-one. Five foot eleven. One hundred and seventy pounds. We start with defib, and we need to get a shockable rhythm. Have one milliliter of epinephrine ready."

The officer conveyed the information. She knew the paramedics could handle the attempt on their own, but she had no intention of letting them.

The car jerked to a stop on the side of the road, and Lori continued the CPR.

You're wrong. He's gone.

The car door swung open and the screech of tires announced the ambulance's arrival. A paramedic dressed in a white shirt shoved the officer aside. Eyes on Daniel's lifeless form. He glanced back at his partner, who was wheeling a clattering stretcher on the run.

"Help me with him," Lori said, breathless from her constant pumping.

They slid him out and, with the second paramedic's help, heaved his dead weight onto the gurney. Then ran it back toward the ambulance.

Blue and white strobes from the emergency lights flashed on their faces. The rear of the ambulance was spread wide, and a large black case rested on the floor, already open. An automated electronic defibrillator, or portable juicer, as some liked to call it.

"You're the doctor?" the first paramedic said.

"Forensic pathologist. You have a cardiac monitor on that AED?" she asked. "A manual override?"

"Both," the first paramedic said. "I'm Dave, he's José. The wound on his head looks pretty bad."

She knew what he meant. You don't just bring back the dead after—what?—thirteen minutes? Particularly those who have taken a direct gunshot wound to the head.

"The bullet didn't penetrate his skull. With any luck we have pulseless V-fib caused by shock. Keep that wound pressurized, give me your AED, and put him on a peripheral IV, wide open. D5-W, we're going to need high-dose epi."

"Almost fifteen minutes?" the one named José asked. They slid to a stop and together the paramedics released the scissoring gurney legs and lowered it to the ground.

Lori dropped to her knees, grabbed Daniel's black T-shirt, and ripped it open with a grunt. "Just hook him up. This isn't over until I say it's over. Either of you do ACLS before?"

"We've been around, Doctor," Dave said.

Not around this, she thought.

"Get an IV into him now. Have the epinephrine ready."

José already had the AED on the ground, gelled the paddles. Dave was working the bag valve mask on Daniel's face. The two paramedics had done this enough to develop seamless efficiency, but she couldn't find any comfort in the fact. Daniel was way beyond the benefits of methodical efficiency. With drugs, electricity, and raw luck, maybe they could beat his body back to life. Like a kick to the jukebox.

"It's ready."

She took the paddles and shoved them into the anterior-apex positions—the anterior electrode on the right, below the clavicle, and the apex electrode on his left, just below and to the left of the pectoral muscle.

"Hold on." Dave was fixing three self-adhesive electrodes to Daniel's torso to measure cardiac activity. He reached across the body and flipped a switch. The nine-inch screen on the AED popped to life. Dark gray lines ran across the lighter gray background. It wasn't V-fib, and her heart sank. Asystole, a flatline.

Okay, it could still work. She looked back at her hands. "Clear."

"We have cardiac activity," Dave said.

She spun her head to the AED screen. The flat line sporadically jerked. The ventricle in Daniel's heart was twitching unevenly, refusing to contract. But the muscles were trying.

Except for in movies, defibrillation was rarely used on patients with a flatline. Recovery was virtually impossible.

"Clear!" she shouted.

"Clear."

José thumbed a switch, and 200 joules of electrical current coursed through Daniel's chest. His muscles quivered as expected. No arching of the back or violent jump. But plenty of juice for the heart to respond to if it was capable of doing so.

The monitor showed one small blip of increased activity from the sinoatrial node, then returned to the scribbled line.

"Again, clear."

"Clear."

José waited another three seconds as the AED recharged, then hit the switch again.

Daniel's muscles reacted again. This time no reaction from the heart monitor.

"Give him the epinephrine!"

Dave already had the syringe hooked up to the IV line. He shoved the plunger to its hilt, flooding Daniel's vein with the clear drug. "Hit him again."

The cardiac monitor blipped once, twice, then returned to a straight gray line.

"Check the contacts," Lori breathed. "Check them!"

Dave did. The lines remained flat.

She glanced at her watch.

Nineteen minutes!

"Clear!"

"Clear."

Another surge of electricity. Another small jerk as the muscles responded.

This time there was no reaction from the monitor. Only a high-pitched tone that signaled no activity. Continued asystole.

Dave was still diligently working the respirator, pumping oxygen into Daniel's lungs. José was still readying the AED for another surge of current. Lori was still leaning over the dead body, knuckles white on the paddle handles.

But something changed in Lori's mind then. The forces of inevitability pulled the plug, draining the last reserves of hope from her.

"Clear," she said. Then whispering, begging, "Come on, Daniel. Please. Don't do this to me."

"Clear."

The body jerked a little. Then lay still.

The line on the monitor ran thread-thin.

Silence settled around them. Lori looked to one side and saw that the officer was watching her. As were the two paramedics.

Dave broke the stillness. "I think..."

"Give him more epinephrine," she said.

"Any more could kill him."

"He's dead!" she screamed, slamming both paddles on his chest. "You can't kill him! He's dead already. Give him more!"

Dave exchanged a glance with his partner, pulled out a second syringe, and emptied its contents into the IV.

"Clear." Quieter this time.

"Clear." The rote reply of someone checking off a list he had checked off a hundred times before.

This time Lori didn't bother looking at the monitor. She just listened for a change in the tone. Only when there was none after five seconds did she glance over.

No change.

"Clear."

Her mind was spinning with vague thoughts. It was all a mistake. Daniel wasn't supposed to die tonight. She'd been so sure, so intoxicated by the prospect of what lay ahead.

They hadn't responded.

"Clear."

"Doctor, he's ... flat. He's fixed and dilated—certifiably dead. His nodes are totally depolari—"

"Juice him!" she screamed. "I know he's dead! Now juice him!"

"Clear," José said.

When the body jerked this time, Lori knew it was over.

He lay on the white mattress, dead. Dead for twenty-one full minutes.

The medical record was spotted with rare cases of resuscitation after long periods of death, the longest being forty-nine minutes in Tyler, Texas, eight years ago. A man struck by lightning had come back to life on his own after being transported to the morgue.

He'd lived for another four days in a coma, then died.

There were several cases of people who'd been brought back after thirty minutes, including one in Poland in which the victim had gone on to live a relatively normal life despite the paralysis of his left leg.

And many thousands of cases in which people had been resuscitated after several minutes. Millions of cases involving some form of near-death experience. But Lori knew all too well that the chances of anyone coming back to life in any kind of normal state after being dead twenty-one minutes were rare enough to be considered impossible.

The still form in front of her confirmed that impossibility.

She settled to her haunches, still clenching the paddles in each hand. She released her grip and heard them clatter to the asphalt. Mind numb, she lifted her hands to her head, covered her face, and tried to think.

Her fingers were shaking, and her breathing was hot in her face. For several long seconds, darkness swallowed her.

Lori lowered her hands and stared at the lifeless form that had been Daniel Clark. Then she touched his bare belly. Pressed her palm against his clammy flesh.

She leaned forward slowly, reaching her other hand

out and touching his chest. What happened next was a product of her basest desire and instincts, not borne of any premeditation or conscious thought.

She lunged forward, shoving the paramedic aside, flung the respirator from Daniel's face, tilted his head back, and shoved her mouth against his.

She filled his lungs with the contents of hers.

"Breathe." It came out as part sob, part whisper.

Another deep breath, closing off his nostrils as she had in the car for the ten minutes before they'd met the ambulance.

"Breathe, Daniel." She blew deep past his cold lips.

Her hand slipped off his chin and his jaw clamped shut on her lip. She grabbed his chin and yanked, sickened by her own desperation.

His mouth flew wide of its own, and a scream filled her mouth.

For a split moment she wasn't sure if it was her scream or his. Then he sucked deep and screamed again.

Lori jerked back.

Daniel's jaw stretched open in a scream that rocked both paramedics back on their heels.

His eyes remained clenched and his face contorted with pain. His jaw snapped shut, and then he began to cry. He was breathing. With quick, short breaths through his nostrils.

The monitor beside her was beeping. *Fast.* Ventricular tachycardia. He was thumping like a freight train. His eyes dilated, his face flung sweat, his lungs hoarded the oxygen. No longer deprived of pulse and breath, he was suddenly animated, frantic and convulsive, an all-inclusive resurrection of life and energy.

Daniel was alive.

Reprinted from Crime Today *magazine, 2008*

MAN OF SORROW:
JOURNEY INTO DARKNESS

by Anne Rudolph

Crime Today magazine is pleased to present the second installment of Anne Rudolph's narrative account of the killer now known as Alex Price, presented in nine monthly installments.

1983

THE DETAILS of what happened to Alex and Jessica after they were forcibly taken from their small home in Arkansas are not easily reconstructed. The memories of those involved have been whitewashed by pain.

The account you are now reading was carefully constructed during several long interviews with Jessica in a quiet corner of the faculty lounge at UCLA, where Jessica now teaches. Dr. Karen Bates, an expert frequently consulted by the FBI on behavioral psychology matters, and I conducted the interviews with the FBI's full support, as part of the criminal investigation directed at Alex and Jessica's abductors. Jessica's emotional stability was always our priority.

Alex and Jessica's thirteen-year captivity is perhaps best understood by the influence it had on their lives following their escape from the backwoods of Oklahoma.

The exact date of their flight cannot be determined, but it was in late October, 1981. At seventeen and sixteen years old, Alex and Jessica knew only a fraction of what most teenagers know at their age. They knew how to read the Bible. They knew how to survive one more day. They knew pain. They knew that even a mistimed glance at either Mother God or Father, Alice and Cyril, could end in pain. They knew that Eve, the evil spirit that Alice conjured each new moon, watched them constantly and repeatedly vowed to kill them if they ever crossed him.

And they knew that twice a day, once midafternoon and once in the dead of night, a train rumbled through the forest south of the shack they all slept in.

They had always been vigorously discouraged from asking questions of any kind, otherwise they surely would have known about trains much earlier. But the curiosity that leads to most children's discovery of the world was squashed from the outset.

Alex was fifteen before he worked up the courage to ask Cyril about the distant sound one afternoon as it passed. "Train," Cyril said.

"What's a train?" Alex asked.

"It's none of your business, that's what it is," Cyril said. Then after a moment he added, "Takes bulls to the slaughterhouse."

A full year passed before Alex told Jessica about the exchange. Although she couldn't bring herself to talk about the details of what happened that day—or perhaps she could not remember them—Jessica claimed it was a very bad day. Alice punished her, and Alex stepped in to take that punishment, which was allowed under Alice's rules.

Later that night, when the rest of the house was asleep, the faint rumbling of the passing train reached their room. They each had a mattress, placed roughly six feet apart, and late at night, while they lay still on their backs as was required of them, Alex would sometimes whisper some of his hidden thoughts to her.

That night, Alex told Jessica that he had been thinking about the train. He thought it might go somewhere. When she asked him where, he lay silent for a long time before answering, "Away from here."

At first Jessica thought he must have lost his mind to talk that way. There was no place but here. And even if there was, it was none of their business. She refused to talk about it and eventually fell asleep.

Still, Alex's comment lingered in her mind, and she brought it up again several months later when they were scooping water into a bucket for Alice's weekly bath.

This time he told her to shut up. There was no train and she had no business thinking about where the train might go, even if there were a train.

She thought he was upset because the next night was the new moon. The new moon, when the sky was blackest, was always a difficult time. So she decided to put the train out of her mind. In their fractured state, neither could grasp the hope that the train might one day offer them. And if they did grasp it, they dealt as quickly with that hope as Mother would deal with any of their indiscretions.

Six months later, Alex brought up the train again. That week, Alice and Cyril had a fierce fight over a woman they'd recently brought home. Both Mother and Father came out of the house soaked in blood as Alex and Jessica looked on.

"Have you seen Alice's whore?" Alex asked Jessica two days later, speaking of the woman. "No," she told him. The far-off rumble of the train reached them. Alex showed no reaction to the possibility of Alice's whore being gone, but the sound of the train brought a rare glint to his eyes.

Then he asked if she would trust him. At the time, she didn't know what he was truly asking, but she knew that her life depended on him. She would have died long before without Alex's protection. She told him she would always trust him and then thought nothing more about it.

Jessica's memory of the night before the next new moon was as vivid as any she had. Sometime past midnight, she guessed, they were both awake, lying as instructed, staring at the ceiling. The window was dark without a moon to light it.

Jessica heard Alex stir and looked over to see that he was slipping out from under the sheet each of them was permitted during colder months. She watched, amazed, as he pulled on his dilapidated work boots and crawled over to her mattress.

He whispered for her to get dressed and follow him as quietly as possible. She started to ask him why, but he silenced her by putting his hand over her mouth. "Trust me," he whispered. Although terrified of what might happen to them if they were discovered, she did as he said for the simple reason that she had always trusted Alex.

They dressed in the brown slacks and white shirts they wore daily, grabbed up the sheets to keep themselves warm, and climbed out the window. The fear of Alice's reprisal forced Jessica to a standstill, shivering under the thin sheet outside. What had gotten into Alex? Didn't they have a warm bed to sleep in and good food to eat, as Cyril always said? "Downright lucky," he used to scream. It was an absurd thought indicative of Jessica's frame of mind.

But Alex tugged at her sheet and Jessica followed him across the yard and into the forest, where he started to run. She would have called out for him to stop if she didn't think she would be heard, caught, and punished. By now Mother had surely checked the room and found it empty. Unable to think of facing Mother God in a rage, Jessica ran after Alex, farther into the woods.

They came to the fence that marked their boundary. Neither of them had ever stepped beyond that fence. But then they were past it and running down a long slope, through trees, up a hill and farther, until Jessica was sure that they were completely lost. But she was still afraid to speak out. Alice's ears were everywhere.

Jessica couldn't remember how long they ran, only that she felt more fear while racing behind Alex than she recalled feeling before that moment. Although she'd suffered years of abuse at Alice's hand, fleeing Alice was what Jessica feared the most. She had no recollection of her birth parents or her first three years. Everything she knew about life and how it was meant to be lived, she'd learned from Alice. She had little information about the outside world and how other families lived.

Fleeing her home of thirteen years felt like a plunge into a terrible evil.

But they'd already committed the sin, and within minutes they stumbled across two long tracks that split the forest. Thinking it was now safe to speak, Jessica demanded to know if Alex was trying to get them killed. They both knew that they wouldn't be the first victims.

Alex ignored her and started walking down the tracks. Once again she followed, ignoring the inner voices that insisted she leave him and run back to face whatever consequences awaited.

Again, time was lost on Jessica, but when the huge, thundering train finally came up behind them, she and Alex ran for the trees. Crouched in safety, her fear of Alice was replaced by an awe that such a long, powerful thing had passed by the house for so many years, and she cautiously emerged to watch.

For the first time in her life, Jessica's desire to know what life might be like without Alice overtook the fear of failing her. And when Alex yelled at her to follow him and ran straight for the train, she realized that her fear of losing him to that train was also greater than her fear of Alice.

The train that Alex and Jessica managed to jump in late October, 1981, was the westbound Union Pacific 98, a freight train that hauled

The root cellar used for punishment

mostly wheat, oil, and cattle. The long train frequently pulled more than a hundred cars through Texas, New Mexico, Arizona, and into Southern California. Any shorter and they may not have made the jump.

The car they successfully pulled themselves onto was a flatbed, and the night was cold, forcing them to huddle up at the front, behind a large container that blocked most of the wind. They crouched in the dark for a long time, watching trees rush by.

The train began to slow. Fearing that they might be seen, Alex be-

came frantic. He insisted that they had to find a way into one of the other cars. They managed to crawl through a ventilation window in a wheat car that was only half full. They buried themselves up to their arms for warmth and stared at the night sky, which they could see through the window.

To say that Alex and Jessica had stumbled upon their first bit of luck in thirteen years would be an understatement. The number of things that could have gone wrong that night is strikingly obvious.

Alice or Cyril could have heard

them opening the window and stopped them before they made it past the backyard. Either one of them could have been hurt as they ran through the forest in the dark, or been killed as they made a grab for the train. They could have failed to find such a rare wheat car, only half full, and with the ventilation window left open so that toxic gases would not fill the open space. They might have been seen, thrown off the train at the next stop, and returned to the Browns.

We can only wonder how events might have changed the world for better or for worse had the children failed in their escape. Some have argued that the only tragedy greater than Alex and Jessica's abduction was their escape. But watching Jessica weep years later as she haltingly recounted what she could remember of her captivity suggests otherwise.

Alex and Jessica did escape. And when they finally climbed out of the train three nights later, they found themselves in a world as alien to them as Mars might be to the average American.

IF NOT FOR the Salvation Army, soup kitchens, and the few homeless shelters scattered throughout greater Los Angeles in 1981, Alex and Jessica might not have survived the sudden and drastic change forced upon them as they moved from rural captivity to bustling city.

A transcript from Jessica's interview with authorities best captures that first month: "We didn't know what we were doing. You know. We just stumbled around, 'fraid to talk to anyone, lookin' stupid in these clothes that everyone kept staring at. We ate out of garbage cans at first, until someone told us about the soup places. We were happy with that. You know. Alex was like, you know, a new person."

And a new person he was, complete with a last name that he insisted they both take since they didn't know Alice's. They would now be Alex and Jessica Trane.

The train that had delivered them to Los Angeles dumped them on the outskirts of Union Station on Vignes Street in old Chinatown. The trail of alleys where they would sleep and soup kitchens they sought steadily led them north toward Pasadena. A homeless man who said his name was Elvis told them about the Union Station Foundation on Colorado Boulevard in Pasadena, claiming it was the best place for a couple of lost bums like them. He stayed with them a week before disappearing.

Nancy Richardson, who volunteered at the USF from 1975 through 1983, remembers Alex and Jessica Trane clearly. "They were just wide-eyed kids, just eighteen if you believed them. At first we were sure they were runaways, but all of our efforts to dig into their pasts or find relatives failed. We had no choice but to take them at their word."

Nancy recalls that Alex was the perfect gentleman, unnervingly quiet most of the time, handsome when he cleaned up. He was always staring, fascinated with the simplest things, like a boy half his age.

At first the workers at the foundation thought he might be retarded, because he preferred to look at people rather than talk to them. But once they got him to open up a bit, they realized Alex suffered only from naïveté, not any lack of intelligence. Both Alex and Jessica were socially inept, especially around members of the opposite sex. Alex in particular seemed to have no interest in women.

"I remember stepping into the washroom once when Alex was cleaning up, about a week after he first came to us," Nancy recalled.

"He had his shirt pulled down past his shoulders, and I saw that his upper back was covered in thick scars. The sight was so shocking that I gasped. He jerked his shirt up and spun around. Before he could button up I saw more scars on his chest. Without my asking he said he'd been in a bad car accident, then he left quickly. It could have been, but I wasn't convinced."

Horrified by what she'd seen, and wondering if the scars had anything to do with Alex's disinterest in women, Nancy questioned Jessica, but the girl refused to discuss the matter. "It's none of your business," she said.

They both refused to talk about their pasts, except to say that their parents, Bob and Sue Trane, had been killed when a train ran over them in Los Angeles.

When confronted with the fact that no such incident had been recorded by the authorities, Alex said their parents were also homeless and the accident happened at night. They'd been told about the accident by someone else and had never actually seen the bodies. Neither the story of their parents' deaths nor Alex's car accident could be corroborated. Left without a choice, Nancy and the director of the USF did the only thing they could for Alex and Jessica: feed them, give them a bed when they needed one, and steer them toward a normal life.

The next year was filled with so many firsts for both Alex and Jessica that they were effectively able to set aside most of the influence their captivity had burdened them with. Like two butterflies who'd escaped their cocoons, they fluttered from one discovery to another, embracing freedom with a newfound passion for life.

They drifted in and out of the USF, disappearing for days at a time, always quiet about where they'd gone or what they'd done. Nancy knew she had to get them into a more stable living environment, but her concern was eased by the eagerness with which Alex and Jessica took on the challenges of life.

Both had discovered books and were rarely seen without a bag that contained at least two or three volumes—anything from novels, which Jessica favored, to history books, and without fail, an old Bible from which sections had been torn out.

One hot day in August 1982, Nancy Richardson introduced Alex and Jessica to Father Robert Seymour, a priest from Our Lady of the Covenant, a Catholic church on the south side of Pasadena. Father Seymour had seen the couple hanging around the shelter and took an interest in them when Nancy spoke of Alex's thirst for learning.

Father Seymour made the Tranes a simple offer: if they would take jobs arranged by him, and agree to stay in the low-income apartments on Holly Street, he would make a curriculum available to both Alex and Jessica and help them attain a GED.

What was a GED? Alex wanted to know. Father Seymour explained that it stood for general equivalency diploma, roughly the same thing as a high school diploma.

Alex's eyes lit up at the suggestion, and after a hasty consultation with Jessica, he enthusiastically agreed. With a passing glance at Nancy, Alex headed down the street with Jessica to "do some stuff," promising to be at the church at nine o'clock sharp the following morning. It was the last time Nancy would ever see Alex. Her mother would soon fall ill, and she would be forced to leave the shelter in the summer of 1983 to take care of her.

"I can still see the look in his eyes," Nancy said years later. "Those same brown, haunting eyes that seemed to swallow the world."

Neither Father Seymour nor Nancy Richardson nor any of the staff at the USF on Colorado Boulevard could have realized the extent of the rage and pain that hid behind those haunting eyes, beneath the scars that had shaped Alex Price, known during the eighties as Alex Trane.

SEVEN

2008

HEATHER CLARK PACED the living room carpet, one trembling hand at her chin. The pain that pounded her chest refused to wane. She glanced at the clock. 1:55 a.m. Where was Raquel? The prospect of even another minute alone sent shafts of fear through her heart.

Daniel was dead.

The bell rang and Heather started. Raquel.

She raced to the front door, peered through the eyehole, and seeing her friend's long dark hair, fumbled to open the latch. Raquel stepped inside, took one look at Heather's teary face, and pulled her tight.

"I'm so sorry, honey."

The door swung shut behind them, and with the soft *thud*, Heather felt her restraint fall away again. She leaned her forehead against Raquel's shoulder and began to sob softly. *There's no end to it*, she thought. *I can't find the bottom of this pain.*

For a few minutes Raquel just held her, whispering her sympathy. Demonstrating the same strong character that Heather had always relied on, Raquel gently led her into the living room and announced that they could both use a cup of coffee.

Several minutes later Heather thanked her, took one sip of the hot beverage, and set it on the coffee table. There was so much to say but no reason to say it.

"You really did love him," Raquel finally said, looking at a large portrait above the fireplace. An artist's rendering of Daniel and Heather at Fisherman's Wharf in San Francisco. "I mean really."

Heather started to cry. She hated herself for crying, but she seemed powerless to stop the tears. She took a deep breath, wiped her eyes, and clasped her hands together.

"Unfortunately. You'd think I'd be over it by now." She tried to force a grin, but her lips twisted wrong. "I left him. I told him this thing would kill him…"

Raquel put her hand on Heather's knee. "It's not your fault. You start thinking like that, I will personally haul you in, you hear me? This was Daniel all the way. As much as we all love him for his confidence, he was completely blinded on this one."

"No! He wasn't the one who wanted the divorce! He begged me back then not to file the papers. He asked me to reconsider two months ago, the last time we talked. But not me, no. Not unless he chose me over all that other…" Her throat knotted, cutting her short.

"And you were right," Raquel soothed. "Dear, you were more right than you can possibly know. You have to let this go and stop blaming yourself. I've never seen a woman love a man the way you've loved Daniel. But he never could let go."

Heather sat back and struggled to maintain at least a semblance of control. "I pushed him away, Raquel."

"*He* abandoned *you*. How many times did you call me, alone, while he was out lecturing on the sins of religion?"

That stalled them both.

"None of that matters now," Raquel said. "What matters is that you've lost him. And I'm sorry. I'm so sorry. In the end the pain will pass, you know that. Right?"

Heather stared up at the portrait and decided then that Raquel had to know everything. Hiding her own obsession now felt like hypocrisy.

"I have something I need to show you," she said. "Something I...I don't know, it's a bit crazy."

"This is me, Heather," Raquel chided.

She stood and walked to the stairwell. Raquel followed without comment. Down the stairs, across the basement. Approaching the door, Heather nearly turned back. No one had seen this side of her relationship with Daniel. The Eve room was more a shrine than the efforts of a good citizen trying to help out the authorities.

She pushed the door open. Turned on the lights. Stepped in.

The fifteen cases were posted in order from left to right, with the date of each woman's death posted above the respective photographs and newspaper clippings.

"You're kidding..." Raquel walked past her and slowly looked around the room, eyes pinned on the photographs. All of the victims were positioned the same:

faceup, hands resting delicately on the ground, legs spread less than a foot, dirtied dresses pulled straight. Pale skin. Fragile. Apart from the pervasive bruising, no sign of trauma.

"You have got to be kidding," Raquel said, walking to the files. "This is all Daniel's?"

It took a moment for Heather to respond. "No."

"Then what's it all doing here? This is…" Raquel turned back from the file she'd opened.

"It's me," Heather said. "My sick, demented way of connecting to Daniel, I suppose." The tears were leaking quietly now, and she made no attempt to stop them. "He taught me a lot about human behavior. Why people do the things they do. Why killers kill."

"You thought helping him find Eve would somehow create a bond."

Heather thought her silence made her agreement clear enough, so she left it at that.

"Have you uncovered anything the FBI isn't aware of?"

She shrugged. "I was chasing down a few hunches of my own. Nothing concrete."

"Okay now, you listen to me, Heather." Raquel glanced at the wall of photographs. "I know you were in love with him. I know this is all just some crazy way to connect with him. But it's over now. This…this can't be healthy. You can't…"

Her eyes settled on a picture of Eve number twelve, a thin, dark-haired girl whose lips seemed confused between gentle smile and frightful grimace.

"There's more," Heather said. "The man I was supposed to meet tonight ended up being a phone call. I think...I think it might have been Eve. He knew about this, about Daniel, about the killer. And he told me that Daniel would die because no one could stop Eve."

"Your informant...It was about this?"

Heather nodded. "He told me that if I couldn't find a way to stop Daniel, he'd die." She walked up to one of the few newspaper clippings that showed Daniel at a crime scene in San Diego. "Not that it matters now."

"It *does* matter now." Raquel touched her arm. "Honey, it does matter. You have to go to the FBI with this. There's a serial killer out there, and you met someone who apparently knows his identity!"

"Maybe. Daniel's dead, Raquel."

"Did he threaten you?"

"No. No." Heather faced her friend. "I think he thought Daniel might respond to me."

"Why do you say that? You've tried to talk Daniel down ever since he took this case."

Silence smothered the room.

Raquel answered her own question. "Because it was a veiled threat against you. He knew that if your life was threatened, Daniel would have responded."

"He didn't say that." Heather walked to the door, snapped the light off, and strode from the room. "It doesn't matter now."

Raquel followed her up the stairs silently. The house felt like a tomb, but at least the flood of tears had subsided. Life as Heather knew it had changed tonight. Raquel wasn't saying it, but she knew Heather would eventually see the bright side to all of this. Without Daniel in the picture, there was no more reason to obsess over him. Time to move on.

"I want you to promise me something," Raquel said, stepping past her in the living room. She waited for Heather's full attention. "Promise me that first thing tomorrow you'll call up Brit Holman or someone else you trust at the bureau and tell him everything. About the phone call, about anything you've learned, any of your theories—I don't care how crazy they seem. Then you drop all of this."

"Eve's still out there, Raquel."

"Exactly." Her friend glared.

"He killed Daniel."

"And he's going to come after you if you don't drop this! You're an attorney, not a federal agent."

Until now, Heather hadn't processed her options concerning Eve. Raquel made perfect sense, naturally. The thought of dropping her own search for him relieved and frightened her at once. Maybe it was appropriate that both Daniel and Eve would disappear from her life in the same night.

"Fine."

Her cell phone rang on the counter, where she'd hooked it up to the charger. The clock read 2:27 a.m.

She walked to the counter, picked up the phone. Saw it was Brit Holman. "Speaking of…"

"Who? That's *him*?"

She snapped the phone open. "Hello, Brit."

"Heather…He's alive."

His words didn't immediately compute. *He's alive*, meaning Eve was alive. Daniel was dead, and they hadn't caught Eve.

"I've had a bad night, Brit. I really don't think I can—"

"Daniel's alive."

The words sounded foreign, like Chinese characters that meant something to someone, just not her, not at this moment.

"He was resuscitated." A pause. "Are you getting this, Heather?"

"Alive?" Her voice sounded like an echo.

"They have him at the ICU at Colorado Springs Memorial, but preliminary prognosis is good. They think he's going to be okay."

Heather's head buzzed with mixed, jumbled, crazy upside-down thoughts.

"Heather? I've got to go, but I want you to call me in the morning. He's going to be okay, I just wanted you to know that as soon as possible."

She slowly closed her phone without acknowledging his request.

"Who's alive?" Raquel demanded.

"Daniel." Heather's arms began to tremble like a track under a train.

EIGHT

DANIEL LAY IN THE hospital bed early the next morning, staring up at the soft hue of indirect lighting that filled his room. Memorial Hospital, Colorado Springs. A dark shadow rimmed the white crown molding that hid what he assumed were fluorescent tubes. Darkness encroaching on light.

Death stalking life.

He could remember finding Eve's sixteenth victim alive in the caves by Manitou Springs. They said the killer had been gone.

Waiting for them, watching his victim. He'd come out of the night and faced down the Suburban, head-on.

Then killed Daniel, one officer, and clipped Lori's arm with a shot. He'd taken the girl. Still missing.

Lori had rushed Daniel to meet an ambulance and managed to resuscitate him after several minutes. Death to life.

So they told him, but Daniel could remember none of it. Not the sight of Eve coming out of the dark, not the shot to his head, certainly not dying or being dead. Or waking. His memory ended with Lori cradling Eve sixteen in her arms as they rushed down the mountain, then resumed with his waking in this bed.

The door opened on his right, and Lori walked in with a man Daniel assumed was a doctor. No smock, just khaki pants and a blue button-down shirt. Daniel could see a guard standing outside his door as it closed.

Lori put her hand on his arm and smiled gently. "How you feeling?"

"A bit of a headache. A bit groggy."

"That's probably the morphine," the doctor said, stretching out his hand. "I'm Dr. Willis." He stared at the left side of Daniel's head. "If you don't believe in divine intervention, now might be a good time to reconsider. That or you have enough luck to walk out of Vegas a rich man."

Daniel looked from one to the other. "You mind telling me what happened?"

The doctor reached for the bandage around his head and began to peel it back. "The bullet struck just above and to the side of your left eyebrow where the upper bone of the orbital socket is at its thickest. An eighth of an inch up or down and you'd be dead."

"I thought I was."

The doctor nodded. "You were, but thankfully your brain escaped irrecoverable damage. The bone diverted enough of the bullet's energy laterally, around the side of your head, so that it didn't actually penetrate the skull. It traveled under the scalp and exited behind the left ear."

"Sometimes having a thick head comes in handy," Lori

said, then moved on as if she was perfectly serious. "The bullet recovered from the side of the Suburban was fired from a .38 special. They're still working on it, but enough of the bullet's trunk is intact to make a type ID. Likely a police-issued Colt Cobra firing a lead semiwadcutter bullet—used primarily for targets, not humans."

"He doesn't like to kill with a gun," Daniel said, shifting his eyes to the ceiling. "His pattern is more about how and why they die, not *that* they die. Death is hardly more than the unfortunate end."

They looked at him, unsure.

"Could be," Lori finally said. "Your mind hasn't shut down, that's good."

"Like I was saying," Dr. Willis said, "pretty lucky. I've seen worse, but this one's worth a write-up."

"And what did kill me?"

"Hydrostatic shock," Lori said. "The bullet's energy transferred to the soft tissue of your head and sent your nervous system into failure. Your heart and lungs went into full cardiac and pulmonary arrest."

"Shock killed me."

"Shock kills plenty of people, nothing unique there." She stood, peered at his skull now exposed by Dr. Willis, and handed Daniel a mirror. "Take a look."

At first he thought the mirror was reversing the sides of his head, but glancing to the right he saw that neither side of his curly blond head had been shaved. His brow was stitched up on the left, just above the eyebrow. Some bruising traced a line across his left temple. He would have a black eye for a few days.

"That's it?"

"That's it," she said.

He sat up in bed, felt his head throb, but let it pass. "So then I'm free to go."

"Not so fast," Dr. Willis said, urging him back with a hand on his chest. "We have to keep you under observation."

"Observation? For your sake or mine?"

"You were dead six hours ago, Mr. Clark. Your brain was starved of oxygen for over twenty minutes. Acute hypoxia. You seem rational enough, but there's no telling what damage has been done."

"Damage. Such as what?"

The doctor frowned. "Apart from more severe effects, which obviously haven't presented? Disrupted fine motor skills, memory loss, possible hallucinations. There's no telling."

Daniel stretched his fingers, wondering if his fine motor skills had been affected. No indication apart from a slight buzz that lit through his whole body. Staring at his fingers, he was bothered by the notion that something had changed. His ability to digest food, perhaps, his sense of humor, his proficiency with logical constructs, his tear ducts, the muscles in his left leg.

Something.

"The point is, you're alive," Lori said. "Montova will be here soon." She stood back, crossing her arms under her chest. "So...what was it like?"

"Honestly, I don't remember. My mind is blank. I remember you giving the victim CPR in the rear seat, and I remember waking up an hour ago in this bed."

"Nothing at all in between?"

Daniel shook his head. "Nothing. Why?"

"Because you saw him. You have an image of Eve locked away in your mind somewhere."

His mind spun with the implications. "You're sure?"

"He was ten feet from you. You had to see him. Lit up by the car's high beams."

"So we have a positive ID." Eve wasn't in CODIS, but a positive sighting could lead to their first real identity break. "What was he like? Blond bangs over deep-set eyes? A strong, pitted jaw? Tall? The farmer next door?" He'd constructed an image of Eve based on a hypothetical history drawn from his own profile of the man.

"I don't know," Lori said, watching him with soft, unblinking eyes. "I didn't see him. I was getting off the floor when he shot you. The girl blocked my view at the side door."

Daniel blinked, searched his mind for a hint of something that didn't belong. Anything that might ignite his memory. But his mind was blank.

"So the first real break in the case is locked in my mind. We have to find a way to get it out."

"A break? How so?"

"I could provide the details for an accurate artist's sketch. We break the case wide open and put his mug shot on every computer screen across America. Information is the greatest weapon we have in the age of the Internet."

"Seems to me Eve would know that too. So why did he risk being seen?"

"Because he didn't bank on either one of us surviving."

She nodded. "He killed you, and he would have killed me if Brit hadn't shown up."

"So it seems."

"What did it feel like?" Lori asked, again returning to his death. "You don't remember, but do you feel anything? Do you think you saw anything? In the mind's eye, that is."

"You mean a near-death experience," he said. "No. Not that a hallucination of that kind would help us anyway."

"No, but hitting the right switches could trigger your actual memory. We'll just have to wait, won't we?"

"For what?"

"For your memory of Eve to resurface. Memories are bound up in chemicals. In your case most likely DMT. Dimethyltryptamine. Excreted in massive doses from the pineal gland during the trauma surrounding death. The hallucinogenic drug thought to be responsible for near-death experiences. It's part of what may have caused the block in your memory."

"You're saying you think there's a way to trigger this hidden memory I have of Eve. Is there?"

"I don't know. Time. Time brings back memory."

Dr. Willis held up the bandage. "Let's get this back on."

"Is that necessary? It's just a couple stitches in front."

"You were lucky, but not that lucky. You have cranial bruising and a good tear on the back of your head. I really think—"

"Please, Doctor, I'm not a child here. My head's not falling apart. Give me a few Advil and I'll be fine."

Dr. Willis shrugged and set the bandage on the over-bed table. "If you insist. I'll check on you again at noon."

"If it doesn't bust anyone's chops, I need to visit the crime scene, while it's relatively fresh." Pain stabbed through Daniel's head, but he didn't react except to lie back on his pillow. "Something might jog my memory. You have a problem with that?"

"For all we know you'll take five steps and drop dead from an aneurysm," Dr. Willis said. "Get some rest. I'll be back at noon." The doctor excused himself and left the room.

For a moment Daniel stared at the closed door, mind oddly blank. He threw off the sheets, pulled the IV out of his arm, sat up, and swung his feet to the floor, ignoring his swimming head.

"So what, I'm a dead man walking?"

He stood to his feet, and Lori instinctively reached out to steady him. "Please, Daniel. There's too much at stake for you to start acting crazy."

"At stake? Eve's at stake. The life of his next victim's at stake. What would you know about what's at stake?"

"Your life's at stake," she shot back, jaw firm. "Now, sit down!"

He took no offense at her frustration. If anything it gave him a small measure of comfort—this never had been a game for the weak.

Ignoring her order, Daniel walked forward five feet and stopped. No dizziness or other warning symptoms that he could tell. He crossed to the door, pulled it open, and stepped into the hall. The door closed behind him.

The nurses' station stood ten feet to his right, currently manned by three attendants, who looked up at him. Only then did he look down and remember that he was still dressed in a hospital gown covered in tiny blue paisleys. Underneath, his boxers. No undershirt.

Daniel turned back to his room and walked in. Lori stood near the hospital bed where he'd left her, wearing a thin, hooked grin.

"Forget something?"

"Where'd they put my clothes?" he asked.

"In the closet. But I wouldn't head out before talking to Montova."

"You know as well as I do that the crime scene is all we have now. No word of the victim?"

"They're combing the proximal area," she said.

"He had another car stashed. Brit's on that, right?" Daniel crossed to the closet and yanked the door open. "I need to be there."

"Of course Brit's on the car," she said. "It was his first assumption—Eve's always planned his scenes down to the last detail, probably months in advance. He knows every possible escape route and has alternative flight paths prepared. They're on it. Question is, what are you on?"

"I'm on the case."

"You're also on an overdose of DMT."

Daniel buttoned his pants and lowered his arms, ignoring his shirt for the moment. There it was again. His memory. The most obvious way to close in on Eve.

Lori's cell chirped and she flipped it open, turning her back on him after a lingering look. "Ames."

Daniel grabbed his ripped black T-shirt, shrugged into it, and wondered if a shower might be in order. But the thought of the evidence response team picking through the cave before he did was burrowing under his skin.

His head throbbed. A slug had smacked him with enough force to trigger cardiac and respiratory failure. He should be on life support or cooling in the basement. He had no business being out of bed, much less heading to the crime scene.

Daniel finished dressing, lifted his wallet and cell phone from the bed stand, and faced Lori as she finished her conversation. "I understand. Immediately." She snapped her phone shut.

"They found the body."

Eve's sixteenth body. Daniel felt his well-fed obsession with Eve uncoil in his gut and shove its way through his chest. The bodies had come once a month for sixteen months, and each time he'd crawled a little farther into Eve's mind by studying that undisturbed body.

He took an involuntary step toward the door. "Okay, I—"

Darkness smothered him midstride so suddenly that he was forced to stop when his right foot landed, two feet in front of his left. The dark crashed over him like a plunger cup, slamming his ears with a percussive blow that left his head ringing.

In that darkness he saw a nondescript form striding for him.

And then it was gone.

Lori had reached him and taken his arm to steady him. "You okay?"

No dizziness, no lingering darkness. His heart slogged through a thick molasses.

"Tell them to stay back," he said, heading for the door. "No evidence technicians until I've had some time."

"What about Montova?"

"We'll call him on the way."

"The doctor..."

"You're a doctor," Daniel shot back, pulling the door open. "Tell me I'm not well enough to look at a dead body."

She finally nodded. "Try to keep your heart rate down."

NINE

DANIEL KNEW BEFORE he'd set foot outside the hospital that Lori was right in suggesting he had no business walking around a room, much less running down to a crime scene. A sharp pain bit his skull with the incessancy of a barking dog. But the morphine took the edge off, and the blackout spell he'd suffered in the hospital hadn't recurred, so he kept his mouth shut and tried to focus on Eve.

Eve. A name tied to the killer's victims as much as to him. Young women trapped between innocence and guilt. As with so many serial killers, Eve was undoubtedly driven by ideology. Faith. Religion. God. Satan. Ideas likely introduced by his mother.

To Daniel's thinking, ignorance bred killers as much as it bred religion. Once a person began to look for answers in a place unbound by the restraints of science and logic, he opened himself up to accept religious edicts that defy reason. To make war on a neighboring country or bomb the World Trade Center. Or kill innocent women every lunar cycle.

Inasmuch as humans used religion to destroy others, religion was an enemy. Daniel explored this idea at length in *Fixing the Broken Among Us*.

"You sure you're okay?" Lori asked, setting her hand on his knee. They sat side by side behind Joseph, a local driver assigned to them by the FBI.

Daniel blew out some air and touched the black headband she'd insisted he wear to protect the entry and exit wounds. "It's just..." The thought faded.

"Just what?"

"Nothing, really. Eve."

She nodded. "Eve. He's crawled inside of you, hasn't he? He lives there."

"Now you're sounding like Heather. My wife."

"I know who she is. Was."

Daniel glanced at her and saw that she was staring out the side window. "Was."

"Hmm."

"What?"

Now it was her turn to play coy. "Nothing, really." Lori faced him. "Eve."

The Suburban snaked up the same road they'd traveled last night. An evidence response team from FBI–Denver had already taped off a perimeter that allowed only one route into the scene, limiting potential contamination. The driver rolled down his window, spoke to the local police officer enforcing the entry point, then rolled into the canyon.

They'd established the perimeter several hundred

yards from the abandoned van's location, curious to Daniel until he saw the black Suburban he'd driven last night sitting cockeyed on the road, under examination by a couple of agents.

A stain darkened the asphalt beside the driver's door. His blood, he realized.

"Anything come back?" Lori asked.

He shook his head.

The driver looked over his shoulder. "Would you like me to stop, sir?"

"Not now. Get me to the body."

Three vans were parked fifty yards farther up the road, still a good couple hundred yards from the cave Daniel had entered last night. The driver parked next to them.

"Right through the trees. Special Agent Holman is waiting."

Daniel followed a yellow-tape corridor through the trees, toward the cliff. Lori followed close behind.

"He took her from the car fifty yards down the road, headed straight into the trees, and worked his way back up the cliff," Daniel said. "This wasn't his entry point."

Lori didn't respond. Several agents stared at them as they exited the path. Only then did Daniel consider how his appearance at the scene after being shot dead must sit with anyone who knew. Which was undoubtedly all involved.

He lowered his eyes and walked past them to Brit Holman, who stared at the cliff, smoking a cigarette. The old habit died hard among those who faced death on a daily basis.

No cave that Daniel could see. "Where is it?"

Brit spun back. Extinguished his cigarette in a red

Altoids can he carried for this purpose. He dropped the
sealed can in his jacket pocket and strode forward.

"I'll be a son of a gun. You've got to be kidding." He
stretched out his hand.

"Better than a dead son of a gun." Daniel stopped and
studied the cliff for an opening. "It appears I owe my life
to the one who studies the dead for a living." He glanced
at Lori, who smiled.

Brit glanced down Daniel's body, an understandable
bit of observation, considering. "You were dead, my
friend. She did bring you back though, didn't she? I've
seen my share of close calls, but…" Brit shook his head.
"You have any…you know…anything happen?"

"Tunnels of light? No. Where's the victim?"

"This way." Brit angled for a large rock, skirted it, and
walked past four agents waiting to enter the crime scene.
He motioned for one of them to hand Daniel and Lori
flashlights, then stepped into a narrow, obscured cave
entrance now lit by a string of battery-powered fluorescent lights that ran along the floor.

"It's an unmarked cave. We found the exit at the top
of the cliff first, then backtracked this way. Watch your
head, it's smaller than the cave we found last night."

Brit led them in, panning the walls with his light.
"No telling how many other escape routes he had. Picks
the one that suits him. Deadpan thinking, not impulsive.
He had a car waiting at the other end—tire impressions
indicate a sedan. There was no way we could have found
this cave or the car in the dark. And he knew it. He's got
a good six hours on us. Could be in Utah by now."

Daniel stopped. Felt Lori close in behind him. "Hold
up, Brit."

The agent looked back. Daniel nodded and stepped past him. "If you don't mind."

Brit made no objection to his taking the lead. Daniel didn't see it, but he heard Lori's breathing close behind him, and he knew she'd stepped past as well. The young pathologist eager to learn. Couldn't be much younger. At the right time he'd ask.

He walked forward slowly, listening to the soft crunch of dirt and gravel under his shoes. Eve would have carried the body over his shoulder to avoid banging her head and feet on the side walls. A strong man, six foot. Easy, unhurried stride. This after plucking his prey from their grasp like a father snatching his child from danger.

Strange thought.

They followed the cave around a forty-five-degree bend and stopped at the entrance to a chamber maybe fifteen feet wide. It narrowed again thirty feet farther in. Beyond, the cave wound its way up to the exit above the cliffs where they'd found the tire impressions, but Daniel wasn't as interested in how Eve had escaped as in what he'd done here, in this chamber.

The girl's body lay on a shelf ahead and to his left. Still dressed in the dirty white dress. No shoes. No head covering. On her back, facing the ceiling, carefully placed.

He knew that the photographer had already recorded the scene, following protocol. The FBI now had a permanent record of the cave. Otherwise the area had been undisturbed since Eve's departure sometime before daybreak.

A musty smell filtered through Daniel's nostrils. A stronger but less pervasive odor hung behind it. The bite of bile. He walked forward, stepped over a clear footprint, and skirted the rock shelf from his left to his right.

He traced the body from head to feet. Positioned exactly as Eve had positioned the other fifteen bodies. Hands by her sides, fingers curving gently, feet slightly parted. Eyes closed.

A pungent odor rose from her body. Before she'd finally relaxed and died, the victim had vomited. A wet spot containing no obvious solids by her left shoulder.

"He doesn't hate them," Lori said beside him.

"What leads you to that conclusion?"

"Her death came from the disease inside of her, not from him."

"Very good, Dr. Ames. And yet when you do your autopsy, I think you'll find that his murder weapon is far worse than a bullet to the head. Why does he infect them?"

"Because they deserve to be infected. But he doesn't blame them or use violence. He isn't angry at his Eves."

She pulled on a pair of green surgical gloves, snapped them around her wrists. Leaning forward, Lori eased the victim's lips apart, pulled her lower lip down to expose her teeth and gums.

"Blood," she said. "From a cut on the inside of her lip that wasn't there last night. Her lips were compressed with enough force to draw blood."

She looked up at Daniel.

He met her eyes. "He kissed her on the lips at the end."

"He needs to watch them die," she said.

"He's obsessed with watching the disease smother them."

"And he's there to taste the last breath."

"Why?" Daniel asked.

They were volleying like tennis partners. Lori had taken a path that landed her a job and title known as forensic pathologist, but he wouldn't be surprised to learn that she had studied far more than the human body along the way.

"What about the other victims?" she asked. "Similar cuts?"

"Bruising. Some blood. But it's always been attributed to the disease."

She stood upright and looked over the body. "When can we get her back to Los Angeles?"

"As soon as she's processed here," Brit said. "She'll be on ice and on a plane within two hours. Unless you want to use the Denver lab."

"No."

"Why would he risk his life to kiss her?" Daniel asked the question aloud, but he was posing the issue for himself. "What is it about their breath that drives him? Eve risked his life without hesitation to take her back from us last night. Why? So he could finish what he'd started. Finish taking her life through a disease."

"Or finish taking her breath," Lori said.

They stood next to Brit, who respected their exchange. Get him with the forensic evidence team, and he'd take the lead.

He spoke after a long stretch of silence. "Montova is at the first site with the ERT. He wants to talk to you, Clark."

"Give me a minute, will you?"

Lori touched his arm, then left with Brit. Alone with the body. He took a deep breath, paced along the rock shelf, formed a steeple with his fingers, and tapped his lips.

Eve had kissed his victim. Sucked the breath from her. Or forcefully smothered her with his lips, but additional evidence would almost certainly undermine such a forceful killing. Eve had never expressed his passion through personal violence.

"You don't *want* to kill them, do you?" His voice echoed through the chamber. "You feel sorry for them."

Pain knifed through his head, then faded. The morphine had worn off and the ibuprofen was wearing thin. Why had Lori checked the victim's lips?

But he saw why. A thin line of dried blood traced her lower lip. The pathologist from Phoenix was unusually observant.

Daniel left Eve number sixteen as she had died, faceup on the shelf, and joined the others outside the cave.

Brit turned to one of the technicians dressed in a Tyvek suit who was checking the power supply to a black light. "It's all yours, Frank. Break it down into quadrants, turn over every rock. Let me know what you find before filing the report."

The black lights would cause photoreaction of fluorescence or phosphorescence in different articles of evidence. Once the cave had been thoroughly scanned for trace elements, secretions, and fibers, floodlights would be taken in for a meticulous visual search. Chips in the rock, scrapes, articles of clothing, weapons, the whole gamut. By the time the cave was dusted for fingerprints, any disturbance created by the dusting itself would be immaterial.

"This way." Brit led them along the cliff wall, where game had worn a thin trail through the brush.

"You okay?" Lori asked.

"You got any more Advil?"

THE CAVE WITH THE animal pens looked like a zoo now, climbing with technicians armed with the tools of the trade. The evidence collected would be bagged and tagged and flown to the LA lab for examination. Only the Tokyo Police and Scotland Yard matched the FBI's capability in extracting patterns from evidence. But the suggestions made between the lines were what interested Daniel.

No sign of Montova.

Daniel spent ten minutes walking through the pens, stepping around technicians sifting through straw and dirt. They had already lifted a wealth of evidence from the scene, but nothing that would lead them closer to Eve's identity. They might catch a break, but fifteen months on the killer's trail had left Daniel with one clear understanding: there was no real trail.

Eve left only evidence that confirmed the profile they already had. He'd been careful not to supply the slightest indication that might expand the FBI's knowledge of him, and Daniel doubted he'd slipped this time.

There was one thing in common among the blue Bic pen found in the third cage, and the razor-clean cut along the goat's sternum, and the metal chair in the girl's cage, and the mud impressed by the bottom of Eve's boots, and the fingernail recovered next to the chair, and a dozen other pieces of bagged evidence: none of it would advance the ID of the UNSUB.

It was the seventh time they'd found a slaughtered animal near the victim. Part of his religious profile.

"Could I see you in private, Agent Clark?"

Daniel turned around and faced Montova, who stood near the cavern's entrance. "Morning, sir. Of course."

The assistant director in charge led Daniel to his car, where Lori leaned against the front fender, arms crossed. She stood when she saw them approach.

The rusted white Dodge Caravan was being loaded onto a flatbed truck, ready to be taken to a secure facility in Colorado Springs for processing.

Montova stared him down, rubbing his jaw between his thumb and forefinger. "You know why I'm here?"

"Not really, no."

"For a lot of reasons that make sense to the bureau. First victim found alive. First agent found dead. To mention a couple."

Daniel nodded. His head ached despite the Advil he'd downed. A cricket in the nearby trees seemed unnaturally loud. The canyon was filled with sounds of the FBI working over a crime scene—subdued voices, the mechanical clicking of a camera, muted radio chatter. To the casual observer, they were just busy bodies working methodically, hardly an image of full-scale war.

Montova spoke. "Consider yourself off the case, effective immediately, Agent Clark."

"Sorry?" Daniel felt momentarily stunned.

"Not only do we face significant liabilities in fielding an agent in your physical condition"—he glanced at Lori—"but we can't afford to put a case of this magnitude in the hands of a broken man."

"Broken?" Daniel felt his left eye twitch, a condition only his wife had called out as an idiosyncrasy. Evidently the twitch came on when he was enraged, a rare enough occurrence that only someone who lived with him for quite some time would notice. So said Heather, his one and only true love.

"I'm sorry, sir," Lori said, "but I believe *at risk* was the term I used."

"In my estimation, *at risk* of a mental breakdown is *broken*, at least when it comes to field duty. You were killed. At least accept that much. Your body made it back in one piece, but did your mind? I'm not willing to sit around and find out. At least not officially."

"I can assure you, I'm fine," Daniel snapped. "Apart from a headache and some occasional dizziness, everything is functioning just fine. You can't just remove me from the case."

"You were dead for—"

"I'm alive, for heaven's sake! Don't penalize me for refusing to die!"

"We aren't. Just questioning your mental stability."

"I'm sorry, I was under the impression that she"—Daniel pointed to Lori—"is a *medical* doctor. I'm the behavioral psychologist. Or did I lose my doctorate while I was under as well?"

"Self-evaluation isn't acceptable. FBI policy. I'm putting you on leave, no discussion." Montova blew out some air. "On the other hand, if you choose to follow up this case on your own, I won't stop you."

"Meaning…"

"You forget already?" Montova's brow arched.

Daniel glanced at Lori. "You're saying I can go dark on the condition that I work with the woman who's declared me unstable."

Lori took his frustration in stride, returning his glare

with the look of an empathetic, maternal partner. *It'll be okay, trust me.*

Montova glanced between them. "That you do everything through Lori, yes. She'll provide you access to necessary elements of the ongoing investigation. And for the record, I think you could use someone to help you process what's happened here."

"You mean someone to keep tabs on me," Daniel said.

Montova dipped his head almost imperceptibly. "Call it what you want."

Daniel stared at the flatbed that was hauling away the white van. "I want to check the tires," he said.

"Stick to the head game, Agent Clark. Leave the tires to Agent Holman."

"The tires *are* part of the head game," Daniel snapped. His head throbbed and for a moment the edges of his vision darkened.

Then it was gone. *Stable*, he thought. Maybe Montova and Lori were on to something.

"The tires tell us where he's been."

"The lab will tell Brit where he's been," Montova said. "Brit will tell Lori. Lori will tell you. You'll have full access, and believe me, I hope you corner him in one of his dark, smelly holes. But it's my job to make sure it's Eve who ends up in the ground, not you. You do things my way."

Daniel decided to accept the man at his word. If he were to be completely frank, he'd thank them both for giving him more than he'd asked for. Lori's involvement could prove invaluable; she'd proven that much in the last hour alone.

"Fine," he said.

Montova nodded. "As of this moment, consider yourself dark."

TEN

HEATHER CLARK WALKED along the concrete sidewalk, angling for the steps leading up to the courthouse, mind still buzzing with the events that had kept her awake through the night. The world seemed to have rolled over and exposed an underbelly not even she could stomach.

An hour earlier, Brit had filled her in on the details of Daniel's death and resuscitation. She had begged him to let her talk to Daniel, but he'd insisted she should let Daniel process the matter first. The death. His health, body and mind, or the lack thereof. The crime scene.

It was then she'd learned that he was actually headed to the crime scene. Any lingering concerns for his well-being fell away. Daniel had been killed and brought back from the brink, but in the end he was still Daniel. His first concern was always the crime scene. He probably hadn't even stopped to consider the pain his rather inconvenient death had caused her.

"Does he know that I know?" she'd asked.

"No."

That gave her some comfort. If he knew, he'd have called to check on her. Unless he finally decided he'd had enough of her lines in the sand. Every person had a limit. The longer a couple is separated, the less likely their reunion, they said. She and Daniel were going on two years.

Heather climbed the steps, mind so far from her continuance hearing that she considered calling the office to pawn it off on Cynthia or one of the other new attorneys.

Her phone chirped and she pulled it from the clip on her belt. Raquel.

"You okay?" Raquel asked.

"As I can be. Find anything?"

Raquel paused. "Bobby ran the plates and came up empty."

Bobby Nuetz worked for the California Highway Patrol, a good friend to Raquel who had dipped into his state resources on more than one occasion for both of them. True to form, Raquel had followed Heather out of the bar last night, watched her step into the black car, then scribbled the plate number on a napkin before going back inside.

"What do you mean *empty*?"

"I mean it doesn't exist. I obviously missed something. You don't happen to remember the make or model of the car, do you? If Bobby had one or the other, he could cross it with part of the license and possibly get a hit."

"No. A black sedan. But there were others who saw me get in, I made sure of that. The valet may know."

"I'll check." Raquel took a breath. "Have you talked to Daniel?"

"Not yet."

"You going to tell him?"

"I don't know yet."

"You need to turn this over. Play with fire and you'll get burned, Heather."

She dipped her head at a dark-suited man who opened the glass door to the court building. "Thank you." She stepped into the busy foyer. "I'll call you after the hearing. I'm at security."

"Call me."

She dropped the phone into her purse, set it on the X-ray belt, and stepped through the scanner. The guard who motioned her through was a retired cop named Roy Browning, and he tipped his hat as he did every time Heather made an appearance at the courtroom.

"Lovely as always this morning."

Her phone was ringing as it passed through the X-ray tunnel—a traditional bell sound that she normally muted before entering any office.

"Thank you, Roy. I feel like I've been scraped off the bottom of someone's shoe."

"You look like an angel. And you can tell the judge I said so."

She picked up her purse, smiled at the man, and pulled out her cell phone on the fourth ring. One more and it would go to voice mail.

Heather flipped the phone open, thinking the call might be more news from Brit, who'd promised to reach her if anything changed in Colorado Springs.

"Hello?"

Static filled the receiver.

She hurried forward, hunting reception. "Hello?"

Only static.

She glanced at the display, saw that she had three bars, and pressed the phone back to her ear. "I'm sorry, I can't hear you."

A soft click sounded. A breathy voice was barely audible. "Heatherrrrrr."

She stopped in the hall. A sea of bodies, most dressed in suits, moved around her, but they fell silent as her hearing homed in on the one small speaker pinned to her ear.

"Heather. Heather—are you there?" A male voice, the same one that had called before, if she wasn't mistaken. Whispering this time. Low. "Heather, Heather. Did you make me a promise?"

"Who is this?" she asked. But she knew already, didn't she?

Still whispering. "I'm your saving Jesus. I'm your worst nightmare. I am Lucifer. It depends on what you want me to be. On what you do."

The voice sliced into her mind and sent a fear unlike any she could quite qualify through her nerves. Her voice came raspy, so quiet.

"Eve?"

Even as she spoke, she doubted he could hear.

"I do love Eve," the voice whispered back. "Do you love Daniel? He's forgetting his promise. He's going to die if you can't stop him."

"What promise?" she said, loud enough now for two men who'd passed her to glance back.

"You can't stop me. He took me from my daddy, my sister, my priest. No one can stop Eve."

Breathing.

"Who are you?"

The phone clicked.

"Wait! What promise?" This time she yelled the question, and a dozen passersby turned to look at her. She stood rooted to the marble floor. Stranded and conspicuous, she snapped the phone shut and forced her feet forward.

Raquel's warning rang through her head. *Play with fire and you'll get burned, Heather.*

She took two steps before slowly turning and walking toward the exit.

THEY BROUGHT THE VAN into the garage for inspection. Daniel slid out of the Dodge Caravan's cab, glanced around, then walked to the back, nodding at the mechanic in charge. He squatted and ran his finger along the edge of the right rear tire. "Decent tread. Can we get this up on a hoist?"

The mechanic headed for the lift levers on the wall. "Sure."

He and Lori had arrived before the technicians, who would get to the van this afternoon. Lori had insisted he return to the hospital for a follow-up after lunch. Evidently the doctor wanted to keep him overnight for a battery of tests. Daniel had agreed, but not before spending some time with the van.

Together they watched the mechanic operate a hydraulic lift that raised the van until it perched just above their heads.

"So no luck on the other vehicles Eve left behind?" Lori said.

"Unfortunately, no. The soil samples matched local terrain. Typical debris from highways. Nothing unique. But the tires on both vehicles were worn thin."

"Less tread, less debris and dirt picked up and sprayed inside the fenders."

"Right." He ducked his head and stepped under the right rear tire. A hundred thousand miles of wear had sagged the springs and corroded the undercarriage. He ran his hand over the lumpy metal surface. Felt like asphalt, which would yield them nothing. Most of the roads in the United States were constructed of the oily tar.

Daniel angled a work light on the tire and turned the wheel. The technicians would remove all four tires and examine every tread for residue. But Daniel was after something different.

"What are you thinking?" Lori asked so the mechanic couldn't hear.

He glanced up at her, saw the fascination in her eyes. "A killer is made in the mind. Years of abuse, a traumatic breakdown. It's all about the mind."

"You're looking at a tire," she said.

He returned his stare to the black rubber. "Am I? You see a tire, I see his choice. More importantly, I look past his choice into his world. The roads he travels. The stores he shops at. The women he stalks."

"Imagination: the making of a killer, the making of a priest," she said, quoting from his second book.

"One and the same. Fortunately, the same imagination that drags a killer into death allows people like us to understand him. We imagine enough, and every once in a while we get lucky and actually peg him. That's what I'm doing. I'm trying to get lucky."

"Hmm."

Daniel returned his focus to the slowly rotating tire. Tiny pebbles lodged in the tread, several small twigs, probably pine from the brush where he'd abandoned it by Cave of the Winds. Some chewing gum or...

"You have a knife?"

Lori disappeared and returned with a knife and an evidence envelope. Her attention to detail was natural for a pathologist, but she seemed to thrive as much on fieldwork. He took the knife and pried a thin milky strip of what had looked like gum out of the gap between two treads.

"Looks like plastic."

"Or wax," she said.

He sliced through the material. Small black grains of something that looked like asphalt were laid into the cloudy substance. Dropping the evidence into an envelope, Daniel made a quick inspection of the other rear tire, then both front tires. Three of them had at least one sample of a similar material.

"Whatever this is, he drove through a wide path of it."

"Assuming it was Eve, not the previous owner, who was driving at the time," Lori pointed out.

Where have you been, Eve? "He already has the next hole picked out. Maybe two or three holes. He thinks ahead of us and puts redundancies in place. Three or four escape routes, more than one mode of transportation, at least two possible killing holes. He's thought it all through like a chess player. Calculated, not passionate."

"To make a point?"

"No. Because he needs to. Because it's his ritual, and it must be observed with reverence."

"He works alone?"

Daniel hesitated. "Yes. At least when he kills."

She held out her hand and he set the sample in her palm. Their eyes met. His wife had accused him of making quick character judgments, and he'd never argued the point. Years of studying behavioral patterns had taught him to read a subject's every movement, every look, every word, every breath.

But looking into Lori's eyes, he felt as much the subject as she. She was studying him, piecing together his profile, deciding if she would trust him, pursue him. They shared a palpable intensity bound by the same passion for discovery.

Daniel's phone vibrated in his pocket. He blinked and turned away from Lori. "Tell them I need the mass spectrometry analysis on that as soon as possible. It may be nothing, but we might get lucky."

"Consider it done."

He flipped open his phone, saw the number. *Heather Clark.*

Daniel stared at the black phone vibrating in his hand. Only one explanation for a call from her: Brit had told her about his death. Heather and Brit talked on a regular basis, he knew that, and he knew that Brit was keeping her updated on any progress with Eve. But the last time Daniel had talked to her was two months earlier. She never called him. Protecting herself, she said. From what? From any unnecessary emotional entanglement. It wasn't like she didn't love him.

The phone stopped ringing. He punched the accept button, hoping he wasn't too late. "Hello?"

Dead line.

"You okay?" Lori asked.

"Fine." He walked away and punched in Heather's number. In all honesty he wasn't quite sure how he felt about her any longer. He'd come to accept the fact that she was right about the barrier between them. Not just Eve, but his obsessive compulsion to hunt them all down.

"Daniel?"

"Hello, Heather."

The line breathed static, and he knew immediately that something was wrong.

"What happened?"

"You okay?" she asked. "Brit told me what happened."

So it was his death. "Crazy, huh? Can't get rid of me that easy."

"No, you always were stubborn. You sure you're okay?"

"Apart from a hole in my scalp, a thumping headache that refuses to stay down, and the dizzy spells, I'm alive as they come."

"I'm afraid, Daniel." She didn't bother with small talk. Never had.

"I'm fine, Heather. Seriously. And if it makes you feel any better, I haven't changed my will. The Ford Pinto goes to you." He didn't have a Ford Pinto, didn't even know if any of the ridiculous old cars could be had.

"I don't want any stupid Ford Pinto!"

"What do you want, Heather?"

The line quieted. Figured.

"I need to talk to you."

"I don't know if that—"

"No. Listen to me. I need to talk to you as soon as possible." A beat. "It's about Eve."

"It's always about Eve. You want me to give up Eve. You want me to let it all go. Tell me I'm wrong."

"Stop it, Daniel! I'm afraid!"

The urgency in her voice was new, he thought. Something had happened. Then he remembered that he'd died, and his concern faded.

"I'll be back in LA tomorrow. Can I call you then?"

"Yes. Come over to the house?"

Something was definitely up. "What time?"

"Eight?"

"I'll be there."

ELEVEN

THE BATTERY OF TESTS that Daniel subjected himself to turned up nothing but what could be expected from a horrendous thump to the head. His loss of memory was normal considering the concussion, his headache would pass, his sporadic narrowing vision was consistent with trauma to the visual cortex. All were predictable presentations of such an injury.

But both Dr. Willis and Lori were more interested in finding presentations symptomatic of death and resuscitation, of which nothing was remotely predictable.

As it turned out, coming back from the dead, as it were, wasn't exactly understood. Defibrillating a heart within a few seconds to even a full minute was no real mystery, but beyond that, luck of the draw had more to do with resuscitation than science did.

Near-death experiences, or NDEs, were a different

matter. They were far more predictable and better known by science, never mind that most people would rather bask in the supernatural possibilities of the afterlife than accept the medical reason for the common experience.

Daniel knew that medical science estimated eight million Americans alive today had experienced NDEs, tunnel of light and all. Some while clinically dead, others during traumatic experiences—everything from giving birth to suffering acute illness.

He, on the other hand, had not, unless his memory of it had been suppressed. Of far greater interest to them was whether he was mentally stable after such a blow. And the answer became clear with each additional test: banged up but stable.

Lori left him at eleven, promising to return at seven in the morning to catch a private flight back to Los Angeles. The crime scene investigation had turned up nothing new on Eve. By all indications it appeared that Eve had done what he believed he was on the earth to do, then casually walked through their fingers to do it again.

The only break they might still pursue was Daniel's sighting of Eve. He'd stared into the killer's face and lived. But his memories had not. With time, those memories could emerge intact. Maybe. It might take days or weeks. More likely months, or never.

Hypnosis, however inexact a science, might jog his memory. At this point he would try anything.

Daniel threw back four Advil and retired, feeling defeated. Half-dead. Trapped by the hopeless cycle of which he was the most protracted victim.

Not true. Eve was a victim. A malicious killer, yes,

but as much a prisoner of his own devices. The deep psychosis of most serial killers eventually drove them to claim themselves as their last victim, if not in death, then by subconsciously yielding to a growing need to be caught.

Eve obviously suffered no such compulsion. Not yet. He would soon begin final preparations to take his next selected victim.

The last time he sneaked a peek at the alarm clock's glowing red numbers they read 1:12 a.m. And then he settled into a fitful sleep.

A scream woke him.

Not a distant shout for help, but a raw cry that crashed through his mind, repeating itself like a looped guitar riff with the volume twisted up full. Behind the piercing cry, a whisper rattled. An indistinct voice. Fear mushroomed like a noxious cloud.

His scream, he realized. The whisper wasn't his, but the scream was. Terror woke him. And that fear became a sledgehammer when he realized that he wasn't really awake at all.

He was conscious, but still trapped by sleep. A black form hovered at the end of his bed. A shadow against the darkened hospital room wall.

Not a face. Just a form hulking in silence, staring at him without eyes. Whispering.

Eve.

Daniel cowered, unable to move. His cry broke and then came again, tearing at his vocal cords.

Oddly enough, he knew what was happening. He was seeing what he most feared in his mind's eye: the hidden form of the man who'd slain sixteen women.

Something smashed into his cheek, breaking him loose from his fixation. The dark form had slapped him?

"I see you, Daniel Clark."

A slap again, on the other cheek.

"Mr. Clark . . . Mr. Clark . . ."

He opened his eyes and gasped. A nurse stood over him, speaking in a hushed voice. "Mr. Clark. It's okay. I can see you, you're fine. It's just a dream. Just relax. Sh, sh, sh."

Daniel sat up, clawing at soaked sheets that clung to his bare chest. He hardly recognized the face staring back at him from the vanity mirror. Drawn and pale—the face of an older man who hadn't been touched by sunlight for a year. Spikes of hair stuck out from the black headband. His chest expanded and contracted with the muscles countless disciplined hours at the gym had formed. From neck down, this was him, staring back.

From head up . . .

Daniel took a deep breath, cleared his throat, and lay back down. "Nightmare."

"No kidding," the nurse said. She was an old, thin rail with short red hair. Actually, his face had looked a bit like hers. Death warmed over. Minus her ruby lipstick.

"You okay?"

"Fine. Sorry about that."

"Happens to us all. That was a doozy, though. You need anything for your head?"

He touched his bandage. Now that he considered the matter, his headache was gone. "I'm fine. What time is it?"

"Six thirty."

Daniel tossed off the sheet and stood in his boxers. "I've got to get ready. My ride's here at seven."

* * *

DANIEL TOSSED THE BLACK headband in favor of a gray beanie Lori had purchased for him, climbed aboard the Cessna Citation, and made it to the descent into LAX before the fear revisited him.

It was hardly more than a flash that spiked through his mind as the plane lined up with the runway, but for that moment Daniel was gripped with a terror so overwhelming that he passed out.

For just a moment. Facing a dark form at the end of his bed.

"I see you, Daniel Clark." Like a clicking insect. "I see youuuu…"

He snapped his eyes wide. Lori sat in the facing seat, watching him with those bright eyes. "You okay?"

A side glance out the window showed the ground coming up—he'd been out for a second or two.

"Fine. Just nodding off." He forced himself to breathe through his nostrils. You don't start hyperventilating while nodding off.

She handed him a bottle of water. "You look like you could use a drink. Head's still okay?"

"Fine, I said!" He took an open-mouthed breath. Closed his eyes. Settled himself and forced as much ease into his demeanor as he could manage. "Sorry. Just tired."

Daniel stared outside and willed himself to find peace. The mind was a mysterious, often misunderstood piece of art only beginning to reveal its secrets to diligent researchers.

The results of a placebo study just released made the

point clearer than anyone could have guessed. The power of belief in a drug (which was in reality only a sugar pill) had eliminated significant pain among 68 percent of subjects tested. It explained the majority of spontaneous "healings" attributed to belief in the supernatural. A prayer or pill, take your pick. Both can trick the mind into spontaneous, genuine healing.

Which was what Daniel needed now, gazing out the Citation's window. Whatever sickness afflicted those who craved priestly prayers could not be more mentally disturbing than the fear he'd now felt twice. Heaven help him.

Mind over matter. He decided then, as the plane's wheels touched the ground, that he simply would not allow the fear to return.

It came again an hour later, as he sat in his office, like a freight train that crushed him in one horrendous blow and then thundered over.

This time his body jerked once, beyond his control. A chill swept through his limbs. He effectively stifled a scream to a soft whimper by clamping his mouth shut.

Once again, the dread left as quickly as it had come.

He glanced back at the door to his office, relieved that he was still alone. Lori had started the autopsy, and he would join her after collecting a few items to take back to his apartment.

Daniel sat hard and stilled his trembling fingers. "Get a grip, man. You're losing it."

"A bit of an exaggeration, don't you think?"

Brit walked in, grinning.

"What?"

"Talking to yourself," Brit said. "You were thumped

pretty good. Give yourself a break." The man put one hand on Daniel's desk. "So it's true?"

"Is what true?" Daniel asked, withdrawing his Eve file from the credenza.

"Montova says you're taking a leave to heal up. Not that you shouldn't. Heck, you haven't taken a day long as I can remember. It's just hard to imagine. You off the case, I mean."

"I'll be keeping tabs, trust me. It's not like I'm dead."

"Touché." Brit tapped the desk with his knuckles. "Anything breaks, you'll be the first to know."

"My primary contact is Lori. Montova told you?"

Brit arched his brow and offered a whimsical grin. "He did."

Daniel set seven files related to Eve alongside his framed picture of Heather in a box, then scanned the room for anything else he might need. He would have remote access to his computer, where most of the information he might need was stored. This was his life: files of Eve, memories of Heather.

Turning the lights off, Daniel headed for the morgue, box under his arm.

He made it through the hall, into the stairwell, down the stairs, and was halfway to the metal door with the word *Morgue* stenciled in black letters above a small observation window when the train slammed into him again.

This time he involuntarily dropped the box and fell to one knee.

He pressed his palm onto the cold concrete to steady himself. *Easy. Okay, just take it easy.* The mindless fear was gone, but now a new emotion flooded his veins.

Panic.

He was losing it. A nightmare was one thing. So was a recurrence, even a third episode. But now panic attacks were closing in. He couldn't ignore the possibility that his mind had suffered more than he'd been willing to admit.

Daniel staggered to his feet and ran for the door.

Reprinted from Crime Today *magazine, 2008*

MAN OF SORROW: JOURNEY INTO DARKNESS

by Anne Rudolph

Crime Today magazine is pleased to present the third installment of Anne Rudolph's narrative account of the killer now known as Alex Price, presented in nine monthly installments.

1983–1986

ALEX AND Jessica Price, known in Southern California as Alex and Jessica Trane, moved into apartment 161 at the Holly Street Apartments on August 21, 1983, with the help of Father Robert Seymour. In order to stay, at least one of them was required to maintain employment. Alex started working as a dishwasher at Barney's Steak House on Union Street the same week.

"He was terrified to go to work the first day," Jessica recalled, seated with one leg swinging over the other in the lounge at UCLA. Her eyes had a far-off look as she pulled the details from her memory. "Not that he was afraid of work—he'd done plenty of that. It was the thought of working with people that got to him.

He was afraid he'd have to work with a woman. He never did have much luck talking to women."

As it turned out, the kitchen had an all-male staff, and as a dishwasher, he didn't have much interaction with the waitresses. A week later, Father Seymour found a job for Jessica cleaning offices at night.

And as promised, Father Seymour set them up with a correspondence course that would give them a GED within two years if they passed the General Educational Development tests, which Alex felt supremely confident of doing.

Now nineteen and eighteen respectively, Alex and Jessica were well on their way to making a healthy transition into a well-adjusted life just two years after their escape from captivity. Or so it appeared to those blind to the full extent of the abuse they'd suffered in Oklahoma.

The furnished apartment the siblings would call home for the next nine years had a basic kitchen with pale yellow countertops, a refrigerator, a stove, and a white ceramic sink. The furniture consisted of eleven inventoried pieces: one kitchen table with four chairs, one brown couch, one oak coffee table, two beds (one in each bedroom), and two nightstands. Beyond that, they were on their own.

The bedrooms, one with a window and one without, were on opposite sides of the living room. Sleeping had always presented a problem for both of them, particularly sleeping in the dark, which was all but impossible. When they finally did fall asleep, nightmares frequently woke them. According to Jessica, a lights-out policy was the main reason Alex had refused to spend much time at the shelter. He would much rather find a streetlight to fall asleep under.

Each of the rooms had an overhead incandescent bulb, but they couldn't afford to keep these on all night, or so they reasoned. There was no way Alex could sleep in the room without the window. For that matter, Jessica wasn't sure she could sleep in her room alone.

Alex came up with a solution immediately: They would both sleep in the living room, she on his mattress, which he pulled from the bed in the windowless room, and he on the couch. They would keep their clothes and private things in their respective bedrooms, but until they figured things out, they would just have to sleep in the living room. With the kitchen light on.

Slowly the apartment began to take shape. "Alex dragged all kinds of things home," Jessica recalls. "I mean, if it wasn't an old beat-up desk he claimed the church gave him, or a lamp from someone's Dumpster, it was some other piece of furniture or trinket. I brought some stuff home too."

Among these trinkets were a variety of framed pictures. The pictures didn't matter; they both favored the ornate frames over the pictures anyway. Soon the apartment's decor began to take shape. They filled it with candles, and anything made from stained glass, and colored rugs to cover the brown carpet.

And crosses. Two or three for each room. Alex had an obsession with crosses, something he'd picked up from Alice, Mother God. "Except he insisted they be hung right side up," Jessica said. "We always thought the long part was the top, but all the churches had them the other way, and we learned to do it right."

From the day they first moved into the apartment, Jessica made it clear they would do nothing the way it had been done in their old home. Alex needed no encouragement.

"I don't blame those who don't believe in Evil; I pity them. The inhabitants of this planet also once thought the earth was flat. It was their lack of experience that failed to inform them of the truth, not any lack of intelligence."

—Father Robert Seymour
Dance of the Dead

"That first year, living at Holly Street, was the happiest year of my life," she later said. "We were both working, we both were studying, often together. We both were so free and hopeful. Not to say we didn't have our problems, but compared to what we'd lived through with Alice, we were practically in heaven."

And Jessica was right. In retrospect, 1984 appears to have been the best year they shared. The problems Jessica speaks of were relatively minor compared to what would come.

Father Seymour summarized his take on the pair that year: "I knew they had issues that could only have been explained by a dark past that neither wanted to relive, but Alex in particular was making progress by leaps and bounds. He seemed adamant about putting the past behind and forging a new life. Both proved to be exemplary students."

What kinds of issues? For starters, the nightmares continued. In fact, unknown to Father Seymour, Alex was suffering them with increasing intensity. He slept less, became more irritable, and struggled with depression. Small incidents could set him off, like the time his boss hired a woman to work in the kitchen. "He came home and threw one of the chairs against the wall," Jessica recalled. "Then he locked himself in his room for several hours to cool off. Luckily the girl quit the next day. I think it might have been something he said to her, although he wouldn't tell me what."

There were other issues: Alex's sudden dislike for overhead lights, which ended in his bringing home seven or eight old lamps and setting them in all the corners. He became more sensitive about his personal space. When Jessica suggested they might consider moving into their respective rooms, he wouldn't hear of it. Instead, he wanted her to keep her side of the living room spotless. Everything had its place, and he became more sensitive about where those places were.

If he couldn't control the mess unraveling in his mind, he could compensate by controlling his environment.

Although Alex refused to move his bed into his room, he began to use the space as his personal sanctuary, a place to which he would withdraw to escape the demons that haunted him. Still he plowed on, putting on a facade of well-being that kept even Jessica in the dark.

Meanwhile, Jessica made a more seamless transition to a normal life, steadily gaining confidence in her ability to merge with society. She suffered from an understandable nervousness around men and preferred disappearing into a book over spending time with anyone who might be considered a friend, but she found herself laughing more and even began to enjoy her work cleaning offices.

Neither made what could be considered more than acquaintances, and certainly not with members of the opposite sex. At the same time, Alex was fiercely protective of Jessica and she of him. And Alex would have it no other way.

On January 17, 1986, Alex and Jessica took the General Educational Development tests under the supervision of Father Seymour. Both passed with ease. It was a time for celebration, and celebrate they did, by going out to a restaurant together for the first time in their lives.

Alex ordered a bottle of wine, and they each had two glasses, though neither was a wine drinker. It just seemed to be the right thing to do. Jessica was now twenty-one and Alex twenty-two. They were legal, had jobs, an education, and held the world by the tail.

A little dizzy from the wine, they returned to the apartment at about ten and fell asleep, he on the couch, she on her mattress in the corner, as always. Just past midnight, by the old grandfather clock Alex had hauled in from somewhere, Jessica woke to the sound of screaming. Fearful that the whole apartment complex would wake, she rushed over to the couch and woke Alex from his nightmare.

He retreated to his sanctuary and locked the door. The next morning he emerged with dark circles under his eyes and issued a new rule. Under no circumstances was Jessica ever to enter his room again. When she asked why, he said he needed the space to heal. And he had to do the healing alone. Then he headed off to work, taking the key to the bedroom with him.

Jessica came home from cleaning at ten that Wednesday night and found Alex already sleeping, exhausted from wakefulness the night before and a long day at work.

Two hours later, she once again woke to terrible screaming. Again she hurried over to him and woke him before he disturbed the neighbors. Again he retreated to his sanctuary.

When a similar set of circumstances repeated themselves Thursday night, Jessica started to grow genuinely concerned. Nightmares of Alice were nothing new to them, but she suffered them with less intensity while Alex was becoming overwhelmed.

"I suggested he talk to Father Seymour about the nightmares, but he said he'd tape his mouth shut before he'd lay all his garbage at 'that pimps feet. Those are exactly the words he used, 'that pimp.' It was the first time I'd heard him talking about the father like that. I figured he was just tired."

That night Alex made good on his promise. When Jessica came home, she saw that he'd strapped duct tape across his mouth before falling asleep.

As crazy as it seemed to her, the tape worked. Unable to open his mouth, his screams were muffled and woke him before she heard. The nightmares didn't subside, but at least he wasn't waking the neighbors. He would retreat to his room, lock the door, and spend the rest of the night alone, often without falling back to sleep. Jessica couldn't recall ever again seeing Alex fall asleep without gray duct tape covering his mouth.

Six months passed without any major incident. But without studies to occupy Alex's mind, he spent more and more time alone in his room, sinking into a depression that no amount of encouragement from Jessica could shake. He forced himself to face life each morning with a courage that made her heart break.

The first significant shift in their relationship occurred on a Saturday in late August of 1986. Both of them had the night off, and Jessica suggested that they go out on the town, maybe drink another bottle of wine. With a little twisting of Alex's arm, she persuaded him.

They walked to Colorado Boulevard and strolled down the street, which was bustling with nightlife. But whenever Jessica suggested they go into one of the bars or restaurants, Alex refused. By this time in her life, Jessica had started taking more interest in men—not so far as to enter into a relationship, but she couldn't help notice the way most looked at her with interest. The attention was beginning to lift her confidence.

Alex, on the other hand, not only steered completely clear of women but was noticeably bothered by the fact that Jessica seemed more comfortable around men. Colorado Boulevard was filled with both men and women on the prowl that Saturday night, as on any Saturday night.

Just past midnight, as they passed by an alley next to Sister's Bar at the quiet end of the street, a group of four young women who'd obviously had too much to drink snickered as Alex and Jessica passed.

"They were just young girls, maybe eighteen or nineteen," Jessica recalled. "Just having fun, that's all."

One of them made a passing comment under her breath, suggesting that Alex "dump that whore for some real fun."

"Alex stopped and turned to them. I told him to keep walking.

That it was okay, just keep walking. And he did until they started to laugh. That's when it went bad."

Infuriated by the insult to his sister, Alex walked up to the nearest girl and demanded that she apologize. When she rolled her eyes, Alex hit her in the mouth. She staggered, stunned.

The other three screamed their outrage, hurling insults not only at him but at Jessica. "It was what they said about me that got to him," Jessica said. "He couldn't care less what they said about him, but he had this thing about protecting me."

Overtaken by anger, Alex hit another woman in the head with enough force to knock her out. But he didn't stop there. He went after the others in a blind fury, delivering sharp blows to each in rapid succession.

It all happened so fast and with such ferocity that Jessica didn't acquire the presence of mind to cry out, much less try to stop him. Not that she could have. The beating was over in ten seconds, and Alex stood over four collapsed figures, panting.

Someone down the street yelled, and Alex snapped out of it. He grabbed Jessica's hand and pulled her down the alley. They didn't stop running until they reached the apartment.

"By then a siren was blaring, and I knew it was for those poor girls,"

Jessica recalled. "I insisted we call the police and tell them what had happened, but he told me we couldn't. He just paced, crying, telling me they would throw him in jail and he couldn't go to jail. If those whores were really hurt, he'd tell Father Seymour the whole thing in the morning."

She finally agreed. And when they learned in the morning that apart from two broken noses, none of the girls had been seriously hurt, Alex persuaded her not to turn him in.

"He cried and expressed real remorse that night," Jessica said. "Part of me thought it might actually be a turning point, because for the first time in months, Alex slept the whole night on the couch. He wasn't awakened by a nightmare."

But the nightmares returned the next night, and within a couple of weeks, Alex had fallen into an even deeper depression. It was then that he began to do small things that reminded Jessica of Alice. "Mostly the way he spoke," she said. "Alice used to tell us how lucky we were, and Alex started telling me how lucky I was to have him protecting me. But he said it just like she would."

Other things Alex said bothered Jessica. He became picky about food and started to call any food he didn't find acceptable "slop," using the same intonation Alice had. The police became "pigs." None of it was enough to spark any real concern from Jessica, but the change in him began to gnaw at her.

They'd made a vow never to speak of Alice again, but when Jessica came home one afternoon and saw that Alex had turned one of the crosses upside down, she could hold back her irritation no longer.

"What's wrong with you?" she demanded. "You're starting to turn into Alice!"

She knew with one look at his white face that she'd said the wrong thing. Alex stood still for a long time, eyes wide and glossy. Jessica immediately began to apologize, swearing she hadn't meant it and vowing never to say it again. Without speaking a word, Alex grabbed his jacket and walked out of the apartment.

As the night grew late, Jessica became worried. He didn't like staying out late because of his fear of the dark. She couldn't remember the last time he was gone so late by himself. Midnight came and passed.

She was finally slipping into an exhausted sleep at 4:00 a.m. when the door opened, waking her. Alex stood in the doorway for a while before stepping in and locking the door behind him. His face was smeared with dust, and Jessica could tell he'd been crying.

"I asked him if he was okay, and he started to cry." Alex rushed over to Jessica, fell to his knees, and began to kiss her hands, begging her forgiveness.

"My heart broke for him. We were both crying, just holding each other and sobbing." Months and years of pain flooded from Alex and Jessica as they clung to each other in the early morning. Jessica swore never to bring up Alice again, and

Alex tried to hush her, insisting that it was his fault. She was right, now that he thought about it, she was right. He didn't know what was happening to him.

There was more Alex said that night. He kept apologizing, saying he didn't mean to do it. He was so profuse that Jessica wondered if he was speaking about more than her comment about Alice. She asked him where he'd gone, but he never did tell her.

Alex finally fell asleep, curled in a ball next to her mattress. He wasn't disturbed by a nightmare that night.

TWELVE

EVE'S SIXTEENTH EVE lay naked on the stainless-steel guttered table, white under the blazing overhead lights. Lori Ames bent over the body, dressed in a white surgical gown and gloves.

She glanced back at Daniel as the door squeaked shut behind him, then returned to her work without a word.

Daniel glanced around the familiar room of the dead. An eerie disquiet settled over him. But for Lori's unreasonable efforts to bring him back, she might well be examining his body at the moment. In this very room.

The tools of the trade sat in their racks: saws, scalpels, chisels, drills. Bodies were disassembled here, not fixed. Thoughts of his own smothering fears eased. Nowhere was the hunt for critical evidence so visceral as on the steel table, under the pathologist's blade.

The victim's clothes sat on a side table, awaiting

meticulous examination by the evidence response team. Other preliminaries had already been completed: fingerprints taken for an AFIS identity check. Blood sample for the lab tests—toxicology, viral, bacteriological.

Lori glanced back again. "Take a look?"

Daniel took a coat off the rack to his right, pulled on a pair of gloves, and approached the table. The victim's skin was translucent and badly bruised, similar to the other victims Eve had left behind. Unlike the others, Eve sixteen had been put on ice soon enough to arrest decomposition.

Lori pulled a suspended microphone down and flipped a switch to engage the recording. Two cameras recorded the autopsy from opposing angles. She picked up a chart and read her findings thus far for the recorder.

"FBI forensic pathologist, Lori Ames. I am examining federal case 62-88730, body as of yet unidentified. A female Caucasian in her midtwenties, blonde hair, brown eyes. Body weight, ninety-eight pounds, four ounces. Sixty-four inches in length."

Lori set the chart on a roll-away table and began to examine the body with her gloved hands, issuing her conclusions with practiced ease.

"External examination of the body shows rigor mortis present in the extremities. There appear to be systemic contusions spread through both forearms. Petechial rash appears to be present on the lower trunk and upper thighs. Pervasive bruising on the torso and extremities. Possible presenting symptom of meningitis."

Daniel looked on, struck by his fascination with watching Lori. She seemed to be in a world uniquely her own, just as he was while studying behavior patterns.

"There appear to be no puncture wounds, no intravenous injections. The only perforations are pierced earlobes."

She looked up at him for the first time. "Classic Eve. Whatever killed her wasn't introduced intravenously. Help me turn her over."

The body turned stiffly under their hands.

"Beginning lumbar puncture." She turned to the operating cart, lifted an iodine sponge, and began to swab the lower back. The victim had been dead for over a day, but the lumbar puncture required aseptic technique to ensure that the CSF sample wasn't contaminated. She curled the body into a fetal position, felt along the spine until she located the space between L4 and L5, and inserted the tip of a spinal needle.

The needle slid in easily. "Dura mater punctured. Drawing 10 cc's of cerebrospinal fluid. Increased pressure indicates infection. As expected."

Daniel knew what they would find. The meninges were small membranes that covered the brain and central nervous system, designed to protect from infection. However, if a virus or bacterial infection permeated the dura mater and infected the inner meninges, the membranes swelled. This swelling placed a massive amount of pressure on the components of the central nervous system. The infection spread throughout the body, breaking down capillaries, thus the contusions and bruising. If the swelling didn't kill the victim first, the disintegration of the organs eventually did.

He knew the results already; Eve had killed this young woman, and he took every life the same way. But Lori approached her first autopsy in the case with the wonder of a scientist examining an alien body.

Daniel glanced at his watch. Twenty minutes and the fear hadn't returned. But the thought of a recurrence made his stomach turn. He reached up and switched the recorder off.

Lori met his eyes. "Yes?"

"I just need a second."

"Give me half an hour and I'm all yours."

"No. No, actually, I'm not sure it can wait thirty minutes."

"Okay." She stepped back from the table, peeled off her gloves, dropped them in the wastebasket, and rubbed her face. "I needed fresh gloves for the heavy work anyway. What gives?"

He nodded. "I uh...I've had a few..." Few what? He searched for an appropriate word. "Episodes. Fear. More like terror."

She lifted an eyebrow. "You've been holding out?"

"They're not serious or anything, not as far as I can..."

The fear hit him then, midsentence, like a battering ram to his gut. For an endless moment he knew he was dying. That's what this was—a replaying of the moment of death, that moment when life is snatched by an unwelcome fate.

He gasped and reached out to the table for support. Felt himself sag. "Oh..."

And then it was gone. He gripped the table, drained.

"Daniel?" Lori grabbed a chair and slid it toward him.

"No, no, it's okay. I just need to..."

"Sit!"

He sat.

"Talk to me."

Daniel took a deep breath and rubbed his temples. Gooseflesh rippled up his arms. "On one condition."

"You don't look like you're fit to be making demands."

"One condition," he insisted.

"Of course."

"This stays between you and me and has no bearing on my investigation. I won't be taken off this case."

"You *are* officially off it."

"You know what I mean."

"Okay. So talk."

He told her about the nightmare and the increasingly violent recurrences of fear that seemed to come out of nowhere, smother him for a few seconds, and then leave as suddenly.

Daniel stood and glanced at his watch. "Twenty minutes. Please tell me this makes sense to you."

"Actually, it does."

"My death."

Lori sat in the chair he'd vacated, crossed her arms and legs, and stared at the victim. "DMT," she said. "Dimethyltryptamine."

"The Schedule I drug? *That* DMT?"

She frowned. "It's still a bit of a fuzzy science, but research indicates that the pineal gland dumps massive doses of DMT into the brain at the time of death. It's thought to be the primary cause of so-called near-death experiences. Hallucinations triggered by severe trauma. A chemical dump that generates a reflection of one's beliefs. Christians see a tunnel of light and Jesus; American Indians see the great Spirit Warrior. DMT."

Daniel's own research calling into question the myth of a supernatural reality clicked into place. "Near-death experiences are triggered by the belief that one is dying. Trick the mind into thinking it's dead, and hallucinations erupt. You're saying my mind still thinks it's dead?"

"I can't see that. But DMT is a natural drug tied into both dreams and memories. It's thought that the drug may be tied to post-traumatic stress disorder, triggering flashbacks as the pineal gland dumps overdoses of DMT into the brain." She shrugged. "Like I said, it's not an exact science yet."

"But it explains a few things, doesn't it? What triggers this release of DMT? Besides death."

"The belief you've died. A board falls on a construction worker's head, and the visual image persuades his mind that he couldn't possibly survive the impact. He has a near-death experience, when in reality he comes nowhere near death."

Daniel rubbed his jaw, thoughts spinning. "Point is, the mind can be fooled into an NDE. Or a nightmare. Or, in my case, reliving the memory of coming face-to-face with Eve."

Her eyes were on him, drilling through his, way ahead. It was as if she'd speculated as much all along but wanted him to draw the conclusion. Why? Because she wanted him to try something only he could decide to do . . .

She averted her eyes. "This dark form you saw—what makes you think it's Eve?"

He shook his head. "Nothing."

"Unless, as you say, your memories from that night are being triggered by something like DMT."

Again Daniel was struck by the sense that she was driving him somewhere. Or leading him.

"DMT," he said. "You're saying that this fear I feel could be a hiccup in my brain—an extra shot of DMT."

"If so, it's the tip of an iceberg."

"The iceberg being my memory of Eve just before he killed me."

She faced him. Her eyes said it all.

"Can a near-death experience be simulated?" he asked.

"It happens every day," she said. "We call it a bad trip."

"Acid?"

She stood, walked to the cupboard, pulled on fresh gloves, and approached the body. "Lift her up, will you?"

He helped her slide a rubber body-block under the shoulders, which caused the head to tilt back and the arms to swing away.

"What about hypnosis?" he asked.

"You're the psychologist, you tell me. But something tells me sleight of hand won't do the trick."

Daniel knew that hypnosis, while occasionally an effective tool in getting the mind to lower its defenses, didn't trigger the recovery of traumatic events—outside of movies.

"Beginning Y incision," Lori said. "You might want to back up."

She covered her face with a transparent surgical shield, lifted the battery-powered Stryker saw from the operating cart, and pressed the power button. The whine was a sound Daniel could never quite appreciate.

She cut from the tip of one shoulder to the other. Very little blood; most of it had already pooled in the posterior of the body. Once circulation ceased, gravity took over. Lori followed the first cut with another, this one from the base of the neck down the trunk, deviating to the left around the navel and down to the pubic bone. She eased off the trigger and let the saw spin down.

Her eyes lifted. "DMT is endogenous, created in the human brain, but it can be synthesized."

The woman's body lay between Lori and Daniel, cut up by the saw, but neither of them was focused on the autopsy now. The implications of what Lori was suggesting had more bearing on the case at the moment.

What waited to be found in the cadaver wouldn't likely shed new light on Eve. What waited in Daniel's mind could very well blow the case wide open.

"The synthetic form is so psychoactive that those who use the drug have to be supervised," she said. "It hits hard and fast; a user will as likely drop the pipe they're smoking as finish the bowl. Or leave the needle in their arm if using intravenously. The trip is extremely intense and reaches its climax within the first minute. Cool-off is five to thirty minutes. A bit like an NDE."

Daniel was breathing shallow. "You're suggesting I consider a trip."

"I didn't say that."

"Face the monster from my dream."

"It's illegal."

"Take his mask off. Demystify him. Unlock his identity."

She stared. "It could work."

"Like hypnosis on steroids. Would I feel the fear?"

The intensity in Lori's eyes lost focus. She frowned and visibly relaxed. "Forget it. It's way too dangerous and irresponsible to even consider. Theory is one thing. Sending a healthy man on the most radical hallucinogenic trip is another."

She revved up the saw and returned her attention to the cadaver. With the Y incision made, Lori spread the skin, made lateral cuts across the ribs, lifted the rib cage, and set it on the cart. The internal organs were now exposed.

Daniel was so distracted by the notion of peering behind his mind's veil that her dissection of the body sat in his mind like elevator music—distant and inconsequential. She continued to work, engrossed in the task at hand or in his dilemma, he didn't know. Starting with the heart and working down to the stomach, she examined and withdrew the organs, looking for signs of trauma, infectant traces, ingested bacteria. They'd not yet determined the method by which Eve infected his victims, concluding only that it was never intravenously.

Worse, they'd never actually identified the meningitis as either bacterial or viral. The symptomatic presentations of bacterial meningitis were all there, but only minute traces of the bacteria itself, not necessarily more than the average human carried at any given time.

"She could have lived ninety years, this one," Lori said. "Her body was in pristine condition."

"No unique indications?" Daniel asked.

"Nothing new that I see. Classic presentation of acute meningitis in the trunk. If I were to guess, I'd say it was inhaled."

Trunk finished, Daniel helped Lori slide the rubber block beneath the head. Working with calm precision, she made an incision from behind the right ear, across the scalp, to the same spot behind the left ear. She peeled the face down over the skull and reached for the saw again.

Daniel sighed and walked to the wastebasket. He peeled off his gloves, glad to be rid of the clammy things.

The saw ground behind him as she worked to expose the brain.

But Dr. Lori Ames, forensic pathologist from Phoenix, had already exposed her mind to him. He'd looked into her eyes and seen himself. They were cut from the same cloth. Neither was saying anything now, but they'd both opened themselves up to doing the unthinkable for the same passion. Uncovering Eve.

The saw quieted. He could see Lori lifting the front quarter plate of the skull. She stared at the brain.

"Take a look."

Daniel stepped up to the operating table and saw what she saw. The entire brain was swollen to the point of epidural hemorrhage. Blood pooled in vascular dilatation, almost black.

"Like the others," he said.

The phone chirped and he crossed to it, lifted the receiver off the wall. "Morgue, Agent Clark."

"It's Riley, Dr. Clark. We have a hit on AFIS."

Daniel caught Lori's questioning eyes. He hit the speaker button. "Go ahead."

"Her name is Natalie Laura Cabricci, aged twenty-four, from Phoenix, Arizona. Her parents are being informed now."

"Any details on her abduction?"

"Only that she went missing six days ago after going to the supermarket for milk."

"Religion?"

"Catholic. Agents on the ground will have more as soon as they finish questioning the parents."

"Thank you, Riley."

He broke the connection. Lori turned back to the body

and resumed her work. The autopsy would take another hour, and he no longer had the stomach for it. With next of kin identified, another pathologist would close up the body and prepare it to be returned to Phoenix. Except for the heart, stomach, lungs, and brain, the other organs would be incinerated.

He'd been through this same requiem of death sixteen times in the last two years, each time feeling just one breath, one glance, one word away from that one piece that could make a perfect picture of this illogical puzzle.

At the moment, the missing evidence felt inconsequential. What was truly of consequence was locked away in his own mind. If there was any way, any possible hope no matter how—

The fear swarmed him before he could finish the thought. Like a pack of wolves lunging for his neck, clamping fangs on his heart and mind. Howling rage through one vicious tearing of flesh.

I see you, Daniel…

Then it was gone, so brutal and so fast that he didn't have time to react until the fear left him. Then he caught his breath and instinctively clutched at his chest. He closed his eyes and warded off a stab of pain through his head with a moan.

"You okay?"

Lori was facing him again. Had he blacked out? It occurred to him that he might have trouble driving.

"Yes." Daniel walked forward on numb legs. Glanced at the recorder. She flipped it off and turned back to him.

"You have to help me, Lori. I don't care what it takes, we have to do something."

She looked at him for a long moment. "Maybe you

don't understand how dangerous this is. There's a reason why it's a Schedule I drug."

"I don't care if it's a bullet to the head! If it can stop this"—he jabbed at his forehead—"we need to try it."

"It's a violation of the Controlled Substances Act. A felony."

"Special circumstances. This could lead to evidence critical to apprehending Eve."

"Its effects aren't predictable. For all we know, another trip might only make things worse."

"That's my decision, not yours."

She hesitated. He had no doubt that she wanted this, but her concern for him gave her pause.

Daniel reached out and gently took her hand. "I can't do this alone."

"Montova wouldn't approve."

"I don't work for Montova anymore."

Her thumb rubbed the back of his hand. Her eyes shifted away. "It could work. We could start with a small dose."

"Can you get it?"

"DMT? I'm sure they have some under lock and key here. If not, the Phoenix lab has some."

He released her hand and paced away. "The sooner the better, right? Tonight. After our meeting with Heather."

"Meeting with Heather?"

He hadn't told her about the phone call. He wasn't sure what had stopped him, but the reason seemed immaterial now.

"She has something to tell us. Tonight. At eight."

THIRTEEN

HEATHER SPENT THE fifteen minutes leading up to eight o'clock trying to keep herself busy in the kitchen. Making coffee. Wiping the counter. Setting the milk out by the coffee. Placing a batch of chocolate chip cookies she'd baked next to the milk and then putting the milk back in the refrigerator after deciding it might get warm sitting out. Then, after removing the milk, deciding to put the carafe of coffee and the cookies on the kitchen table, where she and Daniel could sit and talk without things getting uncomfortable.

For starters.

It had been two months since she'd talked to Daniel. Six months since she'd seen him. Considering the undeniable fact that, as Raquel put it, she was smitten by him, it was no wonder that her palms were moist with sweat.

Perhaps *smitten* was too strong a word. She had been

the one who controlled the relationship, not he. To say that she was subdued or smitten by him mischaracterized the relationship.

Obsessed maybe. But that was even worse. Mutually respectful. Enamored. Afflicted with a very real case of liking. Loving. Daniel had always fascinated her, not as a mere object of interest but as a passionate man who tore through life with acute focus. Unfortunately, acute focus only benefited a relationship when the object of that focus was the relationship itself.

She had been Daniel's focus once. The fulcrum of his life. His living passion. And he claimed as much to this day. But she'd drawn her line to test his love, and he'd failed miserably. His leaving her for seven out of twelve months to serve his career despite repeated cries for help had been the final straw.

Maybe she was a fool to love him; maybe she was as twisted as he; maybe she was the one who needed a year or two of therapy.

More likely they were both so screwed up that neither deserved more than the misery they found themselves in. Their mutual obsession with Eve had crossed another line. For the first time in her life she was truly afraid for Daniel's life. For her own.

She glanced at the kitchen clock, a round white plate without marks. The minute hand had passed vertical. Daniel was running...

The bell chimed.

...late.

Heather took a deep breath, wiped her hands on her jeans, and crossed the carpet. Stepped onto the wood floor leading up to the front door. Daniel had insisted on wood over carpet when they remodeled. A good choice.

"Here goes," she breathed, pulling the door open.

A woman stood on the porch next to and slightly in front of Daniel. The idea that Daniel might not come alone hadn't even crossed her mind. She expected he would come to be with her as much as for what she would tell him. Clearly not.

Before Heather could properly process her disappointment, the woman stuck out her hand. "Hello, Heather. Dr. Lori Ames, FBI. Daniel thought it would be helpful for me to hear what you had to say."

Lori was dressed in jeans and boots, a blue halter top covered in part by a cropped cotton jacket. Shoulder-length blonde hair tucked behind the ears revealed silver hoops.

Heather took her hand and looked at Daniel, who looked a bit distracted. Even worried.

"Hello, Daniel. So nice of you to bring your friend." He wore a gray beanie to cover the wound on his head. Ten years younger and he might look like Justin Timberlake.

He smiled sheepishly and nodded. "Hey, Heather. You good?"

She released Lori's hand and stepped back, refusing to acknowledge such a dumb question. *Fantastic, Daniel, particularly now that I've met your sweet girl pal.*

"Come in."

They walked in, and Daniel gave her a peck on the cheek. One of his sweet habits she normally loved. At the moment she couldn't help wondering where else those lips had been. The jealousy was completely cold considering what Daniel had been through in the last two days, but she couldn't shake it off.

Heather led them into the living room and watched them take seats on the sofa. She considered offering them the cookies and coffee but decided getting straight to the point would serve them all better.

"You okay, Daniel?"

"A bit banged up, but all things considered…"

"Frankly, he's a mess," Lori said. "Lucky but not well. All things considered."

She didn't sound cheeky. Just a cut-to-the-chase kind of girl. Daniel's type.

"What do you mean?"

Lori deferred. Heather looked at the man whom she'd sworn to love till death and felt her heart tighten with empathy. The confidence he typically wore so nonchalantly was gone. He looked gray and haggard now, with bags under his eyes.

Now with more force, "What's wrong, Daniel?"

"Well, I did die, didn't I? I can't remember dying, or the events surrounding my death, but they tell me I saw Eve. It turns out that when your mind thinks it's dead, it sends out electrical signals and chemicals that wreak a bit of havoc. Except for a couple of scalp wounds, my body is fine. But my mind doesn't seem to know it yet. That about sums it up."

"What Daniel's trying to say is that he's having nightmares. Sometimes while awake."

"I wouldn't classify them as nightmares," Daniel said. "Unexplained paranoia."

His blond hair curled out of the beanie. Beneath those gentle curls, a mind that was rarely shaken. Until now.

Daniel looked at her with sad blue eyes. He didn't have a lot of facial hair, but if she wasn't mistaken, he hadn't shaved today.

"What kind of nightmares?" Heather asked.

"Just...fear. Like a hammer to the head."

"Which would make sense, right? You were shot in the head." Heather sat back and crossed her legs. "You're alive, that's what's important. They told me you were dead."

He cleared his throat. "You mean before I was resuscitated?"

"Yes."

"I'm sorry." Understanding crossed his face. "I can't... Brit?"

She nodded. Tried to push those few terrible hours from her mind.

"You're right, I'm alive. That's what counts."

They exchanged a few more polite remarks, mostly about the good doctor's new assignment as the forensic pathologist on the Eve case. Daniel had been asked to take a leave, which he would do. But only formally.

Short of a straitjacket, they would never keep him off the case.

It wasn't until Heather finally decided to serve them the coffee that Daniel pressed the issue that hung over their heads.

"So, you wanted to talk about Eve."

Here it was. The strange phone call that had forced her to abandon her hearing to one of the other attorneys felt distant and foolish now. Daniel was suffering the side effects of a shot to the head, and she was running scared from a prank call.

She'd intended to show him the room. Maybe even run

through a few ideas she'd been working on. They were just wild theories, but they all knew that wild theories eventually distilled into those that proved true.

Looking at Lori, she knew she didn't dare show him the room.

"It's probably nothing, but…" *Not true, Heather. Just spit it out.*

"Heather, I know you better than that. Something's scaring you. Please, just tell me."

The way he said it reminded her of a time during their short engagement when he demanded to meet Bill, a local prosecutor who'd made some off-color, potentially threatening comments to her during a trial. Daniel confronted the man at a bar, and although he refused to tell her what was said, the attorney had given her a wide berth ever since.

She set her coffee cup down. "Okay." She told him about the call she received the night of his death. They both watched her with increasing interest. Or incredulity, she wasn't quite sure which.

When she finished, Daniel was staring, wide-eyed.

"That's it?" He stood and paced. "This was before or after I was killed?"

"During. Or just after."

"So he didn't know. He was making idle threats. And we know it couldn't have been Eve."

"The point is, he knew the sixteenth Eve had been found. How many people knew that? And he made it clear you would die if you didn't back off."

Daniel crossed his arms.

"Unless he's not working alone," Lori said. "It's not a new theory."

"No, but we've never run into anything so definite."

Daniel crossed the room toward the kitchen phone. The purposeful look on his face could hardly be associated with a trip to the refrigerator.

Heather stood. "What are you doing? You can't call this in."

"Don't be ridiculous. We have to find the driver, the car. We need resources."

"We already ran the plates. They don't exist," Heather said, standing. "He's not that stupid and that's not the point!"

Daniel turned back, receiver in hand. "And what is the point, Heather?"

"You. *You're* the point!"

The tone of her voice stalled him. She pushed while she had the advantage.

"Listen to me! Whoever this guy is, he knows it all. For all you know he's *with* the bureau. The moment you push this, he knows you're doing exactly what he insisted you not do."

"That's a risk we have to take."

"That's not a risk *I'm* willing to take!" she snapped. "I'm not ready to lose you."

Thinking she was showing too much, she eased back into the chair and set her hands on her knees.

"He called again," she said.

Daniel set the phone back in the cradle. He came back into the living room, glanced at his watch, and sat down.

"And said what?"

"The same thing."

"You're sure it was him?"

"Not completely, no. He was whispering, and his voice sounded like it was coming through a box. Distant."

"Tell me what he said."

"I told you, pretty much the same thing."

"No." He shook his head. "Tell me exactly what—"

Daniel stiffened and inhaled sharply. For a second, maybe two, he looked like he'd been electrocuted. Then he sagged and exhaled.

Lori stood and put her hand on his shoulder. "You okay?"

His voice came out ragged. "That's something you don't get used to."

"That was what you were talking about?" Heather asked, alarmed. "A panic attack?"

He didn't respond. The fierce color had gone out of his eyes. They sat in silence for several beats. He was in more emotional pain than he let on, she realized, then chided herself for not showing the concern that gnawed at her. She should be reaching out to him, comforting him. Under his show of strength he was hardly more than a wounded child, desperate for relief. And she knew how to give it to him. A gentle touch to his cheek, a soft word of encouragement, a promise of solidarity.

Instead she'd been frozen by the unexpected intrusion named Dr. Lori Ames. Part of her knew she should express her love for Daniel; part of her wanted to slap the lug for being so insensitive.

The latter part was winning. The same part that had brought them to a divorce in the first place. Honestly, she didn't know if her choices had been noble or plain selfish.

Daniel was staring at her. "Tell me what he said. Exactly as you remember it."

"That if I didn't keep my promise you were going to die."

"Use his words. As you remember them."

She'd played the words through her mind a hundred times, but she wasn't sure if her current version was precise. The voice had asked if she loved Daniel. She decided the detail wasn't pertinent to the FBI's investigation.

"He asked if—"

"No, use his words."

"I am!" She glared at him. "I asked who it was and he said, 'I'm your Jesus. Your worst nightmare. Lucifer. It depends on who you want me to be. On what you do.' Something close to that. Meaning if I can't stop you, you're going to die."

"What makes you think that?" Daniel asked.

"Because he said it! He said, 'He's forgetting his promise. He's going to die if you can't stop him.'"

The skin around Daniel's eyes twitched. "He used those words?"

"Yes. Or something very close. Then he said something about his daddy and a priest... I don't remember exactly. My mind was on what he'd just said. About you."

"What daddy? What priest?"

"I told you, I don't remember. He said no one can stop him."

"Speaking of himself? Those were *his* words?"

"I'm not one of your witnesses, and I'm sure not one of your patients. His words were *him*. No one can stop *him*, meaning someone else, whoever *him* is. Eve."

"Did he say—"

"No, he didn't say *Eve*. I'm just assuming. Who else would *him* be?"

Daniel stared at her, mind working. She'd seen the look a thousand times, lost in speculation, measuring, always measuring. It was one of the things she loved about him, this wild pursuit of truth. Just not when it supplanted his interest in her.

Lori Ames broke her silence. "He mentioned his father and a priest. Paternal care and religion."

Daniel stood and crossed to the fireplace, seemingly ignorant of the portrait of him and Heather hanging above the mantel.

"Reference to predominant informative factors in his life," he said, turning. "For all we know Eve was abused by both."

His jaw muscles bunched up with frustration. If there was one thing Daniel was known for in the field of behavioral science, it was his outspoken stand against ideologies that bred hatred for others and justified acting on it, subservience to some supernatural deity being the standout culprit.

It was one of many arguments he made with outstanding clarity in his books and lectures, Heather thought. Whatever his shortcomings, Daniel lacked nothing in the intelligence department.

"This scares me, Daniel."

"Don't let it."

"Eve's killed sixteen women. How can you stand there and tell me not to be afraid of him?"

"He's after *me*. I'm closing in, and he knows it. Something I've done is ticking him off, and he's trying to scare me. You're honestly suggesting I walk away now?"

"Yes." She stared him down. "Because I believe him."

"She has a point, Daniel," Lori said. "You're officially off the case. That's a start. Maybe it has more benefit than we realized."

Daniel settled. Now that his little doctor friend had suggested the same thing Heather had, he was actually listening. She didn't care. At the moment she only wanted him to drop the case.

"Back off Eve," she said. "Take another case. Any case. I don't care how much of your time it takes." A slight pause. "I want you to come home."

Her words struck him broadside—she could see it in his face. He stared, silenced.

Then she clarified, to be sure he understood. "Just drop Eve. Please."

Looking into Daniel's blank blue eyes, she couldn't possibly know what was on his mind. Other than recurring terror.

"I'll think about it," he said.

FOURTEEN

TEN O'CLOCK

THE APARTMENT DANIEL had taken two years earlier had two bedrooms, one of which he'd converted into a fully equipped office. The other contained a king-size bed without a headboard, one nightstand with a large brown ceramic lamp, and one built-in closet.

The living room had a green sofa and love seat he'd found at Rent-to-Own and a glass coffee table Heather had let him take. Two floor lamps with black shades.

A square, glass-topped kitchenette set rounded out the apartment. He hadn't expected to stay more than a few months when he'd set the apartment up, and he'd been too busy to flesh out the place after it became apparent that he might be here longer than anticipated.

Two weeks earlier he'd purchased and hung two large paintings that reminded him of the mountains near Helena, Montana, where he'd spent his first eighteen years before heading to UCLA and starting a new life destined for the FBI.

His mother, Claire, would have approved of the paintings but not much else if she were still alive. His father wouldn't have cared as long as Daniel was ladder climbing at the FBI. Rudolph Clark's only son had done him proud.

In all honesty, Daniel couldn't tell if Lori approved or not. She walked into the apartment, took one look around, and said, "Is it sparse or just plain neat?"

"Both," he said. The apartment was immaculate, a reflection of Daniel's own mind, Heather would say, though she'd never seen the place. "I haven't had time to do much with it. Where do you want this?"

Lori glanced at the white box containing the small sample of DMT she had taken from the lab for testing purposes. "You sure you don't want to give this more thought? It'll keep in the fridge."

He set the box on the coffee table. "I've given it thought."

His thoughts were twofold. One, he needed relief from the bouts of fear that persisted every thirty to forty-five minutes. If there was any chance that giving his mind a chemical shock would interrupt the cycle, he would willingly accept the risk of failure.

But second, and more important, he simply could not pass up the opportunity to jar his memory by taking a chemically induced trip approximating the one that had wiped Eve from his mind in the first place.

The dark form that had stood at the end of his hospital bed had a face. Eve's face. The urge to reach out and pull that face from the night of his mind was overpowering.

"How do we do this?"

"I'll take that as a no." She shrugged off her coat and draped it over a chair. "Do you have a belt? Or some rope?"

"For what?"

"I don't want to take any chances. The dose I'm going to give you isn't much, but DMT isn't predictable. We don't know how much the mind actually releases at the moment of death."

"I'm not following. What does dose have to do with a belt?"

She stepped out of her shoes and crossed to the sofa. "I need to restrain you." She looked up, brown eyes soft.

"I thought you said we'd start with a small dose."

"I did."

Daniel waved her off. "Fine, restrain me. I'll get a belt."

"Three belts."

"Three belts."

He knew she was only taking every precaution in the event he became violent. They'd discussed the negligible risk of addiction with controlled use as well as the typical side effects: increased heart rate and blood pressure, dilated pupils, dissociated hallucinations. Potentially violent reactions that could result in him swinging his fists unawares. She was evidently concerned that he might smash the coffee table, cut his wrist, something along those lines.

Daniel slipped off his shoes and returned to the living room with three belts.

She'd laid out a white cloth from the morgue on the glass coffee table. A syringe rested next to a length of surgical tubing and a small bottle containing half an inch of the cloudy liquid.

DMT.

Daniel handed her the belts and stepped back. "I need a drink of water. You want one?"

"Thanks." Her eyes followed him to the kitchen.

Surreal, this covert bit of drug use. Daniel had never even considered injecting his body with an illegal narcotic, never mind that this one was endogenous, created by the body itself. He found the prospect of doing so now distasteful.

Subverting FBI protocol was slightly less distasteful—he'd been forced to give the red tape a wide berth before. But this ... this shooting up to see Eve's face was nothing short of lunacy.

The fear crashed through his mind as he reached for two bottles of mineral water, forcing him to still for a moment until it passed. Which it did, leaving him with a slight tremble in his outstretched hand.

He was getting better at coping physically with the onslaughts, but his mind fared no better. Terror was terror, and every time it visited him, it scraped his nerves raw.

Lori was still watching him when he crossed to her with the bottles in hand. He didn't want to discuss the fear—they'd beat the subject to death a dozen times already. So he rehearsed a more familiar script.

"I was thinking we should take a trip to Phoenix," he said.

She just looked at him.

"We have to assume the investigation of the victim's abduction will turn up something. Never give up hope. There's always a chance."

"Of course."

"Someone who saw something. The victim being picked up, pulled into a van, talking to a stranger, anything."

"Just like the other fifteen victims," she said.

They both knew that he was stalling, trying to buffer his mind against that needle on the glass table. But neither seemed interested in hurrying the process now that the needle was before them.

"Come on, Daniel. We both know there won't be any witnesses." She spoke in a soft, soothing voice. "Like you said, Eve knows their habits too well to take them anywhere they can be seen. Natalie Cabricci was on foot when she was taken. The route she normally took to the store crossed two parks and three parking lots. The local uniforms have already canvassed the area. Never give up hope, but a trip to Phoenix isn't going to open up this case."

Before leaving to meet with Heather, they'd spent an hour poring over interview transcripts and several investigative reports filed from the Phoenix office. Brit was hauling in the data as fast as he could get it, but sixteen months on the case had convinced them all that when the break did come, it wouldn't be from an expected source.

The FBI estimated that at least thirty serial killers operated in the United States at any given time. At least half of those would never be caught. Unless a pattern killer broke and decided he'd had enough, he only became more elusive with each killing, contrary to what the public believed.

Yes, the FBI did gather more evidence with each event, and yes, as a pattern became evident, anticipating a killer's next move became easier. But a killer who remained at large after killing sixteen women did so by being good in the first place, and he refined his evasive skills with each kill.

On a one-to-ten scale of skill sets, most garden-variety killers operated at a two or a three. Most successful serial killers operated at a five or six.

In Daniel's estimation, Eve operated at a nine or ten.

"You ready?" Lori asked.

Daniel took a deep breath and blew it out. "As I'll ever be. Tie me down."

"Do you mind taking your shirt off?"

Daniel pulled his knit shirt off, dropped it on the floor, and sat on the couch dressed only in jeans.

"Arms by your legs," she said. "You can lie down."

"Wouldn't it be easier on the floor? More room."

"If you want."

He lay down on his back, spread his legs a little, and pressed his hands flat against his hips. Lori slipped a belt under his upper thigh and cinched it around his wrist.

"You can pull your hand out if you try, but this will keep your movements restricted."

"Good to know, Doctor." He tried to smile.

"Other hand." She tied his left wrist down to his side, then looped the last belt around his ankles.

Using a cotton swab and some alcohol, she cleaned the peripheral vein on his right arm, speaking as much to fill the silence as to give him any useful information.

"The sample I have was synthesized using dimethylamine, lithium aluminum hydride, and oxalyl chloride. I'll be injecting one cc of the drug into your vein. You'll feel the initial effects within twenty seconds and probably black out within the first minute as the DMT spreads to the capillaries in your temporal lobe."

"So out in five minutes?"

"Up to thirty minutes. Don't worry, I'm right here." She put her hand on his chest and slowly moved it down to his belly. Her eyes followed her fingers as they touched his skin.

She looked into his eyes. "I never told you how it was. Bringing you back to life."

"How was it?"

"Words can't describe what I felt. When your breath filled my mouth..." She smiled, and Daniel ignored a sudden urge to sit up and kiss her.

"Thank you," he said.

She exhaled, patted his stomach lightly, and reached for the surgical rubber band. Working quickly now, she twisted the tourniquet around his upper arm, pulled it tight with one end in her mouth. She inserted the syringe's needle into the bottle of DMT, withdrew one cc, set the bottle back down, and cleared the syringe.

"Close your eyes."

He did. His heart was hammering already.

The prick on his arm was hardly more than a mosquito's bite. And then the needle was out.

Daniel began to count the seconds down. He got to twelve before the first hammer fell on his mind.

He felt his body jerk once as a bright light exploded before his eyes.

A second blow seemed to strike him between the eyes, then a third in rapid succession. Two more white-hot eruptions made him gulp air.

Then a fourth hammer fell, and this one brought pitch-black darkness.

He began to thrash.

FIFTEEN

DANIEL HAD BEEN ON two drug-induced trips in his life. The first: when his brain dumped DMT into his system upon death, spawning a so-called near-death experience that he could not remember.

The second: when Lori injected a small amount of synthetic DMT into his right arm two hours after he'd promised Heather to think about dropping the Eve case—a promise he had no intention of keeping, not until Eve was chained down on death row.

He knew that both trips were induced chemically, triggering reactions in the mind that called up euphoric emotions, lights, sounds, colors—a plethora of sensations that nature had perfected to ease severe trauma to the mind.

He knew that neither had any bearing on a future or other reality except for their ability to reach backward into memory and project what had once been seen, heard, smelled, touched, or tasted by the brain.

Daniel knew all of this, but all of it became meaningless in that moment of darkness. Whatever memory the fear was accessing to flesh itself out hardly mattered in the moment.

What did matter was that the bouts of fear he'd experienced throughout the day paled next to this new fear. He was dimly aware of his own screaming. His violent convulsions.

And then a starburst of blue-and-white light filled the darkness. In the space of a single breath, the fear fell away. Euphoria swelled through his chest and boiled over in what he thought might be real laughter, bubbling from his own lips.

Wow. Now, now…now this is a trip, he thought, grinning stupidly.

Images flew past him: A long tunnel of light, swirling with lazy light. His mother, smiling, kissing his father. A large white limousine with a smiley sticker on the rear windshield.

Heather staring at him with dark eyes.

Daniel's laughter stilled.

And then here it came, another sledgehammer, swooping down from the sky, black as oil. It hit his chest.

I see you, Daniel…

His world turned dark and he began to scream.

And the trip ended. The fear dissipated like spent steam. The pitch-blackness was replaced by a slightly red darkness that he realized was the back of his eyelids.

Daniel opened his eyes and looked up at Lori, who was kneeling over him, staring into his face.

"Sh, sh, sh, it's okay, really. It's going to be okay."

"What...what happened?" He was breathing hard. Hot. Wet with sweat. "What happened?"

"You okay?"

Daniel tried to push himself up and succeeded only when she helped him. "How do you feel now?"

"Besides a headache, not terrible. How long?"

She glanced at her watch. "Twelve minutes."

"That long? It felt like a minute." He shivered. "Man, that was a trip."

"Let's hope you didn't wake the neighbors."

"I was that loud? Man..." He stood shakily, walked to the couch, and eased himself down. "Man..."

"So?"

"So."

"Did you see him?"

The intense emotions had pushed the objective from his mind. "No."

"No? Nothing at all?"

He thought about it as carefully as he could, head throbbing as it was. "Nothing except some pretty radical emotions. I saw things from my past. Light. Darkness. But mostly I just laughed like a fool or screamed bloody murder."

Lori sat down and leaned back. Crossed her legs and arms, lost in thought. "Well, that's not terribly helpful. Is it?"

The failure of the experience hit him then. "Unless it's taken my fear. That's possible, right?"

"Possible. But you didn't see Eve. I realize you want to relieve yourself of this fear, but I was hoping..."

"Yeah. Well, now I know."

"Know what?"

"What an NDE feels like. I saw the light, the tunnel, the whole works." He took a long pull from his bottle of water, noted that his fingers were still trembling. "Heaven and hell in the space of one minute. You should try it."

"No thanks." She sat forward and began putting the drug paraphernalia back in the white box.

"You seem pretty disappointed," Daniel said.

"Aren't you?"

"If the fear returns...more than you can know."

She nodded. "Something else is bothering me."

The sweat on his chest had dried. He considered putting his shirt back on but decided to wait until he'd taken a shower.

"What if it was just a bad trip?" Lori said.

"It was. I don't follow."

She shrugged. "A synthetically induced drug trip that approximates the effects of death."

"A fake NDE," he said. "All NDEs are essentially fake. Illusions created by a flood of electrochemical reactions."

"That's not my point. When a brain dies, as yours did in Colorado Springs, it suffers trauma we can only guess at. The neurotransmitters and receptors are in synaptic chaos. The hippocampus and amygdala die. The entire nervous system is flooded with DMT, like you just were, but there's more. Somewhere between the chemistry of the temporal lobe and the lack of oxygen to the rest of the brain, the critical processes become acutely confused. It's like developing a thirty-year case of Alzheimer's in a minute and a half."

"Not just a bad trip induced by a few chemicals."

"Chemicals can kill the brain, don't get me wrong. A higher dose of DMT, for example. Which is the problem."

"The dose of DMT I would need to re-create what I lost in death would probably kill me," Daniel said.

"Exactly."

They watched each other for a few long seconds.

"You going to take your wife up on her offer?"

"Heather's not my wife. We've been divorced for two years. Do I have a choice?"

"She seems like a sweet lady."

He let the comment pass.

"No, I suppose you don't have a choice. You couldn't give up on Eve if a gun were put to your head."

"Is there?" he asked. "A gun to my head, I mean."

Lori stood, walked around the coffee table, and stepped up to him. She stopped with her toes resting gently against his foot.

"There is. A gun to your head." She leaned over and kissed his forehead, then stood, picked up the white box, gathered her jacket and shoes without putting either on, and strode toward the front door.

"Sleep well, Dr. Daniel Clark. No nightmares."

Daniel locked the door after her, took a shower, and threw on his sweats before realizing that an hour had passed since his DMT trip.

The fear hadn't returned. He went to bed at midnight, feeling relieved and grateful. For peace and other small things in a world of chaos. Like friends. Like Lori.

Like no nightmares.

His sentiment honored him with six sweet hours of sleep. And then the fear returned. And when it did, he might not have been able to keep himself from slitting his wrists if he'd been awake and a razor had been within reach.

He woke in a full-throated scream, vocal cords already raw and raspy because he'd worn them out screaming at the dark, faceless form standing at the end of his bed.

I see you, Daniel...

Reprinted from Crime Today *magazine, 2008*

MAN OF SORROW:
JOURNEY INTO DARKNESS

by Anne Rudolph

Crime Today *magazine is pleased to present the fourth installment of Anne Rudolph's narrative account of the killer now known as Alex Price, presented in nine monthly installments.*

1986–1989

NEITHER ALEX nor Jessica knew their actual birth dates, only those assigned to them by Alice, but they'd estimated approximate dates which ended up being quite accurate. They decided that they weren't both born in October, as Alice had said, but in September, she on the seventeenth and he on the nineteenth, one year apart.

Alex had just turned twenty-two, roughly a month after his breakdown in Jessica's arms in the fall of 1986, when he walked in one afternoon and made an announcement.

After much thought and deliberation, he'd decided to become a priest.

Jessica didn't know what to think about his idea, but when he ex-plained his reasoning, she thought he might be on to something.

He was convinced that becoming a priest would be a kind of absolution for past sin. It would be a clean break from Alice's twisted religion, which turned out to be an amalgamation of Christianity, Islam, Hinduism, secularism, and Satanism that Alice called Eve's Holy Coven. Alex needed order in his life, he said, and the priesthood was all about order. In fact, he urged Jessica to consider becoming a nun.

But was he qualified? She wanted to know.

If he wasn't, he would become qualified. He had his GED and was an excellent student. All he needed was four years of seminary. It fit his love for the truth, he said. And he certainly wouldn't have a problem with the vows of chastity. The very idea of marriage made him queasy. If ever there was someone cut out to be a priest, it was him. Watching Alex's burst of enthusiasm, Jessica thought the priesthood might be exactly what her brother needed.

He'd talked to Father Seymour about the idea, and although the priest didn't agree to sponsor him, he didn't reject the idea outright. "The idea was a little outrageous," Father Seymour recalled. "Alex was a tortured soul. But the Catholic church doesn't hold past sins against those who seek to serve God. God knows I would never have qualified if it did. You don't decide on a whim to accept this sinner over that sinner; it's a matter of the heart. If Alex could prove his heart, the rest would sort itself out. As it did."

When pressed about his failure to recognize and stop Alex then, while there was still time, Father Seymour only shrugged. "If we all recognized evil for what it is, the world would be a utopia, yes. But the Maker of all this is winning handily despite our ignorance. There's cheering, not cowering, in his corner."

Alex embraced Father Seymour's challenge that he prove his heart by returning home with a pile of theology books from the library. He began to read these on the couch by lamplight rather than in his room. "He even brought a Bible home," Jessica recalled. A whole Bible, not the one Alice had introduced them to, which had all the New Testament except for the book of Revelation torn out.

Alex was on his way. He didn't relax his insistence on cleanliness and order, and his nightmares didn't stop, but his new focus eased his depression. He began to see himself as a priest and bought himself several black shirts, which he wore buttoned to the top, though he didn't go so far as to wear a collar.

But even in those first few weeks, Jessica noticed signs that studying for the priesthood would prove to be a difficult road for her brother. With increasing frequency he would slam a book closed, mutter something about sloppy thinking, and retreat into his room without the books.

She came home one night to find pages from the Bible torn out and scattered throughout the living room. Hearing her enter the apartment, Alex came out of his room and picked up the pages without speaking. When she pressed him for an explanation, he muttered something about cleansing the room. The next day Alex moved all of his theology books to his sanctuary, where he claimed he could study without distraction.

> "Destroying all forms of light is evil's primary occupation. Its secondary purpose is to do so without being detected. I would say that every human brushes up against the most abject form of evil at least once a day. But they might notice only once every ten years."
>
> —Father Robert Seymour
> *Dance of the Dead*

In late November, 1986, Alex finally convinced Father Seymour that he was fit to earn his sponsorship at the St. Peter's Seminary College in Pasadena. "It was like he'd won the lottery," Jessica said. "He was going to be a priest. The fact that he was having difficulty studying those theology books never seemed to be an obstacle for him. He was going to be a priest and nothing else mattered to him."

Two hundred seventy-three students were enrolled in St. Peter's Seminary College for the spring semester in 1987, and many of them remember the shy student dressed in black who sat at the back of his classes. "He wore this black shirt, same one every day, buttoned tight around his neck," recalls one student. "He looked like a gangster with his hair slicked back all clean."

But it was Alex's demeanor that drew the attention of most students. He wasn't only shy; he generally refused to look others in the eye, shifting his attention to other parts of their face when he was forced to talk to them. And by all accounts he had a very difficult time talking to women.

Sister Mary Hickler remembers an incident that struck her as curious that year. Studying in the library one day, she had a question about a course assignment. Seeing only Alex seated at a table in the back, she approached him. She sat across from him and pulled out her book. He immediately stood and moved to another table. Offended by his behavior, she approached him again. This time he sat still but refused to look at her.

"I was young and a bit feisty back then. And I wanted him to tell me if he always ran away from women. When he didn't answer, I asked him to look at me, which he also refused to do. He didn't blush or show signs of embarrassment as I expected, but irritation. His jaw muscles tightened and his breathing seemed more deliberate. Even for me, it was a rather frightening experience."

Two months later, Sister Mary Hickler was walking behind Alex when he dropped a book. She picked it up for him. Evidently recognizing her from the library, Alex turned and walked away, leaving her with the book. She hurried to catch him, and placing the book into his arms, she gave him a piece of her mind.

"If you want to be a priest, you'll have to learn to love more than yourself. Including women." Then she left.

Jessica remembers the day as well. It was in the fall of 1987, Alex's second semester at the seminary. He came home pacing and chewing his fingernails as he'd taken to doing as part of his cleanliness routine. He wanted to know if she thought he loved her. Of course, she replied.

But her assurance didn't calm him. He wanted to know if she thought he was selfish. "Well, we can all be selfish," she answered. But he wanted to know if he was especially selfish. Because a priest couldn't be selfish. Then he told her what had happened, spinning the details in his favor, claiming that a recovering whore had thrown herself at him, and when he refused her she had said he would have to learn to love women, because even Christ loved the adulteress.

"That story in the Gospels never made sense to Alex," Jessica said. "And I couldn't make sense of it either. Sex was one thing off-limits to us. It always had been. Alice was very strict about even the suggestion of any sexual behavior. There was no sex at the Browns'. I was severely punished the first time I menstruated, and every time after. It seemed to me that the adulteress in the gospel story should have been corrected."

Neither of them ever spoke of the incident again.

For all of his social limitations, Alex proved to be an exceptionally bright student. His thirst for knowledge became evident to his teachers, who saw him as a wounded soul who probably understood pain more than most, and as such might very well make a good priest one day.

Gradually Alex began to open up to his teachers, who encouraged him to engage the class in discussions. By the fall of 1988 he began to do just that, not frequently, but with an articulation that gained him a little bit of fame. Instead of being seen as the freak in the ridiculous black shirt, he was known as the smart one with something to say.

"His thoughts were always highly organized, and his arguments, though challenging, were quite persuasive," his eschatology professor recalls. "I can't say I agreed with many of his arguments, but they did provide a balance."

Alex still suffered from his general aversion to women, but he soon recognized that his peers' newfound respect for him was threatened only by this odd behavior. He couldn't blame shyness any longer, so he set out to at least tolerate the women he was forced to come into contact with.

"I was very proud of him," Jessica recalls. "Every night, he would talk about how everyone looked up to him. He would go on about how even the teachers couldn't refute his arguments. It was a huge confidence booster. He asked me to help him deal better with women, which was the first time he'd ever even admitted that he had a problem with them."

While Alex was relishing his newfound power as a respected student, Jessica was discovering a genuine interest in men. Because her brother was so protective of her, she didn't tell him about the passes that interested suitors made, but she knew that eventually they would have to discuss the possibility that they wouldn't be living together their whole lives.

Now twenty-three and gaining self-esteem, Jessica spent more and more time wondering what it would be like to have a romantic relationship with a man. In the fall of 1988, she left the cleaning company that had kept her steadily employed since 1983 and took a job as a waitress at a Denny's restaurant three blocks from the Hope Street Apartments.

She told Alex about the change after she'd made it, and he reacted the way she thought he would—with anger. He argued that she didn't belong in a job with so many men eager to ruin the lives of the first beautiful woman they met, which would definitely be the case with her. In Alex's mind, Jessica was not only the most beautiful woman he knew, but perhaps the only beautiful woman he knew.

Jessica's timing was calculated. With Alex eager to adjust to the women at St. Peter's, he wasn't exactly in a position to refuse her the same courtesy, now was he? After a few hours of debate, he finally agreed and the matter was dropped.

He never even quizzed her about the men at her work or, for that matter, any other men in her life.

By the winter of 1988, Alex and Jessica were leading lives that on the surface appeared perfectly normal to all concerned, including themselves. They were so well-adjusted, in fact, that Alex began to develop a healthy desire to know who their biological parents were.

Up to this point, he'd never told Jessica that he believed they'd either been adopted or taken as children. They'd both grown up believing themselves to be the Browns' natural children. But a number of inconsistencies led Alex to believe differently.

For starters, Alice's abhorrence of sex and her claim to be a virgin would have prohibited her from having children, a fact Alex hadn't put together until he was in California. There was also the vague memory he had of another mother and father when he was very young. The memory was burned into his mind when he was fourteen. He'd found an old pair of pajama pants with the name Alex Price sewed into the elastic waist. Upon learning that Alex found the pajamas, Cyril burned them the next day.

When Alex sat Jessica down one night and told her about his theories, she broke down and wept. But he told her for a reason: he'd decided that they should search for their real parents. Jessica immediately agreed.

They would have to be careful, because according to all legal documents, they were now Alex and Jessica Trane. Exposing themselves as Prices would identify them to the Browns, and neither had a doubt that Alice would find a way to have them killed if she ever learned their whereabouts.

Using his resources at St. Peter's, Alex began to hunt for newspaper records involving individuals by the last name of Price, starting in Oklahoma and then in surrounding states. Assuming that an abduction would have occurred when they were very young—three or four, judging by the size of the pajama pants he'd found—he needed newspapers dating back to the late sixties. Unfortunately, the surrounding libraries kept no record of newspapers from other states so far back. He would have to find another way to access the records.

Investigators would later trace Alex Price's obsession with law enforcement and forensic science to the search he conducted for his biological parents during the winter of

1988. For a highly successful student who had a voracious appetite for knowledge, the step from investigating religion to investigating crime was hardly a leap.

There were simpler methods for going about finding the truth, but Alex chose the one that interested him most. He undertook the task of writing a paper for his hermeneutics class at St. Peter's that compared biblical investigative and interpretive methods to those employed by law enforcement in contemporary society. His teacher, Dr. Winthrow, thought the idea was a good one.

With the full support of his teacher, he meticulously laid out an argument that researching evidence in the biblical record was essentially the same as researching the veracity of facts found in the criminal record. To complete his paper, he needed to pick a reported criminal event and attempt to determine whether that event had actually occurred, using only recorded reports.

As part of his research, he insisted that he should interview a professional involved in such things on a daily basis. Someone from the criminal records division of the FBI, for example. Eager to lend a hand, Cynthia Barstow from the Los Angeles field office agreed to Dr. Winthrow's suggestion of a phone interview with Alex.

It was only a matter of time and several clever interviews before Alex had what he needed. His paper used a purported murder case in Texas as an example, but during the course of his interviews with Cynthia Barstow, using a series of "what ifs" and "for examples" to better understand how the FBI kept records, he learned that a widely publicized kidnapping of Alex and Jessica Price had indeed been reported in Arkansas on January 15, 1968.

He also learned that the siblings' father and mother, Lorden and Betty Price, had died in an automobile accident when another car slammed into their truck in 1976. No surviving children. The abduction case was still unsolved.

When Jessica returned home from waitressing that night and learned the truth about the fate of their true parents, she wept. Alex, on the other hand, seemed strangely unaffected. He was far more bothered by the confirmation that they were abducted by the Browns.

"I couldn't understand why at first," Jessica stated. "He was upset, but the emotion wasn't sorrow or regret or anything like that. Then I realized it had to do with Alice."

The abduction case was still unsolved, and they, Jessica realized, had the information needed to solve it. They could simply tell the FBI who they really were, and tell them to look for the Browns somewhere along the train tracks in Oklahoma.

But Alex rejected the idea. He threw out all sorts of arguments. The Browns (he refused to use Alice's name, Jessica said) were too smart for that. They'd long ago moved and covered all the evidence. They were probably in California, waiting for news of Alex and Jessica to leak. Opening up the case now was way too risky and wouldn't prove a thing. Their real parents were dead anyway.

Jessica argued for justice, but he only became more agitated, begging her not to force him to relive anything that would bring him closer to "that whore."

But there was more, she thought, and she made the mistake of suggesting it to him. "That's not what this is really about, is it? You want to protect her. You actually want to protect Alice the same way you protect me!"

The moment the words left her mouth, she tried to retract them. Alex flew into a rage, tearing around the apartment, smashing trinkets and throwing books. Then he stormed out and slammed the door.

As he had done once before, Alex stayed out late as Jessica worried and paced. And as before, when he returned early in the morning he crumpled at her feet and sobbed like a child, begging her forgiveness. Jessica thought he'd done something terrible, but she didn't have the heart to confront him.

Instead, she embraced him and cried with him. He was right, she reasoned. They'd suffered enough and shouldn't have to relive any of their childhood, not even for the sake of justice. For all they knew, the Browns were dead. Sobbing together, brother and sister reaffirmed their love for each other and their vow to leave the Browns out of their lives forever.

Little did Alex or Jessica know how this choice would lead to an unraveling that would make their abduction from Arkansas pale in comparison.

SIXTEEN

2008

DANIEL WASN'T SURE which of his growing troubles was worse: the fact that he wasn't closer to finding Eve, the fact that Eve had killed him and left him with a terrifying case of recurring fear, or the fact that Eve had evidently threatened to kill him again if he didn't drop the case.

There was no way he could spend more than a few minutes at the field office in his deteriorating state. His going dark had been a stroke of blind brilliance. Little could he have known that doing so would protect him more than the integrity of the case.

To say that the fears came back after DMT had given him a brief respite would have been a falsity of offensive proportions. The fears were indeed back, but DMT had *not* given him any respite. It had only coiled around his mind like a snake, waiting to strike with doubled ferocity.

After waking from his nightmare at 6:00 a.m., he'd successfully fought off two more bouts of terror, one every ninety minutes or so. Each had been severe enough to force him to the bathroom floor and the couch respectively. He simply could not stand under the assault. Or brush his teeth. Or talk on the phone. Or take a shower. Or cook eggs.

Or drive.

He called the field office at nine, five minutes after the second attack, feeling reasonably certain he was safe for an hour or so. As he expected, Lori was already in the lab.

"Good morning, Dr. Clark."

"Morning."

She wasted only a breath before dropping the big question. "Did you sleep well?"

"I did. For about six hours."

"That's fantastic. Good, right?"

"Then I was awakened by a nightmare that made the one I had in the hospital seem like a wet dream."

Lori stayed silent on the other end.

"Any update on the case?" he asked.

"Always. Skin and hair tests came back positive."

"Eve's."

"Full report from the Colorado evidence team on the Caravan. It was reported stolen in Billings, Montana, six months ago under a different set of plates. Looks like our boy slipped up."

Daniel leaned back in his office chair. "No. He doesn't care that we know he was in Montana six months ago. Or that he stole the Caravan from some poor sap in Billings. Brit will chase it down to its bloody end, but if I know Eve, it'll lead nowhere."

"He was in Montana for a reason. Why?"

"Because he was stalking a woman in Billings," Daniel said. "Or because Montana happens to be between Vancouver and Florida. He was just passing through and needed a new van. It could be anything."

"Brit's following up Montana," Lori said.

"He'd be a fool not to. For all we know we'll catch a break. I'm just telling you what my experience with Eve has been." Daniel leaned forward, picked up a black fountain pen that Heather had given him for his fortieth birthday, and turned it in his fingers.

"Do we have the personal physical effects from the van yet? It should have been flown up on a red-eye."

"The reports are—"

"No. I want to see whatever they found. His personal habits. What kind of food he eats. Anything that sheds light on the man. If it's there, I need to see it as soon as possible."

"Hold on."

Although all recovered evidence was critical to any investigation, Daniel preferred to focus on the details that weren't necessarily related to the crime itself. Eve would carefully remove any incriminating evidence from the crime scene, but it was harder to cover traces of mundane details related to everyday life. Evidence that fleshed out the man more than the crime.

Lori came back on in thirty seconds. "It's here."

"Can you pick me up? I don't want to drive."

She hesitated. "That bad?"

"Worse," he said. "Not as often, but worse. Much worse."

"Give me an hour?"

"Actually..." An hour might put him on the brink of another attack. Then again, he couldn't run into hiding every ninety minutes. He would have to find a way to deal with the fear throughout the course of a normal day, however abnormal that might be. "That's fine."

Daniel hung up and checked his e-mail. Mostly trash, even the stuff his filter allowed through. He opened a note from Montova asking him to copy the new SAIC—Brit Holman—on any and all Eve-related information Daniel might run across during his medical leave. The next paragraph made it certain that until a full psychological workup cleared Daniel of any adverse side effects, he would continue his convalescence.

Daniel reached for the phone to call Heather at the office, then decided against it. Six months ago he might have seriously considered her suggestion to drop Eve and take up another case if it meant getting back together. But she must know that his interest in rekindling the relationship had waned. Two years was a long time to be systematically rejected. He still loved her, he thought, but living apart from her had become synonymous with being himself.

There was the matter of Eve's threat to kill him, assuming it had been Eve who made the call. But letting Eve off the hook to save his own skin struck Daniel as morally reprehensible.

He spent the next thirty minutes setting up an exhaustive search for the driver who picked up Heather. He couldn't spill the beans about the actual threat, but he gave his contacts at CHP and the Santa Monica Police Department enough to call in favors. Chief Tilley immediately agreed to send a couple of officers down to the bar that evening to canvass for witnesses.

He was a little more straightforward with Brit, who agreed to keep the investigation clear of Heather on the understanding that the caller might present a threat to her if he knew she was talking to the authorities.

Satisfied the gears were in motion, Daniel shut down his computer and pulled on his shoes. If the caller had left any clue as to his real identity, they would find it. Daniel doubted he had.

Lori picked him up just after ten, as promised, drove him to the field office, and hovered as he opened a plastic evidence bin she'd retrieved for him: the personal evidence Eve had left in and around the scene where he'd killed his sixteenth victim.

The bin contained a pile of clear evidence bags, which Daniel spread out on the table in the evidence room.

Three red, white, and blue Baby Ruth candy bar wrappers
One crumpled aluminum Cherry Coke can
One Heath toffee bar wrapper
Three feathers, labeled chicken
One dirty white sport sock
One empty roll of gray duct tape, and another with about an inch of tape left
One piece of dried-out jerky
One stick of Big Red gum, still in its wrapper

Daniel slid the eight plastic bags to one side, leaving a ninth in front of him. "This is new."

Lori shook her head in amazement. "Same thing every time, huh?"

She'd read the file. He glanced at the spread of bags

he'd moved aside. "He practically lives on candy bars and Cherry Coke. Fairly typical of obsessive-compulsive personalities to limit their patterns of eating. Health means nothing to him."

"No receipts for this stuff? Where does he get his money?"

"He's never left a receipt. No wrapper has ever had a price tag with a store name on it. He leaves these knowing they won't help us narrow his traveling patterns. The rest is conspicuously absent."

She picked up the bag with the old sock. "He subdues his victims with an inhalational general anesthetic."

"Generic sock, sold in every Target and Wal-Mart in the United States. Seventh one we've recovered. If it hasn't already, the lab will find traces of halothane on it."

Lori set the bag down. "Why does he leave such clear evidence of his abductions behind? You'd think such a careful person would leave nothing so incriminating."

"He doesn't care about incriminating evidence, as long as he doesn't get identified and caught. In this case he clearly thinks it's more important we know that he makes his victims unconscious before giving them a fatal disease."

"Like our own society," she said, looking at him. "Some would say."

"Very good, Doctor."

The last bag contained a wrinkled page that had been ripped out of the first book of the Bible. Genesis. Chapter three. King James Version.

Daniel lifted it up to the light so that he could see the tiny type on the opposite side. No marks that he could see.

"May I?" Lori reached for the bag and held it up. "The story of the fall," she said. "Adam and Eve."

"Eve is tricked by the serpent and eats from the tree of the knowledge of good and evil. I've pored over every word of the story two dozen times. We've been pretty sure he was taking his cues from the account of Eve, but this is the first time he's left corroborating evidence."

"Question is, what does meningitis have to do with the fall of man?"

She faced him, eyes bright, and answered her own question. "The meninges shield the mind from disease. Like a layer of innocence."

Impressive. It had taken him a year to draw the same conclusion, without the benefit of the extensive profile she'd read, granted. Still. Maybe it was the doctor in her.

"Destroy the meninges, destroy the mind," Daniel said. "That's right. Our boy is reliving the fall of man by introducing a disease that pierces the veil of innocence and kills the victim. Who'd have thought that the third chapter of Genesis could be such a lethal weapon?" He indicated the bag. "Have it scanned for any marks that aren't indigenous."

The blackness from his nightmare lapped at his mind, darkening his vision. He instinctively steadied himself with one hand on the table. No fear. The darkness seemed to stall, and for a moment he thought this change might indicate a reprieve from the episodes of—

The fear came, like a sledgehammer from heaven, slamming into his throat.

Every nerve in his body stretched tight as if set ablaze with kerosene. The air was sucked from his lungs, leaving him vacant. But it was the darkness...A pit of bitter cold despite the heat.

Horror.

Daniel felt his legs buckle. His chin struck the table before he could catch his fall, and with that blow to his head, the fear was gone.

"Daniel." Lori knelt over him.

He heard the door open. "Daniel?"

Brit rounded the table as he struggled to his knees. He quickly checked his chin and was relieved to find no blood.

"You okay? What happened?"

He got up with Lori's help and brushed his slacks. "Okay, that was embarrassing. I missed the chair." He forced a whimsical grin. "You pull the chair out?"

The agent's eyebrow cocked.

"You see this?" Daniel handed Brit the wrinkled page from Genesis.

Brit took the bag, eyes on Daniel's trembling hand. "You sure you're okay?"

It took every ounce of his concentration to keep from quaking head to toe in the brutal fear's aftermath. Daniel sat. "I hit my head on the table," he said, adjusting his beanie. "I'll be fine."

Brit set the evidence bag down on the table. "I've already had it processed. One latent print matching Eve's. They found this page crammed in a dash vent."

Daniel had to get to a therapist, despite knowing that therapy would offer no help for his condition. A sedative, on the other hand, might.

Brit left them alone again a few minutes later, and Daniel's resolve to hold strong broke the moment the door closed. He placed both arms on the table and rested his forehead between them.

Lori's cool hand touched the back of his neck and began to knead his tight muscles. She remained silent, a small gift that he appreciated. There wasn't much that could be said. He had to find a way to stop the fear.

Any way.

"Maybe we should try a stronger dose," he said.

Her hands moved to his shoulders. "Let's pretend you didn't say that."

"You think you can *massage* it out of me?"

"You prefer me to beat it out of you with a sledgehammer? Because that's what a stronger dose of DMT would do. It could kill you. Out of the question."

"Then what?"

"Time."

Daniel stood and walked toward the door. "I don't have time." He opened the door and stepped into the hallway before remembering that his car was still parked at the apartment.

"Can you give me a ride home?"

"Already?"

"Now. I can't be here."

SEVENTEEN

DANIEL WORKED FROM home the rest of the day, although *worked* perhaps mischaracterized the way he spent the hours.

He refused to speak to Lori about the recurring episodes despite her questioning on two different occasions. She suggested discussing the developments in the Eve case over dinner, but the prospect of having a panic attack while waiting to be seated at a restaurant was enough for him to padlock his door.

No, he needed some time alone. He instructed her to fax the reports as they came in. He'd study them from home, where he could focus without worrying about collapsing on a crowded street. He sounded calm and reasoned on the phone.

Alone, he paced his apartment like a tiger, searching

his memory and his texts for a morsel of anything that might ease his torment.

And when his memory came up blank, he exhausted Google, drilling as deep as the search engine would allow, searching for case studies with similar signatures. Even remotely similar. Psychosis. Near death. Acute paranoia. Delusional disorders of any kind that attacked the nervous system.

His suffering was characterized by nondelusional anxiety, that much was clear. Most likely a form of post-traumatic stress disorder brought on by his death experience. But the acute symptoms he was facing weren't adequately explained in the literature he scanned.

In fact, only those cases that involved near-death experiences approximated his own symptoms. This whole business of the mind reacting to death by washing itself with overwhelmingly strong electrochemical stimuli was just plain annoying. The victim's brain would be forever short-circuited if he didn't actually *terminally* die.

In the end, his search rewarded him with nothing but the general understanding that the human brain was a mysterious, little-understood organ that made computers look like blocks of concrete by comparison. But he already knew that.

He asked a colleague who was also a physician to call in a prescription for Ativan, a relaxant commonly prescribed to calm anxiety. Relatively confident that he wouldn't suffer an attack within thirty minutes of another, Daniel chanced a drive to the Vons drugstore at six that evening.

He took two Ativan and a sleeping pill he already had in his medicine cabinet and readied himself to fall into a deadened sleep. Strange how quickly his priorities had changed. His whole rationale for going dark had been borne out of an obsession to find Eve. Now he only wanted out of this new darkness.

Two Ativan with the sleeping pill should have laid him out flat. They did. For two hours.

He jerked up from his sofa at nine, wet from a cold sweat, heart slamming through the powerful drugs' effects like a ship's pistons.

The fear passed, but now a new kind of horror emerged. If a double dose of Ativan couldn't give him any peace, nothing short of an anesthetic would. And even then, what if the anesthetic put him under but didn't stop the fear? What if he was forced to lay incapacitated as terror racked his mind? A frightening prospect.

Daniel lay on the couch and began to seriously fear the next onslaught.

Surviving another case of horror at eleven, he almost called Lori to come and sit with him. But the idea that he, a renowned behavioral psychologist who hunted society's vilest killers, could only fall asleep in the arms of a beautiful doctor struck him as ridiculous.

He finally drifted off to sleep at two the next morning and awoke to the phone's shrill ring at ten. He'd slept through the night? Relief washed over him.

Then he remembered that he hadn't slept through the last eight hours. In fact, he'd been repeatedly awakened by the dark form at the end of his bed.

He let the answering machine pick up the call from Lori, who was worried about him. The report on the stolen van from Montana had come in. Someone from the Santa Monica PD had called. They were turning up nothing definitive on the car or the driver but would send what they had to his e-mail.

"Call me, Daniel. I'm worried about you."

He took a shower, brushed his teeth. Drank a glass of orange juice. Tried to ignore the anxiety brought on by the anticipation of having to live through another day of fear.

He wondered where the term *basket case* came from. Maybe they'd caged lunatics in large baskets at one time, before the padded cell was introduced as a more humane form of imprisonment.

He couldn't remember the last time he'd actually called in sick. Although he wasn't technically sick—or maybe he was—Daniel decided that he would stay in for the day. If anything came up, Lori would call. Brit would call. Montova would call. They all needed him. At least when it came to Eve, they needed him.

The doorbell rang at noon. Daniel hurried out of his office where he'd been studying cases of NDEs, which helped him tolerate the time between his anxiety attacks. With any luck this would be Lori, he thought, then immediately wondered why he hadn't just called her up if he wanted to see her so badly.

Because he was sick. In the head. And to be perfectly honest, a bit embarrassed about being sick in the head.

But it wasn't Lori. It was the police, following up on several complaints that had been called in last night. Evidently someone in the vicinity had been heard screaming during the early morning hours. Was he aware of the disturbance, and had he heard anything himself?

"Screaming, as in someone who's being tortured screaming?"

"We're not sure. Just screaming. But it was enough to wake two different parties, and it happened three times for about a minute each time. You hear it?"

"No. You sure it was here, not down the street?"

"We're checking all the houses. Probably nothing, but if you hear anything, please give us a call." The officer tipped his hat. "Afternoon."

Daniel closed the door and engaged the dead bolt. How this had happened to him, of all people, was beyond him. He wasn't some stray psychotic who needed a straitjacket. He was the one who put stray psychotics *in* those straitjackets.

Lori called an hour later, and he explained that he had been making some progress on a new theory of his. He wasn't ready to run it by her yet. Give him a couple of days and he'd test it out on her.

Did he need some company? Was he coping? Maybe he should get out and take a walk.

He did have some company, haunting him from the end of his bed, but he didn't say that. He said he was coping just fine. He just needed a few days to sort it all out.

The reasonable part of him wanted to beg her to spend the night with him, holding his hand, with instructions to muzzle him if he started to scream. But he couldn't stoop that low.

That night Daniel took another two Ativan and added a Seroquel—all told, a dangerous but just tolerable dose for a healthy male his weight. The medication knocked him out, a good thing.

He woke screaming two hours later. Not a good thing.

He'd forgotten about the police visit until now and, fearing the neighbors might be even now crawling out of their windows to isolate the sound, he resorted to a thought that had come to him earlier that afternoon.

Still groggy from the drugs, Daniel retrieved a roll of duct tape from the toolbox in his garage. Stumbling back to bed, he ripped off a six-inch length, plastered it tight over his lips, and lay back down.

An hour later he woke screaming into the tape. He didn't like the taste of the adhesive, but at least the tape had worked, he thought, and he succumbed to the mind-numbing drugs once again.

DANIEL MANUFACTURED AND effectively delivered a dozen excuses not to see Lori over the next two days. They spoke at length around noon each day, reviewing new data that had trickled in, none of it particularly helpful, then again on both evenings, satisfying Lori that he was indeed okay.

She had to know that he wasn't. No matter where the discussion went, he always found a way to bring it back to the ND effects, as he called the anxiety attacks. He assured Lori the effects weren't getting any worse, but he feared the tone of his voice betrayed the truth.

In reality, not only were the ND effects growing stronger, but they also came at him with greater frequency. And with more form. A faceless Eve was there, staring at him out of the darkness as he had the night in Manitou Springs, mocking Daniel's death.

He was so desperate for relief by the end of that week that on the second night of his isolation, he called Lori back an hour after they'd hung up.

"Hello?"

"Hey, Lori."

"Daniel?"

A fist lodged itself in his throat, refusing him air, much less a voice.

"Daniel, are you okay? I'm coming over."

"No. No, it's fine. I just..."

"No, it's not fine. It's worse, isn't it?"

"No, not—"

"Stop lying to me, Daniel, for the love of—"

"Okay! It's worse!" he gushed, unable to stop himself. "It's a lot worse, but there's nothing anyone..." He closed his eyes and tried to settle himself.

"Okay, that's it, I'm coming over. You hang tight, I'm—"

"Please, Lori. No. I'm not... Really, there's nothing you can do. I wish there was, believe me." He wanted to tell her more. So he did. "I'm sleeping with tape over my mouth."

"You're *what*?"

"To keep from waking the neighbors. You know... duct tape. It's just a practical thing."

The line remained silent.

"It's been a week and it's not getting better, Lori. I don't know what to do."

"You should check yourself back into a hospital, that's what you should do! I know a doctor at Cedars-Sinai who specializes in severe—"

"You're not listening, Lori. Short of putting me under with anesthesia, I'm alone to face this fear."

"You don't know that."

"I *do* know that! I have a doctorate in behavioral science, or does the fact that I'm barely hanging on change that too?"

"I'm sorry."

They talked another fifteen minutes and accomplished nothing more than passing time. Once more she asked him if she could come over, and once more he rejected the idea.

Daniel spent another night soaking his sheets with sweat and screaming into duct tape.

The next day proved to be the worst day yet. Eve had gone quiet, as he always did between lunar cycles. The investigation had settled into a quagmire of guesses based on new evidence that offered nothing new.

Lori didn't find it within herself to call and check on Daniel, and he doubted it was because she was too busy. He knew how effectively repeated rejection dampened any relationship. He'd now been on both sides.

It was his fourth full day at home, and with each passing hour he couldn't escape the growing certainty that at some point his slow descent into terror would become too much. A certain straw would finally break this camel's back.

He could not know that the straw would come at five thirty that very evening with a single knock on his door.

Daniel opened the door wide, hoping it was Lori, because as strong as he needed to be, his strength was crumbling.

It wasn't Lori. It was Brit Holman. And his face was pale.

"Hello, Brit."

Brit dipped his head. "Daniel. Can I come in?"

"What's wrong?"

"I . . . Well, I should probably—"

"Just spit it out, Brit."

"It's Heather."

"What about her? You talk to her about the phone calls?"

"She missed our lunch appointment today. When I called the office, they said she'd missed a court appearance this morning without calling in."

Daniel reached for a chair. "She has to be home."

"I called. There's no response."

What was the man saying?

"I think Heather may be missing, Daniel."

The fear descended on him then, while he stood in the doorway. A brutal kick to his chest that made him gasp, not unlike a dozen other similar barrages of fear he'd endured that day.

But this one didn't ease up. And it screamed through his head with one word.

Eve.

EIGHTEEN

DANIEL MOVED WITHOUT clear thought or consideration. Past Brit, knocking the man to one side. Over a small hedge that bordered a low-maintenance rock garden. Through the garage's side door.

"I'll come with you!" Brit said. Daniel barely heard him.

His black Lexus sat in the dark, undisturbed for four days now. He slid behind the wheel, punched the garage door opener, and fired the engine.

Only then did he remember the near-death effects. How long they left him alone might determine how long he lived. But the drive to Heather's house was only fifteen minutes.

For the first time he was thankful he'd forced himself to dress respectably each morning—an ineffective ploy to convince himself that all was fine. He tore out of the garage, leaving Brit at the door, jerked the wheel hard to his right at the end of the driveway, and shot into the street in front of a white sedan that swerved to miss him.

The fear that had stormed him thirty seconds earlier hadn't abated, but he knew it wasn't an ND effect. The near-death effects hit hard and throbbed through his nerves like giant waves of energy.

The fear he faced now pushed a steady chill along his nerves.

His phone chirped and he grabbed it. Brit. He spoke quickly, before Brit could. "I'll give you a call, Brit. I'm just going to check the house and then I'll call you."

"I can follow you—"

"No. I need to do this alone. I'll call you." He hung up.

There were a dozen possible explanations for Heather's disappearance, if she had indeed disappeared, and he reviewed each one.

Fallen and knocked herself out in the basement.

Headed to the mountains, furious at his decision not to accept her proposal. It had taken a lot of courage for her to suggest the compromise. Maybe he'd been a fool.

A weekend on Catalina Island with a friend.

But she would have called someone. And she wouldn't have missed a court appearance. Not Heather. Not ever.

He took the next corner with a squeal of tires. Punched the menu button and scrolled through calls received until he found Lori's call to him last night. Hit send.

She answered on the third ring. "Hello, Dr. Clark. Nice of you to—"

"Heather's missing, Lori."

"Heather's what?"

"Missing. It's Eve, it has to be. I hope this is a mistake."

"Calm down. Where are you now?"

"I'm on my way to her house."

"You're driving?"

"She's *missing*!"

"Okay. I'll meet you there."

"No. I need you there."

"I was headed out. It's almost six."

"Stay there, Lori. Don't move. I'll call you in fifteen minutes."

He hung up and tried to push an image of Heather alone in the kitchen from his mind. The image was replaced with another, a dark form and Heather. In a root cellar. He dropped his open palm onto the steering wheel and cut through traffic, horn blaring.

It took Daniel twelve minutes to reach the house. He bounded up the sidewalk, found the door locked, and retrieved a key from under the ficus plant to the door's right.

The lights in the house were off. All of them.

"Heather?"

His voice sounded hollow.

"Heather! Answer me!"

Daniel ran through a vacant living room, up the stairs to the master bedroom. He yelled her name into each room, checking under and behind furniture. In the bathroom, back down to the main floor, in the garage.

Her white BMW was parked in one of two bays.

Muttering a curse, he ran for the kitchen and checked the answering machine. Nine new messages. The first from Raquel at seven thirty this morning.

He scrolled through the caller ID numbers, found Raquel's cell, and called it.

She answered in a chipper voice. "Hey, girl. Where you been hiding out?"

"It's Daniel, Raquel."

"Daniel? Oh, I'm sorry. I didn't mean to interrupt."

"I called you. Listen to me: I need to know when you talked to Heather last."

"What do you mean? Yesterday, we had a drink after work."

"What time?"

"What's wrong, Daniel? You're saying she's not there?"

"No, she's not. What time did you leave her?"

"At about six. I called and talked to her at ten."

So Heather had made it home.

Raquel's voice now betrayed concern. "What's happening?"

He clicked the phone off and set it on the counter. For a few moments he couldn't move. Heather had been taken.

Or was she doing this to get his attention? Could it be? It wasn't like her. But there were other possibilities. This wasn't Eve, couldn't be. For starters, he always took his victims as the moon was waning, never approaching a full moon.

Eve had been in Colorado a week ago and would have had to ditch his car, find another, work his way unseen into California—all things that took time.

Then there was Heather, who'd never been associated with any religion. Eve had only taken women with some religious affiliation thus far.

For that matter, Eve was far too careful to waltz into a house and abduct Heather simply to send a message to Daniel.

The basement.

Daniel hit the light switch in the stairwell and took the steps two at a time. Storage boxes were stacked up along one wall of the unfinished game room. The door to the back room was closed.

He hurried across the concrete floor, twisted the brass handle, and pushed the door open.

The room was dark. He felt the wall for a switch. Found one. Flipped it up. Fluorescent bulbs stuttered to life.

At first the illuminated scene confused him. The walls were covered with information tied to Eve. And him. It was almost as if the killer himself had set up the room. He stared in stunned silence.

But the writing was Heather's. The computer, hers. Everything about the room, hers. Heather had been stalking the case.

Stalking Eve.

Daniel walked forward, legs numb. All this time she'd been hounding not only Daniel but the killer. Eve. Which said more about Heather than he could possibly have guessed.

The ND effect hit him with a fresh wash of dread as he stood in the middle of the floor. And this time the form at the end of his bed loomed over him.

I see you, Daniel...

He shook but refused to fall.

When the fear passed moments later, leaving only chills, he was trembling but still upright, still staring back at the newspaper clippings, still defying the fear. In so many ways Heather had defied them all. For all he knew, she'd gone after Eve on her own. Maybe she hadn't been taken by him; she was taking *him*.

Daniel turned around, scanning the walls. A purple stain on the floor pulled his eyes downward. A broken wine glass on its side. A small lump of white next to it.

It was a sock.

He'd seen a sock identical to this one seven times in his life. Each time in a clear plastic bag. Each time the sock had been used to knock out a victim.

Eve had taken his seventeenth Eve.

The fear came again, triggered by the sock...by the knowledge that Heather was gone, had been gone for almost twenty-four hours.

Now he did drop, hard, onto one knee. He pushed himself up, fighting the waves of horror with a clenched jaw. She was in Eve's possession because of him.

Daniel managed to get his phone out and hit send again. Lori picked up on the first ring.

"Did you find her?"

His voice trembled. "Eve took her."

"You're sure?"

"Stay there, Lori," he said.

"You're scaring me, Daniel."

"Stay there, I'm coming to you."

"Tell me what you're thinking."

He took a deep breath and let it out slowly.

"I know what to do, Lori. I know how to find her."

Reprinted from Crime Today *magazine, 2008*

MAN OF SORROW:
JOURNEY INTO DARKNESS

by Anne Rudolph

*Crime Today magazine is pleased to present the fifth installment of
Anne Rudolph's narrative account of the killer now known as Alex
Price, presented in nine monthly installments.*

1990

NINETEEN NINETY marked the beginning of the end of Alex Price's entry into any kind of normal social existence.

Having accepted and then dismissed their true identities, both Alex and Jessica pursued their new lives with purpose and enthusiasm through the winter of 1989 and early 1990. Jessica's varied schedule at the restaurant allowed her to keep unpredictable hours, some of which she began to spend with friends she made at work. She started to talk more openly with men, not about her past but about her life and dreams, both of which were evolving with increased freedom.

She rarely spoke about her brother outside of his life as a seminary student at St. Peter's. Although none of them had met Alex, all of her new friends knew that Jessica Trane's brother was becoming a priest and doing it better than most.

The environment at home began to wear on Jessica, but not enough to make her push for any change. Alex still slept on the couch and she still slept on the mattress, not for her sake, but for his. At her request he'd tried to fall asleep in his own room on a couple of occasions, but he said he just couldn't sleep in there.

She suggested that they set up two beds in her bedroom, just to get the mattress out of the living room, but he recoiled at the idea of invading her personal space. They simply could not sleep together in the same bedroom now that they were adults. It wasn't right.

The only solution was the living room, and all things considered, Jessica didn't mind too much, except when Alex's nightmares woke her. If anything, they had become worse. He woke every night, screaming into the duct tape that covered his mouth, then retreated into his private room.

Inside his room, he hung a black blanket from the ceiling so that even when he opened the door, the room could not be seen. When asked if she ever wondered what he was doing in his room all that time, she only shrugged. "He was weird that way, but I understood it. Private space was very important to him. He'd grown up in a house without any, and now he wanted to have his own place of safety."

It wasn't that Alex didn't feel safe with her, she said. It was that most of his struggles had nothing to do with her and, as he said, they all had to fight their demons on their own.

Alex continued to excel as a student, now in his third year, and grew bolder with his verbal arguments and even bolder in his papers. Studying to become a priest had become his purpose for living, the one thing that gave him meaning.

He would attend class in the morning, return to sleep for an hour or so in the afternoon, and walk to the restaurant where he still worked a three-hour shift as a dishwasher. Returning home by four, he would then labor over his controversial theology and philosophy papers till Jessica came home, often late at night. After telling her about his day and hearing about hers, he would prepare himself for a fitful sleep, which would usually end in a nightmare around two or three in the morning. For weeks on end, Alex lived through the same cycle.

In April of 1990 that cycle came to an abrupt end. He presented a paper he wrote titled "God," in which he argued that God, as defined by most of the major world religions, including Christianity, Islam, and Judaism, might be understood as nonexistent. Catholicism, he argued, might fare better as a religion that held the belief that God was an extension of man.

"His argument would have been dismissed as philosophical banter if he hadn't argued the case with so much conviction," his former theology professor Herman Stiller said. "He had a reputation as someone who thought outside of the box, but reading the paper I wasn't certain Trane didn't believe what he'd written."

When confronted, Alex at first defended his position but then backed down. The matter was dismissed and he continued with his studies.

Up to this point, Alex had been seen by other students as a strong critical thinker with a healthy dose of cynicism. But he'd never proposed doctrine that would be seen as heresy by the Catholic church until he wrote the paper on God's nonexistence. When word of the paper leaked to a few of the students, their attitude toward Alex began to shift.

> "I have seen the face of evil, and if not for the grace of God himself, I would have cut my own throat so as not to face it ever again."
>
> —Father Robert Seymour
> *Dance of the Dead*

Meanwhile, Alex was having trouble hiding his own true feelings about religion and faith. In truth, he didn't believe in God, not the way the rest of the students did. His was a far more subjective faith—a strange brew of secularism that used the term *God* as if it were a label for anything unexplainable.

"I did notice that some of the things he said sounded a bit too familiar," Jessica confessed. Alex used terms like *demon-greased souls* and *babies for Lucy*, both terms that Alice had used to describe sinners. But none of this concerned Jessica because, as she put it, "He wasn't adopting Alice's ways. I thought he was rejecting them and anything to do with false religion."

Indeed, Alex appeared to be taking the same path many children take once they find their freedom. Having been indoctrinated with certain beliefs as children (such as the belief in God's existence), they enter the world and find those beliefs challenged, often turning against them.

In Alex's case, he had been both indoctrinated and abused by Alice's religion. Although he seemed to think at first that Christianity was the superior religion, he couldn't dismiss his resentment of religion in general. In fact, the more he studied doctrine, the more he turned against all religion and faith. Like the proverbial frog in a pot of hot religious stew, his faith began to die. And it was only a matter of time before his beliefs, or the lack thereof, became evident to others.

What started as a few isolated comments to students quickly spun out of control. When presented with clear questions of faith in open discussion, he demurred with a clever and often confusing answer.

Amazingly, Alex didn't appear to see the case building against him. In March he turned in another paper, this time systematically dismantling the supernatural in all its forms without actually claiming that there was no supernatural reality. "The arguments were all there," Herman Stiller recalls, "so the fact that Trane drew no definitive conclusion was immaterial. The conclusions were implied."

For a week, Alex heard nothing, and then he was called into the dean's office. Present were his professor, Herman Stiller; the academic dean, Bradley Ossburger; and his priest, Father Robert Seymour. For an hour Father Seymour carefully quizzed the bright student about his personal faith, and try as he did, Alex could not cover up his profound doubts about the validity of any faith.

"It was the way he looked at me as much as what he said that bothered me," Father Seymour said. "His glare chilled me to the bone. He frequently substituted words. *All-seeing One* instead of *Almighty God. Kingdom of light* for *Kingdom of God.*"

A simple question near the end brought the interview into clear focus. "As a priest, would you swear your allegiance to Jesus Christ, Son of the Most High God?" Father Seymour asked.

Alex shifted uncomfortably in his seat and gave his answer: "That depends."

"We need a yes or a no," the dean pressed.

"You do, do you?" came the response. "And why do you suppose you, who by your own admission are mere mortal men, can know more than I?"

Ossburger wouldn't let the question go. "A yes or a no."

Alex leaned forward and stared the man down, eyes angry. "Then no." He leaned back, clearly agitated. "How can you sit here and demand that I offer conclusions when I haven't even finished my studies? I'll give you an answer when I've studied all the evidence."

The dean had heard enough. After excusing Alex for a few minutes, they called him in and gave him the news: they were excusing him from studies at St. Peter's, effective immediately.

Alex stood in shock. He demanded they reconsider, but the decision was final. In a diatribe that went on for ten minutes, Alex Trane finally came clean, telling the panel exactly what he thought about their so-called religion. The Catholic church was a farce, because the nuns and the priests served a god who did not exist, in a fanciful battle against a Satan they'd made up as an excuse for their own pitiful, whore-mongering souls. Which, by the way, didn't exist either. The only reason none of them would rot in hell was because all of them would simply rot in a grave.

Trane's true beliefs, delivered in the colorful argumentative style he'd become known for, had finally betrayed him. Any hope of serving humanity as a man of the cloth was decidedly vanquished in those ten minutes.

Father Robert Seymour walked Alex to his car and expressed concern for his spiritual health. They talked frankly, leaving the father with little doubt that the board had made the correct decision. Alex Trane's issues were disturbing, to say the least.

Alex tried to talk his way back into St. Peter's three days later by placing a deeply remorseful call to the academic dean, but Ossburger politely declined and suggested Trane try his mind at science or psychology, both subjects in which he'd demonstrated repeated brilliance.

But Alex didn't want to be a "rocket scientist or a head shrink," as Jessica put it. He wanted to be a priest, and they had taken that away from him. "He was really crushed. Not just upset or angry. I mean completely crushed. The one thing he thought he could do to make everything better was gone."

After the initial anger at being kicked out of St. Peter's passed, Alex redirected his frustration from the staff and students at the school to himself. Without the distraction of classes to fill his days, Alex took to moping around the apartment, wondering where he'd gone wrong. "Pitiful," Jessica said. "I felt so sorry for him."

But they were right to dismiss him, she said, although she never admitted this to him. Alex and she talked about seminary many times late into the night, and it became clear to her that Alex would not have made a good priest. He really didn't believe in God or Satan or anything remotely similar to God or Satan. How could anyone serve a God he didn't believe in?

Alex's answer was simple: "You don't serve God. You serve people who think they believe in God, but when push comes to shove, really don't. People just like me. I am the perfect priest because I am everybody."

His anger gone and his self-confidence crushed, Alex slowly sank into a deep depression. He was searching for meaning. For substance. Even for love. And he shared his thoughts with his sister in a monotone that broke her heart.

There was now only one thing in his life that had any meaning, he often told Jessica. "You. I love only you."

"You don't mean that," she would say. "What about yourself?"

"I hate myself."

And Alex Price was speaking the truth.

NINETEEN

DANIEL WAS TWO BLOCKS from the FBI field office on Wilshire when the next bout of near-death effects swallowed his mind.

He sucked at the car's stale air as darkness clouded his vision. But he couldn't black out. The office was only a minute away. Hunting down Eve was now beyond his own need for accomplishment or to rid society of an evil it had spawned. Heather's life was now in his hands.

And his hands were on the wheel, jerking spastically as he fought off the darkness. His body began to convulse, and for a moment he thought he might actually throw up.

He spread his eyes wide and maintained vision. Unfortunately, the effort resulted in less control over his arms. The car veered to the right and plowed into a flashing barricade. Horns blared.

The fear lifted then, as the Lexus nosed for a hole in the pavement. He stood on the brakes and came to a halt three feet from the worst of the road construction.

Daniel glanced behind, saw that several cars had stopped twenty yards behind, threw the car in reverse, and backed out of the construction pit. He drove back out onto Wilshire and sped down the coned lane, leaving more than a couple of drivers gawking.

He parked in a visitor's spot and headed straight for the basement. Only one other worker saw him—a secretary from the third floor who nodded on her way out for the night.

The viewing window in the morgue's steel door was lit at the dark hall's end. Daniel slowed to a walk. Like a man headed for the light in a near-death experience, he walked toward the morgue's light. Silent except for his breathing and the padding of his feet.

He ran the last ten feet, shoved the door open, and faced Lori, who was leaning against the steel exam table, arms crossed, waiting for him.

For a moment they stared at each other, Daniel calming his breathing, Lori searching his eyes with steely inquisition. They both knew a turning point had been forced upon them, he thought. He had, at least, and he hoped she, too, would accept the truth.

"Lori."

"Hello, Daniel."

Beat.

"You know there's only one way to do this, Lori."

"Do I?"

"Something happened to me back there in Manitou Springs. I was killed. My brain was subjected to an electrochemical barrage that washed Eve's face from my memory and short-circuited my mind. Isn't that what happened?"

"Yes. Yes, that's what happened." ·

"I have to go back to that moment, Lori. You know that's the only way now."

She was silent.

"You have to kill me, Lori."

"Don't be a fool."

Here it was, then. The standoff Daniel knew it would come down to.

"Eve's taken Heather," he said, voice strained. "I'm the only one who can help her. I know what Eve looks like; he's locked in my mind."

"I'm not going to kill—"

"You *have* to!" Daniel walked toward her, not caring that he'd yelled. "His image is locked in here." He jabbed his head. "Nothing out there can help her, and you know that as well as I do."

"And if I can't resuscitate you, that image will die with you! With time, it could come out on its own."

"We don't have time! Eve has Heather."

He gingerly touched his throbbing forehead, then turned away from Lori, eyes closed. He'd done the research himself over the last two days and was reasonably confident that she could pull it off. But it was madness; they both knew it.

"Look," he said, turning back. "I know it's crazy, but you have no idea how much pain I'm in. He's got her, Lori. Eve has his seventeenth victim. Putting me under is risky. It may get us nowhere, but if you don't help me, I'm going to find someone else to do it."

"I worked so hard to keep you alive!" She lowered her arms and strode past him, jaw firm. "You have no idea what you're asking. This isn't some late-night movie here."

"You're wrong. I do know what I'm asking. And I know that we can raise the odds to over 75 percent. You're familiar with the cases involving the Romanian heart surgeon, Dr. Cheslov? Before the advent of heart-lung technology, he experimented with alternatives to open-heart surgery by stopping and restarting the heart externally, a kind of rebooting to deal with—"

"He was an unethical quack. There's no documentation. He experimented on enemies of the state, for heaven's sake."

"You're saying it wouldn't work? New drugs improve my chances of resuscitation. I understand why the medical community doesn't experiment in uncontrolled environments, but this situation is already way beyond our control." He paused. "You know how to do it, don't you?"

She remained silent. But he'd already gotten to her, he thought. She'd been thinking along the same lines ever since the injection of DMT had failed, four nights earlier.

They were running out of time.

Daniel walked up to her and pulled her tight against his chest. Whispered softly by her ear. "Please, I need you to do this for me. Inject a peripheral vein close to the heart with a large dose of a myocardial relaxant. Force my heart into ventricular fibrillation. It'll stop pumping blood. My brain will begin to starve of oxygen and enter sympathetic shock. That's what I need, Lori. I need my mind to think it's dying."

She breathed steadily into his shoulder. He'd rehearsed

the specifics a hundred times over the last two days. He drew back. Brushed a strand of hair from her forehead.

"Only then will my brain do whatever it is brains do as they die. Without adequate blood pressure, my nerves will shut down and all remaining energy will be shifted to my brain in a last-ditch effort to survive. My temporal lobe will release memories. Sensing the end, my brain will drain DMT from the pineal gland. Neurotransmitters will go into massive confusion, crossing electro-chemical circuits in random order. I'll have a near-death experience."

"What if I can't bring you back?" She looked into his eyes. "Seventy-five percent—"

"Is a risk I'm willing to take. You can bring me back. You'll leave me in ventricular fibrillation for one minute and then innervate the heart muscle with massive doses of epinephrine and atropine into the same vein. A 360-joule shock will stop the heart completely, and it will restart on its own automatic contraction."

Leaving little doubt as to what he'd been up to the last two days, he stepped back and watched her. Lori's face had paled a few shades, but she wasn't shutting him down.

"It would be murder, you know."

He pulled out his wallet and withdrew the note he'd signed. "This will get you through."

"Assisted suicide isn't legal, under any circumstances. A note won't keep me out of prison if you die—it's not even a holographic will. A court won't admit it."

She was right, of course. The FBI would probably let her off, all things considered, but it would be their call, not hers.

"Then you'd better bring me back."

The color slowly came back to her face.

"It's not rocket science, Lori. We have everything we need in this room. We could be finished in half an hour."

She turned away. "I can't believe we're talking like this."

"There's a chance it could work, isn't there?" he asked.

"That's not the point."

"It's possible I'll see Eve and remember him this time."

"Possible, but—"

"That this short circuit in my brain will be rewired by the shock of another death."

"That's not—"

"That as a result of my risk, I may learn something that will save my wife!"

Lori crossed one arm and lifted the other to rub her temple. "She's not your wife."

"Possible?"

"Yes! Possible! But we don't have a clue what will really happen!"

"That's where you're wrong. We know that if I don't do this, Heather will be dead in a matter of days, maybe sooner."

Daniel walked to the stainless-steel table and faced her. "I need you to kill me, Doctor, and I need you to do it now."

AS IT TURNED OUT, plotting his death was far easier than facing it. What had started as several marathon sessions of sifting through hopes and hypotheticals had delivered Daniel to a deathbed, facing the white ceiling of a morgue.

"The door is locked?" he asked again.

"No one's coming in here, trust me. This is not only the most morally reprehensible thing I've done in my life; it's also completely illegal."

"Forget that. Just bring me back."

"There's no way you're not walking out of this room on two legs tonight," she said.

She was saying the words, Daniel thought, but he couldn't help seeing some eagerness in her eyes. In retrospect, she had been the one to introduce the idea to him. They were similar, he and Lori.

"Turn your head toward me," she said softly.

He turned, and she wiped the left side of his neck with a disinfectant.

"This will sting." She inserted a long, flexible needle sheath into his neck and opened the IV as she spoke to calm him. "This is going into your internal carotid vein, about as close to the heart as I can get without going into your chest."

She taped it off, satisfied. Three large syringes lay on a metal tray next to the bed. The drugs in each would enter his vein through the IV needle.

It occurred to him that he was due for a near-death attack.

"How much longer?"

"Don't be in such a hurry to die. Almost there."

She attached the adhesive patches from the electronic defibrillator to his side and chest, checked the voltage once more. The electrical impulses would countershock the heart's sinoatrial node while he was under, sustaining ventricular fibrillation until Lori was ready to restart the heart with a 360-joule burst. It was this advance in technology that separated their attempts from others.

She lifted a bag valve mask that was connected to a small green and silver canister of oxygen and took a deep breath. "Okay, you'll feel the air flowing, but I won't turn on the oxygen until we restart."

He nodded.

Lori leaned forward, kissed him lightly on the lips. "I know you have a strong heart, Daniel. Promise me you'll come back."

"I will. Please, before I lose my courage."

She set the mask over his nose and mouth and cinched it tight. Then she lifted one of the syringes, cleared the needle, pressed it into the IV nipple, and filled the reservoir that fed the line.

"One hundred milligrams of benzodiazepine. Heaven help us..."

She released a block, and Daniel watched the amber drug swirling into the solution that snaked toward his neck. She adjusted the flow regulator to allow the full dose into his carotid vein.

It took less than ten seconds for him to feel the powerful tranquilizer's first effect. Pressure swelled in his chest as the muscles surrounding his heart reacted to its sudden slowing.

Pain shot through his left arm, and he was suddenly sure he'd made a terrible mistake. He was going to die. For the second time in one week. How could he tempt fate twice and expect to survive?

The inevitability of death filled his mind, and he felt panic nudging close.

Pain gripped his chest and his whole body stiffened. He moaned.

"I'm sorry, Daniel. Please, I'm..."

He couldn't hear the rest. Already his brain was shutting down his organs to preserve valuable oxygen for itself. He felt his lungs settle, like deflated balloons.

His eyes were closed, but his vision seemed to narrow, tunneling into a deeper darkness. Panic began to batter him. His body was shaking, he could feel it on the table, bouncing through a seizure.

Only then, as the pain of his death spread to a mental certainty, did Daniel realize his mistake.

He was going to die. Really die.

And then the pain lifted and the darkness swallowed him, and Daniel knew that he was dead.

TWENTY

DEAD BUT ALIVE, he thought. At least alive some-where in the deepest recesses of his mind where the brain's last gasps produced a kind of magical life.

Light exploded on the horizon of his mind. The exhila-rating bursts of a DMT trip—he'd been here once. But it was larger this time. A hundred times brighter. On the table, his lungs had shut down and his blood lay still in his veins.

In his mind he was floating through enough raw energy to light up a hundred stadiums.

And then the light was gone, as if his mind had flipped a switch. Memories flooded his mind—childhood, his first date with Heather, the speaking circuit. His introduc-tion to the Eve case. Dozens of snapshots, some of which he hadn't thought about in a long time.

The time he'd pretended to drown a mouse his father

had caught in one of those catch-them-live traps. A hidden memory brought to life now for reasons beyond him.

How many other memories did the brain store in the deep freeze, warmed to the imagination only when certain circuits fired?

Daniel became vaguely aware that he was meant to be brought back to life by Lori. In the next moment, the vagueness of the notion fell away, and he thought maybe she'd already done it because he was standing, breathing. Alive.

But this wasn't the morgue. He stood in a cobalt black room, dressed in slacks, no shirt, no shoes, electrodes still stuck to his chest.

The room was roughly thirty feet square; all four walls and the ceiling were made of a perfectly smooth material that was so black they seemed to suck the color from him.

An excruciatingly familiar emotion eked from his bones, as if sucked out by the walls. His hands began to shake.

The fear.

He knew immediately that his mind had entered the place from which his fear originated. It had formed this image of its final gasps of life. But knowing this didn't give him any reprieve.

This was the place in the human experience men sought to explain with terms like *hell*. The wailing and gnashing of teeth. A lake of fire.

Raw fear.

The floor was a checkerboard of black and white. Cool under his toes.

It was almost like he was in a kitchen, or a huge black oven with the kitchen floor rather than a rack underfoot.

He walked to the nearest wall and lifted his hand to

touch the black surface. But he stopped inches away, certain that if he touched the wall something worse would happen. Much worse.

The sound of a child giggling echoed around the room. Daniel spun, but he couldn't see anyone. There wasn't a light source, other than the white squares on the floor, and they didn't light the corners well. Still, in such a small room he would have seen them by now.

Maybe it was him laughing?

The giggling came again, behind him, where the cold wall was. He jerked around, alarmed to see that he was now on the opposite side of where he'd thought he was. The whole room lay in front of him. It had flipped around. Or maybe not. Each wall was identical. He had probably just gotten mixed up.

The giggle rippled again, the innocent laughter of a young child to his right.

And there, in the corner to his left, squatted a child facing the wall. He was bent over something amusing, like a boy playing with marbles in the corner.

"Hello?"

Daniel's voice bounced off the walls. The boy caught his breath and froze. But he didn't turn. After a moment, he resumed his playing. Then giggled again.

Daniel walked toward the room's center, eyes fixed on the child. The boy (assuming it was indeed a boy) looked about six or seven years old, spine and ribs pressing through smooth, nearly translucent skin. Dark hair hung to his shoulders. He wore ratty tan shorts. No shoes.

"Hello? Can you hear me?"

The boy froze. But he still didn't turn.

Daniel walked closer, edging to his left so he could see

more of the boy who seemed to be intentionally ignoring him. This was him, as a child?

But nothing about the room looked like a memory or something from a distant past. It seemed as real as if Daniel were in his own apartment.

A door emerged from the shadow beyond the boy, he saw. Closed. Maybe the child had come in while his back was turned.

Daniel edged a little farther, then stopped and stared at the object that was capturing the boy's attention. It was a doll. One of those fat baby dolls with blonde hair, wearing a white diaper. Something oddly familiar about the face, but he couldn't place it.

The boy had dug the eyes out and placed them on the floor. Two black holes stared up at him. As Daniel watched, the boy stuck one finger into the doll's eye and wiggled it deep, then pulled it out. The eye socket spread as if the doll was made of soft clay. Or wax.

The boy chuckled, mildly amused.

Daniel was about to speak again when an insect crawled from the doll's eye. A honeybee, then another from the other eye socket.

Eve, Daniel. You have to find Eve.

The voice whispered through his mind, yanking him from his fascination with the surreal sight of the boy playing with the doll. His breathing came thick, like a diver's breath hissing through a regulator a hundred feet under the surface. The black walls seemed to amplify all sound, even the boy's breath. Steady, in and out, in and out.

Another giggle.

"Where's Eve?" Daniel asked.

The boy froze, crouched over the doll. Slowly he lifted his head and stared at the door ahead of him.

"Eve's in there," he said.

The innocence carried by the boy's voice eased Daniel's tension. The child was trapped in here, too, he thought, an image of Daniel's childhood. Although what a wax doll with bees crawling from its eyes had to do with his childhood, he had no clue.

He looked at the doll again. Even more familiar now.

And then the face became clear in his mind's eye. It was Heather. The boy was playing with a doll that looked strikingly similar to Heather.

He took a step forward, alarmed. "What's...is that... is that Heather?"

The boy moved his head around slowly, showing his face for the first time. Only it wasn't the face of a boy of six or seven.

His skin was stretched tight, flattening his lips, pulling his eyelids open to bare jet-black eyes. The incongruity of such a twisted, malignant face on a child could hardly be overstated.

Every muscle in Daniel's body contracted in repulsion. If the room held his fear, this child was fear itself, and the power of that fear hammered his mind with such intensity that he accepted the awful truth of his predicament.

He was dying. This was the final moment of death. Blackness would swallow him now.

The boy's lips twisted into a snarl. His voice came out low and gravelly now, slow, cutting to Daniel's nerves with each crackling syllable.

"You made me a promise," he said, and his voice sucked the air from the room.

Daniel began to scream.

And with that scream, the darkness was dispelled by white brilliance. The overhead light in the morgue.

He was back.

IT TOOK DANIEL SEVERAL minutes to calm down while his body adjusted to the fresh influx of oxygen. His mind had come out of death surprisingly active, but every muscle begged for sleep.

"Wake me up," he stammered.

"I am. Just give the drugs a minute."

Slowly the grogginess faded. Only when his brain had satisfied itself that he was out of danger could he dip back into memories of the time under.

Fifty-six seconds, according to Lori.

Memories of stray events throughout his life. The dark room. The boy. The checkerboard floor.

"I remember," he said into the mask.

Lori nodded and removed the mask. "Your oxygen saturation is fine." She seemed surprisingly at ease with his death and resuscitation, he thought. What had they been thinking?

"I remember it all," he said.

"I'm going to have to keep you on some pretty heavy doses of drugs to keep you from..."

A fresh memory blossomed to life.

Where's Eve?

Eve's in there. The boy had pointed to the door.

He hadn't seen Eve?

Daniel sat up, ignored the throbbing pain.

Lori put a hand on his chest as if intending to urge him

back, then peeled off the electrodes instead. "So? What happened?"

"Eve's behind the door."

An image of the wax doll filled his mind. Heather.

Daniel slid from the table, took one step, and crumpled to his knees.

"Whoa, slow down!" Lori steadied him. "This is going to take some time. We talked about this."

"It's her," he said, struggling to stand. "Eve has her."

She steered him toward the table, but he pulled away and used his right arm to support himself.

"There was a doll, he was playing with a doll. I think it was her."

"Who was? Eve was?"

"No. The boy. But..."

Daniel spun to her. "The mass spectrometry on the tire sample from the Dodge Caravan recovered in Manitou Springs, what came back?"

"Wax. Beeswax. Why?"

Daniel's pulse thickened. "What else?"

"I don't remember. Brit is following it up."

"Can you hand me my phone?" He pointed to the counter, where his phone was perched on top of his shirt.

He took the phone from her, saw that Brit had called several times over the past half hour, trying to track him down. The SAIC answered with a tight voice. "Daniel. You okay?"

"He has her, Brit. I found a sock in our basement. It's Eve's."

"You're sure?"

"There's not a doubt in my mind." How did he say

this? "You got the mass spec results on those samples of wax we retrieved from the Caravan's tires?"

"Beeswax. Standard garden variety. Could have come from a hundred sources. We haven't drilled into the analysis yet."

"Why not?"

"Phoenix and Montana took priority. We'll get to it tomorrow."

"No. I need you to get to it tonight. Don't ask me to explain, call it a hunch. We need to locate that beeswax."

"Heather?"

"We know Eve scopes his sites months in advance. Until we get a better lead, we work with the wax."

"Coal," Brit said.

"What about coal?"

"There were traces of coal in the wax."

Daniel shivered. It wasn't much, but it was a lead, a sliver of hope. "How soon can you get in here?"

"You're at the lab?"

He glanced at Lori, who was watching him.

"Yes."

"Doing what?"

"Looking for my wife."

TWENTY-ONE

THE DRUGS LORI HAD given him cleared Daniel's mind and took away most of the pain, and by the time Brit returned to the office, Daniel was feeling well enough to avoid an interrogation about the pallor of death that had grayed his face for the first hour.

Colleen Hays, a junior agent following up on the wax, accompanied Brit. They joined Lori and Daniel in what had become known as the Eve room, a conference room with Eve-related pictures and reports plastering the walls.

"Old, but yes, plain beeswax," Colleen said.

"Traces?" Daniel demanded.

She blew out some air and traced her finger down the sheet. "Hydrocarbons, 14 percent; monoesters, 35 percent..." She skipped to another section. "Traces of goldenrod pollen."

"Goldenrod," Brit said. "Limited concentrations of the pollen. Northern United States. So we have a Dodge Caravan that drove through a large concentration of wax formed by bees that deposited goldenrod pollen on the wax, placing them anywhere in the upper half of the United States."

"And coal," Daniel said. "What kind of coal?"

Brit pulled out another report, snapped the paper. "Unwashed coal," he said. "Striations suggest a short wall mine. Again, could be from anywhere. Mined in Pennsylvania or Virginia, for all we know, and distributed across the United States."

He set the report down and looked up. Removed a pair of reading glasses from his face. "I don't see where this is taking us, Daniel."

Daniel stood and dug into his pocket for the Advil Lori had given him. He crossed to the drinking fountain and downed four pills with a single gulp. An hour had passed without fear.

But it hardly mattered. If his bouts were gone, they'd been replaced by a desperation for Heather's safety. He could barely stomach the knowledge that she was in Eve's hole at this very moment. Was she conscious? Cut and bruised? Alive? Praying to whatever forces governed fortune that Daniel would find her?

He'd failed her so often he couldn't remember what it felt like to save her.

He glanced at Lori, who leaned against the far wall with arms crossed, forced back his emotion, and spoke to Brit. "Assume that we know she's on the bubble."

"Heather," Brit said.

Daniel looked at him but refused to acknowledge, which was enough acknowledgment by itself. "Eve takes her last night, knowing that we'll discover her missing within twelve hours. He wants her in place before we can begin a search." He looked at a large map of the United States dotted with pins that indicated each of the sixteen killings.

"Let's give him a twenty-hour drive from Los Angeles." Brit walked to the map. "As far north as the Canadian border, down into Baja. As far west as the Colorado–Kansas border. That's a lot of ground."

"Cross every known honey farm in the United States with coal production," Daniel said. "We're looking for an abandoned coal mine."

They all faced him.

"Just do it, Colleen."

She looked at Brit for approval, then nodded and left the room.

"An abandoned coal mine in the Northwest?" Brit asked. "Not exactly confidence inspiring. The coal could have come from anywhere."

"We'll find out soon enough, won't we? It's the honey farm that will tell us if we're close."

Brit didn't look remotely certain. Daniel couldn't blame the man. They'd chased a hundred similar leads over the past year, never finding more than frayed ends.

"I'm going to add this to the bulletin," Brit said, walking from the room.

Daniel sat down, leaned back, and closed his eyes, struggling to maintain composure. "We're missing something," he breathed.

"You need to rest," Lori said. "This is crazy. You have no business leading an investigation in your condition."

"What would you suggest? Just let him kill her?"

"No, but you're not in any condition—"

"It's my condition that got her into this!" he snapped. "It's my condition that could get her out!"

"Because your mind associated the beeswax you found on Eve's tires with Heather's abduction?"

Neither had said as much yet, and Daniel had done his best to ignore the implication, but they both knew that what he'd seen while dead was at best his mind's desperate attempt to draw meaning from loose associations stored in his memory.

Wax. A doll that looked like Heather. A boy angry at that doll. A classic case of an inner child taking out his frustration on the person who'd wounded him most.

"Maybe," he said. "But that doesn't mean those associations are wrong."

"No, but you're grasping at straws, Daniel. If there's a connection between the wax and the coal, they don't need you to find it."

"And if I'm right?"

She sighed and slipped into a chair. "If you're right, then we'll have to reconsider the whole NDE business, won't we?"

"Don't go getting supernatural on me. You're right, I just made some natural associations, a square room with a door. And behind that door is the elusive face. My biggest mistake was not opening that door."

Lori looked away. "Have you ever considered the possibility that you're discounting the existence of the supernatural too quickly?" Eyes back on him. "I mean, if there was ever a person who lived a week immersed in the supernatural, it's you."

"That's exactly what the jury needs to hear. Next you'll suggest that Eve is being driven to kill innocent women by the demons that have possessed him."

"I'm not saying that, but you have to at least accept the strong possibility that Eve thinks it does."

"I've accepted that!" he snapped, leaning forward. "Read the file! That's *exactly* what he thinks. But that has nothing to do with me or these ND effects."

"Don't jump down my throat. I don't exactly believe in God or the devil. This isn't familiar territory."

"It's as familiar as hell," he said. "That's the whole point."

"Then maybe it's too familiar. Take a step back." She sighed. "Look, I'm sorry. You have no business subjecting yourself to this kind of stress so soon." She forced an encouraging smile and reached for his hand. "I need you to sleep for a few hours; promise me that much."

He nodded, forcing back emotions he didn't know he could succumb to so easily. He'd become a blubbering fool, he thought. Losing a wife and dying in the same day could evidently do that to a man.

"You're right, Lori. She's not my wife. But I feel sick for failing her when she was."

Her hand was still on his. "She's lucky to have someone as loyal as you. It's not over yet."

His voice fell to a hoarse whisper. "We both know he'll kill her." Tears misted his eyes and he turned away.

"Don't say that." She squeezed his hand.

"The sad truth is, it wouldn't have ever worked between us. We loved each other, and heaven knows I'd do anything for her. But it's too late for us."

"Stop talking like this is all in the past," Lori said,

releasing his hand. "She needs you now. And you're no good in this condition. You need sleep."

The door opened and Brit filled the gap, face drawn. "We have a hit. Our ride's standing by."

Daniel stood. "Where?"

"Wyoming. Medicine Bow Honey Farm, largest in the country until the late fifties, when USGS discovered a rich coal seam. The short wall mine was abandoned in 1978 and declared a hazardous property by the state of Wyoming. It's one of two locations in the country that match your parameters. The other is in Pennsylvania."

"Too far." Daniel was walking already. "Striations match?"

"We won't know without a comparison sample, but the operations manager of Consolidation Coal Company is on his way to check their records of the mine as we speak. He was asleep with his wife in Maryland."

"How long's the flight?"

"Two hours."

Daniel checked his watch. Ten till eight. Wherever Eve had Heather, he would wait for the darkest hour. It was a hopeful thought.

"Have Wyoming Highway Patrol lock down the access roads and hold tight. We take our own team. God help us."

Reprinted from Crime Today *magazine, 2008*

MAN OF SORROW:
JOURNEY INTO DARKNESS

by Anne Rudolph

Crime Today *magazine is pleased to present the sixth installment of Anne Rudolph's narrative account of the killer now known as Alex Price, presented in nine monthly installments.*

1991–1992

BY THE spring of 1991, Alex Price's nightmares had become so disturbing and occurred so regularly that he could rarely sleep more than an hour without waking with the sweats, screaming into the gray duct tape that he placed over his mouth before lying down on the couch.

It was difficult for Jessica to speak about this dark time of her brother's life without breaking down. She is adamant to this day about her conviction that her own mistakes somehow contributed to Alex's evils.

She shouldn't have left him alone during the day.

She should have gone to Father Seymour much sooner than she did.

At the time, however, they both agreed that he had to continue work-ing at the restaurant if for no other reason than to get him out of the house. Between the nightmares, the unrelenting depression, and his lack of purpose, Alex felt trapped. He repeatedly told her that he was afraid he might be losing his mind.

For reasons neither of them fully understood, the nightmares were much worse at night than during the day. Alex seemed to have a psycho-somatic link to darkness dating back to his abuse as a child. Whether it was day or night, his eyes were shut when he slept, he reasoned, so his mind should not know the differ-ence. But it did.

More and more he chose to stay awake all night and sleep during the day. Without morning classes, he could fall asleep at dawn and get up at noon, in time to make it to work by one. Gradually his daily routine changed, and by the summer he rarely if ever slept at night. After Jessica retired, he would slip into his room where he would spend the next five or six hours without disturbing her.

When asked why she didn't press Alex to see what he was doing in his room every night, Jessica said she did on several occasions. "He claimed that he was working on a book. He was going to call it *Man of Sorrow.* He wanted to keep it a surprise."

She repeated her reasoning that Alex deserved his privacy after such a horrible childhood. Apart from his strong bond with Jessica, time in his room seemed to be the only thing that settled his spirit. This and the fact that Jessica was actually asleep for most of the hours Alex spent in his room was enough to ward off any alarm.

Another benefit resulted from Alex's decision to sleep only during the day: Jessica could now move out of the living room. It was actually Alex's idea. He'd always needed her nearby to fall asleep at night. She was like a child's security blanket to him. But he'd grown accustomed to falling asleep on his own when the sun was up.

Now in her own room and feeling independent, Jessica took other strong strides on her journey to full adulthood. In July 1991, when she was nearly twenty-six, she became romantically interested in a man two years younger than her named Bruce Halstron, the brother of her best friend, Jenny Gardner, a hostess at the Denny's restaurant where she still worked as a waitress.

There could hardly have been a better match for Jessica, and she knew it. For reasons that none of her coworkers could know, she'd turned down numerous men who'd shown interest in her. But in Bruce she recognized a kind, gentle man who was more taken by her own soft-spoken nature than by her face.

Although Jessica glided through her daily duties at the restaurant with the face of an angel, only she knew that ugly scars covered her body beneath her uniform. Her self-esteem had improved over the years, but the thought of being seen naked terrified her.

Bruce was the kind of man she thought she might one day trust with her body, and for this reason more than any other, she accepted his invitation to join him for a meal on a Wednesday night.

Alex was now working a five-hour

shift, having added janitorial duties to the dishwashing, and his day ended at six. Jessica left a note on the table that evening, explaining that her shift had been changed and she wouldn't be home till eleven. Her date was set for seven. She left the apartment at five forty-five, nervous as a mouse, sure that if Alex saw her all jittery, he'd know something was up. Not that her social life was any of his business, but she didn't want to explain herself.

Her night with Bruce at the Casablanca Steak House could not have gone more smoothly if she'd dreamed it all. Bruce treated her like a queen, opening the door for her and ordering the rib eye steak she'd chosen from the menu. She was discovering romantic love for the first time, and desires she never knew she had flooded to the surface of her mind.

She was so taken by the blond Swede, his eyes sparkling in the candlelight, that she decided she had to know sooner rather than later if he would have a problem with her scars. She wouldn't risk becoming attached to him if he would only reject her later. So she told him she'd

Handwritten pages recovered from Alex Price's files

been in a car accident that had left her badly scarred and watched for his reaction.

Without a beat of hesitation, Bruce told her that was good, because his right leg had been badly burned in a gasoline fire at the auto shop where he worked. There was much more to life than physical attraction, he said. Love was about the heart.

Jessica knew then that she'd found a rare man indeed. One who was as wounded as she, at least physically. One who trusted her with a secret similar to her own. She wanted to see his leg immediately, then chided herself. New at these matters of love and courtship, she would take the relationship slowly, but she already knew where it would go.

She floated home at ten thirty, trying to convince herself that it was way too soon to think she was in love. She failed miserably.

When Jessica got home, she found Alex seated on the couch with his head in his hands, crying. He knew? She felt a surge of anger that he would stick his nose in her relationship, but when she asked him what was wrong he offered an unexpected explanation.

He'd been fired.

Alex told all. He'd overslept and

shown up for work late eight or nine times in the last two months, ever since he'd started staying up during the night. He'd begged, but the manager had refused, suggesting that he was a freak.

Jessica had encouraged him to get a better job many times—he certainly had the mind for a higher pay scale. Each time, Alex refused, citing his fear of people and new environments. His personal space was critical to him, and the slightest change bothered him—a pillow out of place or a dirty glass in the living room, none of it escaped his attention. The prospect of finding a new job in a new place working with new people was more than he could handle.

Once again, Jessica held her brother as he wept. "It wasn't just losing a job," she said. "Everything that made him normal was being stripped from him. And he was terrified."

She loved the broken boy in her arms with a compassion that would defy most human beings' understanding. But most human beings had not suffered the abuse she and Alex had.

Most human beings did not have a brother who had repeatedly stepped in to spare them from even more abuse.

Most human beings did not have a brother who had helped them escape captivity, learn to face the world, and grab hold of a new life.

Alex had his problems, but somehow they would get through this and find a way to fully recover.

For the next several days, Alex settled into a frightful self-loathing that triggered Jessica's guilt and made it difficult for her to pursue her budding relationship with Bruce. How could she go around with a light step and a sailing heart when Alex was at home, barely able to get up off the couch?

She mentioned Alex's depression to Bruce, and her new boyfriend suggested a therapist. Amazingly, Alex agreed to see the man.

No records of Alex Trane's twenty-seven appointments with Dr. Chuck Alexander survived the fire that swept through his office four years later. Dr. Alexander himself died in a boating accident while on vacation in Florida last year. The wealth of information that might have been gleaned from this source is lost to the field of behavioral science. Only Jessica's very limited memory of what Alex told her during a few conversations remains.

"For the most part he refused to talk about his sessions with the therapist," she said. "But as long as it was working—and I really thought he might have killed himself without them—I was okay."

Two things stand out in her memory besides the belief that the sessions were helping Alex. The first was that Alex came home from one of his first appointments mumbling about maybe joining the FBI and becoming a behavioral psychologist. He could run circles around them all.

The second, which came several months later, just before his breakdown, was that he'd been wrong about there not being a god. There was a god, and his name was Psychology.

It soon became clear to Alex that his therapy sessions weren't the solution to his deepening depression. If anything, they only convinced him that there was no hope. He'd tried religion, going so far as to embrace priesthood. He'd thrown himself into academia and excelled as a student. He'd exposed himself, at least in part, to a therapist. If none of these could give him release, what could?

Beginning in the fall of 1991, Jessica saw a subtle but unnerving change in her brother. For the first time since they'd escaped their captivity eleven years earlier, he started to withdraw from her.

Even through his depression he'd

always shared his struggles with Jessica. He depended on her for comfort. Since childhood they relied on their strong bond of friendship to deal with the hurdles they faced. And above all, they always protected each other, with Alex taking the lead. Perhaps his withdrawal from Jessica was an attempt on his part to protect her from the greatest obstacle they would yet face.

Himself.

Apart from his biweekly therapy sessions and an occasional trip out to the library or for food, Alex remained mostly cooped up in the apartment, sinking deeper and deeper into himself. His skin paled and he lost weight.

Jessica, meanwhile, was finding greater and greater freedom in the company of her boyfriend, Bruce Halstron, whom Alex still knew nothing about.

The siblings' lives were drifting apart, and Jessica didn't know what she could do to stop it. "I thought it was a good thing. Not his depression, but the fact that we didn't have to talk about it. My happiness only made him frustrated. The less we saw each other, the better for both of us."

One day in early November, Alex came out of his room as Jessica was preparing for work. He walked into her bedroom, something he never did, and stared at her as she pinned her hair up. After a moment she asked him what was wrong.

"I think I know how to fix this," he said.

Mentally dismissing the claim as yet one more in a long string of failed attempts to find light in his dark world, she just nodded and told him that was good, because she didn't know how much more of it she could stand.

He stared at her a long time, then slowly turned around and headed back toward his room. She heard the door close and the dead bolt he'd installed snap shut. Feeling guilty that she'd sent him away so flippantly, Jessica considered knocking on the door to apologize, but out of respect for their privacy rules, she decided against it.

She left the apartment and walked to Denny's, putting the matter out of her mind.

When Jessica returned that night after a quick dinner with Bruce, she found a very different Alex waiting up for her. The one who had haunted their apartment like a walking dead man over the past few months was nowhere to be found. Alex was sitting at the kitchen table, eating calmly and reading a book on the FBI. Looking up, he asked her how work was. "Fine," she told him. He smiled gently and replied without effort, "That's good. That's good." Then he bit into the sandwich he was eating, flipped the page, and continued reading.

Jessica asked him if he was okay, and he responded with assurance. "Yes, Jessica. I'm fine. And you know I'll never let them hurt you."

Encouraged by his confidence, Jessica boldly put her hand on his shoulder and told him that she appreciated his concern, but she really wasn't sure she wanted him to protect her from anyone. She even considered telling Alex about Bruce, but she couldn't. Not yet.

That night they talked about sensible things for the first time in weeks. "He was tired, and he looked like he'd crawled out of a casket, but he was acting like a perfect gentleman, soft-spoken and confident. When I asked him why he was in such a good mood, he just shrugged and said it was about time."

He told her that his book was coming along nicely. With any luck he could get *Man of Sorrow* published and make up for her shouldering all the bills these last few months.

But the most surprising change in

Alex came at midnight, when he said he was going to try to sleep. Jessica watched him tape his mouth, wished him a good night's sleep, and retired to her bedroom.

She found him sleeping on the couch the next morning.

That night Alex went a step further. He not only slept the night through, but he did it in his bedroom.

Jessica's hopes soared over the next week. The nightmares were still visiting her brother each night, but not with enough intensity to wake him, he said. He still spent most of his time in his room, writing and brooding, but he emerged each evening and talked to her, almost like a father figure, calmly, with purpose and understanding.

Alex was a new person, and Jessica told Bruce the good news at the end of that first week. Her brother's depression was gone. She hadn't told Bruce about the Browns or any details about Alex's dysfunctional life, but he knew that her brother's depression weighed heavily on her, and Bruce shared her excitement.

She headed home early that day, determined to finally tell Alex all about her relationship with Bruce. They were thinking of getting married—it was high time her brother knew the truth.

Nothing could have prepared Jessica for the sight that greeted her when she opened the door to apartment 161 at the Holly Street Apartments on November 23, 1991.

TWENTY-TWO

2008

HEATHER SAT ON THE chair, trembling as much from the cold as from fear. The smell of earth leaked through the bag he'd placed over her head. Sweat dripped past her temple, mingled with mucus from her nostrils, and wet the corners of her mouth, a milky, salty mix that oddly enough helped her feel alive.

Her hands were bound behind her, and she could feel the chair's cool metal along her arms. Her feet were tied together, then somehow looped to the chair legs, she thought. Her mouth, taped.

Eve hadn't spoken to her. She'd felt his breath and smelled his musky skin, neither of which was offensive. But she hadn't seen him and she hadn't heard his voice. She wasn't even sure he was in the room with her.

It had all happened so quickly, her taking. So uneventful, really. No real struggle, no violence, no threatening words.

She'd come home after having drinks with Raquel, checked the answering machine for a message from Daniel, then busied herself with a few odd tasks around the house before taking a glass of wine to the basement as she often did.

To the Eve room.

She'd stepped in, flipped the switch on, and was standing under the blinking lights when Eve reached around from behind her and smothered her nose and mouth with the sock. A strong medicinal odor flooded her nasal cavity, and she dropped the wineglass.

She had grabbed at his hand, but before true fear could grip her mind, she passed out.

The true fear came sometime later, when she woke up bound and gagged with tape in the back of his vehicle. She knew she'd been taken by Eve, and for the first few hours she'd lain still, telling herself to stay calm. She could beat him. She *would* beat him. Nothing she could do or say now would help, but at some point an opportunity would present itself—it always did. Always. And when it did, she would be ready.

But the thin veneer of courage wore ever thinner as the hours stretched on in silence. What might be an *always* with any other killer was more than likely a *never* with Eve. The man driving the van had already calculated the eventuality of every potential opportunity that might come her way and made the necessary arrangements to remove them completely.

She knew this because she knew Eve.

They'd driven for a long time, maybe a day. She couldn't tell because he'd placed a bag over her head. She'd been forced to urinate on the floor, through her jeans.

He'd fed her from behind once, a bottle of water and a Heath bar.

She'd asked one question with the tape off her mouth. "Who are you?" But she knew he wouldn't answer, and so she resisted the urge to ask him more. The time would come.

Or it wouldn't.

It was dark again when he taped her mouth and carried her from the van into the cave in which she now sat, trembling with renewed fear.

Something shifted to her right, and she stilled her breathing. A pebble rolled. He was there, to her right.

The bag came off her head. Heather stared into blackness. Not shadows or darkness, but the kind of pitch-blackness found in caskets, six feet under.

Fingers dug at the tape stuck to her lips. Slowly pulled it off. She whimpered once but swallowed a cry of pain from the ripping adhesive.

A lighter sparked to life a foot ahead and to the right of her face. She started. The orange flame licked at the dark, and for a brief moment she saw dirt walls, old beams embedded.

But her attention shifted immediately to the hand that held a red Bic lighter. Clean nails. Little or no hair on his arm. He stood behind her, reaching forward so she couldn't see his face.

"Do you like the light, Heather?"

It was the first time Eve had spoken, and his voice surprised her. She didn't know what she'd expected—perhaps something gravelly, not the smooth, low voice that spoke in her right ear.

His breath smelled like toothpaste.

Then the flame went out, plunging her back into the blackness.

"Eve?" Her voice trembled. She tried to stop shaking.

"No. Would you like to meet her?"

"What's your name?"

No answer.

"Are you going to kill me?"

"No. I don't kill people."

"Then why am I here?"

He moved to her left, several feet off now. "Because he broke his promise to leave me alone. He made a promise to Eve. That's why she let him live again. But he lied."

This was all pointless, she knew. He was going to kill her. The disease was going to kill her. "Are you going to hurt me?"

"I saw the room in your basement," Eve said, speaking slowly. "You don't know very much, do you? I was going to be a priest, did you know that?" A deep breath. "But I didn't believe. Heather, do you believe?"

"Believe what?"

"That the serpent is real. That it eats away at the mind."

It was his first reference to the meningitis, the disease that broke past the protective layer of meninges and poisoned the brain. Heather shivered. This was it. He was leading up to something.

"Please...please don't hurt me."

For ten or fifteen seconds nothing happened. Eve breathed evenly behind her. She shivered in the chair. Then his fingers touched her cheek. A tender caress.

"Have you ever heard of Daisy, Heather? Daisy Ringwald, born in 1934 in Milwaukee."

"No."

"She was born blind. Without an optic nerve. Died blind."

A tear slipped down Heather's cheek.

"But she saw. Blind as a bat until she died on the operating table on January 23, 2002. When they brought her back she told them what she'd seen. The heart surgeon's emerald class ring on the table next to instruments that she described with perfect detail. She saw it all, Heather. What the nurses were wearing, their jewelry, the layout of the bed and the lights. Even the cover of a copy of *Huckleberry Finn* that had gone unnoticed for five years on the top of a cabinet in the corner."

He breathed deep and his thumb brushed her cheekbone.

"How did she see it, Heather? If she was blind."

She was shaking too badly to respond.

"Are you blind, Heather?"

She almost said no, but in the context of his story, she changed her mind. "Yes."

"Conventional wisdom would say that what I'm planning to do with you is a mistake. They will accuse me of breaking my own rules. Of making the stupid move that gets the criminal caught. I'm telling you this in case you're later tempted to wonder if I've made a mistake. Don't be."

"I believe you," she whimpered.

"Don't be afraid. I'm not going to hurt you," he said. "I'm going to help you see. All of you."

But Heather was afraid. Very afraid.

* * *

THE FLIGHT INTO LARAMIE, Wyoming, aboard the Citation, took two hours and seven minutes from wheels up to wheels down, and with a little help from Lori, Daniel managed to sleep an hour and a half of it.

The raid was a long shot, Brit had told Montova, but they all knew long shots broke cases. The Wyoming HP had set up roadblocks on every road in and out of the abandoned Consolidation Coal Company operation east of Laramie. Daniel and Brit would go in with Lori and a local for backup this time. State police would remain back at a five-mile perimeter.

Before the mine, the two-hundred-acre plot had housed the Medicine Bow Honey Farm, the largest known bee farm on record, owned and operated by a family of settlers until a surveyor had found a seam of coal on the land in 1959. Strapped with debt, the family sold the mining rights to a subsidiary of the Consolidation Coal Company, which began mining operations in 1961.

They'd moved the bees in swarms and flattened more than a hundred thousand hives—something to do with the competition and low quality of honey.

Unlike most mines that tunneled deep or dug large open pits, short wall tunnels rarely exceeded 150 feet, relying instead on thick veins that could be cut from the side of the mine. According to the operations manager they'd awakened in Maryland, the Medicine Bow mine consisted of one colliery with four entry points, three of which had collapsed in 1977, after which the mine had been shut down. The striations of the coal appeared to match the FBI sample, at least in type.

Daniel let Brit drive the rental Suburban, a dark-green

late model that suited the task. Mark Tremble from the Laramie PD rode shotgun, Lori and Daniel behind.

He felt Lori's hand on his knee. "You good?" she whispered.

Five hours since he'd been brought back and still no recurrence of the fear, unlike the trial with DMT. Whatever his brain had done during those fifty-six seconds seemed to have worked wonders. So far. He nodded.

She squeezed his knee, then removed her hand.

For the second time in a week they drove quietly through the night, bearing down on Eve's suspected location. Beyond that similarity, the raid was hardly familiar.

This time Daniel had died to be here.

This time Heather would die.

They came to a gate with a rusted chain and padlock. "Before we busted them, this used to be a hangout for potheads," Tremble said. "The lock doesn't actually work."

He jumped out, peered ahead, then unlatched the gate and swung it open. A squeal disturbed the quiet.

"What's he doing?" Daniel snapped. "He'll hear that. Go, go!"

Brit moved the truck forward, slowed for Tremble to climb in, then pushed ahead.

"How far?" Brit asked.

"Open shaft is about a hundred yards."

"When we hit the ground, you stay put." Brit killed the lights. "No sound, no radio, no cell phone. If this guy's here, he's watching and listening."

Tremble sat still.

A large conveyor belt reached toward the hill on their

left like a black claw draped with chains and belts. The mine it pointed to looked like a black throat on the side of the hill.

"You ready?" Brit asked, stopping the vehicle.

Daniel already had his gun out. Engaged. He eased the door open and whispered to Lori. "Stay to the rear ten yards. Brit's got my back."

Then he was running on the balls of his feet, straight for that throat.

According to Tremble, the entrance had been boarded up, but a gaping hole on the left side would let them in. Their shoes scattered coal, and the moonlight caught the golden tan surface of what remained of the hives. The beeswax had survived thirty years only because this side of the hill had been mined last, and trucks had approached the shaft from the far side, leaving the wax mostly undisturbed.

A wax doll. Heather. If the boy wasn't Eve, who was he?

Daniel slid up next to the mine entrance and waited for Brit to reach him with the floodlight. The moon grayed his face.

"Ready?"

Daniel nodded.

And then they were in, two abreast, facing darkness. Brit flipped the halogen lamp on. Light glared to life, flooding a long, black tunnel a hundred feet in. Large pillars ran along the left wall. Tracks down the middle.

No sign of Heather.

Daniel ran forward, stepping over rocks and lumps of coal.

No sign...

An ache spread through his chest where his heart raced. They were way beyond any pretense of stealth.

"Heather!" His voice bounced off the walls. Brit's light revealed a slight turn to the left ahead, and Daniel sprinted for that bend, desperate for the image his mind toiled to see. A chair. A woman in that chair.

Daniel spun around the turn, gun extended, and pulled up hard, panting. Then Brit caught up, and his light revealed the sight as though it were day.

An old coal car lay toppled at the end of the track. And beside the car, a steel chair.

An empty steel chair.

Daniel's hands trembled badly. Brit walked past him and stepped up to the chair. He shone the light on a brown Heath bar wrapper that sat on the rusted seat.

Daniel felt his strength go. He settled to one knee and lowered his gun.

"They were here," Brit said.

Lori rounded the bend and stopped behind Daniel, breathing hard.

Daniel struggled to make sense of the scene. Brit was right, Eve had been here. But he'd anticipated them. How? He took a deep breath and forced his mind to calm.

"No." Daniel pushed himself to his feet, turned around, and walked past Lori, ignoring her sympathetic eyes. *No, you're wrong, Brit. You're dead wrong.*

"This is only one of four entry tunnels," Brit said. "He was here. He could still be in one of the other tunnels." Then, keying his walkie, he said, "Bring them up. I want every tunnel shut off now. Let's go!"

"You're wasting your time, Brit."

"I'm not willing to take that chance."

"He's way ahead of us!" Daniel yelled, spinning back. "He knew we'd find the wax in his tires and track this place down." He thrust his finger out at the chair. "That's what the Heath wrapper says."

"So..." Lori looked between Brit and Daniel. "Where does that leave us?"

Daniel turned and strode toward the night sky. "Dead," he said. "She's dead."

TWENTY-THREE

AN EXHAUSTIVE SEARCH OF the tunnel turned up nothing more than the metal chair and the Heath bar wrapper. Daniel paced the grounds, nudging lumps of coal, running his hands through his hair, doing his best to avoid Brit and Lori.

Grappling with a senseless thought that refused to dislodge itself from his mind.

An evidence response team was already on its way from Cheyenne. Footprints would show that one, not two people had entered the mine shaft recently. Not Eve and Heather. Just Eve.

Fingerprints on the metal chair and wrapper would match those they had for Eve. Tread marks near the entrance would show that the Dodge Caravan driven by Eve had been here several times at least. It was one of numerous locations he'd chosen ahead of time.

The Cessna Citation was fueled, ready to take them back to LA as soon as Brit was satisfied with the ground operation. An hour of pacing and Daniel began to feel the familiar dizziness that had preceded some of his panic attacks.

He found Lori speaking in hushed tones with Brit just inside the mine's entrance. He stopped twenty feet shy and let them talk. Whatever steps they might be considering, he was now beyond caring.

There was only one way to find Heather.

Lori broke the conversation off and walked up to him. "Come on, let's get you back to town."

"When are we heading back to LA?"

"In the morning," she said.

Daniel stopped her. "The morning? No, we have to get back now!"

"Brit wants some daylight. There's nothing we can do in LA that we can't do here." She headed toward the Suburban. "We have rooms at the Marriott in Laramie. Let's go."

The senselessness gnawing at his mind turned to dread. "No, no—we have to get back tonight." He needed to make the point with Brit, but Lori grabbed his arm as he turned.

"What you need is rest, if I have to force you into bed and hold you down myself!"

"You know as well as I do that he usually kills them within the first three days. That gives us another thirty-six hours. We can still stop him. We can't just sit around for twelve hours."

"This is a major departure from his pattern. We have no indication he'll proceed before the next new moon."

"I'm not willing to take that chance! He's not going to hold her for a whole month before…" His voice faltered.

Brit looked at them from the tunnel entrance.

She took Daniel's arm and guided him to the vehicle. "Get in."

He stepped into the passenger's seat. Still no wave of fear. The key was there, in the protective layers of his mind. In the meninges.

Lori started the car, whipped it through a U-turn, and roared down the dirt road. They remained quiet for the first five minutes, Daniel because he didn't know what to say, what he wanted to say. Lori because…

He studied her set jaw. Lori because she already knew what he wanted to say.

Sitting in the bucket seat beside her, Daniel was overcome by the hopelessness that had brought them to this point. That black space where the only alternative is no alternative at all. A mother forced to choose between the deaths of two children. A cancer victim given one last chance to ride his horse, knowing being jostled in the saddle will break all of his ribs.

A dead man walking who chooses the injection over the electric chair.

Pressure swelled behind his eyes, threatening tears. He was too tired to resist, so he let them slip down his cheeks in the dark. Lori glanced at him once, but he refused to return the look.

"I'm sorry," she finally said, breaking the quiet.

"You know there's no other way."

Lori drove through a red light and headed up the main drag.

"The fear hasn't come back," he continued.

"I know."

"I'm alive."

"And I'd like to keep you that way."

"She's going to die."

"Even if we did think it would do any good, it's way too early to try again. Your body needs time to recover."

"Eve's behind the door, Lori. All I need to do is open that door."

"And if you don't come back, Heather will die anyway. Have you thought about that?"

"I've beat the thought to death," Daniel said. He twisted and gripped her arm. "Listen to me. The *only* advantage we have over Eve is my memory. I saw him before he killed me. We know how to recover that memory now. We have to do this. I'm begging you."

"Even if you do walk through that door and recover that memory, what good will an image of Eve do in the short term?"

The point hadn't been lost on Daniel. Being able to identify Eve, reproduce the killer's face for an airing on television, putting it through the FBI's system—they could and probably would lead to Eve's capture at some point. But not in time to save Heather.

He released her arm and shifted in his seat. "I don't know. But I have to do this now, while I know she has time. Not tomorrow, not in a week. Tonight."

Lori's knuckles were white on the steering wheel. But she didn't immediately throw out another argument. This was her way of processing. Denial and rejection, knowing all along that she would agree and accept. She was as eager to stop Eve as he was.

"Where can we do it?" he asked.

"Stop it! You're acting like this is a line of coke we're talking about!"

"How I deal with my death is my issue, not yours!" They were yelling now.

"What we did last night wasn't only completely unethical; it was insane!"

"*He's* insane!"

"So to stop him, we have to become like him?" she demanded.

These were useless accusations borne out of frustration, he knew.

She swallowed hard, shook her head, then spoke through her teeth. "I can't believe I'm even listening to you."

"Because you know I'm right. And you know it's my choice, not yours."

"You haven't read up on assisted suicide, obviously."

"Fortunately we both work for the FBI. That gives us certain rights."

"Like killing ourselves?"

He let the comment go. They passed a Super 8 Motel and a 7-Eleven on the right. They were in Laramie, driving through traffic lights, but he could hardly remember any of it.

"Will the hospital here have what you need?"

She shook her head again. "This is crazy."

"Will it?"

Lori slammed the brakes, searched the rearview mirror, then pulled the Suburban into a U-turn, cutting across the street.

"Where are you going?"

"The hospital," she said. "It's behind us."

TWENTY-FOUR

"**T**HERE ARE TWO WAYS to do this," Lori said, following a blue sign indicating that the Ivinson Memorial Hospital was located off a side street to the right. "With the hospital's full cooperation, which will mean convincing—"

"Alone," he interrupted. "No one knows."

"That's not going to be easy."

"We don't have a choice. Maybe it would be better to get what we need from the hospital and do it in a motel room."

"It's more equipment than you realize." She took another corner and headed for a lighted sign that read *Emergency*.

"Better for you to go in dead."

"Dead? What do you mean? Kill me out here?"

She frowned. "Pretty much. Yes. I have the benzodiazepine in my bag. For that matter, I have the epinephrine and atropine. It's the rest I need."

"You brought them?"

"Just the drugs. Epinephrine and atropine are standard. To be honest, I don't know why I brought the muscle relaxant. Point is, I have it." She pulled the vehicle to the curb and put it in park.

"I could call ahead, clear a room with a defibrillator standing by, inject you with the benzodiazepine here."

"Isn't that dangerous?"

"Dangerous? It'll kill you." She looked at the emergency doors ahead. "The drug takes at least thirty seconds to stop the heart. If the ward was ready, thinking you were already dead, and we got you in within a few seconds of injecting you…" She faced him. "No more dangerous than killing you on the bed."

"So you'd just inject me while I'm standing outside the door?"

"Close enough. Directly into the same vein we used earlier." Lori closed her eyes. "This is nuts."

"If I went in dead, or close enough, the emergency room would only be concerned with my resuscitation," Daniel said. "Right? What would you say to the agency?"

"An acute cardiac failure resulting from the stress of losing Heather. You died a week ago—I think I can make the case."

Montova would freak, but Daniel was beyond caring at the moment. "Okay. Tell me what you need."

"Get in the back."

She retrieved a small black handbag from the back, filled a syringe with the same powerful muscle relaxant she'd killed him with last night, and slid into the backseat.

The light from the streetlight under which they were parked paled her complexion. She quickly cleaned his neck with a disinfectant patch from one of those sealed packets, cleared the syringe.

"You're sure about this?" she said.

"Make the call. We're running out of time."

Lori snatched up her phone, punched in 9-1-1, and stared into his eyes. Her tone was urgent.

"This is Dr. Lori Ames with the FBI. I have an agent who's suffered a heart attack, and I'm transporting him to Ivinson Hospital. Can you patch me through?"

Her eyes didn't waver from his. Her own apparent concern began to unnerve him.

She reached the emergency ward, introduced herself in a terse voice, and demanded to speak to the physician in charge immediately. Not until she was connected to the party she needed did she shift her eyes from his.

"I'm about a couple minutes out. From what I can tell, the patient is in cardiac fibrillation. I need a gurney standing by outside, everything else in the closest available room. Manual defib, epinephrine, atropine—all of it."

She listened for a brief moment, then snapped her phone shut.

"Okay, here's how we do this. You're going to lie down on the seat. I'm going to insert the needle and have you hold the syringe while I drive around the block. Don't push the plunger until I say. Empty the syringe, pull the needle free, and apply pressure with this gauze. Is that clear?"

"Yes."

She took a deep breath. "Lie down."

Daniel lay flat, legs dangling off one side.

Lori swiped his neck once more, turned on the overhead light. "This will sting."

It hurt like hell.

She took his hand and put it on the syringe. "Got it? Don't touch the plunger until I see that gurney. Clear? I don't want that drug in your system until I know they're ready."

"I'm counting on it, trust me."

She climbed through the seats, pulled the Suburban into gear, and drove.

"You okay?"

The needle in his neck shifted with the jostling vehicle, forcing him to grip it with both hands. But the thought of a needle inserted into his jugular was more disturbing.

"Fine. How much longer?"

She didn't respond.

His neck stung and he wondered if he'd pricked the inside wall of his vein. Did veins have nerves? He was about to ask her, when the car surged forward.

"Okay, I can see them with the gurney, two paramedics right by the street. This should be good, it should be good. Okay...okay, do it. And get that syringe out quickly."

Daniel held the syringe with his left hand and pushed the plunger to the hilt with his right. He yanked the needle out, pressed his neck with the gauze pad. Dropped the syringe.

"Daniel?"

"Done." The pain kicked in faster than he remembered. Like a mule. He instinctively grabbed his chest, closed his eyes.

As before, the certainty that he'd made a terrible mistake settled on him as his heart began to fight the deadening drug.

"Oh, God..."

Ben Kingsley had said those words as Gandhi being assassinated. *Oh, God.* The next scene was his funeral procession. A white casket. But in that casket, a black room.

Daniel felt his consciousness waning. Lori was yelling orders, he could hear that much. Then his body was sliding down the seat. Handled roughly onto something flatter. A gurney.

He was dead. Even if his heart hadn't stopped beating yet, he was dead.

But his heart had stopped beating. And his lungs had stopped breathing. The oxygen in his mind was running out fast. Soon it would go into those extreme throes of survival that generated the electrochemical responses he desperately needed to open the door.

A violent flash of light. A flood of images.

And then Daniel's world went dead. Only he wasn't dead, dead. He was in the black room.

He heard a deep, long, sucking sound, a breath that echoed softly around the square room. Daniel scanned the walls. Then turned slowly to each corner, expecting to see the child.

But he found himself in an empty room. No boy, no giggling, no wax doll with bees crawling from empty eye sockets.

"Hello?"

His voice filled the room. Then it, too, was gone, leaving only the sound of his lungs pumping air. And time was running out. Was there any correlation between the length of a near-death experience and the time one was dead?

Then Daniel saw the door, just visible in one shadowed

corner. The boy's voice rang through his memory. *Eve's in there.*

He walked toward the door, took the silver knob in his right hand, then thought twice about opening it. Behind it was—what—the wailing and gnashing of teeth?

He twisted the handle and pulled the door open. Stepped tentatively inside another room with black walls. From all appearances, identical to the first room.

Same walls. Same checkerboard floor. Same absolute stillness.

Same giggling.

Daniel spun to his right and stared into the corner. The boy squatted on his haunches, staring at him with the same ghastly black eyes and taut-skin face, smiling. The single most disturbing image Daniel had set eyes on.

So disturbing that he couldn't speak.

"Hello, Daniel," the boy said, in the innocent voice of a child. "I see you."

Daniel felt suffocated. He began to breathe in quick, shallow pulls.

"I was hoping you would come back."

"Where's Eve?" Daniel managed.

The boy's voice changed from a sweet child's to a rasping growl midway through the second word. "I am Eve," he said. But his smiling face did not change with this voice.

Daniel took a step back. He'd heard the low voice before, once, just before being pulled back into the land of the living the first time he'd left it. Staring into those black eyes, that stretched mouth, his blond hair hanging loosely around thin shoulders—Daniel wanted to scream.

"Do you want me to poke your eyes out?" the boy said, voice now innocent again. "I can, you know."

"No," Daniel said.

"Then why did you break your promise?"

"I didn't. What promise?"

Beat. Now in a low, crackling voice, snarling mouth, leaning into each word: "The first time you met me, when he shot you. You don't remember—too bad—but you promised me you would back off, let me continue killing. I allowed you to come back because of that promise, otherwise you'd be in a pine box, six feet under. I let you live."

A twisted grin split the boy's tight face, revealing black teeth. "Now I'm going to poke her eyes out."

Heather.

Daniel tried to protest, but he couldn't speak. A small voice in his own mind within this mind was asking him if he was speaking to himself as a child. Who was the boy? Eve...but who was Eve?

"What's the matter, you a dumb mute now?" the boy asked. He stood and waddled toward Daniel on bowed legs.

Daniel stumbled back, horrified. He hit the wall, shivering with fear. The boy stopped just beyond arm's reach.

"Is...is this my mind?" Daniel asked.

The boy cocked his head, amused. "Foolish doctor." A foul stench carried his voice. "You can save her. One last chance to keep your pincushion alive, foolish doctor. I'm gonna stick her like a pig from the inside out."

"Please..."

"Southhhhhhh." The boy spread his lips. "Only you."

Daniel couldn't pull his eyes away from the grotesque face staring him down.

In a child's voice again, "If you tell that little sow, I'm going to make Mama scream for a long time."

The boy lifted one hand and motioned Daniel with his index finger. "Come here."

Eve wanted him to lean down? Daniel might throw up. Surely the boy could say what he wanted from this safe distance.

"Come here!" The boy's voice cracked like a whip.

Daniel bent.

The boy placed his clammy cheek against Daniel's right cheek and whispered slowly.

"We're going to be best friends, Daniel."

Something soft and wet touched his ear. The boy's tongue.

Daniel recoiled. His heart was pounding and his chest was heaving. He was having another heart attack. His arms and legs began to jerk through a frightening convulsion that he could not control.

The room blinked off. Light blinded him. Voices: "We have him...That's it, Daniel. Easy, easy."

Only half-aware of Lori and two other emergency staff who stood around the bed.

Fully aware of a child's smooth, tarry voice.

I see you, Daniel.

He bolted up and screamed.

MAN OF SORROW:
JOURNEY INTO DARKNESS

by Anne Rudolph

*Crime Today magazine is pleased to present the seventh install-
ment of Anne Rudolph's narrative account of the killer now known
as Alex Price, presented in nine monthly installments.*

November 23, 1991

JESSICA UNLOCKED the door
to the apartment on Holly Street,
eager to unburden herself from the
secret she'd held for all these months.
If there was ever a time when Alex
was prepared to learn that she'd
fallen in love and planned to move
out, that time had come.

She quietly closed the door behind her and locked it. Turning to the
living room, she dropped her coat
and looked around the apartment. As
always, the room was immaculate.
Every wall hanging was perfectly
squared, every knickknack properly
positioned. A rocking chair now sat
in the corner that her mattress had
filled for so many years.

She was about to call out for
Alex, figuring he was in his room

working on his book, when she saw
the red smear on his door. Her first
thought was ketchup. But Alex hated
ketchup. And he would never be so
sloppy.

A loud crack followed by a sharp
cry reached past his door. She stood
frozen by the front door, trying to
come to grips with what she'd just
heard. The sound came again.

This time a chill shot through her.
She couldn't mistake that sound, not
in a million years, not after hearing
it so many times as a child. It was
the crack of a whip followed by a cry
of pain.

Memories of Alice weighed her
down to the floor. Had she not been
immobilized by terror, she might
have fled the apartment. Her mind

flashed back to dark nights, strapped to a table.

Alice had found them!

Or had Jessica just awakened from a long nightmare to find that she and Alex had never escaped their hell in Oklahoma? Then another possibility crossed her mind.

Alex, not Alice, was whipping someone.

"Alex?" She took several steps and stopped at the end of the couch. The door to Alex's room swung open, revealing a man standing naked in front of her. His hands were bloody. Several long cuts on his chest leaked blood. He wore a mask of red; he'd smeared the stuff on his face.

Alex.

Jessica couldn't speak. Alex stared without expression for a few seconds, then told her what he'd done in three simple words. "I fixed it," he said.

Then tears snaked down his face and his shoulders began to shake. He rushed out and fell to his knees, grabbing her hands before she could pull them back. "I've done it, Jessie. I've done it."

She could see his back now, covered in fresh cuts, and she knew that only a whip embedded with glass or metal could account for such dam-

age. She stared, horrified, and all the while Alex kept sobbing, telling her he'd fixed it.

Jessica came to and jerked her hands from his. He dived for her feet and wrapped his arms around her ankles. Lying prone and naked at her feet, he wept.

"Debates about the existence of Satan and God are the stuff of foolish children who are arguing about whether the world ends at the tree line in their backyard. An afternoon adventure into the woods would settle the matter for them. Take a trip with me, sir. I'll show you the forest. And when you start to scream, I promise to hold your hand."

—Father Robert Seymour
Dance of the Dead

She stood over him, torn between competing emotions. On one hand, her fingers trembled with relief at finding that Alice had not found them and that this was not the nightmare she most feared.

On the other hand, her fingers trembled from the realization that

Alice had found them, and this was a nightmare she feared more. Alex was Alice, and he'd brought the nightmare to life.

Then again, Alex wasn't Alice at all, but her wounded little doll, stripped and whipped to appease the demands of her holy coven. Jessica felt revulsion and pity at once, and she didn't know whether to join Alex on the floor or kick him in the head.

"I'd never felt so angry at him," she recalled. "Frustration, sure, but not the kind of bitterness that I felt standing over him. I felt sorry for him, but I was more angry at him for doing this to himself the way Alice might have."

Something snapped in Jessica's mind as she gave in to the anger and rejected her empathy for the man at her feet. She tried to pull her feet away, but he clung to her with strong arms. So she grabbed a white pillar candle off the end table and smashed it against his head.

Stunned, Alex let go. His sobs quieted and he looked at her, stricken. Slowly he stood, dazed and confused. Jessica finally recovered her voice. She asked him if he'd whipped himself. He just looked at her. When she pressed him, he nodded.

Why? she demanded. Why had he done what only Alice could possibly do to him? Why had he brought Alice back into their lives?

He said nothing and headed back into his room, leaving the door open to the black blanket that hid his private world. When he emerged five minutes later, Jessica had cleaned up the carpet, and he'd wiped most of the blood from his face and body, but some of it was seeping through the blue shirt he'd put on.

For a long time neither spoke. Finally she asked again why he'd done it. Why had he brought Alice's sick sewer of religion into their home after so many years?

He looked away. "She was wrong," he said. "God and Satan do not exist. They are in the mind."

"That's what she used to say," Jessica retorted.

Although Jessica found it much easier to remember her years in California than her years as a child living with Alice, she was able to draw at least an outline of the convoluted beliefs that drove Alice and Cyril to the brutal abuse of such young children.

Alice's unholy concoction, which she called Eve's Holy Coven, appeared to draw on every major world religion, often in direct contradiction to the underlying premise of those religions, namely finding God.

Throwing in some animism and a healthy dose of satanic ritual, what emerged was the gospel according to Alice.

She demanded order and created rules. No exceptions. In the end, people's judgment would be determined not by how well they served some omnipotent being called God, but by how much power they took from this life to become God.

In Alice's mind, she was God.

It's doubtful that Alice really believed in a God outside of herself at all. Or for that matter, a Satan. For her, the notions of God and Satan were merely instruments she used to invoke powers that ultimately resided only in her.

The rules of the universe were crystal clear. One had to stay pure in order to maintain power in this life. And although she believed that she maintained an almost virginal existence in virtually every aspect of her life, there was always a little evil that slipped in and watered down that purity. Only a vessel truly pure could tap the power of evil rather than be contaminated by it. She simply had to maintain purity if she hoped to achieve the power she needed to stay pure. Hopeless circular reasoning. Secular humanism with an ugly mask.

Borrowing sacrifice from Judaism and appeasement of the gods from ancient South American tribes, Alice found a way to deal with the impurity that threatened her. She needed an unspoiled lamb—which really meant an innocent virgin—to pay the required price for any lingering evil that would dilute her power.

For this purpose she needed young children, kept pure through a vigorous system of rules and punishment. She then made them pay for her evil once a month, during the new moon.

In Alice's twisted mind, the only woman to truly accomplish perfection was Eve. Virginal and completely unspoiled in the garden, she was able to trick Lucifer into giving her his power, which she then passed on to the human race. All wars and sickness and every kind of evil came from Eve, who beguiled the snake. There has never been such a powerful woman since. Thus the name of Alice's tiny cult, Eve's Holy Coven.

Satanic ritual was nothing more than a way for Alice to experiment with different ways to trick Lucifer the way Eve had.

Of course, all of this was a metaphor for her own struggle against herself, because in the end good and evil, God and Satan, lived inside her. In every worthy person. Alice was God; Alice was Satan.

Looking at a bloodied Alex in their apartment that night, it appeared to Jessica that he was following in Alice's footsteps, punishing himself to find purity and power—as Alice had punished a much younger version of him to the same end.

The fact that Alex had so quickly zeroed in on this central part of Alice's philosophy alarmed Jessica. God and Satan do not exist. They are in the mind.

She pushed Alex further, accusing him of embracing Alice's religion. Instead of reacting with repulsion, as he had in the past when she suggested any lingering association with Alice, he sat down at the kitchen table, crossed his legs, and asked for her forgiveness. He calmly explained that he was simply proving to himself that he could face the pain of his past with defiance so that he could finish his book, *Man of Sorrow*. Shocking as it might seem, what he had done was only an experiment. A test that he'd passed. It wouldn't happen again.

But Jessica needed more reassurance, so she pushed even further. How could she know that he wasn't regressing? And if he could whip

himself as Alice had whipped him, what was to say he wouldn't one day snap and try to whip her, the way Alice had?

Alex recoiled at the suggestion, and for a few minutes he became the old Alex she knew so well. He stood up, shocked. Through misted eyes he asked her how she could ever think he'd hurt her. He would die for her! He nearly had, on several occasions!

"He was just a wounded kid again. It was so sad. I couldn't just ignore that pain." Jessica recalled the defining moment through tears. "But for the first time, I was afraid of him."

She finally broke down and comforted her brother, and when he refused to go to the emergency ward for treatment, she cleaned and dressed his wounds. They agreed to keep the incident between them, as they did with all things related to Alice. Questions would lead to exposure for her as well as him. Neither was ready to expose their past to the world. News would leak. For all they knew, Alice was still out there, waiting for word.

The next day, life in their apartment continued as though nothing had happened. But Jessica began to wonder more and more what life without Alex would be like.

JANUARY 3, 1992. The day was overcast, but the new year brought a thrilling surprise to Jessica. On New Year's Eve, Bruce Halstron had taken her to the swings at what was known to the locals as Lovers' Park, swung her high in the air, and told her that he wouldn't stop until she agreed to marry him. Delighted, she agreed halfway through the first swing.

Three days passed before Jessica decided she had to break the news to Alex, who was his normal brooding self. Her engagement to Bruce meant that she would be moving out of the apartment when they wed, probably in the summer.

Nursing more than a little trepidation, she asked him to sit down and brace himself because she had a wonderful announcement. He grinned and asked her to go on. She was in love with a man named Bruce Halstron, she told him.

He continued to smile in silence, but his grin now looked forced. When he didn't react negatively, she decided to get the rest out quickly.

And, she told him, she'd accepted Bruce's proposal of marriage.

Alex's face turned completely white. "He'll live here?" he asked.

She sat down next to him, placed a hand on his knee, and explained her heart. "No. We have to move on,

Alex. I'm getting married. That means—"

But he stood and cut her off. "I know what it means!"

As she'd half expected, he launched into a tirade, reminding her of their special circumstances. He didn't have a job and couldn't afford the apartment. He would be lost without her. His whole life revolved around her! Quickly his anger turned to fear and then to panic. How could she even think of abandoning him?

But Jessica knew her brother well and was prepared. Again, she approached the subject with reason, explaining that she wasn't a little girl any longer.

Alex slapped her. Stunned, she sat back and lifted a hand to her stinging face. Seeing her shock, Alex dropped to his knees and begged her to forgive him. He didn't know why he'd slapped her. She was his life, and the fear of losing her had made him crazy. He laid his head on her lap and cried his remorse.

Rather than engage him, she pushed his head off her, walked to the kitchen, and poured herself a drink, knowing he would follow. He did, and now he told her that she had his full support. Of course she had to leave. She deserved her happiness.

She couldn't live the rest of her life in this pigpen with him.

Did he mean that? Yes, yes, he really did. She was right, they weren't children. They had to get on with their lives.

Relieved, Jessica embraced him and thanked him. For a long time they just held each other. Their crazy life in the apartment was finally drawing to a close.

Then Jessica told him about Bruce—how they'd met, where they went on their first date, how wonderful she felt around him. All the while Alex listened with a brave grin, forcing polite questions. Trying to live without her would be difficult, he said.

"There was a hollow look in his eyes," she recalled. "But I was used to it. He was being very brave, and I respected him for that."

Unable to hold back any longer, Jessica told Alex something else. Bruce had kissed her. And what was more, he'd seen her scars. He'd touched them.

The look of horror on her brother's face seared itself into Jessica's mind. But Alex didn't object. "He was just trying to make sense of it all. We never talked about sex. It was off-limits, you know, because of Alice. We just couldn't go there."

The discussion ended shortly after her confession, and she excused herself, walked into her bedroom, and closed the door. That night Jessica fell asleep with a smile on her face. She'd finally taken the last step in finding freedom from Alice. Or, more accurately, she would, when she left Alex for Bruce.

TWENTY-FIVE

DANIEL LAY SHIVERING in Laramie, Wyoming's Ivinson emergency ward, grappling with an acute awareness that he stood on a cliff with a hand on his back, pushing. The cliff being the boy's demand that he head south on his own, despite his physical state. The hand pushing him being his motivation to save Heather.

And at the bottom of that cliff, the concrete reality that a single slip of the foot would mean a bone-crushing demise for them both.

Fifteen minutes had passed. The room was clear except for Lori, who checked his vitals yet again and, satisfied, settled on the bed next to him. She spoke in a near whisper.

"You have no idea how close that was. They wanted to give up."

"How long?" he asked.

"Two minutes, twenty-five seconds. Never again, Daniel. That's it."

He nodded.

Lori glanced at the pulled curtain. "Tell me it was worth it."

He considered telling her everything, then discarded the notion, thinking that until he figured it out himself, telling her might be dangerous. For all of them.

"Did you see the door?" she whispered.

"Yes."

"You opened it?"

"Yes."

"And?"

How did he explain the fact that the near-death experience he'd just had didn't make sense, at least not entirely? He could understand why his mind had seen the boy again. In fact, he'd expected the experience. The demand that he remove himself from the Eve case made sense— he'd subconsciously struggled with guilt for two years for pursuing the case at Heather's expense.

But this business about heading *southhhhhhh*, as the boy put it, was less obvious. There were only a few explanations for why his mind had dredged up the thought: maybe something else had happened in that moment before Eve killed him in Manitou Springs; maybe the killer really had visited the end of his bed while he slept and said something Daniel only now remembered.

Or maybe his mind, confronted by death, was grasping at straws.

Lori could guess as well as he could, but none of it would be more than speculation.

"Please, just tell me what happened," Lori said, brow wrinkled in concern. Her hand took his.

"That's just it. Nothing really happened."

"You said you opened the door!" She gave the slit in the curtains a quick look, then lowered her voice. "You didn't see Eve?"

"No, I did. The boy said he was Eve." He lifted a hand to his head and considered asking for more pain medication, but quickly decided admitting pain now would only slow him when he made his break.

The thought caught him off guard. He was going to follow the boy's demands, wasn't he? If there was even a slim chance that doing so might save Heather, he would do it and he would do it alone, as the boy had ordered.

"No." Lori shook her head. "No, that can't be right."

"Of course it can. The boy is my subconscious lashing out at me for my failings. For failing Heather, for failing to stop Eve."

"Yes, but... Nothing else? You're saying this had nothing to do with seeing him that night?"

He couldn't tell her his intentions. If, by some strange twist of fate that he couldn't yet understand, his heading south did lead to Eve, she couldn't know about it. If Eve had demonstrated one thing over the past year, it was that he could and would do precisely what he said.

"I don't think so, no. Nothing to do with that night."

"Which means what?" she demanded.

"That we're back to square one." He sat up.

"Lie back," Lori snapped, clearly disturbed by more than his sitting. "You need rest."

"I've got enough epinephrine in me to keep a horse

awake for a week. Trust me, rest isn't in the picture, not without drugs."

"Then we'll get some. Nothing's going to happen before dawn at this point."

"No drugs. I'm done." He looked at the clock—nearly two in the morning.

Southhhhhhh. The boy's putrid breath hung in his nostrils. *Southhhhhhh, Daniel. I see you.* Daniel swallowed, trying to ignore the urgency nudging him. *Southhhhhhh now, Daniel. Now!*

"Some ibuprofen for the swelling and this headache, maybe," he said. "Nothing more."

Lori looked at him, then stood. "This whole thing was a mistake. We're lucky you're alive." She shook her head. "I can't believe we did this. Again."

He nodded his agreement.

Southhhhhhh, Daniel. Want me to poke her eyes out?

"I'm alive."

"Thank goodness."

"I could use the ibuprofen."

She walked to the curtain, glanced back with a frown, then stepped out.

Daniel yanked the IV from his arm, slid out of the bed. His legs were shaking, and it took him a moment to steady himself. They'd stripped off his shirt and laid it over the back of a gray chair on the other side of the hospital bed. Holding the bedrails with his right hand, he stumbled around.

He grabbed the shirt and shrugged into each sleeve. As absurd as his attempt to leave was, the notion of heading south—just south, no destination in mind—was even worse.

As he'd hoped, the keys to the Suburban were in Lori's

black handbag, the same one she'd stashed the muscle relaxant in. Which, once again, struck him as interesting. It was as if she'd anticipated the possibility of his wanting to die again.

He took a deep breath and slipped out from behind the curtain adjacent to the bed. His hands were trembling, so he shoved them into his pockets. A patch of gauze was still stuck to the inside of his right arm, and he thought about tearing it off. Instead he withdrew his left hand and covered it as naturally as he could.

The door stood open past the nurses' station—they would undoubtedly wonder what he was doing up so soon. But his trek across the emergency room floor wasn't as much about avoiding curious stares from the nurses and doctors on duty as getting out without Lori knowing.

He kept his head down and walked easily, as if all was in perfect order, never mind the sweat bathing his face.

"Sir?"

He glanced over at one of the nurses who was staring at him. "Tell Dr. Ames I went to the bathroom."

"We have one around the corner." She wagged her finger in the opposite direction, eyes still questioning.

"Okay, hold on one second."

He picked up his pace, exited through a wide, white door, and entered the hall. Both directions clear. Thank goodness for small favors.

Daniel was halfway down the long wheelchair ramp on the right when he heard Lori's voice from the emergency ward. He scooted forward in a fast walk that struck him as safer than a sprint. No need to stress the heart in his condition. Whatever that was.

"Daniel!"

Daniel slipped outside, eased the door shut, and headed through the parking lot toward the vehicle. He had to assume the worst, that she would find the bathroom empty and immediately run to the car.

Cool night air whispered past his neck, through his exposed hair. The Suburban chirped when he pressed the remote. Orange lights flashed twice.

Lori burst through the emergency doors as he slid into the seat.

"Daniel!"

Fumbling with the keys, he managed to shove them into the ignition. Fire the engine. Drop the Suburban into drive.

Lori stood her ground in front of the door, yelling something he couldn't hear. It didn't matter at this point. There was no way she could catch him, and she had no idea where he was headed.

How could she? He himself didn't.

Southhhhhhh...

The Suburban surged out of the parking lot and around two corners before roaring onto the main drag.

Daniel shook his head of an image of the boy whispering with lips stretched over black teeth, breath so rancid he could almost see it.

"South. Why south?"

No sign of chase in his rearview mirror. He was driving a rental; he absently wondered how far he would be taking it. How long was he supposed to drive south before realizing that this recklessness was a fabrication of his mind after all?

He drove under a sign that told him Interstate 80 was a mile ahead. More east than south, but it joined Interstate 25 roughly fifty miles farther.

His cell phone buzzed on the passenger seat where he'd left it. He glanced at the screen, saw it was Lori, flipped the phone open. Then thought better of answering and snapped it shut. If he was going to do this, clearly a decided matter, he had to do it to the letter. Alone, in every respect.

Traffic was thin on I-80 and he made good time, pushing ninety. Then a hundred.

The fact that he *wasn't* actually headed south yet kept his palms wet and slimy on the steering wheel.

The fact that he *was* actually following the advice of the boy with black teeth that he'd met in his mind while dead cooled his neck with chills. A week ago he wouldn't have run from the emergency ward to do the bidding of an alter ego who insisted that he was Eve. Then again, a week ago he hadn't yet been dead. Three times.

Thirty-six minutes and four more ignored cell calls later, Daniel hit the 45 MPH ramp onto Interstate 25 south doing sixty, sixty-five, then promptly accelerated to the century mark again. He was FBI, after all. Speeding tickets couldn't touch him.

Still, his heart pounded. Still, his palms greased the wheel. Still, chills raked his neck like a predator's talons.

The tires hummed. His head ached. He was headed south, right? This was what *southhhhhhh* meant, south on the interstate, not straight south out of Laramie. What if he was wrong about that? What if Heather was stuffed in a root cellar just south of Laramie?

What if there was no south to Eve at all?

His phone rang again, and he only gave it a side glance, fully expecting Lori's or Brit's number. Out of state. Area code 508.

At three o'clock in the morning...

He lifted the phone, eyes fixed on those ten numbers. Would Eve use a traceable phone?

He flipped the receiver open and brought it to his right ear.

"Clark."

The responding voice was confident. Low. "I understand you're headed south. There's still time if you hurry."

"Who is this?"

The caller waited four or five seconds, as if considering the question with some uncertainty. "I'm sorry. I didn't expect such a stupid question from you. Go south. Take 40 East. I'll call again with a different phone. Please hurry. Heather's not so good."

The line went dead.

TWENTY-SIX

DIED?" BRIT SAID. "As in…"

"Acute cardiac fibrillation. His heart stopped. Think of it as an aftershock. But as I said, we were able to resuscitate him at the hospital." Lori gripped the phone in her right hand and paced her hotel room the next morning at nine. They were due to take off in an hour, and Daniel still hadn't returned or made contact.

"Why wasn't I informed?" Brit demanded. "It's been seven hours and I'm just now hearing this?"

"I'm sorry, I should have. It just… We brought him back, and it was late." She walked to the window and looked at the parking lot. "You heard what I said, though…"

"That he was gone. You just told me you brought him back. How can one person die twice in one week?"

Three times, she nearly said. "No, *gone*, as in he took the Suburban and left."

This time Brit came back slow. "After he came to? To where? I thought he was in the hospital."

"He walked out of the emergency ward, got in the Suburban, and took off. To where, I don't have a clue. To clear his head, for all I know."

"So he could be dead on the side of the highway for all you know. And you didn't bother calling me?"

She'd spent the last seven hours thinking the same thing. "I thought he was just blowing off steam. The highway patrol would know. I called, no reports involving a Suburban in a five-hundred-mile radius."

Brit remained silent on the other end.

"So, what do we do?"

"We delay our departure and find him," Brit said.

"And if we can't?"

"If he doesn't turn up by this afternoon, we head back and keep our fingers crossed. He'll either show up or we'll find him. We have the Suburban's license number and can track his cell phone."

"I'm sorry, I really thought he'd be back before now."

Brit ignored her apology and asked the obvious question. "Any reason to think he may have gone after Eve on his own?"

"Heather."

"Of course. But as far as you know, he didn't have any information we don't know about."

Yes, he saw a boy in his mind who called himself Eve, she thought. Although how that might prompt Daniel to take off alone, she had no idea. If he had gone after Eve, he'd learned something from the boy that he refused to share with her.

Her own desire to tell someone what she did know pounded through her chest like a freight train.

"Not that I know," she said. "He'll be back."

"I hope you're right. I really hope you're right."

But she wasn't sure she was right. Not even close.

"I'm worried about his heart giving out, Brit. I don't think it can take much more."

TWENTY-SEVEN

DANIEL GUIDED THE Suburban down the over-grown gravel road slowly, eyes peeled for the cattle guard Eve had said he would find past mile marker 97. The night was black. Trees rose on both sides, like dark sentinels watching the lone vehicle roll past, knowing what only a fool could not.

This was a one-way trip.

Using a series of phone calls to pay phones, Eve had drawn him to Oklahoma, south of Interstate 40, into the woods. Forty-five minutes had passed since Daniel last saw the lights of another vehicle. Eve had meticulously laid out the route, probably the same one he'd used to transport Heather once he'd turned south on I-25.

Eve's ploy made unnerving sense to Daniel. Eve had taken Heather to draw him. He'd calculated Daniel's required refueling stops and the time it would take to reach each one. He'd stopped at each himself and written down the numbers of pay phones, planning that at any given time, Daniel would only know the next leg of his journey south.

None of this was particularly disturbing to Daniel. He would expect nothing less from such a meticulous adversary.

What haunted him was the fact that Eve intended to expose himself. How could he know that Daniel hadn't reported the calls? That a tactical team wasn't following by air at this moment, ready to smother Eve when Daniel reached his destination?

I see you, Daniel.

Yes, there was the inner child, that boy in his mind's eye who claimed to be Eve. But the mind's invention did not a flesh-and-blood adversary make. The boy couldn't inform Eve of Daniel's calls any more than the killer could transport himself into the vehicle for a quick peek.

No. Eve, or whatever his real name was, had something much more dangerous up his sleeve.

He had Daniel himself up his sleeve. How, Daniel couldn't be sure, but Eve knew him nearly as well as he knew himself. Knew that Daniel was desperately loyal to Heather. That only his obsession with Eve drove a wedge between them. That Daniel had been worn down to the loose ends of a frayed rope over the past week, haunted by fear so unnatural that he was willing to kill himself not once, but twice since Eve had killed him.

That after such a long hunt, Daniel wouldn't risk losing either Heather or Eve by reporting his whereabouts to the FBI. That if he did, Eve would know. How, exactly, Daniel didn't know, but Eve had repeatedly proven that he was far too smart to risk his exposure without having covered every possible danger.

What if…Just what if, however unlikely, the supernatural was real and Eve was a supernatural being? A demon, as the religious nuts called them. A presence who was operating with the killer, and had visited Daniel in his death, in his dreams?

Leading Daniel south to his final death.

The temptation to call in his location had badgered his mind for hours. But Eve was right: Daniel couldn't bring himself to risk Heather's life. Or to risk finding a resolution to the abyss that had swallowed him since his first death in Colorado.

When he lost cell coverage half an hour earlier, the temptation had been removed.

I see you, Daniel. One last chance to keep your pincushion alive.

He took the Suburban around a long bend, and its headlights illuminated a fence. A cattle guard bridged the gap in the barbed wire.

His arms tensed. Nothing past the cattle guard that he could see, just more overgrown road with grass down the middle and twin graveled paths where the growth had been discouraged by the occasional passage of trucks. Hunters, perhaps.

The Suburban's tires rattled over the steel piping.

There was a distinct possibility that Eve had already infected Heather with the disease. That Daniel would find her on a chair, eyes rolled back, convulsing as the lethal strain of streptococcus ravaged her mind and body.

Daniel eased the gas pedal down. The sound of crunching gravel under him became a muted roar. He wiped the sweat from his eyes and stared at the fuzzy line between the headlights' reach and darkness.

An old shack down the road, Eve had said. But he hadn't said how far.

Exhaustion had forced him to pull over at a rest stop just after he crossed the Oklahoma state line. He slept thirty-seven minutes before jerking awake and resuming his push.

Upon further reflection, the notion that the boy in his mind's eye was something more than an electrochemical reaction felt hollow. Nevertheless, however foolish notions of the supernatural were, he now understood with surprising clarity why 98 percent of the world's population put its faith in them.

Explaining his experience in supernatural terms would be acceptable to any less-informed person. And, even for him, it was tempting. He knew that hell was real because he'd been there and met the devil himself: a little boy who called himself Eve. When the killer had killed him that night in Manitou Springs, Daniel had met the boy— this demon called Eve—and evidently made a promise to back off the investigation in exchange for his life. That was how Lori had been able to bring him back.

Now Daniel was paying the price for failing to keep his end of the bargain. That was the religious explanation for what was happening to him.

In some ways the explanation rang true. Only the names were wrong. Hell was the mind, the devil was actually a little-understood chemical called DMT, and the boy was an even less-understood electrochemical reaction best known as the conscience.

The light reaching out into darkness broke on an old

shack. Daniel shifted his foot to the brake, heard the tires skid, then eased off. The fear hadn't returned since he'd left Wyoming, but panic made a pass now. Then retreated.

The shack was maybe ten by ten—too small, he thought. And then the headlamps found a large compound, and Daniel knew that he'd arrived.

He stopped the Suburban and stared out at the clearing. A small square house rose from overgrown weeds on his left. Old gray boards hanging off the walls, half the roof missing, broken windows.

A small hill rose ahead before meeting the forest. What looked to be an old rusted plow leaned into the brush at the base of the hill. Beyond, a rotting wood fence.

Three thoughts crowded Daniel's mind. The first was that neither the shack nor the house fit Eve's profile.

The second was that he was out in the open, lights blazing, in the crosshairs of anyone staring out of the forest.

The third was that his chest was aching badly.

He reached for the key, shut the engine off. The hum that had been his constant companion for the past seventeen hours was replaced by a soft ring in his ears. The clock read 8:13.

Daniel turned off the lights. A half moon cast just enough light over the clearing for him to make out the house's outline against the black forest. A quick glance at his cell confirmed that he was still out of coverage. Eve must have used a satellite phone.

He sat with both hands on the wheel, letting his eyes adjust to the darkness. He'd considered countless scenarios, but stranded in the clearing now, none of them seemed to matter. Eve was already watching, waiting.

Daniel had only two options. He could turn around, drive the half hour to cell coverage, and call the location in. Or he could search the compound and trust his instincts.

Instincts that told him method killers like Eve depended on their compulsions to the point of addiction. Eve killed women on the new moon for reasons powerful enough to prevent him from killing Heather now. Whatever he had in mind, it wasn't a straightforward killing spree.

However unlikely to a logical way of thinking, there was a possibility that Eve had done all of this to serve as a warning, to show his mastery over the situation. *That* would fit his profile.

Daniel pulled his weapon from its holster, chambered a round, and stepped out of the vehicle. He closed the door and stood by the front fender, searching. For what, he didn't know. Movement. Sound. Anything to suggest a course of action.

Crickets sang in the forest. The Suburban's engine ticked loudly as it cooled. Otherwise the compound was quiet.

He stepped into the brush on his right, intent on keeping the forest close to his back. In any other circumstance he would sweep around, keeping low, attempting to find an advantage through stealth or speed. But the idea of trying to get the upper hand on Eve after being led here seemed foolish.

So he turned to his right and walked out into the middle of the compound, where he stopped. Still nothing. He held his gun in both hands, lifted halfway.

"Heather!"

His voice carried through the clearing, then dissipated

into the trees. Daniel took three steps toward the house
and yelled again, louder this time.

"Heather! Can you hear me?"

This time a faint cry drifted across the compound.

Daniel jerked his gun up and sighted right, then left. It
could have been a product of his imagination, that cry. Or
an animal in the forest. An owl, or a...

It came again, but he still couldn't tell from which
direction.

"Heather!" He headed for the house, running in a low
crouch, gun still in both hands but directed at the earth.
He picked his way quickly over fallen branches, several
rocks. The house's door was missing. Just a gaping black
mouth.

Daniel pulled up against the wall, then spun in, gun
extended. By the faint moonlight he could see that the place
had been trashed long ago. Not Eve. None of this fit Eve.

"Heather?" Softer.

He stepped over several rusted paint cans and peered
through a doorway on the right. Two shredded mattresses
littered with empty tin cans lay on the floor, one in each
corner. An old bedroom.

Daniel was turning from the room when he saw the
dark stain on the wall, just visible by moonlight. One
word, splashed over the decaying wood. A name.

Eve.

He stared, mind spinning. Not the same style the killer
used, but definitely the same name. Written here years ago.

The killer had drawn him to a location linked to his
past. His childhood or his teenage years. It was a hot
night, but the room seemed to have cooled. Gooseflesh
rippled up Daniel's arms.

For the first time in twenty-four hours, the fear raged through Daniel's nerves. He felt himself gasp, felt his muscles quivering and his knees buckling.

He reached out with both hands, searching for something to steady himself. The gun thudded to the floor. His right hand found a sharp edge on the doorjamb—a nail or a sliver sliced into the flesh at the base of his thumb.

But the terror that swept through his senses blanketed the physical pain. He staggered, felt the skin on his hand tear, caught himself with a quick step forward.

And then the fear passed, leaving him trembling in the chilled air.

He stood and tried to settle his mind. The gun sat two feet to his right, and he bent for it. It occurred to him then, as he stood back up, that his breath fogged the air.

The chill he felt wasn't a matter of nerves. The temperature had fallen drastically. How was that possible?

Another cry reached his ears. With a parting glance at the stain that spelled Eve's name, Daniel ran from the house, breathing steady now. The onslaught of fear and its subsequent easing left him more cautious of his own mind than of Eve. He couldn't live with whatever battered his emotions with such savagery.

Facing Eve was a preferable prospect. The air was hot.

A cry cut the night, this time clearly from his left. The direction of the hill. He sprinted through the tall grass, nearly spilling when his foot landed on something hidden in the weeds. Pain spread up his leg, but he ignored it and ran across the road.

Turned to the left and slowed to a quick walk around the base of the rise.

"Heather!"

No cry this time. But he didn't need one to guide him, because rounding the hill, he saw the black hole that led into the ground.

Daniel pulled up hard, panting. Thick timbers framed a wood door propped halfway open. A root cellar.

Images of the other root cellars where Eve had killed his victims skipped through his mind. Missing pieces that made up Eve's puzzle settled into place. The child who'd become a serial killer had returned home.

Daniel walked up to the door, gun tight in his bloodied palm. "Heather?"

A soft whimper from inside.

He was beside the doorway now, eyes straining into a dull, flickering glow. He knew that entering the cellar could not end well for him, but he also knew that not entering could not end well for Heather.

Daniel stepped past the doorway into the root cellar.

Shifting flame light moved shadows over large rail-road ties that supported the sagging ceiling. The large cellar smelled of dead rats and creosote. Quick breathing echoed softly. Another whimper.

Daniel jerked his eyes from side to side, looking for Heather. A table to his right, piles of debris, a couple of fallen timbers. But the sound was directionless.

He took two steps and spun back.

Heather sat in a metal chair, arms bound behind her back, ankles strapped to the legs with duct tape. Shivering.

There was a bag over her head.

No sign of Eve.

"Heather…" He crossed the dirt floor in four long steps. "I'm here. It's Daniel. It's okay, I'm here now." He whispered quickly, searching for the killer.

They had to get out, he knew that as clearly as he knew how unlikely it was. He glanced back at the entryway. Still clear. He started to tug at the tape around her ankle, but the going was slowed by his grip on the gun. He couldn't release the gun.

Heather was still shaking, hyperventilating. She'd cried out more than once, why now so silent?

"It's okay, Heather. I'm sorry, I'm so sorry."

The tape came free and he attacked the second leg.

"Forgive me." Emotion rose through his chest. "I'm sorry, I'm so sorry..."

He got the second leg free, but she made no move to stand. Daniel stood and faced the inevitable. When he pulled the bag from her head, he would discover if she'd been spared the disease.

He hesitated a beat, not sure he could face the answer. Then he reached out, took the seam of the bag in his left hand, and pulled it off her head.

Heather's hair was matted with sweat. What was left of her mascara smeared flushed cheeks. Mucus stained her upper lip. Duct tape sealed her mouth.

But the terrified eyes that frantically searched his were clear of the disease. She'd been spared.

A quick check of the doorway assured him they were still in the clear. "We have to go! We have to get out of here."

Her hands were still bound to each other and her lips taped shut, but she was freed from the chair. They didn't have time to untie the knots behind her back.

He started to pull her up, glancing again over his shoulder. "Come on, please, we have to get out of here."

Her eyes rolled to the right and left, bright with fear.

She was trying to tell him something. He released her and grabbed the edge of the tape.

It was then, while Daniel's hand was on the tape, that Eve spoke. Not from the doorway behind them, but from the shadows beyond the chair.

"Put the gun down."

Daniel jerked up and stared at a man dressed in dungarees and a plaid flannel shirt, holding a gun on Heather. He'd stepped from the darkness, but his face was still in shadows, giving him the appearance of having no eyes.

For several long breaths Daniel stood rooted to the ground. The moment had taken him off guard. Yet here it was.

He should have known the duct tape was a recent addition, applied only moments earlier.

He dropped the gun and stood back.

Then the man stepped from the shadows behind Heather and looked into Daniel's eyes.

"Hello, Adam."

TWENTY-EIGHT

EVE REPLACED THE BAG over Heather's head before hauling her from the root cellar, but not before turning her around to see Daniel.

Eve had hog-tied Daniel behind her back, then chained him to one of the railroad ties that rose along the wall. Duct tape ran over his mouth and around his head several times. He lay on his side, eyes shifting between Heather and the man behind her.

Eve hadn't allowed her to see his face. Something that could bode well for her.

Daniel, on the other hand, was staring at Eve now.

Her hands were still tied, otherwise she would have put up a fight here and now, to hell with consequences. The tape was still across her face, otherwise she would have cried out her love for the man on the floor. Demanded that Eve take her instead of Daniel.

"I'll give you a drink when I get back," Eve said to Daniel.

Then he pulled the bag over her head, turned her around, and forced her from the root cellar.

The hot night air smothered her. She had no idea where they were, only that it was a long way from Los Angeles—a day's drive. She'd seen the inside of the root cellar but nothing more.

Eve guided her over uneven ground for a hundred paces, then stopped her.

"Please relieve yourself," he said.

She was so far removed from shame in the wake of her ordeal that she gratefully did so with his help.

They walked a short way before stopping again. He opened a sliding van door and nudged her inside. He'd never been rough with her. Never shoved or yanked her. Only his initial assault on her had required any force at all.

Even in his speech, Eve struck her as an intelligent, cautious man who was motivated by ideology rather than violence. And it was through those few spoken words that she'd learned more about Eve than a year of obsession had taught her.

She lay down on the van's carpeted floor. The door slammed shut. She lay in silence for thirty seconds before hearing the growl of another engine.

He was moving another car. Daniel's.

She didn't know tear ducts were capable of producing the volume she'd wept over the past two days. None of her anguish had moved the man who'd taken her. He felt no sorrow, but neither did he relish their pain, she thought.

The gravel crunched under his feet as he approached.

He climbed into the car, started the engine. The van moved through a turn, then sped up.

Heather wasn't sure why he'd gone to so much trouble to bring her all this way if his objective was Daniel all along. An obsessive mind often followed its own convoluted reasoning, Daniel often said. It was guided by principles obvious only to the faithful. Yet another way in which he connected killers and religious fanatics.

Maybe Eve wanted Daniel in the root cellar for this reason. She'd studied the room during hours of waiting. Someone had carved *Eve's Holy Coven* on each overhead beam, facing the back wall. Rusted torch rings were fixed to the vertical railroad ties.

But it was the table along the near wall that said more about the room's purpose than anything. Holes had been drilled in each corner, and from these holes hung leather restraining straps. The pitted surface was stained with dark blotches. She'd stared at the table and imagined animals tied down and slaughtered. She'd imagined worse, but then refused to dwell on it.

They drove for an hour, and Heather let her mind wonder what would happen to Daniel. She lay on her side and wept at the thoughts.

Slowly the rumbling under her right ear called her to exhaustion, and she embraced a deep, numbing sleep.

THE NEXT TIME HEATHER opened her eyes, light seeped through the neck of the bag over her head. She'd slept through the night and part of the next day.

The van wasn't moving.

Heather lifted her head and listened. She could hear Eve

in the front seat, eating something. A plastic wrapper being torn, then another bite. Then a long drink. He was having a candy bar with a soft drink, she thought. Cherry Coke.

No other sounds that she could hear. She laid her head back down. But her rest lasted less than a minute before Eve's door squeaked and he climbed out. The van door slid open.

"Would you like to relieve yourself?"

She sat up with his help. Scooted to the edge of the van, swung her legs down, and stood. He eased her head away from the roof and guided her along a hard surface. A sidewalk or street.

They entered a room that smelled like a freshly cleaned bathroom. They were at a rest stop?

Eve asked her to sit in a corner, then taped her hands to a cold pipe and washed up in a sink.

"Two things you should know. The disease takes three days to set in. If the FBI gets lucky and finds us before those three days have passed, I'll kill him before they arrive."

A beat, then he spoke again. "Don't try to outthink me. It'll only get more people killed. Letting you go is not a mistake unless you make it one. For you, for Daniel."

Then he left.

It took her several minutes to realize that he really wasn't coming back. He'd left her alone in a rest stop bathroom to be found by the next traveler!

She tried to free herself, but the tape job proved too secure. She tried to scream through the muzzle, but the strain on her vocal cords wore them raw. So she settled down and prayed the driver of the next vehicle to pull in would be a man with a burning bladder.

She didn't have long to wait. A man, a teenager by the

sound of it, haltingly hammering out the lyrics to a rap song she didn't recognize, opened the door. She normally hated rap. But in that moment rap became the sweetest-sounding music she'd ever heard.

The would-be rapper's lyrics caught in his throat as he shuffled into the bathroom.

But instead of rushing up to free her, the boy fled. Heather screamed into the tape after him, but he was gone. She'd never considered what effect the image of a bound and gagged woman in a men's restroom might have on the casual passerby.

Pounding feet washed away her fears. The boy had gone for help, and it was coming fast.

"Ma'am? You okay?"

She gave the stupid question a stupid, muffled cry.

Then hands were on her arms, ripping away the tape. The bag lifted off, and Heather stared at a large, dark-skinned man who looked like he might have been a running back in college.

"You okay, ma'am?"

The man eased the tape off her mouth.

"Do I look okay?" She was frantic to be free, completely unbound. "Untie me...Get this stuff off me!"

Tears flooded her eyes and she started to cry, as much from relief as anything. But her own rescue was poisoned by the knowledge that Eve was on his way back to Daniel.

"Get this stuff off me!"

"Tyrone!" the man snapped.

The man's son, presumably the rapper, shrugged off his shock, yanked out a pocketknife, and made quick work of the tape that bound her wrists.

They had to help her to her feet. She stared at her hands, calming.

"Thank you. Thank you, thank you!" She threw her arms around Tyrone and kissed his face without restraint. "Thank you, thank you." She hugged the running back tight.

"You sure you're okay?"

Heather stepped back. Sniffed. Wiped her nose and mouth.

"You have a cell phone, Tyrone?"

He fished an iPhone from his pocket and handed it to her.

"Where are we?"

"Just outside Trinidad," the man said. "Colorado. I-25."

She punched the number in with an unsteady hand and looked up at the man, who was still watching her. "Thank you." She touched his arm. "Thank you so much."

A twisted grin nudged his lips, and he dipped his head.

Brit's voice filled the phone. "Hello?"

"Brit?" She knew it was him, but she wanted to hear him say it.

"This is Brit Holman. Who's this?"

"It's Heather, Brit."

"Heather?"

"It's Heather—"

"Are you . . . are you okay?"

She leaned into the wall and started to cry again. "He's got Daniel, Brit."

Reprinted from Crime Today *magazine, 2008*

MAN OF SORROW:
JOURNEY INTO DARKNESS

by Anne Rudolph

Crime Today magazine is pleased to present the eighth installment of Anne Rudolph's narrative account of the killer now known as Alex Price, presented in nine monthly installments.

January 7, 1992

ONE WEEK after accepting Bruce's proposal of marriage in Lovers' Park, Jessica looked forward to a walk in the same park to discuss wedding plans that evening at ten.

Alex had accepted the news with as much grace as she could have expected of him. In fact, with more than she'd expected. He'd withdrawn after his initial outburst and subsequent apology. They talked each day, and he showed no concern about Jessica's relationship with Bruce. She referred to it once and he changed the subject. Best to give him space to adjust, she thought.

Jessica's shift was supposed to end at ten, but an irritated customer who refused to pay his bill delayed her fifteen minutes. By the time she stepped into the cool night outside the restaurant, it was almost 10:20. And no sign of Bruce.

Lovers' Park was only a block away. She made her way across the quiet street to find him by the swings, where they often met. He'd once surprised her from the bushes at the entrance to the park, and although he'd rolled on the ground laughing, she found the fright not the least bit funny. Still, the thought of it now made her smile. She kept her eyes on the bushes as she approached.

Life with Bruce would be an adventure she could hardly imagine. Like a trip to outer space for most people. She might even be able to have children with a man like Bruce, although the thought terrified her.

She walked into the park with a wary eye and angled for the swings. There was no one else near that she could see. When she reached the swings and saw no sign of Bruce, she became concerned. He'd never been late, and it was now twenty minutes past the time they'd agreed to meet. Had he left already? What if he'd gone to their apartment?

A moan from the slope to her right made her spin around. There in the draw was a form. Bruce? She rushed over, calling his name.

Bruce lay prone, trying to move, groaning. She dropped to her knees beside him and only then saw the extent of his injuries. His face was mangled and bloody. His shirt was torn to ribbons, revealing long gashes on his chest and sides and forearms.

Through sobs, she tried to help him, but he slipped into unconsciousness. She raced back to the restaurant, screaming for an ambulance, then returned to Bruce's side.

All the while one word kept drumming through her mind. *Alex.* Alex had done this. Alex had beaten Bruce and whipped him with a cat-o'-nine-tails. Jessica ran to the bushes next to Bruce's prone body and threw up.

The ambulance arrived at 10:31 and rushed Bruce to the emergency room. Jessica watched the paramedics roll him into the ward, hardly able to think for the rage she felt. She'd told the doctor on duty exactly what she'd seen, which was nothing more than he could see. Someone had attacked Bruce in the park and left him battered and bruised.

He would live, the doctor said. The blood made the wounds appear worse than they were. They would keep him in the hospital overnight and probably release him sometime the next day.

Jessica rushed home. "I was a crazy mess," she recalled. She entered the apartment and eased the door shut. As expected, no Alex in the living room. Several candles were burning on the table. He was there, in his room.

Blinded by rage, Jessica stormed to his door. She tried the handle but it was locked, so she threw her shoulder into the door, screaming at Alex. Surprisingly, the door frame splintered, and she spilled past the opened door, past the black curtain, and into Alex's room.

She pulled up, panting. For the first time, her brother's private space filled her eyes. Two dozen candles on candelabras and pedestals lit the room. All four walls had been painted black. A table with holes drilled in each corner sat against one wall. Dozens of upside-down crosses had been nailed to the walls, intermixed with the heads of chickens with pins sticking into their eyes. *See no evil.*

More books than Jessica could have imagined filled three large bookcases. Legal and medical volumes. Books on religion and philosophy. A rocking chair sat in one corner, a mattress on the floor to her left. One sheet only, no blanket. No pillow. The closet door opposite the mattress was closed.

Alice might have lived here. Jessica saw it all in a glance and froze. It was as if she'd stepped back into Alice's coven.

Her brother sat at a desk, stripped to his waist. Several fresh cuts on his back seeped blood. He turned slowly and stared at her with sad eyes, showing no concern or shock at her sudden intrusion.

Jessica marched over to the closet and threw the door open. At least a dozen whips hung from a wooden spindle. Knives and razors and rattraps lay among other paraphernalia, all neatly placed.

She spun around and faced her brother. "You've become her!"

Alex stared at her wide-eyed. "I'm protecting you," he said.

"No, this is Eve's doing! The unholy spirit is making you do this!" she cried.

Alex's face changed, eyes narrowing to slits, skin stretching tight. When he spoke, his voice growled. "You ever try to stop me, sow, and I'll kill more of them than you know how to bury. And I'll know. I'll know if you breathe a word. Because I can see you, sow."

Jessica watched, frozen to the floor. Slowly Alex's face reverted to its normal form and he stared at her, lost.

"The fear that filled me . . . I'd never felt it, not even when we were kids. I knew then that I couldn't touch Alex without paying a terrible price."

Realizing that he'd made a mistake, Alex dropped to the floor and begged her forgiveness. But this time it was too much even for Jessica, who understood his terrible wounding and loved him the way only someone who'd suffered Alice's horrors could. She ran from the room, threw her most important belongings in a bag, and fled the apartment.

WHEN ASKED why she didn't report the incident to the police,

Jessica's answer was simple: "I was terrified!"

And the events of the next few days only strengthened her fear. Returning to the hospital, she found Bruce sleeping, so she checked into a motel nearby and waited for morning. Exhausted from the ordeal, she fell asleep in the dark morning hours, and without an alarm clock, slept until the maid pounded on the door at noon.

She rushed down to the hospital and discovered that Bruce had been released. He'd left a note for her at the nurses' station. It was written on the hospital's stationery in his handwriting. The blood drained from her head as she read the note.

My dearest Jessica,

I have to leave for a while to get my head straight. My heart is crushed, but I don't know what else to do. You mean too much to me.

Please know, my love, that I am doing this for you. I really don't think we can be together for now. You must know why.

Maybe some day. Please forgive me. I am so sorry.

Bruce

Jessica left the hospital numb and made a series of frantic calls in an attempt to find Bruce. She finally reached his sister, Jenny, who told her that Bruce had left the state and didn't want to be reached. Every other path led Jessica to a dead end.

She knew what had happened. Alex had threatened Bruce with something that drove a stake through his heart. Or had it been Eve who terrified Bruce?

Surely there was a way to stop her brother, but everything she thought of ended in a no-win scenario. She was afraid that if she went to the police, Eve would know. The danger to her and Bruce was too great.

She wanted to go to Father Seymour. The priest had made several attempts to pull Alex back into attending Mass, but Alex refused to talk to the man. Father Seymour had expressed his concern and comfort to Jessica. Surely he would understand.

But Jessica thought going to the church would only force her to the police. Surely not even a priest could hold all these things in confidence. A crime had been committed. And she had no confidence that the very clergy who'd thrown Alex out of seminary could protect her or Alex from Eve.

Jessica's inability to go to the police—a course that any normal human being would surely have taken given her circumstances—perhaps illustrates better than any other evidence just how deep her wounding and fear ran. For two long days, Jessica paced and fretted in the motel. She finally took the only course available to her: she returned to the apartment on Holly Street.

Nothing had been disturbed in the living room, the kitchen, or in her room. The place was immaculate, and it appeared as though the carpets had been shampooed. Jessica hurried to Alex's room and pushed the door open.

The room had been stripped and scrubbed down. Not a speck of dust, not a stray hair, only black walls and shampooed carpet. Alex was gone. Jessica sat in the doorway, lowered her head into her hands, and wept.

The next two weeks passed like a nightmare for Jessica. She knew Alex wasn't coming back. He had fled for her sake, not for his own, she realized. Protecting Jessica from himself had been his final gift to her. He knew she was right, that he couldn't be trusted any longer. The only solution was for him to remove himself from the one person whom he loved more than life itself.

But she couldn't bring herself to move out of the apartment on the chance that he might have a change of heart. She felt sick with guilt, and disgusted for feeling sick with guilt.

No amount of searching turned up Bruce. He was simply out of her life, at least for now.

After two weeks, Jessica finally went to Father Seymour and told him that Alex had moved out of the apartment and threatened to never come back. They'd had a fight, she said, and she didn't think she could stay in the apartment with all the memories.

Father Seymour allowed her to stay in a small studio flat off the parish house, where she lived for four months. On May 17, 1992, the father received a call from the manager at the Denny's Restaurant where Jessica worked. She'd missed two shifts.

He approached her flat fearing the worst. When he opened the door, he found an empty apartment. He immediately began placing calls to anyone who might know of her whereabouts. When the calls turned up nothing, he filed a missing-persons report and began walking the streets.

Over the next week, Father Seymour and a handful of trusted confidants kept an eye out for the pretty girl who'd come to them off the streets. The week stretched into a month, then two.

Two years later, he received a letter bearing a North Dakota postmark that simply read:

> *Wanted you to know that I am alive and well and studying to be a teacher. Please don't try to find me. Thank you for all you have done.*
>
> *Jessica*

Father Seymour's search for a Jessica Trane from Oklahoma turned up empty. He would not see her again until many years later, long after Alex had become Eve, the killer who had taken the lives of so many women.

TWENTY-NINE

THEY SAT AROUND THE conference table, haggard from two days of late nights and little sleep. Brit Holman wore a loosened blue tie that lay askew, white shirtsleeves rolled to his elbows, his chin rough with two days' growth. Montova stared at Heather with cutting eyes. She'd always thought that his shiny face and slicked hair were a better fit for a Mafia movie poster than a recruitment poster for the FBI.

Darkened shadows edged Lori Ames's brown eyes. Her hair was disheveled and stringy. The lines of concern etched in her face made Lori look ten years older than the woman Heather had met in her house a week earlier. Lori cared for Daniel, and Heather felt surprisingly comfortable with the knowledge. Perhaps because she was now an ally.

Heather sat at one end of the table after a two-hour

debriefing in the LA field office. A Colorado Highway Patrol officer had taken her to a local Wal-Mart for clean clothes and then to the Trinidad municipal airport, where she'd waited for her ride back to Los Angeles. They'd let her freshen up and suggested she rest before the debriefing. But she had no inclination to rest.

"So that's it then," Montova said after a long pause. Several agents had come and gone during the meeting, but only the four of them remained. "What do we have, Brit?"

The special agent now in charge of the Eve case tapped his pen on the yellow pad in front of him. "He's in a root cellar. Crickets and other night sounds Heather heard indicate a forested region. Within fifteen hours—"

"No, twelve," Heather interrupted. "That's three hours less. Of search area."

Brit peered up at her without lifting his head, a gentle expression of the frustration he felt at her constant interruptions. Heather knew she was on edge, but she made no attempt to hide or change the fact.

Daniel was out there. And over the hours since her release, one fact had drummed itself into Heather's mind: although the FBI could be an enormous help, she, not they, was the only one who could actually save Daniel's life, however unlikely that was.

Two things you should know. The disease takes three days to set in. If the FBI gets lucky and finds us before those three days have passed, I'll kill him before they arrive.

"Best estimate is that it took Daniel at least half a day to find the location. Say fifteen hours."

"We still don't know if he was on the move the whole

time," Lori said. "He left the hospital at roughly 2:00 a.m., but he could have stopped anywhere for any length of time."

"If we believe what he told Heather, we have three days," Brit said. "Less now. We have to make certain assumptions. Until we know better, we assume he was on the road."

He pushed himself up, walked to a map of the United States on which they'd pinpointed Eve's victims with small red pins. Three yellow pins marked Laramie, Wyoming; Trinidad, Colorado; and Long Beach, California.

"A fifteen-hour drive from Laramie..." He made a large circle with a pencil. "We'll get more precise measurements later. Twenty-four hours from Long Beach..." Another circle. "Twelve hours from Trinidad..." A third circle.

Brit dropped the pencil in the tray and returned to his seat. "The overlapping areas of all three circles are our search grid. Most likely at the perimeters."

"Texas, Oklahoma, Iowa, Missouri, Kansas..." Montova broke off. "He could be anywhere."

Brit nodded, then turned back to his pad. "We know the root cellar is someplace Eve's known for a long time. Eve's Holy Coven is new, but the marks were old. Our boy's returning to his roots."

"He was going to be a priest," Heather said.

Another look from Brit. "We know that he wanted to be a priest. That his motivation is clearly religious. We're already running searches on Eve's Holy Coven and the Daisy Ringwald case he cited to Heather. The goat in Manitou Springs and the table in the root cellar indicate that animal sacrifice is part of his shtick. All long shots that confirm Daniel's profile but may do little to help us isolate his current location."

There was something about the business of Eve wanting to be a priest that gnawed at Heather, but she couldn't narrow it down.

"We still don't know what triggered Daniel's departure in the first place," Brit said. "He found Eve, which means he had access to critical information that he decided not to pass on." He shook his head. "Makes no sense."

"A near-death experience," Lori said.

"So he saw something in his mind while he was dead. Like I said, makes no sense."

"Eve seems to have a unique appreciation for near-death experiences," she said.

"Does that help us locate either of them? Is there anything in that fact at all that might shed light on who he is, where he is?"

Lori shifted her eyes from the man. "No."

Brit leaned back and sighed. "There's a handful of smaller considerations. We'll run with everything we have. I hate to say this, but it doesn't look too encouraging."

"So that's it then?" Heather demanded. "That's all you can pull out?"

The other three looked at her without responding. Brit was right, of course, but Heather refused to accept it. There was something else here that Daniel would have fished out. A clue to Eve's childhood, his personality, his likely rearing. Something. Anything!

"You sound like it's over," she snapped.

Brit shook his head. "It's never over."

Lori stared at the map, eyes glazed over. The confidence she'd carried a week earlier had vanished.

Montova stood. "I want every possible resource on this. Update me with anything you get, I don't care how insignificant." He glanced at Heather, then left the room.

Brit blew out some air. "I'm sorry, Heather. Don't think I've given up hope. And don't count Daniel out. He's still our best shot at this point."

Heather stood and headed for the door. "I was there, Brit. If Daniel's our best shot, he's dead." She pushed through the door, leaving Brit and Lori to sit in their own hopelessness.

But they're right, she thought. *It is hopeless.*

HEATHER SPENT THE NEXT three hours in her basement, poring over analyses of near-death experiences from every conceivable perspective. And there were a lot of them, mostly dismissed. The pictures on the wall had new meaning to her now, but none of that meaning slowed time or brought her any closer to Daniel.

She knew what they'd gone through. What Daniel was going through right now. Although Eve hadn't infected her with the disease, she'd lived through the terror of anticipation, strapped to the chair, bagged, hearing his voice.

It was three in the afternoon. Eve was still driving back to the root cellar, where Daniel lay sweating on the floor.

Hello, Adam.

What would Daniel make of what they'd learned? No one could climb into his mind the way she could. He might understand Eve better, but she thought she understood Daniel better than he himself did.

Eve was replaying the fall of Adam and Eve, infecting his victims' virginal minds with a disease. But more than that, he was offering them up as a way to find atonement for his own sin. For losing his faith. They were his sacrificial lambs.

None of this was helping her. And time was ticking. They were right. It was all hopeless.

She turned her attention back to the near-death cases. The fact that Daniel had died and been resuscitated twice now was unique enough on its own. The fact that he'd evidently gone after Eve after having a near-death experience in Laramie was mind-boggling.

The fact that Eve had cited a near-death experience—Daisy Ringwald's—as his trigger for believing in the supernatural was downright scary. Needless to say, Heather had dug into the cases with a newfound respect.

She was familiar with all the reasons why NDEs were nothing more than electrochemical reactions in the brain at the time of death—Daniel had explained the phenomenon to her a dozen times over the years.

But the evidence that supported a conclusion other than chemically induced hallucinations was surprisingly persuasive.

Admittedly, most of the cases were nonsense. She had little doubt that the vast majority of near-death experiences were indeed chemically induced. Eight million Americans alive today had experienced an NDE, and too many of those had turned their stories for profit, undoubtedly embellishing to the point of quackery at times.

But not all. Heather focused on the cases of those born blind, as Eve himself had.

Daisy Ringwald, born in 1934 in Milwaukee. She saw several references to her case, but they added nothing to what Eve had told her.

But a thirty-patient study of NDE effects over a two-year period by Dr. Kenneth Ring and Sharon Cooper added more than Heather could have imagined. It seemed that Eve's Daisy was not alone. Among the numerous documented cases in which blind people had NDEs, a full eight percent could describe events and objects during their deaths.

How does a person born blind describe something she's never seen? In many of the cases, the subjects had "seen" for the first time in their lives and were able to describe what they saw.

If they hadn't ever seen these objects with their physical eyes, what had they seen them with? Clearly, there was more to the human being than electrochemical reactions.

Eve's question whispered through her mind. *Do you believe, Heather?*

Believe what, Eve? That you're a psychopath caught in your own sick, twisted version of reality? Yes, I believe.

I'm going to help you see, Heather. All of you.

And how are you going to help Daniel see, Eve? Because he's as stubborn as a mule.

I was going to be a priest, Heather.

The doorbell rang, startling her from her reverie. She set the file down and hurried upstairs. Lori stood in the doorway, arms crossed. They'd found something?

"Hello, Heather."

"What's happening?"

"Can I come in?"

Heather stepped away from the door. "So what's happened?"

"Nothing new." But the lines on her face betrayed something more. "I just…"

The woman was distraught. She was acting more like a mourning spouse than a forensic pathologist who'd seen this a hundred times.

"I love him, Lori."

"I know you do. Please, don't worry. This has nothing to do with Daniel and me, not in that way. I haven't been with him and never will."

Well, that was out.

"Okay. So what is it? Forgive me for being a bit distracted, but unlike you, I've given myself to Daniel from the day I met him. He means everything to me, I don't care how that sounds."

Lori nodded. "I'm afraid. For him, I mean."

"We all are."

"I killed him, Heather."

The statement sat between them, like a dumb rock. Meaningless.

"What, so now *you're* Eve?"

"No, I mean Daniel convinced me to force his heart into fibrillation in an attempt to have a near-death experience. I did it twice."

Heather didn't know what to do with such an absurd admission. Then again, this was Daniel they were talking about.

"Tell me everything."

Heather led Lori to the basement, sat in a chair opposite her, and heard it all. The trial with DMT, the morgue experience, the way they killed him in Laramie, the fear that drove him to it, the visions of the boy in the black room. It took half an hour, but five minutes in, Heather already knew that Daniel had been onto something.

Something beyond them all. Locked in Eve's mind.

"I'm surprised none of this disturbs you more," Lori said.

"I wouldn't put anything past Daniel. What disturbs me is the fact that he's in a root cellar with the same boy in his dreams." She swallowed a lump in her throat. "Trust me, I would believe or do anything to get him back."

Lori stood and walked up to the corkboard covered in newspaper clippings. "A week ago you received a call at the courthouse."

Only a week, and yet those two calls seemed a lifetime ago. "That's right."

"Something about being taken from his—"

"His priest!" Heather bolted up. The caller's words rasped through her mind like a saw. "'They took me away from my daddy, my sister, my priest'! He was *going* to be a priest. That means he wasn't a priest. He was taken *away* from the priesthood, not kicked out of a church—they would never kick out a wayward soul. But a seminary would. He was expelled from a seminary."

Heather crossed to the phone and punched in Brit's speed dial. She quickly told him, listened to his response, made a few quick suggestions, and snapped her phone shut.

"That's a lot of seminaries. East Coast ones are closed, but they'll canvass the West Coast immediately. How many students are kicked out of seminaries for heresy? Or losing their faith? It can't be that many."

She slid onto her chair and swiveled around to the computer. "How many seminaries can there be?"

"The field office is on it, Heather. They'll have at least a partial list of students dismissed from West Coast seminaries within the hour." She walked to the door and turned back.

"About what I told you—"

"It's immaterial. Daniel killing himself is no one's business but ours."

"Thank you." Lori smiled. "I had to get that off my chest."

"But I would like a favor from you," Heather said.

"Anything."

"Seeing as I basically have your career in my hands, I suppose I can trust you."

Lori hesitated. "Go on…"

"I didn't quite tell them everything."

Lori raised a brow.

"Eve told me that if the FBI approaches the cellar, he'll kill Daniel early. And I believe him."

She could see Lori's mind absorbing this new detail.

"If you get any information, anything at all, get it to me first?"

"I can't withhold information from Brit."

"I'm not asking you to. Just give me a shot. Do you doubt Eve's promise?"

"I see your point," Lori said. "I think Brit will let me run point on this—it was my lead. You'll be my first call."

LORI'S CALL CAME fifty-three minutes later, ten minutes after she'd pulled into the office.

"We have a hit, Heather. Two students were kicked out during that time. One of them lives in Seattle and works as a fireman. Dead end."

"And the other?"

"Disappeared after he was expelled for heresy from St. Peter's Seminary College in 1990."

"Where?"

"Pasadena."

"Here?"

"Here."

"What was his name?"

There was a tremor in Lori's voice. "Trane. Alex Trane."

Heather mouthed the first name. Alex. Tried to imagine Eve named Alex Trane, but nothing connected.

"Try the priest," Lori said.

"Priest?"

"The one who kicked him out," Lori said.

Three calls later, Heather had the phone number and address of the priest who'd sponsored Alex Trane to attend St. Peter's Seminary College in the spring semester of 1987, and later gotten him expelled. Father Robert Seymour, retired, now living in Burbank.

She dialed the number and prayed to the priest's God that Seymour would pick up.

An old, gruff voice crackled over her phone. "Hello?"

"Father Seymour?"

"Yes, darling. What is it?"

"This is Heather Clark. I'm calling about a seminary student you once sponsored. Does the name Alex Trane ring any bells?"

Silence.

"Father?"

"You've found him?" The gusto had left his voice.

"No. I'm looking for him. I think he may have kidnapped my husband."

Another long beat.

"Father, you remember him?"

"How soon can you be here?"

THIRTY

EVE'S HOLY COVEN.

Daniel lay on the cool dirt floor, drifting in and out of sleep. Consciousness. Sanity. Dreams. Nightmares. Fear.

He'd attempted to free himself from the chain but learned within minutes that Eve hadn't stumbled in his preparation of the restraints. Eve didn't know how to stumble.

Which meant that he would be gone for a long time, Daniel realized. He was going to release Heather, and doing so anywhere near Oklahoma would help the FBI narrow their search grid. He would be alone twenty hours or more.

Without food or water. Without a bathroom.

As the hopelessness of his situation settled in, Daniel felt his desperation begin to yield to resolve. Not to live, but to let the end come as it may.

There was something wrong in Eve's Holy Coven—he knew that because of the sounds and the smells and the rising and falling temperature. Perhaps Eve's Holy Coven was his mind, and he was losing it.

The first indication that his mind was falling apart came with the pungent smell of urine. He blanched, tested the air again, and confirmed that it did indeed smell like a very potent urine. From where or how he didn't know. It wasn't his.

The odor had come and gone. As had the sounds. Creaking at first, which would have been plausible in the house but not in this root cellar. Then the boy's voice, whispering.

I see you, Daniel.

He'd jerked his head and stared into the shadows at the far corner the first few times he heard the voice.

I see you, Daniel.

Wind moaned. But he didn't think there was any wind outside.

I'm going to take you, Daniel. We'll be good friends.

He knew then that his mind was indeed going. If not for the recurring bouts of fear, which brought enough terror to dwarf any other consideration, the irregularities might have kept him in a constant state of anxiety. When exhaustion forced him into unconsciousness, the fear woke him, screaming into the tape.

He told himself that profuse sweating would only speed his dehydration, but he was powerless to control his glands. And eventually his bladder.

Heather's release provided him with a measure of absolution that helped him endure the mind-numbing fear, the cramps that locked his muscles after the first seven or eight hours. And the knowledge that he was going to die in this cellar deep in the woods of Oklahoma.

But his dying act had been to save Heather. The old cliché, *What goes around comes around,* came to mind. The pain he'd caused her over the years was now visiting him, condensed and purified so that instead of paining his heart through many sleepless nights, it was ravaging him through one week of horror.

The fear in her eyes when he'd pulled the bag from her head refused to move from his memory. Misted eyes, peeled back because she knew that Eve was behind her, biding his time.

But Daniel had seen something else in her eyes. He'd seen anguish. *Why, Daniel? Why did you tie me in this chair? Why did you leave me? Why did you let my heart break?*

He considered the possibility that Eve had made a mistake in breaking from his routine—taking then releasing Heather, the first victim he'd done so with. He'd hoped it was a mistake, tried to nurture that hope.

But in the end, the hope collapsed on itself. Eve had taken and released Heather only to lure his first Adam. If Heather did manage to shed new light on the case and bring agents back with her in an attempt to rescue him, he had no doubt that it would end badly.

Eve was working in ways that reduced FBI prowess to an amateur effort.

Daniel shifted again, tried to ease a cramp in his lower back. The cellar was cold. It was summer outside, but the earth underground felt like winter, another trick played by his decaying mind.

He'd long ago given up the spiral attempts to figure

out what was happening. Why so much fear? How had he been directed by his mind to head *southhhhhh*? Why was Eve now calling him Adam?

Actually, he had the answer to that last one. Eve was going to kill Daniel, his first Adam, the same way he killed his Eves. By infecting him with a disease that attacked the protective layer around the brain, and in so doing re-create the fall of Adam and Eve. The loss of innocence.

Eve was taking the lives of others as an atonement for his own sin. Daniel didn't know that as a matter of fact, but he knew enough to be sure it was at least close.

Either way, Daniel would die. Either way, Heather would live. And good for her. She did indeed deserve to live after what he'd put her through.

The breath from his nostrils fogged. Cold.

He heard the breathing behind him then—not the boy's whisper but a man's lungs at work, like bellows.

Daniel twisted to look at the doorway. Eve stood looking at him, hands loose at his sides, eyes unblinking. He was handsome, squared jaw, large with strength, not fat. Green dungarees. The plaid shirt was gone, replaced by a black pullover.

Eve walked over and unwound the tape around his head, freeing his mouth. "You can drink."

He pushed the bowl close, and Daniel lowered his head into the cool water. He drank deep, grateful despite the circumstances.

When he finished, Eve unlatched the chain, hauled Daniel to his feet, and walked him to the metal chair, which he'd placed by the bloodstained table.

All without a word.

Daniel sat still, but Eve made no move to fasten him to the chair. His arms were bound tight behind his back—he wasn't going anywhere, not in his current condition.

Eve stepped behind him, then touched his hair with his fingers. "You call me Eve?"

Daniel said yes, but it came out hoarse and indiscernible. He cleared his throat. "Yes."

"My name isn't Eve. My name is Alex Price."

The name wasn't familiar. But Daniel hardly cared. He cared far more about the fact that Alex Price had given up his name because the information would die with him.

"But I know where Eve is," Alex Price said.

Daniel cleared more phlegm from his throat. "Who is she?"

Alex moved in front of him, studying him. "You came to save Heather. I knew you would. You're a good man, Daniel Clark."

"You're going to kill me?"

"No. No, I hope I don't have to. I haven't killed any of them."

"But Eve has," Daniel said.

Alex walked to one side, eyes fixed on Daniel's face. "I studied psychology once. On my own. Enough to earn a master's if I'd gone through all the dreary paperwork. I read your books. Mostly inaccurate. And I should know."

"Maybe. Unless your point of view is bent." Daniel looked up at the dark timber directly in front of him. "You grew up here, didn't you?"

"Yes. Eve's Holy Coven. That's my mother's religion. Not my real mother. Alice. She tied me and my sister to that table and punished us every dark moon."

He said it so nonchalantly, not what Daniel had expected.

"Now you've become her. Or are you hating her? It's always one or the other."

"I've become her," Alex said, just as naturally. "Do you believe in the devil, Dr. Clark?"

It occurred to Daniel that they were already in the killer's rite. This was probably how Eve approached all of his kills. He should at least go through the motions. Keep the man talking, buy some time.

"It depends what you mean by the devil."

The corner of Alex's lips curved gently upward. "No, of course you don't."

"I do believe in the devil, Alex. Just not the one you believe in. Does that make me wrong?"

"I didn't always believe, you know. I was wrong."

"Then maybe I am wrong."

"You don't mind finding out?" Alex asked.

"Finding out what?"

"If you're right or if you're wrong."

The fear hadn't returned since Alex's entry. Neither had the sounds or the odor of urine. The whole scene somehow seemed perfectly natural to Daniel, which was in and of itself a bit discomforting.

Daniel stared at Alex, unclear if he was expected to respond.

"Do you think I'm a man of my word?" Alex asked.

Considering the man's profile, Daniel had little doubt. "Yes," he said.

"Then if I swore not to kill you, you would believe me."

"I suppose I would."

"Eve wants to make you a friend," Alex said.

"I know. I spoke to Eve."

"Will you allow it?"

"I think I already have, Alex. I think we all make friends with our Eves."

"Not the inner child. I know we all have memories and influences that shaped us during our formative years. I'm not talking about that Eve, as you call it."

"Then what, the devil?"

"No. The boy you met in the box. The one who speaks to me, who led you down here."

A chill washed down Daniel's back, then was gone. It sounded so innocent, this talk of devils.

"So you won't have a problem asking Eve to become your friend to."

Daniel hesitated.

"If you do, I'll give you my promise not to harm you in any way," Alex said. "I'll leave you here and go on about my business. Your friends will find you and you can continue going about your business. Hunting me. With more than enough new information to make my life difficult."

So this was it. A deal of sorts. Oddly unnerving despite being so childish.

"But you have to invite Eve into your heart," Alex said. "Ask him to be your friend. Tell him that you love him and will let him make his home with you."

Hearing it framed in those words brought a tremor to Daniel's fingers. Whatever Alex Price was or had been, whatever experiences had brought him to this place, he was a true believer in the power of evil.

And he was likely insane.

But what choice did Daniel really have? He could refuse, for no good reason other than a sudden unreasonable fear. Or he could accept, face the consequences of another horrifying dream perhaps, and hope that Alex would keep his word and leave him.

Then again, Alex had already insisted that he himself would not harm Daniel. Eve would do that. If Daniel refused to play his game, what harm would come to him?

"No," he said. "I won't invite Eve into my heart."

"Because you know that he would kill you. Because you know that everything you've ever written on the subject is nonsense. Is that why?"

"No."

"Then you have nothing to fear. If you refuse, I will be forced to leave you alone with Eve. The boy will eventually talk you into doing what he wants. By then you'll be mentally worthless."

Meaning Eve, his own mind, would eventually get the best of him. The argument made perfect sense.

"If you insist," Daniel said.

"No, I'm not insisting. It's your decision, not mine."

"You're forcing me. You have a proverbial gun to my head."

"You're saying that the idea of inviting Eve into your heart frightens you? That you wouldn't do it under normal circumstances? That you do believe in hell?"

Insane, but intelligent.

"No, I'm not saying that."

"Then don't pretend you'd only invite Eve if forced."

Daniel knew he'd been backed into a corner, not by Alex's arguments but by his own, made in a hundred lectures. Alex was only asking Daniel to back up his own claim that there was no substance to faith in or allegiance to the supernatural.

Still, the whole business trumped Daniel's poise. "The boy I met when I died—he's a figment of my imagination. An image formed by my subconscious in a moment of crisis. You've heard of chasing the dragon."

"I don't want to talk about hallucinogenic drugs," Alex said. "It bores me. I want you to decide. Just satisfy a deluded psychopath. Invite Eve to be with you, and I will leave you alone with him."

"With myself then."

"So be it. Yes or no."

Daniel looked around the cellar and saw what he expected to see: a root cellar dug a century ago, supported by railroad ties. A table formed of wood, used to feed Alice's sick religion. Packed earth underfoot.

Nothing else.

No devils or boys with black teeth who called themselves Eve.

He looked into Alex Price's eyes.

"Yes."

THIRTY-ONE

NIGHT HAD FALLEN AND the traffic had thinned. A single porch light brightened the front yard of the old white home off Vine Street in Burbank. The grass was thinned to dirt in spots, and the short hedge that bordered the lawn was in need of a trim. A two- or three-bedroom house, at best. This was the life that Catholic priests retired to?

Priests like Father Robert Seymour, anyway.

She made her way to the front door, stepping over patches of grass that had forced their way through the cracks in the concrete sidewalk. A rather hasty Internet search on Father Seymour had turned up more than she would have guessed.

He'd served at Our Lady of the Covenant, a Catholic church on the south side of Pasadena, for fifteen years. Apart from serving on a number of boards, he demonstrated no political aspirations or interest in bettering his

position in the church. He was a simple man—a bit of a
legend on a number of blogs, known for his humility and
wisdom, particularly in his later years, after he returned
from an extended visit to France in 1992. He had authored
a book about that time titled *Dance of the Dead*.

Something profound had happened in France. What
exactly, Heather didn't know. The references were
oblique, and his book was obscure. Evidently he'd gone
to France to study under the tutelage of a famous bishop.
But he'd been forced to step down from the program due
to personal reasons. The year of study became a yearlong
sabbatical, during which Father Seymour recovered from
the effects of an exorcism ritual in which he'd assisted.

Heather knocked on the door and stepped back. She'd
seen pictures of a young Seymour on the Internet; the
man who opened the door not only looked much older,
but thinner.

"Hello, Heather. Come in, dear. Please, come in."

"Father Seymour?"

"You didn't expect someone so young and vibrant?
Come in."

She stepped past him. He had gaunt cheeks, but the
lines etched into his face seemed to smile.

"Sit." He ushered her to an old Queen Anne chair
opposite a brass-rimmed coffee table. The room was
small, decorated with period pieces that had undoubtedly
been collected and passed down. An old black piano sat
against one wall.

"Do you play?" Heather asked.

"When it gets too quiet," he said, pouring two cups of
tea. "I assume you won't refuse a cup?"

"Thank you. Are you alone here?"

"No." Father Seymour handed her one of the white china cups. "But without other people, it sometimes feels like it."

She glanced around the room, half expecting to see a ghost watching them, then smiled at her own foolishness.

"So you say that Alex Trane has taken your husband?"

Heather returned his gaze. Staring over the china cup with bright green vines painted around the rim. Discussing Daniel's abduction over tea.

The cup clinked against the saucer in her other hand, suddenly unable to hold steady. She set it down.

"It's going to be okay, darling. If I can help you, I will. Tell me everything."

She sat back and crossed her legs. In the space of a few minutes, the father had managed to earn her whole-hearted trust. She'd never actually talked to a priest. A Protestant pastor now and then, mostly in her teens. Yet looking into this man's smoke-blue eyes, she knew she could and would tell him anything, everything.

"Have you ever heard of a serial killer known as Eve, Father?"

"Eve. I've read something, yes. Alex Trane is Eve?"

Heather started to tell him about the phone call she'd received from a man she believed was Eve, but Father Seymour stopped her. "Start at the beginning, Heather. The very beginning."

"He's killed sixteen women. It would take awhile just to give you the highlights."

"Alex has killed sixteen women?" Whatever he'd read about the case, it wasn't much.

"Yes."

"Do you want my help?"

"Yes."

"Then tell me everything."

Three days, Eve had said. They weren't going to make it.

"He's going to kill my husband, Father."

"Then I suggest you talk quickly."

RECITING THE EVENTS as Heather knew them only took an hour, and that long only because the father kept stopping her with questions, mostly about Eve's precise words and Daniel's near-death experiences. Father Seymour sat through the details of several victims, then asked her to summarize the gruesome details. He didn't need to hear the same thing over and over, he said.

So she did. The gender of the victims, the fact that each had been found underground, the nature of the disease that had killed them. The name *Eve* written over each victim. Daniel's entire profile of the killer.

But it was the words Eve had used that interested Seymour more than anything. He stared at her with glazed eyes as she haltingly told him about her encounter with Eve in the root cellar.

Father Seymour held up his hand. "Adam? He called Daniel Adam?"

"Yes."

"So he's re-creating the birth of evil, proving that evil has true power, as with Eve in the garden. Something he rejected in seminary."

Heather wiped a tear from under her right eye. "We have to find him, Father. And to do that we have to know where he grew up. He's there, I'm almost sure of it. He's holding Daniel in the same place his mother hurt him as a child. For all we know, he's already infected Daniel with the disease. We don't have much time."

"Have you considered the possibility that it's not a disease?"

"We have solid medical data that identifies the cause of death. A form of meningitis."

"A form of?"

"Yes, well, it's not certain. A new strain."

"Then it may have another explanation," Seymour said.

"Not one identifiable to the medical community."

"And what would the medical community have to say about a woman born blind who can describe objects in a room after dying?"

"Nothing."

"No, my dear. They would say it is impossible, never mind that it happened."

"You're saying it's not a disease?"

Father Seymour stood and walked to the bookcase behind Heather, then returned with a thick leather-bound book. He set it down and withdrew a black-and-white picture, which he laid on the table.

"What do you see?"

The picture showed the side of a woman in a dress, lying on a couch. Her arm, stretched out by her side, was lumpy and badly bruised. A cut by her elbow was bleeding.

"A woman with a disfigured arm," Heather said.

"I didn't take the picture, but I was there. Her name was Martha. She was twenty-six years old and lived in

Monte Carlo. Twenty minutes before this picture was taken, her arm was as normal as yours. The cut on her elbow was made by a book that had been sitting on a table ten feet away."

Heather knew where he was headed.

"What would the medical data lead you to conclude in regard to Martha's disfigurement?"

"I don't know."

"She spent a week in the hospital after the exorcism. The evidence showed that she'd suffered some kind of bad fall or been smitten by one of several rare diseases that result in heavy internal bleeding and bruising. It's one of three exorcisms I've witnessed—I have no desire for a repeat performance. Father Gerald, the attending exorcist, spent two months recovering."

Heather looked at the picture again and tried to imagine the events Father Seymour was suggesting. She couldn't.

"I'm not sure this helps us find Daniel," she said.

"It helps us understand Alex," he said, sliding the picture back into the book. "I'm not saying that each of his victims didn't die of some rare form of meningitis, as you assume. But I am suggesting that Alex himself may be drawing on more than medicine. You yourself said that he claims that Eve, not he, is doing the killing."

"He's mentally unstable, Father."

"I doubt it. The Alex I knew was very sane. I saw the signs back then, and honestly, I've prayed more than once that this day would never come. I find myself culpable."

"I still don't see how any of this leads us any closer—"

He swiveled one hand in dismissal. Frankly, I suspect that most cases of possession are psychosomatic

expressions of human evil. I don't know. But there are
cases that defy anything science can throw at them. And
only a few ever get flushed out."

"I'm sorry, Father, I just..."

"Trust me, the Roman Catholic Church has no interest in encountering or publicizing any of this. Most
bishops find the whole business an embarrassment, for
good reason—most people find it preposterous. But even
those bishops have difficulty ignoring the evidence once
presented with it."

She found his methodical, reasoned explanation fascinating. "And?"

"In most cases evil's encroachment, so called possession, is a gradual process, hardly understood by the
victim. Contrary to what many assume, most victims are
intelligent. But their possession usually revolves around
a single fixation."

"Eve's fixation, that's what you're after."

He frowned. "Find Alex's fixation and you find
the man. Isn't that the mantra of every good forensic
psychologist?"

"We *have* found him. His name, his history, his
motivations—"

"No, not his name or his history. There is no Alex
Trane. I know, because I've searched. They came to us
with a story about losing their parents in an automobile
accident, but there was no accident, not in the police files
anyway."

"They?"

"Alex and his sister, Jessica. Two wounded souls with
a hidden past that they tried to dismiss. But Eve has found
them and made them his own. At least Alex."

Heather stood and paced, rubbing the right side of her neck. Regardless of the veracity of Seymour's suggestion that Eve was some devil haunting Alex, the priest had just opened a new can of worms. She couldn't help thinking that somewhere in that can lay a clue to the location of the root cellar.

"Alex's fixation...He was expelled for his arguments against faith. Do you have anything he wrote?"

"I think I know his fixation," the father said. "But, yes, I asked for his papers. They're in a shoe box somewhere around here."

He stood and started for a coat closet near the door.

"And what is his fixation?" Heather asked.

He opened the closet door and rummaged around. "It was here..." he mumbled, then withdrew empty-handed. Headed for the kitchen.

"What was it?" Heather asked again.

Father Seymour stepped from sight and began opening and closing cabinets. "His fixation?"

"Yes."

"Here it is." He came around the corner holding a brown boot box. "What's the one thing Alex keeps going back to?"

She thought a moment. "Eve."

"And who was Eve? Whose holy coven?"

"Eve's," she said. "His mother."

"His mother, whom he hated. Whom he was forced to either kill or abandon, but whom he could not escape. What was it he said to you in the courthouse? 'They took me from my daddy, my sister, my priest'? Who separated Alex from his father, his sister, his ambition to become a priest?"

"Eve did."

"Eve, his mother. His mother—"

"Took him from his father."

"His real father," Father Seymour said.

Heather felt her pulse surge. "Alex and Jessica were kidnapped."

"I've been living with Alex and Jessica for fifteen years"—he tapped his head—"up here. After hearing what you had to say tonight, it's the only thing that makes sense. A lot of it."

Heather dug into her pocket for her phone and called Lori, who picked up on the first ring.

"This is Lori."

"He was kidnapped. Trane isn't his real name. He was kidnapped and changed his name."

She could practically hear Lori's mind spinning. "The priest knew that?"

"Not exactly. That's his guess after hearing me out. Why?"

"He's right, Trane is a falsified name. No record of Alex Trane before 1983. He was taken from his daddy, you said. Brit's running a systemwide search for abduction cases involving a brother and sister going back fifty years." She paused. "Smart priest."

"This could be it. How long will it take?"

"If it's an FBI case, not long. If they have to make requests from other jurisdictions, longer. And this is all assuming there was a kidnapping, of course."

"I hope so. Call me."

"I will."

She closed the phone. Father Seymour stood holding the box, eyes fixed on her. He held the box out.

"It's got ten or so of his more memorable papers, some poetry, notes, et cetera. If you believed, I might warn you that reading them could tempt you to toss your faith out the window. I don't know how it works for Alex, but Eve isn't his only fixation. Somehow all tied up in Eve is the knowledge of good and evil, belief in the supernatural, God, Lucifer, the snake."

Heather took the box.

"I would be careful," he said. "Don't let that snake bite you."

"Thank you, Father. I'm very grateful."

He crossed to the bookshelf. "One request, if you don't mind."

"If I can."

"You can and I insist." Father Seymour withdrew a book and handed it to her. "*Hostage to the Devil*" by Malachi Martin. Please read it. Read it soon."

She took the book and looked at it politely.

"I know what you're thinking," he said. "Trust me. Read it."

THIRTY-TWO

IF EXHAUSTION HADN'T overwhelmed Heather, she would have read all of the pages spread out on her kitchen table last night. But the concepts were heavy, and no amount of determination could keep her tired mind focused after several hours.

Heather walked around the table in the morning, coffee in hand, staring at the stacks of pages. The clock on the wall read seven fifteen. No call from either Brit or Lori yet.

She'd covered half of Alex's papers, mostly skeptical philosophical arguments that undermined the supernatural with a clarity that would have impressed even Daniel, she thought. They were arguments he himself had made, though Alex's were perhaps slightly less pretentious. And yet made with compelling confidence.

None of it was particularly new to Heather—most of

it boiled down to existentialism recast in fresh language, even now, fifteen years after their writing.

She sat down and picked up the next paper, five dog-eared pages titled simply "God" in small print. By Alex Trane. The body of the paper was written in larger, more traditional print.

Heather read the paper quickly. Same tone as his others but in more direct terms. A layered argument for the nonexistence of God. She was having a hard time concentrating on the words. A month ago the papers would have been gold in her hands. What Daniel could have pulled from them...

She set them down and let her mind wander to the root cellar. Eve, now known to them as Alex Trane, would have returned last night. The man had been gentle with her, but then he'd expected to release her.

No. No, he'd never left evidence of force. The disease had done his dirty work. This disease that Father Seymour suggested might be a different kind of disease altogether.

The doorbell chimed, a soft *bong* that Daniel had chosen over the typical *ding-dong* that resonated through most houses. "A house of peace needs a mellow bell," he said.

Lori stood on the front steps. She'd changed into jeans and a green shirt, but she didn't look like she'd slept.

"Morning, Heather."

"Come in. You look awful."

"I feel awful."

"You drove all the way down?" Heather asked. "Of course you did, but why?"

Lori closed the door behind her. "I shouldn't have, I know. I told Brit I would last night, but—"

"Last night? What, you found him?"

"Daniel? I wish it were that simple."

"What? Come here." She took Lori's hand and gave it a tug, towing her down the hall, toward the living room.

"Now tell me."

Lori stared at the kitchen table. "What're those?"

"Some papers I told you about. I'll get to them, mostly rubbish. Tell me."

Lori spoke without sitting. "The good news is, they found a case involving two kidnapped children in 1968, about the right age. Right names. Alex and Jessica Price were taken from their home in Arkansas. An extensive search came up empty."

"Alex Price."

"Son to Lorden and Betty Price. Both deceased."

"When did you find that out?"

"About eleven."

"Eleven? That was eight hours ago!" Heather sat back and crossed her arms. "So give me the bad news."

"The bad news is, there is no more news. His name is Alex Price. He was abducted with his sister, Jessica Price, when they were young children. They emerged in 1983 as Alex and Jessica Trane, then both disappeared in 1991, never to be heard of again."

"Regardless, we need to find Jessica Price."

Lori picked up one of the pages. "So these are his writings."

"Yes." Heather sighed. "Mostly philosophical bantering."

"I didn't realize there was so much," Lori said, walking along the table. "It should be at the lab for analysis."

"To give us what, his fingerprints? We have them."

"His mind."

"Lovely, Alex Price's precious little freaked-out mind!" She closed her eyes. "Sorry, I'm just a bit frustrated. Take them if you want."

Lori walked behind her, touched her shoulder gently, then slid into the seat at the head of the table.

"Have you been through all of it?"

"I've organized them, as you can see. These papers I've read, cover to cover." She indicated the pages to her left.

"These?" Lori picked up a stack of loose-leaf pages in one corner.

"Poetry, handwritten notes, miscellaneous stuff."

"Poetry, huh? You have more coffee?"

HEATHER REREAD THE GOD paper, energized by Lori's enthusiasm to give the pages one pass before getting them to the analytical team at the field office.

Lori pored over the handwritten notes with wide eyes, making occasional comments, mostly regarding Alex's tendency to repeatedly return to the same subjects. God and Lucifer, which he equated with psychology and parapsychology.

He spoke of his nightmares in his poetry, and Lori took her time with thirteen pages that she set aside, referring to them as his poetic musings.

"Listen to this: 'The boy comes at night, whispering lies in my head; The kingdom of light, but it's darkness in my bed. Take the tape off, take the tape off, I want to hear you scream, traitor, traitor, you, mother, mother, mother—'"

"Tape…" Heather's mind spun back to what Lori had told her about Daniel's nightmares. "You said Daniel…"

Lori just looked at her.

"Maybe the father isn't so crazy."

"Father Seymour? About what?"

Heather told her about the exorcism rite the priest claimed to have witnessed in the south of France. Hearing herself repeat the story in the quiet morning with Alex's papers strewn in front of them was even more unsettling than hearing it from the priest.

The papers in Lori's hands shuddered as the pathologist listened in rapt attention.

Heather finished and looked down at the table. Outside, Santa Monica was working its way through another weekday, oblivious to the notion that evil might stalk in the ways described by Father Seymour. A jet hummed high above. Panther, a black Labrador three doors down, was barking at a passing car again. The clock on the wall ticked, unnoticed in all but the quietest moments.

This was Santa Monica, a life of plastic and concrete and metal and a billion electronic circuits that pulled it all together in a way that made them all watch in wonder.

But Daniel...Daniel was in an old abandoned root cellar that smelled of urine and had the words *Eve's Holy Coven* etched into tar-covered railroad ties.

"Heather?"

She looked up. Lori was staring at a piece of paper in her hands.

"What?"

"I think I just found something."

"What?"

"He wrote a poem in pencil. Then erased it."

"And?"

She read it in an unsteady voice.

In the Brown grass the serpent waits;
Alice of wonderland the children takes.
An apple to feed Eve's lust;
Or thirty lashes will do.

Lori let out a short gasp. Heather set the page down and looked up expectantly. What?

Lori blinked. "Eve's lust…"

Heather slid the page over. "More than that. He's capitalized some words. The names."

The words *Brown, Alice,* and *Eve's* were capitalized and slightly darker, even erased. "'Alice of wonderland the children takes.' You're saying that Alice is Eve."

"Brown Alice. Or Alice Brown…"

Heather quickly read the poem again. Thinking in terms of names, the meaning seemed obvious. Alice Brown was the snake in the garden, preying on innocent children. Eve would pay for her sin by taking thirty lashes.

Or making a sacrificial offering, take the lashes for her.

Heather stood. Paced, thinking frantically. "We can't tell Brit. Not yet."

"Heather—"

"Listen to me, you know very well that if this is true and we do locate this farm registered to someone named Brown, that Brit will take a team down and Daniel will die!" The words came out in a torrent. "They have no idea what we're up against!"

"And you do?"

"I believe Alex Price!" she screamed. She'd gone over the edge, but she knew of no other way to make Lori listen. "That's my husband down there! Now, all I'm saying is that we take a deep breath. We're the only ones who know."

"And if we do find Alice Brown or whatever her real name is? Then what?"

Heather set her jaw firm. Ground her molars. "Then I go. Alone."

"No way."

"You made me a promise!"

"You were upset."

"I'm upset now!" She took Lori's arm, pleading. "You know he'll kill Daniel."

"You're a lawyer, not a field agent."

"If he wanted me dead, he would have killed me. He won't kill me, he's not like that. I know him!"

Lori stared at her, face flushed.

"I'm begging you."

Lori was right. Heather wasn't an agent, but the attorney in her had laid out a strong case, and Lori was having difficulty putting up a defense.

Slowly her shoulders relaxed. The fight fell from her face.

"I hope you're right."

Heather released her arm. "Don't waste your hope on me. Let's pray this Alice Brown wasn't a squatter."

THIRTY-THREE

ONE OF EVE'S THREE days was gone by the time Heather boarded United flight 465 from Los Angeles International Airport to Oklahoma City at eleven o'clock that Tuesday morning.

How Lori kept the information from Brit, she didn't know or care. Only that public land records indicated that a small plot of land deep in the woods of southern Oklahoma had indeed been owned by an Alice Brown between the years 1958 and 1993. The state had taken possession of the abandoned claim in 2003.

She sat in a window seat, staring out at the clear blue sky, one leg crossed over the other, feeling like a wrung-out dishrag. Looking like one. The two seats next to her were empty, and the teenage rocker seated across the aisle kept glancing at her. But she was beyond caring.

At thirty thousand feet, the world appeared serene and

perfectly ordered. But down there on the brown surface, evil lurked. The events that had led to its exposure in her and Daniel's lives still struck her as something taken from a mythic horror tale, disconnected from reality. The other fifty or so passengers aboard the 737 occupied themselves with novels and iPods, or chatted quietly among themselves about mundane matters.

Did any of them have a clue about the nature of the Eves of this world? If so, the knowledge hid in the deepest folds of their minds like a latent virus, working in anonymity.

Someone was talking to her. She turned her head and stared at the flight attendant, who'd rolled a cart up the aisle. "I'm sorry?"

"Would you like a drink?"

"A drink? Water."

She put the bottle of spring water in the seat pocket without cracking the lid and pulled out the book Father Seymour had given her. *Hostage to the Devil.* The author, Malachi Martin, a former Jesuit and professor at the Vatican's Pontifical Biblical Institute, had assembled five documented cases of possession. A serious academic book highly regarded by the *New York Daily News* and *Newsweek,* among others. Why hadn't she heard of this? Or had she and dismissed it?

She thumbed through the pages, then began reading a case that caught her attention: "Father Bones and Mister Natch."

She soon lost herself in the meticulously laid-out case of a wayward priest.

The author seemed to suggest that most exorcists were profoundly affected by their battles with the forces they encountered and were rarely able to direct more than a few exorcisms during their lifetimes, most of which took weeks to set up and perform.

She flipped back and read another account. The exorcism was taped.

The Voice, as the author referred to it, was a layered mess that came from all sides of the room, spoke before lips moved in several octaves at once, spoke backward and forward at once. Only by reversing the tape could some of what was said become clear. A human impossibility. Absurd. All of it, preposterous.

Heather checked the front and back of the book repeatedly, reviewed the author's credentials. If she didn't know better, she would assume this to be a work of fiction.

But it wasn't. Rather, it was simple documentation. Published by HarperSanFrancisco, 1992. The author a *New York Times* bestseller. Enough to curl her toes.

Heather closed the book, mind awash in apprehension as the plane made its final approach into Oklahoma City. The world she'd read about wasn't remotely similar to her own. Or was it? If anyone should identify with Malachi Martin's detailed analysis, she should, having crawled into Eve's mind these past months.

There was no proselytizing here, just an objective reporting of cases that had been authenticated by the tape recorders, and the police officers, and the psychologists, and the clergy present at each case.

Heather deplaned, found her way to the Hertz counter, collected her Ford Explorer, and set out on the route Lori had laid out for her. She called in, eager to hear a familiar voice.

Lori answered, high-strung. "You're there?"

"I'm driving. Anything new?"

"I have to give them the papers, Heather. I can't with-hold this much longer."

"I'm almost there. Just give me four or five hours. If I haven't called in, give it to Brit. I've come this far. You can't turn me over now."

They both knew she was right, and the silence that followed spoke clearly enough.

"I can't believe I let you go down alone," Lori said. "He said no FBI. Maybe I should call it in to the state police."

"We already talked about this. He won't kill me, Lori."

"And if you're wrong?"

"It's a risk I'm taking on my own. Daniel deserves at least that much."

This was all a way to process emotion, Heather knew. They'd already talked through every eventuality.

"Is there anything else I can do?"

Heather looked out the side window at a passing corn-field. "No."

"Call me when you get closer."

"I will." She hung up.

Thoughts of devils and exorcists and the battles between them faded quickly, replaced by a more imme-diate concern: a serial killer named Alex Price, who'd murdered sixteen women in the name of his mother's twisted religion.

An image of what she would find if she was able to locate that root cellar played through her mind like an old black-and-white movie that had lost its frame and kept jumping off track.

She would find Daniel, bound to a chair either with

Alex Price or alone, sweating as the disease slowly overtook his body. Three days. One had passed. If caught early enough, even the most aggressive strain of meningitis could be turned back with the large doses of antibiotics Lori had given her to inject into Daniel's bloodstream.

She'd lost an hour during the three-hour flight. It was close to six before she realized she was almost there. The sun hung like an orange on the western horizon. The two-lane highway she'd been on for the past hour ran a straight course through flat, barren land interrupted with occasional patches of trees.

She approached the cutoff and slowed. Stopped at a gravel road that turned south. She checked the map. This was it.

Heather turned onto the road.

The miles passed quickly. It occurred to her that she hadn't seen any houses for some time. Or vehicles. She checked her cell phone and saw that she'd lost coverage. Lori would have to sit tight—she wasn't about to turn back and hunt for a signal. Maybe she'd reacquire one soon.

But no, she wouldn't, would she? Alex Price knew what he was doing.

A new thought drifted through her mind. What if Alex had told her about the three days and warned off the FBI not because he wanted to be left alone, but because he wanted her to return? Alone.

If so, why had he released her? No, that didn't make sense. But Eve was too smart not to expect her return. There was something else here she couldn't finger.

The flat land gave way to trees, and the trees blocked the sinking sun. She was alone, rolling down an abandoned gravel road without any way to contact the outside world. Grass grew down the middle and on each side of the road.

Close, she should be close.

Her palms felt slimy. Blowing on them didn't help much, but it cooled her fingers. Her tires thumped over a cattle guard. She flipped on her lights, but they made no visible difference in the gray dusk.

The clearing with the dilapidated house dawned on her so suddenly that she gave a short gasp and jerked the wheel, swerving, then correcting. She slammed the brakes and jerked to a crunching halt.

Blood thumped through her veins. She gripped the wheel tight and stared at the compound in front of her.

The old house rose from weeds ahead on her left; a ramshackle shed to her right. No sign of any activity. This was it? Heather eased off the brake and rolled slowly forward. Into the center of the clearing, nearing a rosebush on the left.

Her eyes fixed on the rise. She couldn't see any opening, but it was the best natural location for a root cellar. She stopped the car again and this time turned off the engine.

Leaving the keys in the ignition, she took her handbag and stepped out. The first thing she heard was the crickets in the forest.

The second was the silence, if indeed silence was something to be heard. This kind was, a heavy absence of life beyond the crickets. The sound of a graveyard. The thin sound of death.

Perfect stillness surrounded by the shrill screams of insects in hiding.

She left the door open and walked forward, each step one more away from the car's relative safety. Daniel was in that mound of earth ahead? She stopped and scanned the compound again. Nothing moved, not even the tall grass.

Yet she couldn't shake the certainty that someone, something, was staring at her from the trees.

She hurried forward, fighting back panic. Panting now. Rounding the rise.

The hole in the ground looked like a framed throat, a large mouth into a massive ant mound. She pulled up hard, half expecting to see a stream of insects pouring past the door, which rested half-open.

She walked over the uneven earth leading up to the root cellar, ground she herself had crossed less than two days earlier with a bag over her head.

Fear crowded her mind. She knew that there was only one way to do this, and so she shoved her last reservations aside, yanked the door open, and spun into the subterranean chamber.

Foggy vapor billowed from her mouth. The cold hit her like a wall of ice and everything in her line of sight slowed. She stared at the corner in which she'd last seen Daniel. Flames from a torch where she'd been held licked the air. Thick black timbers ran along the wall. All the same.

But Daniel wasn't there.

The ground smelled of feces and urine. She pivoted to her right and stared at the end of the cellar, where the light barely parted deep shadows.

Daniel sat on a metal chair. Hands taped behind his back. No tape on his legs.

A small gunnysack covered his head.

"Daniel?"

Her eyes darted around the cellar. No sign of Eve. Alex Price.

Heather crossed the barren earth between her and Daniel in five long steps and pulled up at the sight of his body. He was wearing the flannel shirt that Eve had been wearing, she saw. Under that shirt, his body was shivering.

"Daniel?" Heather set her bag on the floor, careful not to break the syringes inside. "It's okay, sweetie, it's okay. We're going to get you out of here." She was aware that she sounded no more confident than a trembling mouse, but she wasn't sure he could hear her anyway.

She had to get the medication into him. All three, Lori had said.

She reached up and pulled the bag off his head. "It's okay, sweetie. It's going to be..."

Heather never made it past the *be*. She'd never actually seen a human body being ravaged by meningitis before, and wasn't prepared for the grotesque sight facing her now.

His eyes were closed. Not clenched.

The skin of his face was pale, bloodless. Stretched tight over his cheekbones and nose. Pulling his lips flat against his teeth.

But it was the slight twist on his face that kept Heather momentarily frozen. The left side of his face was skewed, higher than the right side, as if strings had been attached to the left corner of his mouth and cheek and were tugging them up toward his temple. The effect made the cheekbone under his skin look as if it had been lifted slightly upward.

Not a single wrinkle on his face.

Heather pulled herself from the horror of seeing him in such pain, grabbed the bag, and pulled out the first syringe with trembling hands.

"Hold on, just hold on." She yanked the protective cap off the needle, squirted some of the clear fluid out the end to clear it of any trapped air. She didn't have the presence of mind to find a vein, so she jabbed the needle into his biceps and eased the antibiotic into his quivering muscle.

Daniel showed no sign that he was aware of the needle, much less her.

"Hold on, hold on...It's going to be okay, sweetie."

She dropped the syringe on the ground, fumbled with the second, and injected its full contents into the same arm. Then repeated the same with the third, this one filled with the adrenaline Lori had insisted she use if she found Daniel unresponsive.

The whole procedure took her less than a minute. She tossed the last syringe and dug for her knife.

Except for her own heavy breathing and the soft crackle of flames from the torch behind her, the chamber remained still.

Heather scrambled behind him and slashed at the tape that bound his wrists. She nicked his skin, deep enough to expose white flesh. The cut did not bleed, but she was too frantic to consider whether meningitis prevented the blood from flowing.

His arms swung free and hung below the seat.

He was loose. With enough antibiotic to kill the strongest strains of the meningitis now working its way through his system.

"Okay. Okay, one step at a time." Speaking to herself. "It's all going to work out."

She had no idea how she was going to lift his dead weight, but the need to get him out of this tomb now raged through her mind.

Heather stuffed the knife back in her handbag and turned back to Daniel. He hadn't moved. But his face had.

The grotesque contortion was gone. His face now appeared relaxed, almost boyish. And his shaking had eased to a very slight tremor. The drug was working.

She knelt in front of him and rubbed his right arm. "Can you hear me?"

Still no response.

She whispered, begging. "Please, Daniel, I need you to hear me. We have to get you out of here. Please." She shook him gently. Then with more force.

But he sat board-still. Breathing steady.

Heather sniffed. "Okay..." She leaned forward, pulled his arms over her shoulder, got under his chest, and heaved him up. She staggered under his limp weight, had to bring her full strength to bear to keep from falling backward.

But she had to carry him; it was the only way.

She stood with Daniel draped over her shoulder and turned toward the door. Still no sign of Eve. Maybe he'd left Daniel to die. It wasn't his normal way, but Daniel was his first Adam. Maybe they were looking at a whole new pattern here. Maybe he'd left, not trusting that the FBI wouldn't find him.

She staggered forward and made it halfway to the exit before remembering her bag. She'd have to leave it. Retrieving it would mean putting—

Daniel's body tightened like a coil and spun off of her shoulder with enough force to pop out of her grip. He slammed into a timber three feet above her head and fell to the earth, face-first.

Heather yelped and jumped back. Her first thought was that the adrenaline had kicked in.

But then Daniel pushed himself to his feet, walked back to the chair, and sat facing her. For a moment she looked into the same soft blue eyes she'd gazed into for so many years. Then he closed them and sat still, hands on his lap.

"Daniel?"

She cautiously stepped closer.

"Listen, honey, I don't know what he's done to you, but it's me. It's Heather. You've been infected. Your mind's disoriented. You have to let me help you."

A soft giggle echoed through the chamber. She jerked her head around. But there was no child or animal or . . .

The sound trailed off and she turned back to the chair.

And then Daniel calmly opened his eyes and stared at the wall to his left with eyes as black as coal.

Heather forgot to breathe. Daniel was no longer shaking as he'd been when she'd found him. But she was.

His voice whispered like wind through tall grass. "I see you, Heather." His teeth were black.

Heather took a step back, gasping for breath. She knew she couldn't leave him. But the prospect of walking back up to him now terrified her.

"Daniel. Oh, please, Daniel."

"No," he whispered, still fixed on the wall. "So wrong. So, so, so wrong." Slowly he turned his head and stared into her eyes. He whispered with complete sincerity. "Will you be my friend?"

"Oh God, oh Jesus!" Waves of fear crashed through her chest.

"No," Daniel whispered. "No, not God, not the other. Adam."

The unblinking black eyes drilled a hole through her.

"Do you want an apple, Eve?"

A slight smile coiled around Daniel's mouth like a serpent's tail. His voice came sinister and thin. "If you come near me again, you little obsessed whore, I'm going to take your tongue and ram it down your throat. Adam's apple."

She took another step back.

Daniel's coy grin lingered another beat, then before her eyes, his face began to shift, stretched back, slightly askew. He closed his eyes.

Heather stood immobilized by the certain knowledge that she was facing much more and much less than Daniel. She started to hyperventilate.

Daniel's eyelids snapped wide, revealing black eyes. He jerked forward and snarled in a low, crackling voice through twisted lips.

"Leave me!"

Knowing that she couldn't leave Daniel, that she couldn't stay, that she was staring down death's throat into hell itself, Heather lost any remaining capacity for rational thought. She backpedaled, nearly tripped on her heels as she turned, and ran into the descending night.

Crickets screamed. Her lungs worked at her throat like a plunger, desperate to clear choked airways.

She reached the car and hit the side of her head sliding

into the front seat, but she felt no pain. The Explorer fired and she threw the gear shift into drive, then bounced off, and back onto, the gravel road in a tight turn.

She did not slow until she reached the paved road. And then only for the turn. The service bars on her phone reappeared for the first time three miles down the highway.

Heather brought the car to a screeching stop on the shoulder and made the call that would change her understanding of reality forever.

THIRTY-FOUR

HELLO?"

"Father?" Heather knew it was Father Seymour, but she lost the direction of her thoughts. The sound of another human voice had never so overwhelmed her with emotion.

"Father?"

"I'm sorry, who is this?"

Tears slipped from her eyes. "It's Heather. Heather Clark." And then her words rushed out frantically. "I need help. I don't know what to do. I'm...I don't know what I should do—"

"Calm down, darling. You should calm down and take a deep breath. Can you do that?"

She sucked in a long breath, felt her lungs hitch, then tried to calm her jittering hands.

"Okay, now tell me what the problem is."

Where did she begin? "What I tell you's between us, right?"

"Of course." His gentle voice was soothing.

"I read the book on the way down. *Hostage to the Devil*."

He waited for her point, but *she* wasn't even sure what her point was.

"That's good," he finally said.

"Is it possible for someone to become…" The words were so foreign on her tongue, even now. "You know… haunted."

"You know…haunted in a short time. Like a day? The cases I read were gradual, over years."

"It's unusual, but yes. It all depends on the nature of the afflicted party." She could practically hear him trying to read her mind. "It's not the book that has you so upset, is it?"

"And the exorcisms took a long time. Too long."

"The exorcism rite itself usually takes only hours, up to a day. But we're a cautious lot in the Roman Catholic Church. Before any exorcism takes place, the exorcist confers with diocesan authorities. The subject is submitted to a full slate of medical and psychiatric tests to be sure the problem isn't merely clinical or psychological in nature. Most are mentally deranged or psychologically wounded individuals who need a good dose of therapy, not an exorcist. Once it's determined that the subject is indeed afflicted, there are other steps, preparations—"

"I understand. Okay, fine. But none of that's necessary. I mean, if it was pretty obvious that a person had a problem, you could do the…perform this rite immediately, right?"

"You could. It's up to the subject's willingness and—"

"They have to *agree*?"

"But of course, my dear. A man has free will. He can't be unpossessed against his will any more than he can be possessed against his will."

"He has to agree?"

"Yes. Definitely."

"And if he doesn't agree?"

The father paused. "Like a drug addict entering rehab, he must participate."

That could be a problem. That she was even thinking in these terms was unsettling. Then again, it was not nearly as disturbing as the images that the root cellar had planted in her mind.

Father Seymour continued. "Now, please, you didn't call me for a Sunday school lesson. Tell me what happened."

Heather told him the whole story, repeating the most gruesome details repeatedly, as much to convince herself of their veracity as to make sure he understood exactly what had happened.

He remained quiet when she finished.

"So," she said. "Is he? And how's that possible? I mean the eyes, the teeth."

"Did you already forget the photograph I showed you last night?"

"No."

"Well, then. That spirits can affect objects in the natural world is well documented. Now you've seen it yourself."

"It's just...no one would believe me." She slammed the wheel with her palm. "Do you know how crazy this is?"

"You're wrong. Many do believe, or they wouldn't be

frightened of movies on the subject, now, would they? *Jaws* terrified the country because people *knew* that shark attacks were real. The reason so many details of exorcism have become clichés in the movies is because they, too, are real. Any researcher will tell you that. Spiderman, Superman... not frightening, make-believe. But the movie *The Exorcist*? Except for a few details, amazingly accurate. And it terrifies us all. I say all of this because you're right to be terrified, Heather. Frankly, it bothers even me."

"So he is. Right?"

"If what you're telling me is correct—"

"It is. I was there." Her voice was pitched too high.

Father Seymour was slow in responding. "You see how it feels to be doubted?"

"Okay, fine. I need your help, Father. We both know that."

"No sign of Alex?"

"No. Can you come?"

"Me? No, I really don't think I could. But I'm sure with a little digging I could find someone to help you. The FBI—"

"No! That won't work." She knew she would have to call Lori as soon as she hung up, but the FBI couldn't help Daniel now. "You know him, Father. And you know Alex is here."

"Forgive me for sounding crass, dear. I'm very sorry for you, but it seems to me that Daniel was so quickly taken because of a profound unbelief. I imagine he exchanged liberties during one of his near-death experiences. Such a man doesn't strike me as the kind who will change his stripes overnight."

Heather shifted the phone to her other ear. "Yes, my husband is as stubborn as they come. But he knows now, and he's as strong as an ox."

The line was silent.

"You have to come."

"I wish—"

"You have to come because you failed all of us when you mishandled Alex Price. He's killed sixteen women with Eve. You're to blame, at least in part."

It was a low blow, but she knew he couldn't dismiss it.

She continued while he was at a disadvantage. "Look, I know that there's a price to pay in all of this, and it's clear that whatever you saw in France scared the living hell out of you. But this is my husband! I'm begging you!"

Another stretch of silence.

"Father...If Alex Price is right, Daniel will be dead in two days. If the FBI comes, Alex will kill him. For all I know, Alex *wants* you to come. Every killer returns to his roots, and you're a part of his."

Heather hadn't consciously considered that until the words came from her mouth, but she realized then that the idea wasn't preposterous.

"I'll be on the first flight in the morning," he said.

"No, there has to be a red-eye. Please."

"Then tonight, if I can make it. Where will you be staying?"

She looked out at the dark. Imagined Eve walking up behind her car and hauling her back to the root cellar. She slipped the car into drive and pulled onto the deserted road.

"In a well-lit town with a busy bar," she said. "I need to be around people."

"I'll call you. And Heather..."

"Yes."

"I have one requirement of you."

"What?"

"Finish the book.

THIRTY-FIVE

LORI AMES WALKED DOWN the hallway with Brit, mind lost in information she was intentionally withholding. She'd filled her mind with enough justification to hold herself back, but the burden of holding back was growing too large to bear alone, and with both Daniel and Heather now gone, she was only hanging on by a thread.

Heather had called and left a cryptic message. She was waiting for a priest to join her before going in after Daniel. Please don't breathe a word. Numerous calls from Lori had gone unanswered since.

"Heather's gone after him," Brit said. Sweat darkened his shirt under his arms and a brown stain ringed his white collar. The SAIC had only left the field office for several lengthy interviews at the seminary Alex Trane had attended. It hadn't taken them long to infer that Alex

Trane was actually Alex Price, kidnapped with his sister, Jessica, from their home in Arkansas when they were children.

But without the page Lori had withheld from the file they were analyzing, the trail had gone cold.

"You're right, it's what I would do in her situation," Lori said.

"They've either found Eve and don't think they can call it in, or he's taken them both and they can't call it in."

"The first, let's hope."

They entered the conference room, where Agent Joseph Reynolds was bent over several Alex Trane papers. "Anything, Joe?"

"His issues with abandonment are clear, but we'd expect that."

"No suggestion about his life in captivity?" Brit snapped.

"No."

Lori stopped by the door, thinking she couldn't keep up this charade and face these people.

"Give me a minute, Brit." She slipped back into the hall and headed toward the bathroom.

Heather's insistence that Eve would kill Daniel if the FBI approached had kept Lori frozen for the last twenty-four hours, and with good reason. She was right. Armed with the information Lori had, Brit would storm Oklahoma, maybe put an end to Eve and certainly to either Heather or Daniel, possibly all three.

Lori couldn't live with that. But she couldn't live with leaving Daniel and Heather alone to face a fate beyond their control either.

She entered the bathroom. Stared into the mirror.

You're playing with fire.

If anyone other than Heather had demanded to go after Alex without her, she would have flatly refused.

Eve had said three days, and he would honor all three. Two had passed. If Lori didn't hear from Heather by morning, she'd do what she knew she had to do.

"God help you, Heather." She stepped up to the mirror and let out a long sigh. "God help you."

THIRTY-SIX

THE MORNING WAS overcast with dark gray clouds. Heather drove the Explorer, respecting Father Seymour, who'd grown quiet when they'd turned onto the gravel road and headed into the trees.

He'd taken a red-eye and arrived at the Super 8 Motel at three in the morning, left a message to wake him at nine, then promptly fell asleep.

Heather read most of the book late into the night and hadn't fared so well with sleep.

The father's single bag sat behind them, containing the religious symbols he'd brought with him: the appropriate priestly robes, a crucifix, two candles, holy water, and a prayer book. He held another small book titled *The Roman Ritual of Exorcism* in his hands, scanning passages.

When she'd asked him about the crucifix and holy water, he patiently explained that they held no power in and of themselves, but as symbols humans associated with Christ, they were deeply offensive to the powers of darkness, and as such offered some protection. Though not necessarily much.

He'd insisted on coffee and donuts, to calm him, he said. They talked about what to expect or not to expect, about the rites of exorcism, about the nature of evil, about Eve. But academics aside, even the father took the ride into the forest burdened by more questions than answers, she thought.

They couldn't know whether Daniel was even still alive. Or what had really turned his eyes black. And there was the question of Alex. Heading into the trees, knowing that a serial killer who had eluded the FBI for sixteen months might very well be expecting them, was enough to turn all the academics of exorcism into a sidebar.

"Would you like to say confession?"

Heather glanced at Seymour, who stared ahead. He was dressed in gray wool slacks and a white shirt, buttoned to his neck. His white hair was combed back, and he looked amazingly fresh despite his long journey.

"I'm not Catholic," she said.

He looked at her with his smoky blue eyes. "I doubt God will hold it against you."

She faced the gravel road. "Well, God knows I've sinned."

"Fine, let's cut to the chase."

"I've been very bad," she said. Her eyes misted.

He remained silent for a moment, then said, "I don't want you to speak if we find him alive."

"You don't trust me, Father?"

"No. I don't trust him. Or it. If you say the wrong

thing, the consequences to you could be disastrous. Trust me, I've seen it."

"France?"

He nodded. The freshness had left his face.

"What happened?"

"I was assisting, as a favor to a friend. The last of three exorcisms I've been present at." He spoke in a monotone. "When Michael became ill after ten hours, I stepped in against his orders. The girl was in terrible torment, and I couldn't bear the sight of it all. You read the case of the Girl-Fixer in the book?"

"Yes." A spirit by the same name had possessed a young man.

"Like the priest there who was nearly killed, I, too, comforted the tormented girl. As one human being to another. But as a human I stepped out from under my protection and was beaten. Not by the girl but by a force that punched me in the gut repeatedly, driving me across the room while the girl rattled off my sins in the vilest possible terms. Sounds like something you might see in a movie, but it happened to me in the flesh and it terrified me. The girl accused me of things I'd never told even the closest confidant, names, and places. Long ago forgiven, but on that day flung about the room like feces."

She'd read of this and other cases last night, but watching Father Seymour's face now, the certainty of such happenings settled in her mind, uncontested. She couldn't think of what to say.

Grass ran in thick tufts down the center of the narrow road.

"We're getting close," she said.

"Now listen to me." He drilled her with a stare. "I want

you to set your fear aside. I pay a price, but they cannot touch me if I toe the line. As for you...for you it's very dangerous. You must not, under any circumstances, step beyond the authority I give you, do you understand?"

"Yes."

"If Daniel isn't restrained, he will need to be."

"Is that really necessary?" She knew it was, but it went against her deepest instincts.

"I'll make the determination, not you. You may not question anything. You may not speak unless I direct you. You will stand where I tell you to stand and leave if I ask you to leave. I need your absolute assurance on this matter."

"Yes. Yes, of course."

Maybe it would have been a good idea to bring some firepower. Brit could have provided at least that.

But Eve had said no.

"The point is I, not you, will make determinations. It would be best for you not to think, if that were humanly possible."

"I get the point."

"If I thought you got the point, I wouldn't belabor it now."

She nodded.

"If there is one thing known intimately by them, it's humanity. They will draw upon weaknesses you hardly know exist—your obsessions, your fears, but worse, your reason. Always, as in most of life itself, a person's reason betrays him. If you want to come out whole, I strongly suggest you let me do the reasoning."

"I understand," she said. "I swear, I get it." The cattle guard came into view.

"For your sake, I hope so."

She slowed. "It's around the corner, up ahead." She gripped the wheel tighter to steady her hands.

Father Seymour stared ahead, silent now. They rolled over the metal guard. The sounds made by the Explorer seemed too loud—the humming of the engine, popping of tires over gravel, whisper of the air conditioner, the slight creak of seat springs.

The deep-woods compound slid into view as the car motored around the last corner. The house on the left and the shack to their right. The mound ahead. A grave.

Undisturbed.

And in that grave, Daniel.

THIRTY-SEVEN

"**S** TOP THE CAR," Father Seymour said.

She already had her foot on the brake. They stared at the clearing, looking for any sign of life. Not even the tall grass moved.

And then the father did. He reached back, retrieved his bag, and stepped out of the car. Without returning his eyes to the compound, he pulled on a long black cassock that covered him from neck to feet, then carefully fastened each button. He slipped into a waist-length white surplice and placed a narrow purple stole around his neck so that it hung loosely to his waist.

"Behind the hill, you said."

"Yes."

"Follow me." He grabbed the bag and began to walk toward the small rise. His apparent calm gave Heather some courage, but she'd been in that root cellar. He hadn't.

She climbed out and hurried to catch up to him. "Father, I think maybe—"

"I didn't ask you to think. I asked you to follow me."

Having no desire to disturb his confidence, she followed. Fighting a deep unsettling, she did so closely, with one hand touching his elbow.

He didn't slow his pace as they rounded the rise and faced the open root cellar.

"That was how you left it?" he asked quietly. "Now you may answer."

"Yes."

He nodded, walked up to the dark entry, and only then slowed. By day she could barely see the shifting torchlight inside.

She wanted to suggest what she'd started to suggest before, that maybe she should wait outside, but she dismissed the idea after scanning the trees. Being alone, even outside, would be a problem for her.

Father Seymour stepped up to the doorway, dipped his head slightly, and disappeared inside. Heather glanced at the trees once again, imagined Eve watching her, and then followed the priest into the root cellar.

Blinded by the light from outside, Heather saw only the black, tarred walls and the single flaming torch at first. Then the chair.

Only now there was no Daniel in the chair.

She blinked and stepped up to the father, who stood holding his bag to her right. "He's gone," she whispered, glancing over. She immediately expected a rebuke, but the priest paid her no mind. He was staring ahead. To the right.

She followed his stare. The long table with corner

holes still sat in the shadows along the wall. Daniel lay on top, hands by his sides, facing the ceiling. He didn't appear to be bound, and even from here she could see his chest slowly rising and falling.

Heather stepped forward, but the priest's hand stopped her.

They stood watching him for thirty seconds. Finally, the priest moved closer, then stopped again, ten feet from the table.

Heather stepped up behind him. Unlike the quivering form she'd found last night, Daniel now looked to be in a peaceful sleep. The chill in the cellar was gone. The entire atmosphere had changed.

"Daniel?"

The priest warned her again. "No, Heather."

Daniel's eyes opened. They searched the ceiling in quick jerks. Then he sat up and looked around with wide, questioning eyes.

Blue eyes.

The change in him, from the tormented victim to this man whom she knew so well, flooded her with emotion. She couldn't restrain herself.

"Daniel?"

He turned to the sound of her voice. "Heather?"

"Daniel?" She moved forward, but Father Seymour's hand stopped her.

"No, Heather. Not yet. Please don't speak."

Daniel slid his legs off the table and looked at the priest, then glanced around the room. His eyes misted. "You came . . . Thank goodness—that was you last night— you gave me the antibiotics."

He stood, felt his torso as if checking to see if he was

okay. "It worked, you giving me the antibiotics. I..." He jerked his head up. "He's gone?"

"Who's gone, Daniel?" Seymour asked.

Daniel's thoughts seemed to clear quickly, and he moved toward the door. "I know who Eve is, Heather. His name's Alex Price. He grew up here, in this pit of a cult. We don't have much time. He was here. I think he has another victim. A girl named Maria Sanchez. He's going..."

Father Seymour was moving to cut him off from the door when Daniel stopped and turned back. "Where's Brit? Lori?"

"We didn't—"

"Stop!" Father Seymour shot her an angry glare. To Daniel: "I would like to ask you a question."

Daniel looked the father's robes up and down. "I can understand why Heather brought you here. If there was ever a place that reeked of hell, God knows this is it. But this is about Eve, not me. We don't have time for this." He glanced back at the door.

"Would you be willing to pray with me?"

Daniel stopped and faced the priest, unimpressed, then looked at Heather. "Are you coming? I assume you have a vehicle."

"Not a word," the father said quietly.

Heather stood still. But she knew then that Seymour was wrong. She'd been mistaken. The antibiotics *had* worked, and she had Daniel back. Alex Price had something else in mind.

While they were sidelined here, Alex was gone, finishing whatever he'd started.

"You can't just stay here." Daniel walked back toward

them, clearly frustrated. "Please, Heather. God knows this whole experience has been torture for both of us. Literally." His face softened and he closed his eyes. Opened them.

Spoke softly. "I can't leave you, Heather. Never again. I was wrong, God knows I was wrong." Pleading now. "We can put this all behind us. Please, we have to get out. If we don't stop Eve now, I'm finished. But we will stop him. We have his name, his childhood, everything."

He reached for her cheek and brushed it with his thumb. "You know I'm right."

It was the first tender touch from him in two years. She wanted to step into his arms; she knew he would take her.

"We're running out of time," he said.

"Then pray, Daniel," Father Seymour said. "Repeat a simple prayer after me so that we can leave."

"I wouldn't believe a word of it."

"For me," the priest said. He walked to the chair and pushed it against the wall. Why, Heather had no clue. "It's just religious jargon, harmless, right? Just satisfy a foolish priest who flew two thousand miles to be here."

"We have a serial killer within reach, and you're suggesting we pause to pray." Daniel kept his eyes on Heather. "Don't be asinine."

"Because that serial killer is Eve," the priest said, returning.

"It's not remotely rational."

"Sit in the chair and pray with me."

A pause. Still Daniel refused to look at the priest.

"You think it's wise to argue with me, Priest?" he demanded.

"Then argue with the power of—"

"Fine, I'll pray your foolish prayer!" Daniel snapped, swiveling his head to face Father Seymour.

His faced sagged, and he looked like he might begin to cry. He walked past them, plopped down on the metal chair, rested his elbows on his knees, and lowered his head into his hands. His shoulder hitched once, then several more times with an uncharacteristic sob.

Heather struggled to maintain control. Her promise to the father seemed to have been voided by Daniel's health. She'd come expecting a snarling captive, body contorted by forces beyond her understanding.

Instead they'd found Daniel. Just Daniel, as agnostic and stubborn as he'd always been.

She looked at Seymour with pleading eyes, but he brushed past her, set his bag on the table, and withdrew the items he had brought. He spaced the candles two feet apart and lit them, then placed the crucifix between them.

Daniel was crying now. Why? She'd seen his soft side more times than she could count. His peers saw him as a bulldog, but she'd spent many nights encouraging him when it all became too much.

She couldn't imagine the horror he'd endured these last two weeks. The deaths, the inexplicable bouts of fear, exchanging himself for her, knowing Eve would infect him.

She started to protest. "Father—"

"Please, is that really necessary?" Daniel asked, indicating the tools of the trade. "I said I would pray with you, confess your lies. So we can get out of here...stop Eve..." He stood and paced, crying openly now. "Not play priest with all the trinkets."

"We are going to pray, Daniel."

"Fine, fine, we'll say your little prayer," Daniel breathed. His ordeal had reduced him to a shell.

He looked at Heather, the skin around his eyes wrinkled. "We have to stop him, Heather. His name is Alex Price. I know what he looks like. He told me that if you managed to save me, he would let us go. That we could hunt him."

Father Seymour faced him, unscrewing a small brown bottle of blessed water.

"You love me, right?" Daniel pleaded. "He's out there right now, Heather. He's out there..."

The father stepped forward, shaking water on his hand. "I would like—"

"I'm going to say this prayer and then we have to leave. Right, Heather?"

"—to bless—"

"Oh, stop it already!" Daniel yelled, slapping the bottle of holy water from the priest's hand.

Heather watched the bottle flip through the air, clatter noisily to the table, and come to rest on its side, spilling its contents on the bloodstained wood surface.

A loud hissing sound sent a jolt of alarm through Heather's nerves. The water on the table began to bubble, then vaporized. All three stared in a state of mild shock.

A hundred questions collided in Heather's mind as the holy water hissed, but above them all rose one: if the father had been right about the water, could he also be right about Daniel?

She spun back to her husband. But he'd moved from where he stood.

He sat in the chair now, elbows back on his knees, head in his hands. Crying.

Father Seymour glanced at Heather. Then back at Daniel.

"Daniel, listen to me," the priest said, dropping to one knee beside him. He had something shiny in one hand. "I'm not here on my own, do you hear me?"

He quickly slipped one end of what Heather now saw were handcuffs around Daniel's wrist. Two feet of chain ran between the shackles.

"Your pain is known and suffered by another..."

Seymour snapped the other end of the handcuffs to a large steel screw eye embedded in the timber behind the chair. She understood why he'd moved the chair.

Daniel's hands rested on his lap now. He seemed unaware of the restraint dangling from his right wrist.

"Another was tormented for the sin of Eve."

Daniel's cries changed tone. His head hung and his shoulders shook, but the tone of his sobs became sharper, the shaking more rapid.

He was crying? Or laughing?

A low chuckle echoed through the root cellar, then grew to a harsh cackle. Daniel lifted his head and faced the ceiling, eyes closed. He was laughing, openmouthed, shaking with each laugh—a breath-robbing chortle that seemed impossibly long.

All the while, Father Seymour casually went about the business of retrieving his crucifix and the prayer book.

The laughter died to a few pronounced chuckles, and Daniel lowered his head, eyes still closed, grinning like someone relishing an amusing memory. "I know," he said. "I know."

The smile vanished and his voice dropped to a whisper. "I was there."

Heather was so taken aback by the complete change in him that at first she didn't hear the words spoken by the father. She wanted out. To claw her way to the door and throw herself into the clean air outside. To run from the clearing, into the trees, to the car, anywhere but here.

Then she remembered that she'd begged Father Seymour to come for this very reason.

The priest was reading from the prayer book. "Do not remember, O Lord, our sins—"

"Too late." Daniel's eyes snapped wide. Black as tar. A grin twisted his lips, one corner up, one down. He swiveled his head and stared at the priest through two holes that peered from the darkest abyss.

"...or the sins of our forefathers. Do not punish us for our offenses, and lead us not—"

"Into the filthy priesthood when we ourselves are so extravagantly guilty of the same sins we hope to absolve the pedophile of."

Daniel was rattling off the interruptions as if he knew what the father would read. Seymour dropped his eyes back to the page and continued quickly.

"And lead us not into temptation but deliver us from evil. Save this man, your servant—"

"You're barking up the wrong tree, Seymour. Yap, yap, yap."

"Let the enemy have no victory over him. And let the son of iniquity not succeed in injuring him—"

"'Cause his body's a temple and his mind's a garbage hole."

"Send him help from the Holy Place, Lord. And give him heavenly protection—"

"A box full of condoms or a book about how it's all about the vibrations and chemicals will do."

"Lord, hear my prayer and let my cry reach you."

Daniel shifted his black stare to Heather. The temperature had fallen—his breath formed vapor.

"Hello, Heather." His voice shifted higher. "Do you want to be my friend?" It was a young boy's voice. "Do you want to join Adam in the box?"

"I compel you in the name of Christ," the priest said calmly, "what is your name?"

The smile on Daniel's face faltered for a moment, then twisted again.

"Would you like Eve in your box? You nasty whore."

The stench of urine smothered her, and for the first time she saw that his teeth were black again.

"The love of Christ compels—"

"What right do you have to compel me to do anything?" But this was not Daniel speaking. He stood; the chain snapped taut. He glanced down, then continued, only momentarily distracted. "You didn't learn your lesson in France? How are your ribs, Father?"

Seymour stiffened.

"Did you tell her why you became a priest? The real reason?"

The priest's mouth parted, but he didn't seem able to speak.

Daniel looked down at his wrist, then back at the screw eye. When he faced them again, his eyes were blue. Normal.

An expression of terrible anguish twisted his face, and

Heather knew that her Daniel had surfaced. She took an involuntary step forward.

"That's it, Daniel. You can do it, you're strong. I love you."

He froze. Lifted his face and screamed at the timbers etched with the words *Eve's Holy Coven*.

She didn't know if this was her Daniel or Eve's Daniel until he lowered his head and drilled her with eyes as black as midnight.

"Love, love all this sick talk of love. You love me? Is that what you told Mitch?" Eve's Daniel asked in a slow drawl.

Heather stepped back. She hadn't told anyone about Mitch.

"What's the matter, Mitch bitch?" Daniel growled. "You don't want the beans spilled?"

She lifted a trembling hand to her mouth.

"The next time you look at me funny, I'm going to split your box with a bat."

Father Seymour had recovered.

"Your vile-mouthed distractions don't change the fact that you are defeated by the power of—"

A roar beyond the capacity of the human throat cut the air for a brief moment, then stopped. Daniel had thrown his mouth wide for a split second, but Heather wasn't sure the sound had come from him.

Then softly, pleading. "Eve did this," Daniel whimpered. "Eve took Adam." His eyes cleared and once again he looked normal.

Her Daniel, torn by anguish, pleading. "Please, Heather, don't let him do this. You know me, you know I would never allow him to hurt you. I came for you. I gave myself for you." Tears spilled from his eyes. "I didn't mean to hurt you. You know my heart…"

"Don't respond!" the priest said. Then to Daniel, rushing his words, "I am speaking to you, unclean spirit. Eve, what gives you claim to this soul who seeks to be free?"

"Please, Heather. Will you invite me into your heart? We can put all of this behind us."

Father Seymour took a step forward. "No!"

But Heather hardly heard him. Daniel's words drew her with a cord thickened by two years of separation from the man she loved.

"I was wrong, Heather. I died and I saw. He helped me see the truth. I've felt the fear running through my bones, and now I know it's real, it's very real."

"Eve, I command you to reveal—"

"Shut up, Father! This isn't Eve. It's Adam. Daniel." To Heather, "We were wrong. But it's not like the priest says. You can help me. Your love. He didn't have any love as a boy. You have to save me. But only you can do it. Love me, take me back, accept me into your heart. Quick, before the boy comes back!"

His words confused her, but a thread of sense running through them reached her. The inner child. The boy was yearning for love. Love covers a multitude of sins, it was said. Daniel had frequently talked about the power of love over faith.

Daniel was crying, begging for her mercy. Everything in her wanted to comfort him. She realized that she was crying as much as he was.

"Do you kill those whom you love?" Father Seymour said.

Daniel blinked, confused for a moment.

"Please, Father, this isn't about you. You're going to get me killed!"

"Does Eve punish those she befriends, making a mockery of that very love? Does she kill them like a sacrifice? Was it Eve who killed sixteen women?"

"I'm trying to get us out of here. Alex Price killed them. But there's something in me, I know that now. Isn't that enough for you?"

"No, it's not."

Heather was no longer sure what to think. This was her Daniel speaking, not Eve's Daniel. She'd learned to trust his judgment, his intelligence, his capacity to understand complex situations like this. Now, confronted with the truth about himself, he had found a way?

Daniel sat hard. "He's going to kill us all."

THIRTY-EIGHT

DANIEL WAS.

But at times he couldn't be sure of that. So it had been for countless hours now, nearly as far back as he could remember.

When he *was* sure, he pleaded with himself not to be sure, because if Daniel was still alive and this wasn't just another nightmare, then something very, very wrong had happened.

Somehow he'd found himself back in the black box. This time he'd invited the boy to be his friend. What had happened then was so confusing that it got lost with the question of whether he really was or wasn't.

But he was.

The fear he'd felt after dying was back, but stronger. At times completely immobilizing. At times he couldn't even move his eyes.

It was as if the fear had actually taken physical form and become boiling black waves made from blood and feces and bile. He'd melted and become a part of it all.

And the confusion…Nothing made sense to him. He'd written hundreds of pages about how the mind fabricated things like evil and hell and sin, and yet if he wasn't mistaken, which he could be, he was drowning in the very evil he argued never existed.

The boy was there, right beside him, screaming in rage at the priest, running naked through his mind. Presenting arguments that made only some sense.

In moments of fleeting clarity, Daniel thought he knew some things. Like the fact that this wasn't simply something in his head. That evil was real and palpable, and that he'd found the worst of its kind.

That the boy was real. Eve was a real thing. A ravenous beast who was disturbed at being interrupted by this priest.

In many ways, he loved the boy and hated the priest. Hated Heather. Hated God, who was real, and Eve, who was at the moment even more real.

Daniel felt his eyes darken.

He's going to kill us all.

"He's going to kill us all."

I hate you.

"I hate you!"

FATHER SEYMOUR STEPPED over to Heather, turned her away from Daniel, and whispered.

"He's speaking confused half-truths. Don't assume because he looks normal he is. You understand that the enemy here is Eve?"

"Yes." She wiped at her tears with a trembling hand. "He's in so much pain."

"He's baiting you. Nothing horrifies them as much as having no place to live. I think the same Eve who inhabited Alice Brown in this twisted religion, Eve's Holy Coven, is with us now. She's a killer, make no mistake."

They were both whispering, urgent.

"I think I can help him, Father. He's in pain—"

"Not in your own power you can't! I don't think you understand what we're dealing with here. This evil may have once been satisfied with torment, but now it takes human life, celebrating the fall of Eve in the garden. It will kill Daniel, and then it will kill you."

He was breathing in long, steady pulls. "Perhaps you should leave."

"No! No, he needs me."

Heather didn't understand what rules or principles governed this order, wasn't sure she wanted to understand. But it bucked every instinct she had about the proper order of things.

A moan sounded behind him. They turned around to face the chair and Daniel.

But it wasn't Daniel sitting in the chair. It was Alex Price.

Dressed in a black shirt and dungarees, legs crossed, hands on his lap. The chain lay on the ground, cuffs sprung.

"Take your eyes off the prize, Father Seymour?"

Heather looked for Daniel, but there was no sign of him. How was that possible? Alex could have stepped out of the deep shadows from where he'd been watching, she thought.

But Daniel...

Then she saw the priest's pale face. He wasn't looking at Alex Price. He was staring at the ceiling above Alex Price.

Daniel's shirtless back was pressed against a thick tarred beam, and his arms were spread wide on the ceiling. But there were no nails or ropes to hold him in place.

He stared down at the top of Alex's head with coal eyes, perfectly still.

THIRTY-NINE

FATHER SEYMOUR LOWERED his eyes. For a dozen heavy beats, Heather's heart pumped blood through constricted veins. No one spoke, no one moved.

Daniel was stretched out on the ceiling, staring down without expression. Bare chest white and dry.

Alex sat directly below him, looking at them without any apparent concern.

Father Seymour kept his eyes locked on the man he had unwittingly let loose on the world so many years earlier.

Heather watched her husband and thought that in that moment, he was neither her husband nor Daniel. A passage from Malachi Martin's book came to mind. Many leaders in the Catholic church, the author said, refused to accept that a person was truly possessed unless certain common physical phenomena presented. In particular, stretched skin or a distortion of the face, violent smashing of furniture, the repeated slamming of doors, tearing of fabric—all without any apparent reason.

And levitation.

When she'd asked the father why, if all this was really happening in the world, it wasn't common knowledge, he'd simply said, "But it *is*, dear. Just not for those who don't want to see."

She now understood with a clarity that shook her bones. This was Daniel. But this wasn't Daniel.

He was alive—she could see the vapor spilling from his nostrils as he slowly breathed the chilly air.

"Hello, Alex," the priest said. "It's good to see you again."

"Is it?"

"Not really, no."

"I didn't think so."

Heather couldn't seem to tear her eyes from Daniel's body, inexplicably plastered above them. A fear she hadn't known until now pressed into her, past her chest, coiling around her heart and lungs. The overwhelming presence of evil wasn't coming from her mind, she knew that wholly.

Horror was a physical presence, united with the air itself, slipping past skin and bone to squeeze that part of her she'd never before acknowledged.

"I've been waiting for you," Alex said. "I've waited for fifteen years."

"You know that Daniel doesn't belong to you."

"No, he doesn't. He's Eve's now. They've become friends."

"That's how you kill them?"

"I don't kill them," Alex said. "She does."

"If this is your act of atonement, what is your sin?"

Alex cocked his head ever so slightly. "You should know. It was you who showed me my sin."

"Losing your faith."

"I was wrong," Alex said. "You were right." He removed his hands from his lap and spread his arms wide. "And now we're here."

"If I helped you understand then, let me help you understand something else now. You were not dismissed for your lack of belief in the supernatural." Now the priest spread *his* hands. "It was your profound lack of faith in the proper order of things that became your downfall. Which is the real reason we're here now."

Alex Price offered him a wry grin. "That's your version."

"That's the only version that can save you, Alex."

A drop of liquid fell on Alex's hand with a light splat. Heather glanced up and saw that another tear was about to fall from Daniel's fixed face. Alex stared at the tear on his hand. For a moment she thought she saw regret.

He wiped the tear from his hand, unfolded his legs, and stood. "In this sanctuary, my version is the only one that counts. I'm afraid I'm going to have to ask you to leave. Both of you."

"Or?"

Alex shrugged. "Or Eve may become upset and take her as well." He looked at Heather. "And we know that this one will be easy for Eve. She's hardly better than he. Even worse, now that she's seen and still doesn't believe."

"I do believe," Heather said, voice high and unsteady.

"The question," Father Seymour said, turning to the table with the two burning candles, "is believe what? What happened in this room to twist your heart into knots, Alex?" He studied the walls and the ceiling, settling on the words carved there. *Eve's Holy Coven.*

"What world beat the truth out of you?"

"A world that you could not survive," Alex said. "Believe me."

"Not surprising. Very few survive this world with their faith intact."

"Exactly, but those days are behind us. Please leave so that Eve can finish what she started."

The priest turned back to him. "Alice beat you here, didn't she?"

Alex didn't respond.

"A sacrificial lamb to pay for her own guilt," the priest said. "Every new moon. Now you're doing the same, taking young women who at least loosely represent innocence, and offering them up to pay for your own sin. Like Alice did with you and Jessica."

Alex stood quiet. Hearing the theory now in this dungeon, Heather knew it was true. The fear pressed against her, unrelenting. She kept looking up at Daniel, but he didn't move.

"You're wasting your time," Alex finally said. But he said it in a voice filled with regret. And Heather knew then that Alex was as much a victim as Daniel. Looking at them both now, she wasn't sure who was worse off.

The priest picked up the crucifix and stepped toward Alex. "You know that I hold a bigger stick, Alex. That the light dispels darkness easily if it is embraced. You've been in this world of darkness long enough to know that it is terrified of the light. Have you asked yourself why?"

Alex's eyes dropped to the ornate religious symbol. "I'm not the one moved by trinkets."

"But Eve is."

"She's not with me now. She's on the ceiling."

Daniel still hadn't budged.

"And what *does* move you, Alex?"

"Nothing anymore. I've made my peace."

"You've done all this for a good night's sleep?"

Alex's face twitched.

"I learned only yesterday that you'd been taken from your parents and brought here for Alice's sick purposes," Father Seymour said. "When Heather told me, my heart broke for you. I can't imagine the horrors that pulled you kicking and screaming into hell itself."

"We don't have time for this."

"You've never experienced true love, have you? Alice beat you to a pulp, and now you're doing the same to other women. This is about mocking the firstborn among women, Eve. And all the daughters of God whom you believe cannot love you. After all, Alice didn't love you."

"Love doesn't exist."

"Your sister loved you."

Alex's lips flattened. "My sister *left* me."

Father Seymour took a breath. "The first time I met you at the shelter in Pasadena, I knew that you were special."

"You don't know Eve," Alex said quietly. It was a warning. "She needs her home."

"I just didn't know how deep your torment ran. Even then my heart was breaking for you."

"If you're trying to stall me to give the FBI time to arrive, you're only consigning Daniel to an early death. Make no mistake, Eve *will* kill him. There is no way for the FBI to stop her."

"Not the FBI, no. But another..."

"No one can save him unless he believes."

Father Seymour continued, undeterred. "Everyone is entitled to believe. Even me. I went to France two years after you disappeared, and it was there that my eyes were opened up to your world, Alex. To hell."

A long beat.

"You have no idea what hell is." Alex's breathing had deepened.

Father Seymour shook his head. "You've been tortured all your life, but torturing others doesn't absolve you. It only spares you from a little pain now."

"Spoken like the perfect priest. Who doesn't realize how close Eve is to shredding much more than the meninges of the corpse over your head."

"What nightmares drove you, Alex? Were they the same as Daniel's? Did the same little boy visit you in the box?"

The noticeable anger that had changed Alex's demeanor swelled, reddening his face. "You lost your *right* to pry into my world when you threw me out of yours," he snapped.

"You never entered my world," the priest said.

Alex took two long steps toward the root cellar's dimly lit door, then spun back, both hands gripped into fists. "Have *you* been whipped by a cat-o'-nine-tails?" he thundered. "Have *you* awakened every night screaming into tape?"

He gripped his shirt and ripped it off his shoulder, revealing thick, ugly scars. "Do *you* walk around with mangled skin?"

Alex trembled.

"Then walk away from Eve!" Father Seymour shouted.

Heather instinctively moved back.

Daniel hung on the ceiling.

The scene shifted from raw horror to surrealistic terror. This battle of wills on the ground while Daniel hung in the air, crucified by unseen hands.

FORTY

CONFUSION SWELLED IN Daniel's mind like a black ocean tide, swirling, smothering the rocks of reason anchored deep in his psyche. And above the thundering black waves, a scream of rage. Not his.

Eve's.

The boy was upset.

And with every fiber in his own mind and body, Daniel could feel Eve's frustration, his anger, his outrage. Because he, too, resented the suggestion that those distant words spoken by Father Seymour, the foolish priest, could be true.

And yet every time the priest spoke, the boy grunted and groveled in his own stew of self-pity and rage.

Why do you hate the priest, Daniel?

Because he's talking in these simple terms, as if his garbage has any real power in the real world.

And are you in the real world, Daniel?

I am. I always have been.

Why are you on the ceiling?

Am I?

Why do you feel so much pain? And fear? Are you afraid of that name?

Daniel had no words for this. Only a boiling fury at all that was wrapped up in that name, that symbolism, that ancient relic called the cross.

The waves of darkness seemed to pause for a moment. That was the dreadful question. What if it were all true? What if he really had been wrong?

Daniel felt a new fear, born of desperation rather than the boy's nightmare, grip his nerves. His flesh began to quiver spastically.

He knew then for the first time what he had to do. He had to look to the priest. However foolish, however offensive, however naive his words, the priest knew something that made the boy cringe.

Daniel had to know what the priest knew.

The boy's face was suddenly inches from his own, black eyes pulsating, teeth bared, snarling.

"I hate you!" Its putrid, steaming breath smothered Daniel. And I'm going to kill you."

Daniel closed his eyes and sobbed in horror.

"Say it! Tell me you want to die."

He said it, panting, wishing for death.

"I hate you..."

HEATHER HAD TRIED TO SPEAK a dozen times, but every time she glanced up and saw Daniel's black eyes staring straight down, her thoughts fled.

He spoke now, unmoving except for his mouth. "I hate you. I'm going to die."

Saliva slipped past his stretched lips, forming a long string. Mixed with blood.

Fear shoved words past Heather's throat.

"Stop it!"

None of them seemed to have heard her. Father Seymour was still coaxing Alex with words of truth. Alex stood unmoving, fists clenched, resilient.

Daniel just stared at her with black eyes. Drooling spittle and blood.

"Walk away from Eve," Father Seymour said again.

"I've tried, a thousand times I've tried," Alex said in a tremulous voice. He walked to the priest, grabbed the crucifix from his hand, and kissed it. Then tossed it aside. "You think that will help me? You think I don't hate every minute of my life?"

"No, Alex. It's this demon, *Eve*, you should hate."

"She can hear you." Alex breathed the warning again. "She has her needs."

But the priest didn't seem to care. "Alice introduced you to Eve's world, and you tried to flee that world. You made it to Los Angeles, to the mission, to me, to the seminary. But she dragged you back and you went. Hate her! Hate Eve!" He shoved a finger up at the ceiling. "Hate this genderless killer who's left so many dead!"

A soft chuckle rolled through the chamber, swallowing all other sound. Heather jerked her eyes up. Saw that Daniel's body had changed.

Where smooth pale flesh had covered his torso, now dark bruises and pronounced veins grew before her eyes. She'd seen the images of Eve's other victims a thousand times, and Heather knew that whatever had killed them was racking Daniel's body now.

His face was shifting, skin stretching so tight over blackened teeth that she was sure it would split.

The chuckle became a soft hissing sound, but in the far distance behind that rush of air, she could hear a soft, echoing giggle. For the first time since he had risen to the ceiling, his head turned.

Slowly. Unblinking. Daniel's gaze locked on her. Eyeing *her* with those black, lifeless eyes.

"Hello, Heather." His voice growled more than spoke. "Do you want to be friends?"

Heather bumped into the wall at her back and began to slide down. She could hardly breathe, much less stand.

"I warned you," Alex said.

Father Seymour stepped back and began to recite from the prayer book in a loud voice. "God of all creation, empower me to do your bidding."

"It's too late, Father," the voice growled, slowly, stretching out each word. "His mind has been mine for a long time. He doesn't believe. Even we believe."

Daniel's whole body shook violently. In Daniel's own voice now, "I told you not to say that! Torture me, you pathetic priest, and I'll rip him meat from meat and then I'll cut his pincushion to ribbons. Neither one of them is protected."

"Stop it!" Heather screamed, cowering on the floor. "Please, stop it."

But Eve did not stop. Two puncture wounds suddenly opened in the center of Daniel's palms. Blood leaked out of the two holes, formed an unbroken stream that splashed on the ground and began to pool. Then the same from his overlapping bare feet. Three streams of blood to flesh out the crucifixion.

Heather turned from the gruesome sight and saw that Alex Price had lowered his head and closed his eyes. Even if he did have the power to stop it, he had no motivation.

The priest continued leveling the rites of exorcism, but his words seemed to do nothing more than torture Eve, and by extension, Daniel, whose condition was rapidly deteriorating.

"Release him. The love of Christ compels you."

The skin on Daniel's side suddenly split. Blood drained in a thick cord.

Alex stood perfectly still, head bowed, eyes closed.

Heather wept, screaming now, unable to lower her eyes.

"Release him!" the priest cried. "Release him!"

Daniel started to giggle like a child.

"Alex?"

The voice came from behind them, speaking clearly, heard just above the din of horror. A woman's voice.

And with that voice, the blood from Daniel's wounds stopped flowing. As if the faucet had been turned off. Silence filled the root cellar.

Heather turned her head slowly. A woman was standing in the doorway, arms by her sides, staring at Alex's back.

"Alex, it's Jessica."

But Heather didn't know this woman as Jessica.

She knew her as Lori Ames.

FORTY-ONE

SOUND AND MOTION CAME to a standstill. Lori stared from the doorway, dressed in jeans and a white blouse, hair scattered by the wind. Heather didn't know how long she'd been standing there—long enough to have taken in the room. She wasn't looking at Daniel on the ceiling. Her eyes were fixed on Alex.

On her brother.

And the rest of them were staring at her. Except Alex, who had snapped his eyes wide at the sound of her voice, then frozen with his head still bowed and his back to her.

The last drops of blood from Daniel's wounds splattered loudly in the spreading pool on the floor. Echoed. It was as if time had stopped in that moment, and with it, the cessation of all motion but the pumping and spilling and clotting of blood.

"Alex?"

Lori, who was Jessica, took a step and then stopped. Heather glanced up at Daniel and saw that his black eyes were fixed on Jessica. Curiosity or concern, she couldn't tell. But the sudden entry of Alex's sister had upset some kind of balance in the room.

Father Seymour stared at Jessica, mouth parted in a fascinated smile. His eyes darted to Alex.

"It's her, Alex. It's Jessica."

Alex's eyes still looked down, but they were spread wide.

"She's behind you."

"My sister is dead," he whispered. "Eve killed her."

"I warned you not to interfere, sow!" The gravelly voice had come from Daniel. "Now I kill them all."

Jessica lifted her eyes and stared at him, bruised and bloodied, staring down at her. Tears were running down her cheeks.

"His blood is on your hands," Daniel growled.

"I can't run anymore," she said softly. Then to Alex: "Listen to me, Alex. It's Jessica. When I went back to the apartment, you were gone. I was sure you were dead."

Her eyes flitted to Daniel. "I was afraid because of the threat...you know...But I never did stop caring and hoping."

She stood trembling now, a frail woman racked by terrible emotions she'd managed to bury beneath years of struggle.

"Then I heard about Eve. For a long time I refused to believe it could be you." Her voice quivered. "But when Heather told me about the cellar, I knew what I already knew."

Alex lifted his head slowly. "Jessica is dead."

A single chuckle from Daniel.

"Turn around, Alex," the priest said. He seemed resolved, as if somehow the reunion of Alex and Jessica meant something to all of them.

"She's no better than the others," Daniel said in his own voice. "They're all hopelessly caught up in themselves. None of them are protected."

But the confidence in his voice had slipped, Heather thought.

Alex's eyes shifted, perhaps sensing the same.

Jessica stepped cautiously forward now, lips trembling, eyes streaming clear tears, tears of remorse and sorrow, nothing else, Heather thought.

"Alex..." She spoke his name as if it hung from a crystal thread. "Alex, what have you done?"

Alex was still frozen, but now staring ahead with shimmering eyes.

"She's a whore, Alex," Eve said. "You took her punishment, and Alice turned her back on you."

Jessica walked toward her brother. "Alex..." She stopped three feet behind him. "Can I see your face?"

Heather pushed herself to her feet.

Jessica reached out and touched her brother's skin where he'd ripped the shirt from his shoulder. She lightly traced one of his scars.

Alex turned then, unevenly, shifting his feet several times to manage the full turn. For the first time in seventeen years, brother and sister saw each other.

"Jessica's a filthy sow, sow, sow," Daniel said. "You should whip her, Alex. Whip her now or I'll have to do it for you."

* * *

DANIEL WAS FEAR ITSELF. And the pain of that fear had so overtaken his body that it couldn't respond. He was above them, bleeding, but they couldn't possibly know the torment raging through his mind. He would gladly offer his skin, his limbs, his blood, his face—anything for relief from the horror.

Daniel had all of these thoughts in a brief moment while the fears regrouped for another charge, as he had come to think of it.

Then it was back. Racking his nerves as if they'd been stripped from his body and strapped to the electric chair to weather the hammering joules by themselves.

He began to scream. How his throat could continue to shred itself as he shrieked helplessly became apparent only minutes ago. He'd been screaming for hours like this, but they couldn't hear him, because Eve had found a way to stop his vocal cords. In their eyes, he was just hanging there, staring at them quietly.

Or worse, laughing.

Still, he couldn't stop himself from screaming. This was Eve's world, and Eve was killing him.

It hadn't always been like this. He'd actually felt like himself when he awoke on the table. Disoriented, but free from any pain or thoughts of evil. It made him wonder later, when he realized he was Eve's captive, whether a person could be Eve's friend for many years before feeling the black paste of fear overtake them.

Fear momentarily retreated whenever the priest began to speak, but when he spoke that name, the flood came crashing in worse than before.

Like the tide momentarily drawing out before a tsunami crashes into shore, Eve was taking her rage out on him, pummeling the shores of his mind with a tsunami of black paste.

Then the girl came in. The room went quiet. Daniel felt his blood stop flowing. For a moment even his screaming stopped.

But it started again almost immediately. Eve was interested in the sister, but that wouldn't interrupt Daniel's suffering. So he screamed on through their silence, unheard.

"ALEX." JESSICA SAID HIS name again, as if she herself couldn't quite accept finding him after all these years.

Her face wrinkled with terrible sorrow. She reached her hand out ever so slowly. Touched his face.

He did not react.

"Tell her to lie down on the table," Daniel said in that awful voice.

She glanced up at Daniel. "Is that what you want, Daniel?"

The priest spread his hands and closed his eyes. His voice was strong. *"Our Father who art in heaven, hallowed be your name."*

"Is that what you want, Eve?" Jessica's voice was a little stronger.

"Thy kingdom come, thy will be done on earth as it is in heaven."

"Is that what you want? To finally kill me?"

"More than you can possibly imagine," Daniel growled.

The priest's voiced rumbled on under them. *"Glory be to the Father and to the Son and to the Holy Spirit. As it was in the beginning, is now and shall be forever and ever."*

Alex seemed to have fallen into a trance, staring at Jessica without expression. She looked at his glazed eyes and stepped forward. "Is that what you want, Alex? To finish what Eve started when we were children?"

The priest continued to pray aloud, making no move to discourage Jessica.

"I love you, Alex. I love you." Jessica leaned forward and kissed him on the cheek.

"Still the priest pressed on. To you do we cry, poor banished children of Eve." Heather recognized the prayer from *Hostage to the Devil*—it was the "Salve Regina," referring to Eve from Genesis.

Alex's face began to tremble.

"Deliver this poor soul from the darkness, Jesus Christ our Lord."

"It's not you, Alex. It's not you killing all those women," Jessica said. "It's Eve."

"Do you want to be my friend, Jessica?"

"Eve's the whore," Jessica said, stronger now. "She's the one who whipped us when we were children."

"Take her to the table and tie her down, Alex."

Jessica stepped back, eyes furious. "Is that what you want? You'll take me and let them go? Is that it, you sick pig? Then do it."

She spun around and stretched out her arms. "Whip me!"

Daniel's body dropped from the ceiling, slammed into the wall, and froze two feet above the ground in the same upright, crucified position.

"Whip her!" The words crashed through the room in an earsplitting snarl.

Alex began trembling head to foot.

"Whip me!" Jessica screamed.

Her blouse tore from neck to waist, ripped down the center back by unseen hands. A whip hanging on the wall behind the table flew across the room and smacked into Alex's hand.

"Whip her!" Eve snarled.

Long, ugly scars covered the skin on Jessica's back. The final piece of the picture dropped into Heather's mind. As Father Seymour had speculated, they'd both been systematically beaten when they were children. Severely. Often. By Eve. Who'd now graduated from mere beatings to ritualistic murder.

Alex held the whip without looking at it. His eyes were fixed on his sister's scars. Father Seymour spoke his prayers with greater intensity. "Within your wounds hide me." And then louder, yelling, face red. "Set him free! Set him free, set him free you hear me?"

Alex began to shake violently. The whip slipped from his hand and fell to the ground.

"Forgive me," he whispered.

"Whip her," Eve snarled at Alex. "Whip her, you little worm!"

"No." His face twisted in anguish. "No, I can't!"

Jessica shook with sobs, but she did not lower her arms or turn to face them.

"Whip me, Alex!" she screamed. "Kill me! Kill me and never kill again..."

Alex began to wail. He tore at his shirt and ripped it down the middle, exposing the same long, ugly scars that covered Jessica's back. He grabbed the whip and turned back to Daniel, who was still on the wall, face contorted, once again bleeding from his wounds.

"It's me," Alex screamed. "I'm the one you want. Take me!"

Jessica whirled, face white.

Alex yelled at Daniel again, a terrible throaty moan as loud as the scream. "Take me! Kill me!" He sucked in air. "Kill me! Kill me!"

"No!" Jessica cried. "Oh, God, no!"

Alex jumped up onto the table and began to lash himself over the shoulder. "Take me, take me, take me!" Tears streamed from his eyes.

Daniel jerked his head to the ceiling and began to scream.

FORTY-TWO

DANIEL STILL WAS. Just was. Barely was.

And all that was, was darkness. A void so deep and so empty that what was left of his life was sucked into this abyss of anguish.

Daniel could do nothing except scream, long bloodcurdling cries of anguish, begging for relief, for help.

He now knew one thing that he'd never understood before: he existed to be and belong, and the dark hole that had swallowed his mind was enemy to both, separating him into terrible loneliness that was so horrifying it brought him a great deal of physical pain.

Which was why he couldn't stop screaming. In complete silence.

He wondered if molten fire had been poured into his bones, so great was the pain. The top of his skull might have been sawed off, and a bucket of lava poured in, searing his nerves.

But there wasn't red lava or molten fire. There was only pitch darkness. Separation from the light.

And this last, singular truth was what now swarmed his mind, spinning around the darkness.

He wasn't meant to be pulled from the light any more than a fingernail was meant to be pulled from a finger.

And that was why. He was. Screaming.

But now even the screaming was running out. The jaws of silence gaped from the very throat of this darkness. He wanted to scream, only to make some sound, because sound itself was something to belong to.

Then the last of the sound faded, and he hung limp on the wall. Slowly a tremble swelled, not through his flesh, but in his bones.

The others couldn't see his shaking—that alone would have offered him some comfort and eased his trembling. To be known and seen and therefore reacted to, at least. Anything but this...this perfect solitude in darkness. This void.

He was not meant to be alone. He knew that now, like an eyeball staring at a razor blade closing in knows it is not meant to be sliced.

If only he could scream, his voice would keep him company.

If only he could cry, his tears would be a welcome companion.

If only he could be seen, really seen in this darkness, he would be understood, and maybe one of them would care. Maybe Heather would care, even after all...

A voice broke through the darkness of his mind. *Set*

him free! Set him free, set him free you hear me, you filthy spirit from hell!

The darkness suddenly receded. Daniel gasped.

The darkness pulled back from his mind like a draining sea, revealing a gray, sandy bottom. The boy, Eve, was racing back and forth on the horizon, frantic. Whirling back and staring for a moment or two at a time, but always returning his attention to the horizon.

Screaming obscenities.

Daniel's breath caught in his throat. But he dared not hope, he could not hope, it was too painful.

He clenched his eyes.

"Help! Help!" The words he wanted to use, the words that would explain his predicament, didn't come. Only that single word, bellowed, hoarse and raw.

"Set me free! Please, set me free..."

He snapped his eyes wide, saw that the darkness was being pulled back, way back, and lost himself completely.

"See me, see me, please, see me. Set me free..." Tears streamed and his shoulders shook in violent sobs. "Please, please, please..."

He heard another distant voice over his own, and he stopped screaming.

"Within your wounds hide me! Set him free!"

This was the priest. He was crying out for Daniel, a voice in this dark wilderness, trying to help him.

The voice came again.

"Here!" Daniel screamed. "I'm here, I'm over here, save me, save me!"

A throaty roar split the air, rose to a shriek, and shook Daniel to his bones.

* * *

"TAKE ME!"

"No!" Jessica cried again. "No, Alex!"

A new voice sounded from the wall. Daniel. Head stretched to the ceiling, groaning out in a cracked, breathy voice. "Yes, yes, set me free..."

They froze as one. There was something monumental about those words screamed by Daniel in this pit of despair. The air seemed to have been sucked from the room.

"Set me freeeee..."

A roar split the air, coming from the timbers it seemed. From the air, the room, the wall behind Daniel. Daniel. But from his chest, not his throat.

His body went limp and dropped to the ground in a pile. His agreement with the priest had set him free.

Eve seemed to have left Daniel, but now unseen hands threw Alex Price onto the table. Flipped him over on his belly, facedown. His left arm was jerked toward one corner, and the old leather strap fixed to the table slapped itself around his wrist and tugged tight.

Then the same with his right arm. And each leg, an invisible power working feverishly with the swishing and slapping of leather restraints.

Alex's shirt peeled away, exposing a strong, muscled back.

They all watched, stunned at the suddenness of it all.

The flesh over his spine parted, leaving a gash roughly two feet in length. Alex screamed in pain. But he did not fight it.

Then another cut, and another. He was being beaten

by an unseen whip. But now more. Bruises rose on his arms and lumps moved over his torso, leaving long blue streaks behind like the sixteen victims in his wake.

A short giggle rippled through the air.

"No!" Jessica threw herself at her brother's body, sobbing. "No!" She covered his back with her torso, stretching out with her arms to protect him from the unseen assault.

"No, oh, God no..." She screamed at the empty air above them, "I love him!" A heavy breath. The tendons in her neck stretched tight. "I love him, you hear me? *I* love him!"

A long, hollow shriek split the cold air and ran around the room, followed by a long cut that sliced the skin on Jessica's back.

She jerked. "I love him!"

And then nothing. Silence.

Alex Price lay still.

He's dead, Heather thought. *Eve killed him.* She/he/it had vacated Daniel in a rage, killed Alex, and fled.

But then his head moved, and Jessica was kissing his head. "I'm so sorry, Alex. Forgive me, forgive me, I'm so sorry..."

Heather spun back to Daniel, who was still sobbing. Shaking.

"Daniel?"

She ran to him. His wounds had stopped bleeding, but the one in his side in particular looked like it could threaten his life.

"Daniel, please, honey, lie still."

He turned his head to the sound of her voice, peered up with misted eyes, and seeing her, he grabbed her sleeve. Tugged her frantically toward himself.

"Don't leave me! Don't leave me!"

His voice was so raw, so wrung with desperation that she wondered if he was still being tormented. His eyes searched beyond her, to the ceiling. He was crying out to whatever, whoever had rescued him, she realized. Not wanting to return to whatever hell had held him in its grasp.

She wrapped her arms around his head and wept with him. "No, no, it's okay, I'll never leave you." She bent over and kissed his forehead. "Sh, sh, just rest. It's going to be okay."

The sound of Jessica's sobs filled the room.

"It is finished," the priest said.

MAN OF SORROW:
JOURNEY INTO DARKNESS

by Anne Rudolph

Crime Today magazine is pleased to present the ninth and final installment of Anne Rudolph's narrative account of the killer now known as Alex Price.

2008

THE EIGHT previous install-ments of "Man of Sorrow: Journey into Darkness," written for *Crime Today* magazine, provide a limited but satisfactory look at the forces that shaped Alex Price into the killer known as Eve.

Most of what we know about Alex's first twenty-eight years came from interviews with Jessica Price, also known as Lori Ames. After pleading no contest to the murder of sixteen women attributed to the Eve killer, Alex Price was sentenced to life in a federal penitentiary. He still refuses to discuss more than what has been recorded in this account.

It's not difficult to imagine what his life might have been like be-tween the time he went missing from Pasadena and the time he reemerged in 2007 as the serial killer known only as Eve.

Did he live in an apartment some-where, poring over theology and philosophy volumes? Did he spend much time on the Internet, vicari-ously wandering through the lives of those who unwittingly expose them-selves for all to see?

Did he kill more than the sixteen women chronicled in this book?

Although we know much about the path Alex Price ultimately chose, we may never know much about the stops he made along the way. One thing is clear: Alice Brown's treat-ment of him as a child ultimately in-fluenced his murder of so many women. But even more than Alice, it was Eve who relentlessly drove him to the brink of madness, demanding that to stay sane, he must feed her lust.

Fleeing Southern California in 1991, Jessica Price made her way to North Dakota, where she changed her name to Lori Ames. Eager to put the past behind her, she studied ambitiously. After spending two years at the University of North Dakota in Grand Forks with the intention of becoming a teacher, she decided to study medicine instead. She earned her medical degree at the UCSD School of Medicine in 2000 and subsequently served with the FBI in Phoenix.

Following her brother's admission of guilt, Jessica left the FBI and now teaches medicine at UCLA in Los Angeles, where much of what happened during her formative years has since come to light.

The full details of her own journey are available in a number of essays published through Children of Hope, her Los Angeles–based foundation, which helps abducted children and their parents recover.

When asked why she didn't reveal her relationship to Alex much earlier, Jessica responds with averted eyes, perhaps wondering whether she made the right decision. But she wasn't absolutely positive that the Eve killer was Alex until Heather Clark was released from the root cellar and described her place of captivity. Naturally, she always had her suspicions, but never any certainty. It was possible Eve had finished with Alex and moved on to some other soul. Indeed, she was driven to help Daniel recover his memory of the killer he'd seen in Manitou Springs so that she would know for certain, based on the description, whether the Eve killer was Alex. Short of definite knowledge, she could not act, and even then only very carefully.

Jessica's fear was primarily motivated by the direct threats Eve had made toward her, threats she believed it would carry out. If the killer was Alex, Eve would be watching should she get too close. Jessica had no doubt that if she confessed her suspicions to the FBI, Eve would know and would do much worse than what Alex was doing already.

On the other hand, Jessica knew she might be the only one who could stop Alex. Faced with the conundrum, she reasoned that she had to get close enough to Alex to stop him without presenting a direct threat to Eve. Which, in the end, is exactly what she managed to do.

It's unclear exactly how Eve's power functioned. Did it possess Alex and his victims at the same time? Although certain aspects of evil are predictable, much is a mystery.

Jessica says that she nearly confessed everything to Heather several times. But she agreed with Heather that Alex would kill Daniel if the FBI tried to help out. Instead, Jessica helped Heather connect the last few dots and let her go alone, hoping that she could save Daniel.

When Jessica finally did make the decision to ignore Eve's threat and go down to Oklahoma after Heather and Daniel, she was terrified of Eve's retaliation. Such was the lingering power evil held over her.

In the end, however unorthodox, Jessica's decision to withhold her suspicions from the FBI proved to be an invaluable link to ending Alex Price's cycle of terror.

Although I've done my best to characterize the events surrounding Alex and Jessica's life, I draw no definitive conclusions about precisely how the forces beyond our natural senses operate. Nevertheless, I do believe that the story told in the preceding pages should make one think about more than whether locking your door each night is a good idea. After all, the forces that drove Alex didn't care much about locks.

The events in this report in no way support or even suggest a sustainable pattern of criminal behavior or victimization related to demon possession. Psychologists are no more likely to become possessed than FBI agents. Not all serial killers court the likes of Eve. There is no connection between any form of meningitis and possession.

If your name is Daniel or Eve or Jessica or Heather, you are no more likely to encounter hidden and disturbing forms of evil than your neighbor.

Which by all accounts is likely enough.

Anne Rudolph, 2008

AN EXCERPT FROM
TED DEKKER'S NEXT NOVEL . . .

THR3E

NOW AVAILABLE IN HARDCOVER

ONE

Friday
Noon

THE OFFICE had no windows, only electric lanterns to light the hundreds of spines standing in their cherrywood bookcases. The room smelled of linseed oil and musty pages, but to Dr. John Francis, the dean of academic affairs, it was the scent of knowledge.

"Evil is beyond the reach of no man."

"But can a man remove himself beyond the reach of evil?" Kevin asked.

Dr. Francis gazed over bifocals at the young man who sat opposite him and allowed a small smile. Those blue eyes hid a deep mystery, one that had eluded him since their first meeting three months earlier when Kevin Parson had approached him after a philosophy lecture. They'd struck up a unique friendship that included numerous discussions such as this one.

Kevin sat with his feet flat, hands on knees, eyes piercing and unmoving, brown hair ruffled. The hair was an anomaly. In every other way the man groomed himself perfectly. Clean shaven, fashionably current, nice cologne. But Kevin's ragged hair begged to differ in a bohemian sort of way. Others fiddled with pencils or twirled their fingers or shifted in their seats. Kevin ran his fingers through his hair.

And he tapped his right foot. Not now and then or at appropriate breaks in the conversation, but regularly, to the beat of a hidden drum behind his blue eyes. Some might consider the idiosyncrasies annoying, but Dr. Francis saw them as nothing more than enigmatic clues to Kevin's nature. The truth—rarely obvious and almost always found in subtleties. In the tapping of feet and the fiddling of fingers and the movement of the eyes.

"Indeed," Dr. Francis said. "Can man step beyond evil's reach? I think not. Not in this lifetime."

"Then all men are condemned to a life of evil." Kevin stared at him, unmoving except for his right foot, tapping away. His innocent blue eyes attracted long stares from the secure and forced the less secure to avert their gaze. Kevin was twenty-eight, but he possessed a strange blend of brilliance and naïveté combined with a five-year-old's thirst for knowledge. Something to do with a unique rearing in a bizarre home—Kevin had never been forthcoming.

"A lifetime *struggle* with evil, not a life of evil," Dr. Francis corrected.

"The question is, does man simply choose evil, or does he create it?" Kevin said. "Is evil a force that swims in human blood, struggling to find its way into the heart, or is it an external possibility wanting to be formed?"

"I would say man chooses evil rather than creates it. Human nature is saturated with evil."

"And with good," Kevin said, tapping his foot. "The good, the bad, and the beautiful."

Dr. Francis nodded at the use of the phrase he'd coined, which referred to the beautiful man, struggling between the good and the evil. "The good, the bad, and the beautiful. Indeed." He stood from his desk and stepped toward the door. "Walk with me, Kevin."

Kevin ran both hands past his temples and followed him from the office, up a flight of steps to the world above, as Kevin liked to call it.

"How's your paper on the natures progressing?" Dr. Francis asked.

"Guaranteed to raise your eyebrows." They stepped into the main hall. "I'm using a story to illustrate my conclusion. Not conventional, I know, but I think you'll appreciate it."

"As long as it makes the point. I look forward to reading it."

KEVIN WALKED WITH the dean, thinking that he liked the man beside him. The sound of their shoes striking the hardwood floor echoed through the hall. He glanced up at the paintings of the divinity school's founders along the wall to his right.

"Speaking of evil, all men are capable of gossip, don't you think?"

"Undoubtedly."

"Even the bishop's capable of gossip."

"Of course."

"Do you think the bishop does gossip?"

The dean's answer waited three steps. "We are all human."

They came to the large door that opened to the central campus. Despite the ocean breezes, Long Beach could not escape periodic stretches of oppressive heat. Kevin stepped out into the bright midday sunlight, and for a moment their philosophical bantering felt trivial in light of the world before him. A dozen seminary students walked across the manicured park, heads bent in thought or tilted back with smiles. Two dozen poplars formed an avenue through the expansive lawn. The chapel's steeple towered over the trees beyond the park. To his right, the Augustine Memorial Library glistened in the sun. The Divinity School of the Pacific, South, was at a glance statelier and more modern than its parent, the Episcopal seminary in Berkeley.

Here was the real world, made up of normal people with sensible histories and ordinary families pursuing an admirable profession. He, on the other hand, was a twenty-eight-year-old who really had no business on these grounds.

"You have a brilliant mind, Kevin," the dean said, gazing out at the campus. "I've seen a lot of people come and go, and few of them have your same tenacity for the truth. But believe me, the deepest questions can drive a man mad. The problem of evil is one of those questions. You'd be wise to court it slowly."

Kevin looked into the graying man's eyes, and for a moment neither spoke. The dean winked and Kevin offered him a slight smile.

"You're a wise man, sir. I'll see you in class next week."

"Don't forget your paper."

"Never."

The dean dipped his head.

Kevin took one step down the concrete steps and turned back. "Just one last thought. In absolute terms, gossip isn't so different from murder, right?"

"Ultimately, no."

"Then the bishop is ultimately capable of murder, isn't he?"

The dean lifted his right eyebrow. "That's a bit of a stretch."

Kevin smiled. "Guilty of one, guilty of all, isn't that how it goes?"

"You've made your point, Kevin. I'll be sure to warn the bishop against any sudden urges to kill his fellow man."

Kevin chuckled. He turned and walked down the steps. Behind him the door closed with a soft thump. He turned back. The steps were empty.

He was alone. A stranger in a strange world. How many grown men would stare at a flight of steps just vacated by a professor of philosophy and feel utterly alone? He scratched his head and ruffled his hair.

Kevin headed for the parking lot. The sense of solitude left him before he reached his car, which was good. He swung his beige Sable out of the lot and merged with the steady flow of traffic on Long Beach Boulevard.

Evil. The problem of evil. Like traffic—never ending.

On the other hand, goodness wasn't exactly running scared, was it? He had more to be thankful for than he ever imagined possible. A fine school with fine teachers. His own home. He might not have a rack of friends to call on at his every whim, but he did have a few. Dr. John

Francis liked him. And Samantha had called him. They'd talked twice in the last two weeks.

Okay, so he had a ways to go on the social front.

His cell phone chirped from the cup holder. He'd gotten it a week ago and used it once to place a call to his home phone to see if it worked. He picked it up, pushed the red button, and immediately knew it was the wrong one. "Green is go and red is stop," the salesman had said.

Kevin lifted the phone to his ear, heard nothing, and tossed it on the passenger seat, feeling foolish for being so out of touch with what most would consider fundamental requirements for life, cell phones leading that list.

The phone chirped again. A horn honked behind him—a blue Mercedes crowding his bumper. Kevin pressed the accelerator and picked up the phone. Red brake lights cut across all three lanes ahead. He slowed down—the Mercedes would have to chill.

This time he pressed the green button. "Hello?"

"Hello, Kevin." Male voice. Low and breathy. Drawn out to accentuate each syllable. "How are you doing, my old friend? Quite well from what I can gather. How nice."

The world around Kevin faded. He brought the car to a halt behind a sea of red taillights, felt the pressure of the brakes as a distant abstraction. His mind focused on this voice on the phone. Did he know it?

"I...I'm sorry. I don't think—"

"It doesn't matter if you know me." The voice paused. "I know you. Fact is, if you really do think you're cut out for this seminary bit, I know you better than you know yourself."

"I'm sorry, I don't think—"

"Shut up!" The caller took a deep breath, exhaled, and then spoke calmly. "Really, I don't mean to yell, but you're not listening. It's time to quit pretending. You may have the rest fooled, but not me, booger boy. It's time to let the cat out of the bag. And I've decided to help you do it."

This had to be a practical joke. Peter? Did Peter from Intro to Psych know him well enough to pull a stunt like this?

"Who . . . who is this?"

"You like games, don't you, Kevin?"

There was no way Peter could sound so condescending. "Okay, whatever. I don't know what—"

"Whatever?" The man was incensed. "*Whatever?* No, I don't think so. The game's just starting, and this time it's for real, boy. I thought about killing you, but I've decided this will be much better."

Kevin stared ahead, dumbfounded.

"The name's Richard Slater. Ring any bells? Actually, I prefer Slater. And here's the game Slater would like to play. I will give you exactly three minutes to call the newspaper and confess your sin, or I will blow that silly Sable you call a car sky-high."

"Sin? What are you talking about?"

"That's the question, isn't it? I knew you'd forget, you stupid brick." Another pause. "Do you like riddles? Here's a riddle to jog your mind: *What falls but never breaks? What breaks but never falls?*"

"What? What's—"

"Three minutes, Kevin. Starting . . . now. Let the games begin."

The phone went dead.

For a moment, Kevin stared ahead, phone still plastered to his ear.

A horn blared.

The cars ahead were moving. The Mercedes was impatient again. Kevin pressed the accelerator, and the Sable surged forward. He set the phone down on the passenger seat and swallowed, throat dry. He glanced at the clock.

12:03.

Okay, process. Stay calm and process. Did this really just happen? Of course it just happened! Some madman who called himself Slater just called my cell phone and threatened to blow up my car.

Kevin grabbed the cell phone and stared at its face: "Unavailable, 00:39." But was the threat real? Who would really blow up a car in the middle of a busy street over a riddle? Someone was trying to scare the crap out of him for some inane reason. Or some lunatic had randomly chosen him as his next victim—someone who hated seminary students instead of prostitutes and really intended to kill him.

His thoughts spun crazily. *What falls but never breaks? What breaks but never falls?* Maybe he should get off the road. Of course he should get off the road! If there was even a remote chance that Slater meant to carry out his threat...

For the first time, Kevin imagined the car actually filling with a blast of fire. He had to get out!

He had to call the police!

Not now...Now he had to get out. Out!

Kevin jerked his foot off the accelerator and slammed it down on the brake. The Sable's tires squealed. A horn shrieked. The Mercedes.

Kevin twisted his head and glanced through the rear window. Too many cars. He had to find a vacant spot, where flying shrapnel would do the least damage. He gunned the motor and shot forward. 12:05. But how many seconds? He had to assume three minutes would end at 12:06.

A dozen thoughts crowded his mind: thoughts of a sudden explosion, thoughts of the voice on the phone, thoughts of how the cars around him were reacting to the Sable jerking along the road.

What falls but never breaks? What breaks but never falls?

Kevin looked around, frantic. He had to dump the car without blowing up the neighborhood. *It's not even going to blow, Kevin. Slow down and think.*

He swung into the right lane, ignoring another horn. A Texaco station loomed on his right—not a good choice. Beyond the gas station, Dr. Won's Chinese Cuisine— hardly better. There were no parks along this section of road; residences packed the side streets. Ahead, lunch crowds bustled at McDonald's and Taco Bell. The clock still read 12:05, but it had been 12:05 for too long.

Now true panic muddled his thinking. *What if it really does go off? It's going to, isn't it? God, help me! I've got to get out of this thing!* He grabbed at his seat-belt buckle with a trembling hand. Released the shoulder strap. Placed both hands back on the wheel.

A Walmart sat back from the street a hundred yards to his left. The huge parking lot was only half filled. A wide greenway that dipped at its center, like a natural ditch, surrounded the entire lot, and he made a critical decision.

He leaned on his horn and cut back into the center lane with a cursory glance in his mirror. A metallic screech made him duck—he'd clipped a car. Now he was committed.

"Get out of my way! Get out!"

With a tremendous *thump* he crashed over a six-inch median and into oncoming traffic. Being rammed head-on might be no better than blowing up, but he was already in the path of a dozen oncoming cars.

Tires squealed and horns blared. The Sable took only one hit in its right rear fender before shooting through the gauntlet. Something from his car was dragging on the asphalt. He cut off a pickup that was trying to exit the lot.

"Watch out! Get out of my way!"

Kevin roared into the Walmart lot and glanced down at the clock. Somewhere back there it had turned.

12:06.

To his right, traffic on Long Beach Boulevard had come to a screeching halt. It wasn't every day that a car barged through oncoming traffic like a possessed bowling ball.

Kevin sped past several gaping customers and zeroed in on the greenway. Not until he was on top of it did he see the curb. The Sable blew a tire when it connected; this time Kevin's head struck the ceiling. A dull pain spread down his neck.

Out, out, out!

The car flew into the ditch, and Kevin crammed the brake pedal to the floor. For a fleeting moment he thought he might roll. But the car slid to a jolting halt, its nose planted firmly in the opposite slope.

He grabbed at the door latch, shoved the door open,

and dived to the turf, rolling on impact. Scrambling to his feet, he raced up the slope toward the lot. At least a dozen onlookers headed his way from the sea of parked cars.

"Back! Get back! There's a bomb in the car!"

They pulled back as one, stared unbelieving for a moment, then turned and fled, screaming his warning.

A siren wailed through the air.

Kevin had run a good fifty paces from the greenway before it occurred to him that the bomb hadn't gone off. What if there wasn't a bomb after all? He pulled up and whipped around, panting. Surely three minutes had come and gone.

Nothing.

So, it was a practical joke after all?

A gawking crowd had gathered on the street at a safe distance. Traffic had come to a standstill and was now backed up as far as he could see. Steam hissed from a blue Honda—presumably the one that had hit his right rear fender. There had to be a few hundred people staring at the nut who'd driven his car into the ditch. Except for the growing wail of sirens, the scene had grown eerily silent. Their eyes were on him.

"You said bomb?" someone yelled.

Kevin looked back at a middle-aged man with white hair and a Cardinals baseball cap. "Did you say there was a bomb?"

Kevin looked back at the car. "Yeah."

But that was just it—there was no bomb. There was his car planted nose-first in the greenway, there were a hundred gawkers, there were cars backed up and growing impatient, and there was him, standing on the lawn like a fool.

But there was no—

A deafening explosion shook the ground, and Kevin recoiled, arms up to protect his face.

The bright fireball rose over the car, spewing black smoke into the sky. The red flame collapsed on itself with a soft *whomp*. Smoke billowed from the charred skeleton of what was only a moment ago his Sable.

Kevin dropped to one knee and stared, dumbstruck.

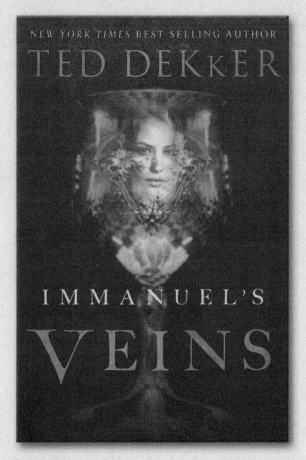